The Map
of Who
We Are

American Indian Literature
and Critical Studies Series
Gerald Vizenor and Louis Owens,
General Editors

The Map of Who We Are

A Novel

By Lawrence R. Smith

University of Oklahoma Press
Norman and London

**Library of Congress
Cataloging-in-Publication Data**

Smith, Lawrence R., 1945–
The map of who we are: a novel
by Lawrence R. Smith.
p.   cm. — (American Indian literature
and critical studies series; v. 24)
ISBN 0-8061-2956-5 (cloth: alk. paper)
1. Indians of North America—Fiction.
I. Title.   II. Series
PS3569.M537575M36   1997
813'.54—dc21   97-11212
CIP

The paper in this book meets the
guidelines for permanence and
durability of the Committee on
Production Guidelines for Book
Longevity of the Council on Library
Resources, Inc. ∞

1 2 3 4 5
6 7 8 9 10

The Map of Who We Are
is Volume 24 in the
American Indian Literature
and Critical Studies Series

Part ornaments are based
on a detail from *La Rumba,*
a painting by Selena L.
Engelhart.

Text design by
Cathy Carney Imboden.
Text is set in Palacio,
which is similar to Palatino.

For my mother and grandmother,
the Missouri tricksters
who taught me that
all language is conjuring

| ACKNOWLEDGMENTS

I would like to thank Gerald Vizenor for his good advice and many insights; Maxine Hong Kingston for her enthusiasm for the book's vision and her encouragement over the years during which it took shape; Evelina Zuni Lucero for her useful suggestions; Allen Mandelbaum for urging me to write a novel in the first place; Ronald Goldenberg, Graduate Dean of Eastern Michigan University, for generously granting leave time to complete the project; and Deanne Yorita, my partner, for her tireless, vital editorial work. Without her assistance, this book would not have been completed.

Portions of this novel appeared in slightly different versions in *Caliban*, no. 8 (1990), *Caliban*, no. 10 (1991), *Caliban*, no. 15 (1995), and *River City* 15, no. 2 (1995).

The Gathering

CHAPTER I | **TRAVELERS**

Power is there, under high-tension lines. Stand quietly to hear it. Look up and feel it polarize the cells of your body, tug at your teeth and eyes, halo the grass at your feet. If you ignore it, slip under it, drive by it, it'll burn a hole in the heart of your favorite song, leave a black tunnel in the air you plan to breathe tomorrow. Power companies say the wires are harmless, but there are no Travelers at Consolidated Edison or Pacific Gas & Electric. You'd think the scars those merchants of darkness have slashed and burned from coast to coast in great swings of electromagnetic frenzy would have totally screwed up the sacred earth-sky grid, undone the Network. But they haven't. We're lucky the grid is on another frequency. The Death Squad controls only a few AM slots; Travelers have all remaining numbers on the psychic AM dial, and end to end on the FM band, the one that connects us with the stars.

Once there was a Traveler, a woman with a name no one could see. She drummed word processor keys and organized for the clerical union in a small university town outside Detroit. Since her father was from Alabama, her mother from Canada, she naturally homed in on a north-south polar hotline in the Network grid. It cut right through the straits, the sacred water crossings, the place we call Detroit. Her mother had been a high yellow beauty, a farm girl from western Ontario, where redwings tend wheat fields on the other side of the river. As a joke, that beauty once stabbed lacquered chopsticks through the twist in her hair. The year was 1942, and it didn't play well on the Ambassador Bridge. Two border guards skated onto the running boards of the old Ford and escorted the family to one side. Hard to convince them she wasn't Japanese, an escapee from a camp in Utah, the authorities not at all amused when she didn't listen to their questions. Whistling a few bars of "Maple Leaf Forever," lost her pucker and could only blow air through her laughter. When she let down her hair, flashed her Billie Holiday kiss-my-ass smile, they finally allowed her back into Detroit. That was 1942: a year before the riots.

Travelers believe in the power of light. They know the shining is always there, in darkness or the stretch of day. It pokes through the planet—rips through sand, clay, rock, and magma—or comes at us straight on, sailing through space in divine transparency. Travelers navigate, transmit, and make preparations. They calibrate turtle shells, adjust our meanderings to the stars, plow heaven, replant the sky with fireflies, exploding corn, the exuberant cries of yucca blossoms. The Travelers have stayed tuned.

The daughter of that sassy Ontario farm girl, Ethel Wright to those with the magic to see her invisible name, crossed different borders: layers of sky, time, energy, and light. Then there were the rituals. She picked ham out of gumbo every time she ate the stuff. In the kitchen she chops onions, green pepper and celery, big flat-leafed parsley, humming "God Bless the Child." Not so much a religious thing on her part, but recollections of her father's Nation of Islam lectures still turn pork to crud inside her mouth. Whisking butter and flour into a medium brown roux, she shouts into the living room, tells Thomas to wake up and turn off the baseball game. *Fait attention!* You got to do a good roux, you got to lace the whole thing with a good Choctaw filé, you got to simmer it up till it slides off the ladle. And to cook a good gumbo you got to use ham—or tasso, smoked down bayou country. For Ethel, all the rest was perfectly OK: crabs, shrimp, oysters, mudbugs, frogs' legs, alligator, redfish, chicken, and duck—just not the ham. She dipped out each stringy piece and laid it by the side of her bowl. *Gombo,* Mandinka for "okra." But not the ham.

Ethel's tight-curled chestnut hair, the makeup that blushed out her tan complexion, the professional white blouses, and her preference for Lou Rawls over straight-ahead bebop, gave no indication she was a Traveler. Travelers and bebop have always been very close. Thelonious had all the marks; it was obvious the first time you saw him. It was just more subtle with Ethel. When she smiled, the diastema between her two front teeth opened the passage to her secret life of nerves and spices. But you had to know what you were seeing.

Dr. Horace Crumlich, her boss at Midwestern State University, could see very little, in spite of bifocals. He couldn't locate Ethel, even if she were the only one in the room. When she left her cubicle of decorative cats to seek clarification on one of his directives, he used his secretary, Karen, a stout platinum woman who seemed to apply lipstick directly to her teeth, as a seeing-eye dog.

Ethel stood in the outer office, leaned through the door. "Dr. Crumlich, I don't think they're going to be happy if you brag about the school's Indian mascot in your speech for Native American History Week."

Crumlich groaned from behind his desk. "Karen, someone there to see me?"

"Yes, Dr. C. It's Ethel."

"Tell her to leave a memo. I'm tied up right now."

"Dr. Crumlich wants you to leave a memo, Ethel."

"OK, I know I'm not here, but if he doesn't listen to me now, he's going to have a couple dozen Indian kids burning sage on his putting rug."

Karen smiled her reddest, most sympathetic smile. "Ethel, why don't you put that in a memo?"

Fumbling with his tweed jacket, Crumlich charged out of his office, aimed for the hallway door. But as he passed Ethel, brushed her arm, there was a loud crackling sound, and a blue flash leaped from his elbow. Staggered, he caught the edge of his secretary's desk and tried to draw a long breath.

"Damnation, Karen, it happened again. Call the campus electrician. There's a short in the wiring under this rug."

Ethel had all the voltage of prismatic light, but that never changed her easy style. She'd talk about any kind of cat, but never herself. So how would anyone guess Ethel knew about people who laid numbers on folks, calling them repeatedly on the phone, chanting, dropping off stuck painted lizards on the doorstoop? A ring and then a dial tone. Two rings and the whisper of flute music. Three rings.

"Hello. Who is this anyway?"

"Papa Legba, Prince of Crossroads, Prince of Shed Blood, open the gate, come and ride this horse."

"Don't you go and try to put a number on me! You better quit or I'll come ride on you."

"Papa Legba, come and . . ."

"Listen here now, don't you feel my words burning? Don't you feel the telephone getting hot on your ear? Right now my words are crawling through that wire and into your brain. When they're finished, they're going downtown to have lunch on your heart. Hello? Do you hear me?"

Dial tone. Sometime after midnight the caller stopped by and tried to undo the injury: castor oil, black soot, Mamman Brigitte's graveyard dirt cast at the doorway. We're talking Detroit now, not the bayou. Ethel didn't deal the stuff, but she sure knew all about it, and she knew who was who on the lowdown hoochie coochie circuit.

The Traveler's Network is what we tell each other when we're gone and no one's listening. It's the map that frays at the desert's edge, reflecting a pattern bigger than everything. It's a chant that enfolds time, measured from points of fire to places we sound out as "then" or "now" or "will be." Travelers sight along the flashing lines of the Network grid, speed across a web of interwoven lives and destinies to wherever they need to go.

When Ethel moved into a big frame house back in the city, she talked to the former owner, a yellow-haired Polish guy who'd died at the Battle of the Bulge. He kept wandering around the house in a blue robe: brushing his teeth, hogging the bathroom. He seemed quiet, kind of sad, and really nice enough.

"Don't worry, I'll be through here . . ."

"Ted, it's time for you to leave. Don't get me wrong. I like you, but you've got to go back where you belong. Your buddies are waiting for you."

"Can I go fishing with them?"

"Fishing it is, then. There's a largemouth bass on your line right now."

Ethel clapped her hands. The yellow hair and blue robe exploded into swirling dust motes; the toothbrush snaked down the drain. And that was it. He never came back. Sorrel on the thresholds and windowsills to keep him out, but such precautions were hardly necessary. The folks on the other side know who the Travelers are. It's funny how few on this side can see them. Or maybe we can all see for a moment here or there, then doubt the whole thing right back into oblivion. Like walking by a window and thinking you've just seen two people having the best sex since the beginning of time. But when you go back for a second look, it's just a dog and a television set.

Travelers carved canals through Venice marshland, channeled into hardpan above the wash that runs through Chaco Canyon. They created the ethereal gridwork of Mars. Travelers built bridges in Brooklyn and San Francisco, rebuilt one by the Chimehuevi reservation near Lake Havasu City, dream-engineered the Rainbow Bridge over the Bering Straits. They vaulted land through air, tongues of water through earth, and why else but to greet the dead, lend a sensual curve to persisting minds. Shoes and moccasins thump out an honor dance to integrate earth, water, fire, and air; to mix bloods, plant the seeds of cities and lives; to travel through a day where everything rings in crystalline octaves; to live in the tightly wound spiral that is formed by all women who have grown large and come together: the lotus, the cactus, and the crimson rose.

Travelers aren't born knowing who they are. Ethel hadn't found out until her late twenties. Jerry Martinez—who sprayed paint for a living at Chaco's Custom Auto Shop in Santa Ana, California— still didn't know. He loved to airbrush fantasy on the sides of vans, low riders, hot rods, cruising machines. Beyond the assortment of gargoyles he laid over pearled finishes and candy apple red, his passion was the natural world: not depictions of RVs and dirt bikes in the desert, but a soft-focused world of buttes, canyons, prairies, mountains, and seashore. The Great Work of his dreams was painting an entire bus. Not an old school bus—splashing on a few colors to whip up a hippie express—but a mint-new Greyhound to transform. It was a grander vision than Michelangelo's biblical wanderings in the Sistine Chapel, and Jerry's was more mobile. Paint the whole thing, even the roof, so the birds could groove on it, and people on bridges too. That's what he was going to call it: "The Bridge to Aztlan." However, most of the jobs he got were filigree, highlights, pinstriping, from the kind of people who install gold trim on their Mercedes Benz. He wished customers without imagination wouldn't waste his time; there were decals for junk work like that. But Chaco never let him refuse a job.

Jerry pushed his masked face closer to the door of the mini-pickup. He was pulling a wing of eagle feathers from the truck's black body, pulling them out of the mist he sprayed with deft turns of the wrist. Knee on bench, hunched over his aerial scene, looking down into the valley. The hangover foot kicked time to the sounds of his salsa box—Jerry riffing inside the ring of percussion, a monkey's collision of gesture and pace, cooking syncopation to open all gates out of the labyrinth.

"Hey, Jer. Come over and sight me out on this mask job." Chaco was calling from the other side of the garage.

"Hold on, man. My eagle's almost done."

Chaco spit into the epoxy dust. "Eagle's never done till he shits on your head."

But Jerry knew that. He once wrote Katherine Davalos Ortega to ask why all our money is gray green, the color of burnt-out astroturf. Jerry had suggestions for alternatives: fuchsia for the ones, the blue of turquoise for fives, sunflower yellow for tens, and black for the twenties if they insisted on keeping Jackson, but persimmon if they could find something else. He assured Katherine he had even more ideas for higher denominations but wanted feedback before devoting any more time to the proposition. And Jackson, after all, wasn't the only problem. Why not dump all those presidential and distinguished colonial faces? Why not hawks, eagles—but not the bird with the arrow up its ass on the back of the one—buffalo, snow geese, snakes, and beavers? Jerry knew it could be done. He'd laid them out on metal for years, and paper had to be easier than metal. To give Katherine a rough visualization, he enclosed bills inked over in various colors with a fine brush. He'd also razored animal pictures in perfect ovals out of *Audubon* and *National Geographic*, and rubber-cemented them over George, Abe, Alexander, and Old Hickory. But Katherine never replied.

He felt disgusted, and was momentarily tempted to abandon his patriotic enthusiasm. Later, Jerry decided it was foolish to let the bureaucracy kill a beautiful idea, so he set about converting his own currency, in exactly the same manner as the mock-ups he'd sent to D.C. Unfortunately, he met resistance in Southern California as well. Whether it was a gas station, a burger joint, or a drugstore, the cashiers would never accept his imaginative money. He reasoned with them. It wasn't counterfeit, after all, and the same old faces, if you really couldn't get along without them, were still right there underneath. You could always peel off the animals and convert back to the boss man's idea of history. But it never worked; no one would accept the money.

One day Jerry decided to take a stand on the issue. He was in the checkout line at Lucky Market, and the checker rang up $23.11 in sundries. He paid with two snow geese, three beavers, and change. At first the checker laughed, then she got mad.

"Hey, you got any regular money? This is no good."

"I'll give you a rattlesnake, if you can break it."

"Joke's over. You got regular money or not?"

"I only have the colorful kind, like the ones you've got in your hand."

"You know I can't take this. If you're not going to give me real money, you got to step aside." The checker fingered her hair and looked beyond him to the next customer.

Jerry leaned over the conveyor belt, blocking the progress of someone's beer and potato chips. "Listen, my money is as good as anybody else's, and I'm not going to step aside. I can wait here as long as I have to. As long as it takes for this country to get its shit straight."

Shoppers in line behind Jerry began to get restless: there were mumbles and finally bad words shouted in a couple of languages.

When the manager arrived, and asked him to leave, the money artist stood his ground. The big man tried to grab Jerry by the shoulder, but each time he brushed the hand away. At the moment of losing patience, just after the manager tried to punch him and he'd countered with a blow to the boss's chest, two cops jogged through the automatic doors. As he held out a sample and began to explain the idea behind his colorful money, Officer Wilkens kneed Jerry's groin and Officer Roman looped a baton over his head from the rear, pulling it tight against the throat. Handcuffs. The whole night in a lockup. Later, back in the streets, his friends couldn't understand why he felt so committed to his experiment. But Jerry still hadn't changed his mind. "Hey, man, that's what this country is all about: flip sides. One side is so beautiful it makes you want to cry. The other's just mean shit and rotten teeth."

His girlfriend, Leslie, who had taken cover behind the cigarette lock box, eased out and snapped a few shots of the cops working him over at the Lucky Market checkout, then took the film to a one-hour developer. When he got back home, Jerry razored out these little tableaux of struggle and rubber-cemented them over the White House and Treasury building.

Travelers make you laugh every time. It doesn't matter if they're dying, or you're dying, but they make you laugh. Then again, when you're in a silly mood they're just as likely to lean over, whisper in your ear, then nip a small piece out of the lobe. It keeps you alert. You have to be alert, because they make up all the rules. When you're with a Traveler, you learn to improvise and hope your instincts will carry you through. Like Bjarni Grimolfsson on his voyage from Vinland back to Greenland in 1012. Their boat had been attacked by sea maggots and was sinking fast. When they drew lots to see who'd be saved, Bjarni was one of the ones to make it into the dinghy. But his foster son screamed at him from the gunwale of the ship, "You coward, promising my father, Orm, you'd protect me, and now you're leaving me to die!" Bjarni crawled out of the dinghy and back onto the ship, traded places with the boy. Grimolfsson, the maggots, and the remaining terri- fied Vikings went down together. He laughed at the boy and at himself. He waved good-bye to the story because he knew he'd always be in it. Bjarni still lives in the settlements there on Rhode Island, where he said the beautiful wild rice grows itself, and you can get drunk on berries and dew. He lives inside the myth that is the map of who we are.

Chief Seattle knows Bjarni. Right now the Seer of the Northwest is standing at the base of the Space Needle, smiling to think of all the people who go up to the top to get the lay of the land. But what's really there they can never see: young Dwamish boys practicing with bows and salmon spears down by the bay, drying and smoking racks with women attending, long cedar houses with hearths cut through their centers to drive out damp and cold. He promised that his people would never leave those lands by the water, and they didn't. He told Governor Stevens they'd only appear to be dead and gone. What Seattle didn't tell the governor when he surrendered the territory in 1855 was that his healing men would be lingering there in the white man's hospitals. When spirits journeyed back to this side of the world and entered white babies, the eagle men were waiting to link the hand of each baby with the hand of a Dwamish earth child. They drew first breath together. Their souls were bound together from that moment on. And when those children grew up and cried out, the universal music could be heard again, no matter how many laws were passed against it.

Neanderthals excited Carla Abruzzese, made her change majors from Spanish to anthropology. UC Berkeley was a good place for that: the shrine of the Kroeber legacy—Ishi, "last of his tribe," the collision of time and evolution in the Golden West. Carla liked to tell a story about fur traders in Outer Mongolia. They swear there are people back in the farthest reaches, in the mountains, who don't look like other humans. In Mongolian they call them *kümün gürügesü*, a name that translates "people animals." There were outsiders who'd heard this talk of "people animals," listened carefully to the descriptions, and had a hunch the mountain people in question might be Neanderthals, or descendants of Neanderthals. Of course, no one but the Mongolian traders had actually seen them. But why should Neanderthals on the lam in Central Asia be particularly surprising? The past keeps hanging around, like smoke from a fire that burned a hundred or a thousand years ago. Diffuse, but still there. Think about it: we already know we're part fish. Any high school biology textbook clearly shows gills on the human fetus in the first month of development. Later, they seem to disappear right into the neck. But we know they're still there, covered by skin, ready to climb with us out of the sea and up the mountainside. There are Neanderthals here too, right here at home. We've all seen them; maybe we haven't noticed them, but we've seen them.

Joey Malone was a young Neanderthal who lived in the little town of Egypt, located thirty-five miles southwest of Rochester, New York. He'd been diagnosed as retarded by a local family practitioner. True, his forehead was more shallow than most, and had a slight backward tilt. But what did that mean to Joey? If the boy couldn't see ordinary water, how could he imagine the duplicity of mirrors? So what if he didn't look and sound like the typical upstater. That wasn't necessarily bad. For one thing, he didn't hit an obnoxious nasal flat with his *o*'s and *a*'s. When his watery hazel eyes focused on a point somewhere behind your head, maybe it was from looking at the sky so much. Joey saw angels and smelled Christmas spices all year round. He tended a garden of radio waves and injured stones. Sure, he had a few problems. He couldn't pronounce the *J* in his name, so it came out "Doey," or "Doughie." He never hit back when kids taunted him by snatching at his spiky hair; he just planted his big bare feet, almost as wide as they were long, and smiled. Returning good for bad, what could be more retarded?

When Joey first heard "Little Egypt" by the Coasters on his old Philco, he thought it was a song about his hometown. The hip-slinky beat didn't confuse him at all. He felt the Lake Ontario basin, its earth and sky, on his skin and in his teeth. It made his pubic hair tingle. And when he looked at lilac bushes in May, he could taste their colors, ride high on purple ink and pearls. That's why he'd always pop a few clusters in his mouth, until his mother or sister caught him and made him spit them out. Whether it was lilac time or hard-hearted winter or leaf burning in October, the world's size and dazzle made him think he couldn't stand any more pleasure. If he looked or smelled or tasted one second longer, he'd spontaneously combust and rise into the clouds. Those were the moments when he'd close his eyes, squeeze lids so tight his huge eyebrows touched his cheekbones. But then the flying animal colors took over, and that mad circus was hard to handle too.

"Hey, Doughie, want a candy bar?"

Tim Shelton, the middle kid from next door, had tripped, kicked, and badgered Joey, but never offered candy. Since the Neanderthal boy didn't speak to people outside his own family—that is, his mother and sister—he nodded yes and held out his hand. As usual, Tim and his neighborhood pals were in uniform, each wearing a pair of khaki cotton shorts and a T-shirt with broad horizontal stripes in muted earthen colors. They'd just come from Danielson's Hardware, where Herb always took them in back and let them try on his work shoes. But Joey didn't recognize uniforms. He wore baggy denim overalls and an oversized white T-shirt, a dozen of which were his vanished father's sole legacy.

He held out his hand, and Tim placed in it a Three Musketeers bar. It was huge. The advertisements for the candy said it was big enough to share with two friends. He opened the wrapper and stared at the wet glob of mud shaped into a rectangle. Tim and his buddies cackled, screeched, and flung themselves into midair twists like the Baptist clowns at the Strawberry Festival. But Joey started to eat the bar—finished it in five bites. When he smiled at his friends, the laughter stopped and they ran away.

Joey actually enjoyed the special bar. How could he explain that he still tasted messages the earth sent, long after the humans he lived with had forgotten the trick? When he sniffed the wind, laughed at what he saw in the sky, or buried his lunch money, his mother could only shake her head. When she extracted him from the mud and his clothes, thrust him into the shower, he saw only his hands, and watched astonished as they crawled and flew through the rain. Maybe Joey could have told his mother some of what he knew, but he just didn't care to explain. Nevertheless, in spite of his silence, or maybe because of it, Joey was a Traveler too.

After the failure of the mud candy caper, Tim tried to think up another prank, one that would indisputably horrify or injure the retarded kid next door. But nothing came to him. At night the Shelton boy stared into the bulb of his Roy Rogers lamp, his hero atop a rearing Trigger on the translucent shade of lashed vinyl buckskin. Roy had smiling Cherokee eyes, trickster coyote eyes, and whether he rode Trigger across the TV screen, Tim's lunch bucket, cocoa mug, or place mat, Roy's eyes dismantled the world, hurled spare parts toward the flash point. He was making it over, redoing the whole thing—not just the Lake Ontario basin, but the big map, the one experts can never imagine how to read. They look at it and handle it, but the language of water and earth eludes them. Tim stared at the lamp, but illumination never came.

Several weeks later, two days before the solstice, Tim and Billy were playing in the swamp near Carlton's junkyard, where Egyptian dead float open-eyed beneath the lily pads. Tim pulled a turtle out of the muck. Billy called dibs, but fat chance—Tim ignored him, held the turtle by the edges of its shell, spit through the curled tube of his tongue, arching a lougie four or five feet to one side with no apparent effort. This ability marked him as a leader among local boys. Billy tried, dribbled over his chin and onto his shirt as he struggled from log to log through the ooze behind the more agile Shelton boy. The two of them walked a country road the Chamber of Commerce had forgotten to name. When they got to the Malone house, Tim hid the turtle in a gravel well outside a basement window, knocked on Joey's back door. Mrs. Malone answered, wiping her hands on a flour-dusted apron, red heart over one hip for a pocket.

"We want to play with Joey."

"OK, boys, but no rough stuff. I'll go get him. Would you like some of my special pumpkin doughnuts? They're fresh from the kettle."

Joey and a plate of the doughnuts descended the rear steps into his backyard. The boys were waiting for him, sitting on a tree stump next to the garage, where his dad had leaned the Chevy's spare tire and side skirts while loading the trunk for his getaway. And there they still leaned, casual in forgotten rust. Joey noticed Tim hiding something behind his back.

"Bet you can't guess what Tim's got."

"Yeah, Doughie, I got a surprise for you." Tim spit cleanly and laid a wad between Joey's oversized feet. "A real one this time."

The Neanderthal boy tried to look behind Tim's back to see what he was holding, but each time he tried to look, Tim moved the surprise out of view. He was getting excited, and a sound somewhere between grunting and moaning came out of his mouth.

"OK, OK, Doughie, take it easy. I'll show you what we got for you." Tim held out the turtle, right under Joey's nose. His eyebrows, nose, and lips danced in a chaos of directions and dissonant quivers.

"Go ahead, touch it."

"No, really, Doughie. Go on and take it." Billy snickered.

Doughnuts into dirt, Joey held out both hands to accept the turtle, but the neighbor boy pulled it away again.

"Wait a second, Doughie. Let me show you how he goes. Look!" Tim lifted the turtle over his head and threw it down hard. The turtle's shells split, both over and under, and a surge of soft flesh, blood, and internal organs spilled over the stump. The two boys turned and dug it out for Tim's house.

Joey stared at the smashed remains of his swamp brother, its feet still quivering from reflex action. Open mouth. Tongue swept over his teeth several times and finally delivered the howl that had been rising inside him. He howled as he ran around and around the house. His mother caught him by an overall strap and took him indoors, but he continued to howl. He howled through dinner, blew peas and mashed potatoes even beyond his plastic Hopalong Cassidy place mat. He howled into the night. Every time his mother or older sister thought she'd calmed him, the modulating howl wormed its way up through his throat into explosions of dust and silence. Joey kept his family busy all that night and into the next day. At noon he stopped howling and began to smile. He lifted his nose, sniffed the mildew-laden Egyptian breeze for the turtle's spirit, breathed it in, and went on.

Carla Abruzzese had a notion; she wanted her friends at Cal to join her on an expedition to search for Neanderthals in Outer Mongolia.

"Don't you see what this means? It'd be wilder than talking to people who stepped off a UFO. You know, like time traveling, going back to beginnings."

"Sorry, I don't believe in time traveling. My best friend in high school talked me into reading science fiction one time. I hated it. It was such rotten plagiarism, like most of the junk Rod Serling did on *The Twilight Zone*. Sorry."

"Who said anything about science fiction? I'm talking reality. You know, like when something comes up and bites you on the ass."

And she did, then and there. The boy was lying stomach down on the grass, reading *Steppenwolf*, so she had a clear shot. She had opened a door for him. Revelation in the California sunshine. She opened another door for him too. Her legs were so strong she could wrap them around the boy's back, when he was in her, and squeeze all his breath out. He liked it. Her pubic hair was black, curly, and rose in an even rug almost to her belly button. He liked that, too, and wondered if it had anything to do with her fascination for Neanderthals.

Carla eventually got to Outer Mongolia. Time dissolved in that twilight meeting on the mountain. And when Neanderthal hands invited with eloquent tribal swoops and flutterings, she walked right into the Network.

Women are powerful, unless they forget other genders they've carried from earlier places. They hold shields, made of human hair and bark from the slender birch, that can withstand most frontal assaults. Men fancy they are powerful too, when they wear armor of metal and hardened leather. But they never forget the hollow spot, the one they're afraid will collapse if they breathe or dream. Their political energy is spent on government, television, and searching for oil. Both men and women, in their present configurations, engage in debate and strategies of delay. But delay brings us back to travel, and we are always, if we only knew it, already there—everywhere and in every time, all at once. Most people don't have the radio turned on, so they can't hear the music—"Blue Monk," "Round Midnight," "Ruby My Dear," "Crepuscule with Nellie." You've just got to stay tuned, listen for the weather report, make sure you know where the sun goes down. For instance, Cherokees had ideas on how to raise children. To teach a child to navigate earth, water, and sky, to keep its feet walking back into sunlight, they always chose a maternal uncle. This freed women up for skirmishes with Creeks and Catawbas, legal debates in the roundhouse. Then the case of Iceland. The Viking women were always there in the same cold and equal place, whether farming or fighting or looking into the future. On this last point, their eyes were much clearer than men's. Red Erik's daughter, Freydis, was an Icelandic wonder wherever and whenever she arrived. She led an expedition to Vinland, then murdered her male partners to get their boats and cargoes.

Bartering bowls of milk drawn from dragon boat cattle, along with pieces of junk they'd planned to throw away, the Vikings took beaver pelts, wolf and fox skins, the tanned and decorated hides of deer and moose. The men with scruffy beards could hardly keep from laughing at the natives, their greed for cow's milk and broken tools. But one *skraeling*, as the Vikings called them, spotted the scam, demanded two bits of brass instead of one for his decorated deerskin. A skirmish, several *skraeling* heads cloven in two, ripe melons to the tempered Viking swords. Later that afternoon warriors returned by the hundreds, caught the Vikings off guard as they worked outside their stockade, drove them into the meadow beyond with large stones inside tanned moose bladders that had been tethered to long poles. As the *skraelings* chased the men with painted hair across the meadow, one of the natives stopped, dropped his weapon, picked up a gleaming axe from the hand of a downed Viking. Entranced by the tangle of snakes writhing on the burnished bronze, he pressed finger to blade, but it bit him, drew blood. He dropped the snakes, picked up his pole again, and sprinted on into the meadow.

"Why are you running from these ragged *skraelings*?" Freydis screamed after her retreating men as she puffed across the field of battle. Eight months pregnant, a little slow on the run, she pulled the sword from the hand of Snorri's son, his skull crushed by a tethered stone.

"Where are the men here? These are only two-legged animals, you fools! Skin their hides and stretch them out to dry!" Turning to face the charging *skraelings*, Freydis pulled her tunic down to the waist and slapped the flat of the sword against her swollen breasts. The natives stopped, terrified at the sight of this fire-haired Death Squad angel, ran back to their canoes, and set up a flurry of churning water as they paddled away.

Consider having sex with Freydis. Since she's pregnant, you'll have to take it easy. The manuals warn that only gentle sex will do at this advanced stage, or you run the risk of dislodging the cervical plug that holds the whole process together. Could anyone have gentle sex with Freydis? If you asked her to roll over on her side and lift one leg, do you think she'd do it? As her belly grows, her breasts get even larger, and she was always substantial: blue veins under the skin are a map to a place you can hardly remember. Blood and milk in abundance. To Freydis, blood *was* milk. They traded milk for pelts with the *skraelings*, then made them pay again in blood.

Her feet were wet and cold with dew when she climbed back into bed a few weeks later with Thorvard the Nameless, her forgettable husband. Now, if Erik's wife had climbed into bed with cold wet feet before dawn and told him she'd just been talking with the neighbor about trading boats, he'd have leaned down and sniffed between her legs. Hell to pay. And if Freydis wasn't wet down there when she slipped between the sheets with Thorvard the Nameless, she surely was when she took a war axe and split the skulls of the five neighbor women. Her backers had grudgingly finished off the men, but they had no taste for chopping up women. It was a pleasure only she could enjoy. If Thorvard couldn't satisfy her, she'd get what she needed on her own terms. A woman all flesh and sharp edges. When a man made love to her, it was sailing into the Western Seas without provisions, risking everything to ice and turbulence.

Even before the Death Squad there were Travelers, riding solar butterflies, sucking waves of electromagnetic nectar. They rode buffalo too. When the Holy Six—North, South, East, West, Up, and Down—bend their vectors to a straight shot, laser through a hole in the fabric of totality, Travelers are calm, alert, and taking names. They sing through war, famine, and pestilence, through earthquakes, floods, and volcanic spewings. They tune harmonic strings in their wild stratospheric spin, play octaves of light to bridge us over the gulf between death and imagination. Flowers for teeth, tongues and eyes of sliding fire. Even when you're sure they've packed up and gone home, the Travelers are still there, ready to ride the last wave in.

The Moon Feast finished, Eagle dancers shed feathers and returned to sleep and their two-legged pursuits, landing hard just after the sun had risen high enough to ignite the edges of the eastern mountains. Even before dawn, the bear women had reclaimed their village faces. Now there were only a few matriarchs in the roundhouse, spooning the remainders of corn pudding and straw-berries into tightly woven baskets for distribution among the clans. John Walkingstick went to the river alone, bathed himself, reached into a pouch of ash he'd gathered from the communal fire, swirled it into circles around his eyes. The raccoon was his power: stealth instead of size, a mind as quick as those tiny hands, knowledge of everything that thrives under the moon. He felt strong after the Moon Feast, thought the celebration's ending a good time for another assault on his daughter's disease. Back to the roundhouse, to toss tobacco on the communal fire, lift his crippled daughter from the mat on the floor where he'd left her. No humans saw this doubled person as he slipped into the brush at the edge of the village, but the healer knew animals always watched and listened, waiting for a sign of weakness. He sang out a challenge.

> Listen to me, you star creatures! Furry runners and wind riders, there is no healer greater than the one you see in my moccasins. How could I fail in anything? Trees bend their branches and adjust their leaves, tell me the secrets they keep. Ha!

Walkingstick carried his daughter eastward through the valley to the feet of the Seven Sisters: the place called Gray Eagle, hotspot on the Network grid. And he sang as he traveled.

> It's only a screech owl that frightened my daughter's spirit. As these words leave my mouth, they harden into laurel, weave a cage to hold that bad moon owl. I'll keep it prisoner until her disease is gone. Ha! Listen to me, all you star creatures!

He knew the culprit wasn't a screech owl, but maybe insulting the bears by not mentioning them, denying the damage they'd done, would trick them into a fatal lapse of concentration. He wasn't sure when the bears had declared war on him. There were signs he'd been marked even before his wife, Chaw Chaw, a bear woman herself, had abandoned the family and gone back to the mountains to live with her hairy kin. Walkingstick had hunted them in anger ever since. His oldest son thought he was crazy to be so vengeful. A good hunter, but not a fast learner, Wiley had disappointed his father in other ways. The Old Raccoon gave up trying to teach him the language of plants. Walkingstick spoke it so fluently, he'd followed Sequoyah's example and written his own syllabary. Not that he'd told anyone about it. Not even his sons knew of its existence; the time was not right. Wiley, contrary to his name, could not understand the dynamics of Network connections. He wasn't even interested in lower-level complexities: the politics of skirmish and negotiation that were bringing the Tsalagi nation to ruin.

Walkingstick had also tested his second son, Pumpkin, in the hope he'd be more receptive. The plant talker made the boy climb a large white oak tree, stay there until he'd heard the stars sing. Walkingstick warned Pumpkin he'd expect a full rendition of that song the next time he saw him. The boy returned to the village four days later, wild with hunger, delivered an atonal version of "Yankee Doodle." The disgusted father bit hard on his knuckles. No wonder Nancy had always been his favorite. She was not only smarter than her brothers but more spiritually insightful than most adults in the village. That's why the jealous bears had taken her down.

Thin, slack muscled, a lack of syntax in her bones, Nancy Walkingstick couldn't move her legs. Her father set her down on the mountainside, doused her arms and feet with cold creek water, unfolded his healing stone from its seven-layered wrap of deerskin. He held the stone up, let sun pass through it, then balanced it on her chest. Held it to the sun again, but now it was cloudy. Praying for the power to undo the curse, clear out the contamination bears had flooded through his daughter's soul.

"Stars, listen to the words coming from my mouth like smoke. Strike down the creatures who've turned my daughter's food to stones inside her gut!"

He touched the bright welts along her inner arms. Auburn hair fell out of her head like broken rope. More creek water, then a pipe smoked in the directions. But no sign came. Even in power places you can fail, even if your dream eyes have seen war and famine and miraculous arrivals. Even here at Gray Eagle a father could lose his daughter and do nothing but watch her cross the long damp fields alone.

Prophesy seized him and spoke through his teeth. "My sons will die a few ridges from here, last holdouts against an army of dead things, gathering my people to march us into winter. And Nancy . . ." The voice disintegrated into bear grunts and mumblings. Even though they were fooling with him again, it was hard to maintain hatred for the bears. This long enmity wasn't really their fault. About the same time humans forgot the multi-tiered language they shared with all other creatures, they acquired a taste for the sweet flesh of their hairy cousins.

Betrayed by President Andrew Jackson, a senior partner in the Death Squad, and all of his cohorts: land speculators, generations of squatters who'd enjoyed Cherokee hospitality and now wanted to drive their hosts away, rednecks hungry for the gold that had been discovered on their land in northern Georgia. This betrayal drove the healer down white oak and honeysuckle paths, basket-making paths, back to the dream caves, where he worked through blood webs of horizontal lightning. He knew the universe was a puppet, those flashing lines the strings that made it jump. Blocked and frustrated by the Death Squad, the healer reimagined death, invented a way to hibernate souls, using basket codes computerized on the old star matrix system. He'd read the white man's Bible, and Revelations gave him the plan, even showed him how to key in the wake-up call. Of course, there was help from Handsome Bear, Chief Seattle, Ethel Wright, Jerry Martinez, and a long Network list he'd transcribed from the dream cave walls. And Thelonious Monk—he wrote the music. For a time John Walkingstick lost family, almost the entire Cherokee nation, but he found a world of pregnant chance beneath the dome of his anger and grief. He fathered the Great Millennial Shift.

"Nancy, listen. I'm going to try one more thing. The sky power of thunder and lightning can heal you—and if I hold your hand, you may live."

The raccoon man kneeled beside his daughter, who lay entranced by their winter house fireplace on a river cane mat. Finally she turned gray-veiled eyes in his direction. "Take me to the open place. If a fire river can't heal me, I'm ready to die."

He touched Nancy on the forehead, lifted the child into his arms, set off for the top of Gray Eagle's dark mountain. As the healer moved through fields of rain-soaked grass, he bent his head to speak into Nancy's ear. She heard him utter the sound of the colored bands that weave to form the evening sky. He asked her to remember the healing light that pulls, when you call it by its true name, dazzle out of gray. He told Nancy to listen for the deep humming reach of the earth's power, and the song of every healing plant that grows through clay skin. He kissed Nancy on both eye-lids, asked her if she could still see the quick-talking points of fire behind the clouds, the ones with a music for eyes that plays only when we sleep. She nodded her head, and Walkingstick shook the air with his bear cry.

Thunder rolled in and out along the jagged horizon. Then the Network light show began. Slashes of light and power, the multiple afterimage explaining that nothing ever dies. Finally, a thick bolt of lightning snaked along, parallel to the ground just to the north of them. Walkingstick lifted an eagle bone whistle to his lips. The snake hesitated, then exploded into fragments, chunks of ball lightning that flew and bounced in all directions. One came straight for the healer and his daughter, blowing across the tops of trees and scattering fiery splinters as it rolled. About to be engulfed, Walkingstick blew his whistle hard enough to pierce the fabric of the world. Nancy's open throat shrieked an even higher note.

| CHAPTER II | **BRIDGES, TUNNELS, AND PASSAGES** |

J. Pierpont Morgan, Supreme Counselor to the Death Squad, sits in his Wall Street office on a mahogany throne, head crowned by a wreath of withered hair. With a flourish he draws a handkerchief from his breast pocket and wipes his moustache, dark bridge arching from chin to nose to chin. His weight holds down delicate inlay—abalone shell and the crushed skulls of railroad strikers from the Revolt of '77. This throne might fly from sheer lightness if it weren't for his groaning laughter, the hard kindling in his mortician eyes that can read the moment of your death, the price your dissected body will bring. In the throne's delicate carving he sees East Indian monkeys flying through a latticed canopy of tree-tops, swinging in a frenzy of loops and spirals. His mind's finger, that can bless or decree death for thousands at a wag, traces aerial monkey pathways. Spirit voyaging back to Bali, Morgan hooks fat corporeal thumbs under the gold chains slouching upward from each hip to meet at his navel, join a gold replica of the planet. But the monkeys, those monkeys . . . As they fly, their tails inscribe circles and ellipses, lines always snaking back on themselves. There is nothing square or predictable about them, nothing like the grave morning-coated monkeys on the Street.

Morgan dreams of circles, dreams of them and awakens in terror. The circles are so light he has to sit hard on his colonial bed to keep night-tripping winds from catching the canopy, billowing it out like the *Corsair*'s spinnaker, sailing him away. He sits with all his might, just as he's now sitting to hold down his throne. His collar stands upright, folds crisply at the points, suppresses a burgundy cravat. The lips beneath his bulbous and ferociously erupted nose align in a smile, parting to allow convenient passage of the latest rattling groan from the pit of his gut. It rises heavy and full, slides through his teeth and across the room, past a medieval French carving of the Blessed Virgin, flecks of gold leaf still adhering to the wood; past the framed golden page of a Celtic Bible; past a Russian icon with ruby stigmata; through the stained-glass window and into the Street. There beyond the window his groan takes the shape of a nightmare spiral: spins into a funnel, gathering force, picking up paper, straw, dry horse manure from gutter and cobblestones, dancing, tipping its head in one direction then another before the portals of the House of Morgan. The King of New York withdraws his gaze from the Street, returns to the grid of names, lines, and numbers he is annotating. Among the names: Freydis, Veranius, Red Swallow, Jonathan Edwards, Andrew Jackson—and a single name enclosed by a black square: Wong Fu Gee.

In Arizona and New Mexico, sun people will tell you to look away from those dust devils, since they have the power to steal a piece of your soul, suck heart's marrow out through your eyes. They'll also tell you that until 1896 the biggest apartment building in the United States was Pueblo Bonito, built one thousand years ago by the ancestors in Chaco Canyon. Morgan financed the plagiarized and slightly larger version in New York, shoved us all a little closer to the edge of the millennium's last crazy century, and no one questioned the independence of his achievement. After all, he knew sun people only casually—if you don't count repeated run-ins with Handsome Bear, and the Counselor's fascination for Red Swallow and her double-hearted hump. But that's another road on the map. Right now we're talking about a hot drought day in J. P.'s city, thirteen years after the end of the Great War Between the States. The sun shone on Morgan's summer festival of cholera and consumption, shone equally on white gloves holding pink parasols and on greasy gingham, barefoot or broken-shoed, loaded into Black Marias, hauled from jailhouse to jailhouse throughout the city. They called these women "revolvers," and their revolution kept them from sleeping in doorways and under stoops, kept them from the sight of J. Pierpont Morgan and his retainers. This evening some of those gentlemen are dining at the Morgan mansion on Madison Avenue, the first building equipped with Thomas Edison's new electrically powered incandescent bulbs. Morgan's guests will be served poached salmon and rack of lamb. In the Counselor's kitchen they are already preparing the primest parts of Molly O'Hara and five of her friends from Chambers Street. Beggars, pickpockets, message runners hang in the meat locker, hooks through their heels, ribs trimmed cleanly out of their sides, naked spines connecting shoulder to hip.

Far above these dazzling July streets former sailors and war veterans bind steel cords together, weave them into cables thick as beer barrels. They ride their wooden rigs down a valley of slouching steel between the Manhattan and Brooklyn towers of the Great East River Bridge. If you could trace vectors through Manhattan smokestacks, the masts of clipper ships in East River berths, the raised fingers of Brooklyn's commercial fantasies, and scaffolds on Bedloes Island, where Liberty prepares an arm thrust through smoke to enlighten the world, they would intersect at the Great East River Bridge—the nexus of American ambition.

This was all John Roebling's idea. He extruded steel beauty from the tangled forest of German imagination, designed a Hapsburg tiara for the Savage Mother. But She, as Dr. Williams has always told us, is a tough mistress. Hegel's favorite student at the Royal Polytechnic admired Her sunshine possibilities one afternoon as he projected an imaginary arch over the East River. John dreamed, but She nudged the Brooklyn ferry into the wooden slip where he stood, crushed his foot. Amputation, water therapy, mathematical incantations, but tetanus took him. This German jeweler of ideas set the stones of his bridal gift in feverish delirium. He felt himself sinking between Her thighs, squeezed and cock-caressed, a hand tightening within Her sweet thing. Tetanus convulsions catapulted him from sickbed to floor. John groaned and came in midair, but he came alone. The bedside crew—son, daughter-in-law, engineering assistants—scrambled to pick him up, return him to his rancid sheets. Two minutes later he was gone. Instead of the tiara, She accepted from John the beauty She'd made of him: lockjawed rictus, the permanent smile of death. Like De Soto's weighted body sinking past monstrous fish into the Mississippi mud, She accepted John Roebling as sperm. Their strange-smiling children would eat logarithm tables, travel a gridwork of concrete pathways beyond calculation.

John Roebling was a genius. His son Washington barely made it through Rensselaer, and tried to substitute labor for inspiration. As he dug deep into the riverbed, laying foundations for the two massive towers, Washington lived six days a week with the tunneling sandhogs. There was widespread praise for this admirable chief engineer, but secretly he dreamed of the Savage Mother, waited to ram those towers up Her two holes, East River and Hudson. Down in the pressurized caissons, She blew Her sweet breath into Washington, the sweat and glory of that dream. But when he rose from Her bedrock, in exhausted satisfaction, re-emerged into sunlight, Her breath sublimed into brain-blocking bubbles. Like the lowest pickaxe or shovel man, Washington Roebling had the bends. That evening his wife found him on his knees in the study, trousers pulled down around his ankles, hands in a gesture of prayer. "I didn't know where to have the bitch . . . where to have her . . ."

"Emily the Amazon," as Washington called his wife, was a wild horsewoman who insisted on riding alone. From the lips of her immobilized husband she took all the mysteries of engineering: vaults, spans, the arching grasp of steel suspended from sky. From the deadly Mistress she took the breath of power. But Emily had no ambition to leave her mark on American history; she only wanted to ride. It was said that every day she delivered orders from her husband, carried on the business of assembling the bridge as he instructed her. The public chose to believe that story; they imagined Washington supervising the project, a telescope thrust out his bedroom window. But the untalented son no longer recognized trousers, trusses, or even the spelling of his own name. When the bridge's road had finally been laid, joining Manhattan and Brooklyn, the chief engineer rode across to check for vibrations. She mounted her best racing buggy, whipped the black stallion to a gallop, traveled straight into the future. Emily Roebling built the Great East River Bridge, and they called it the most magnificent engineering achievement of Modern Man. She rode alone.

Jimmy McMullen, Oliver Flanagan and Ezekiel Smith stood on their open platform two hundred feet above the river, cranked the steel-winding winch around and around the body of the cable. Below, everything from clipper ships to coal boats loaded and unloaded on the Brooklyn and Manhattan sides, where painted brick walls advertised ship's chandlers, clothing for men and boys, liquor, lager, and cigars, and Whitman's ferries shuttled back and forth along cable-thrown shadows. A Yankee clipper passed directly beneath the platform, her sails filled hard and full, lines singing in the wind. Ezekiel sucked on his pipe, proud to hoist this giant steel rigging, watch his city sail into its dreams, run before the wind. The wind of those dreams blew out of the east and whistled due west. Ezekiel looked over the jumbled rooftops of Manhattan factories to the golden band called the Hudson, and to the green hills of New Jersey beyond.

Morgan's pestilent wind sprite moved down Wall Street to the East River, touched water, turned northeast against the current, swept its spinning animal form past ferries, sloops, and barges, working its way upstream.

"Do you think 'twas bad wire that perished those two boys?" Ezekiel grasped his beard with one hand, tugged at the hem of his smock with the other.

"Mighty poor rubbish, that wire. And it'll be killing us all, if we don't mind our bones and knuckles. Jack, they say he'll live, the poor creature, but his leg . . ."

"I'll go bail there's no death on that Jack, so I will." Jimmy had no patience with Oliver's compassion. "And 'tisn't no poor creature neither, Ollie. The man's rotten with money."

"He's a bit close, ain't he, Jimmy?"

"Does a gull shit white? I can tell you he is then, and a great deal better, if you go to that of it. The man heard money jingling in his mother's pockets before he was born."

Oliver stared down toward the river as the three returned to pulling the cable-wrapping machine, a ship's wheel embracing a winch. "Maybe he'll leave something for the workingmen's fund."

"A duck could swallow all the gold and silver he'll be leaving us, that's certain." Jimmy stamped a boot on the wooden platform. He was vain about his new boots, with their fancy Western stitching.

Ezekiel unclenched his teeth, pulled out his pipe. "Aw, Jimmy, you wouldn't know Jack Murphy if you saw him in the street."

"Oh, I wouldn't now, would I? Why, I'd know his skin in a tanyard. The fat little runt, rather jump over him than walk 'round him. A stinking runt. Damn it to hell, Ezekiel, what're you smoking in that pipe of yours? It's enough to make a man sick to his death."

"You know very well you're smelling coal smoke, Jimmy McMullen, or maybe you're smelling your own cursed upper lip. And don't you run away from it, man. You envy Jack Murphy; you wish you were as well on your way as he is."

Jimmy hitched up his trousers with both hands. "I've little need for gold; I have my Kitty. She's the whole world in a kit sack. And don't you be preaching to me, Ezekiel Smith. You been hearing your mother so much, you sound like a damned Ulster Presbyterian."

"Don't you be talking about my mother, Jimmy McMullen. You may well remember, I don't live at home with mother and sister like someone or another up here on this rig. And what am I to suppose you'd be doing with a woman?"

"The devil take the hairs in your skinny nose and braid them up proper!"

"But I do have a nose on my puss, don't I, you puny red-freckled pug!"

"Enough from you two!" Oliver put a hand on each man's chest. "We know your Kitty's a trim girl, Jimmy. There's no denying it. And your sister, Eileen, too; she's a lovely woman. But it's a bad right you have to talk of mothers up here."

"Minding your naughty boys again, Mother Flanagan?" Jimmy snapped Oliver's short-billed cap with a flick of his middle finger.

"Better keep the hat on, Ollie; save that noggin of yours from frying. Meanwhile, as the two of you reckon out the culls, I'll be taking me a piss."

Jimmy unbuttoned his fly and turned upriver, his back to his mates and the wind. He shot out a thin yellow wire, lifting it up into an arc before the wind fanned it to misty rain as it fell toward the river.

"Lordy, boys, it's making a rainbow! Pot o' gold! Lucky pot o' gold! I'll be rich, after all."

Ezekiel and Oliver turned their heads from their work, looked toward Jimmy on the off chance there actually was a rainbow. That's when the wind sprite lifted up off the water, reached high, stretched out, caught the three unaware in their high-altitude nonchalance. Oliver held fast to the wrapping wheel, but Jimmy and Ezekiel were brushed off the platform. As they fell toward the river, they heard laughter, a deep rattling groan.

There was shouting on the Manhattan tower of the bridge. Down below men leaped into small boats, put out into the river in hope the boys might have survived the fall; but Jimmy and Ezekiel never surfaced, their bodies were never found. No mention of the incident in the papers. Accidents on the bridge were considered bad luck, bad publicity for a city about to leap into the twentieth century, to invent it and monopolize it, as Gertrude Stein would later claim. Bridges required falling. That's why Joseph Stella fell through the city's psychedelic crust thirty years later, when he painted the steel superstructure, a mad spiderweb concerto. No one could save him from his glorious descent, nor could anyone save Hart Crane as he threw himself repeatedly against the Bridge, tearing skin on guy wires, bolts, steel reinforcement bars, ripping a hole in the top of his head. He slipped unnoticed into the sea, searching for the secret passage. Steel fleece, blood, and sky juice to make this cat's cradle, the machine of the Marvelous—ready to help us travel everywhere and nowhere. Marcel Duchamp declared the Brooklyn Bridge, the entire city of New York, the greatest work of Dada ever created.

A month after disappearing into the East River, Jimmy McMullen and Ezekiel Smith rode a column of bell-shaped bubbles to the surface of the Pacific Ocean, on the outer edge of Monterey Bay.

As they tumbled up this inverted waterfall of oxygen, angels shrieked, the world expanded inside and out, exploded from their lungs as California sunshine. They broke surface into a swarm of stars, church bells pealing jumbled octaves, and the radiation generated by an open east-west hotline on the Network grid bouncing madly between sky and sea. Tangled in blood kelp, caked in grease the color of unbleached lard, the two men tried to tread water and look for the Manhattan tower of the bridge.

A gaff hook reached down from the sky and snagged Jimmy by the seat of his britches. He fluttered as he and his cargo of kelp were dragged up the side of a Chinese junk. Ezekiel heard his mate squeal, called out to him, but in another moment he too was gaffed and hauled aboard. The two bridge-building sky sailors lay spitting and gasping, surrounded by flopping sharks, pomfret, whitefish, shiners, ling cod, jack mackerel, sheephead, snapper, and one long misshapen fish, or eel, with black spots and wicked-looking teeth. There was little difference between the fish and the other newly landed creatures: Jimmy's red matted hair had turned to sea grass, Ezekiel's hair and beard spiked out in sea urchin prongs, now shot through with white and gray, as if he'd been partially electrocuted. A scramble of bare feet over the deck as an amorphous smock, wearing an old felt hat tied to it with a red bandanna, leaned over, put a face into Jimmy's, and screamed. Jimmy saw the gap, the open gate where the smock's two front teeth had been.

"Aiya! Aiya! *Bok kuei*! Bad luck!"

Another voice joined in. "Aiya! *Say la*! Throw them back!"

"No more good fish, all full of worms! Aiya! No money. Bad luck! Throw back the dead fish!"

When the gate-toothed man took to yelling in Ezekiel's face, he reached to feel for his own, snapped them together, but found them intact.

The fishing boss stared for a moment at the entire catch, then sauntered away. When he returned from the poop deck, he shoved an earthenware flask of tiger bone wine at Ezekiel. Taking a couple of swigs, the bridge-building sailor inflamed his throat and stomach with the liquid, but it allowed him to breathe more easily. The toothless crewman with the red bandanna gave tarps to both men, so they could wrap up and get out the chill. Jimmy gagged and spit, cursed the tarp for its stink of rotten fish, then crawled under it and fell asleep.

Ezekiel licked the salt from his lips, sucked it out of his moustache, worked his mouth as if he were chewing cud. Brine dripped from his hair and beard onto the weathered boards of the junk. His eyes rested on the two men by the salt barrel, whacking and scraping as they shouted at one another in Cantonese. Blood and piles of green and brown intestines began to spread in a semicircle around their feet. The man with the black skullcap grabbed a pomfret by the tail, slammed the contorting fish over the head with the side of his cleaver, wedged it underfoot, then drew the sharp edge through its belly. After pulling out the guts and scraping the ribs that lined the cavity, he cut the head off behind the gills, spread the fish flesh side down, scaled it, flipped it over, reached into the salt barrel, sprinkled a handful on the flesh, slammed it several times with the flat of the cleaver, then threw it into the open hatch. Ezekiel felt a twinge of pain under his sternum that took his breath away; he'd never seen anyone clean a fish so fast.

The Irishman noticed that his boots were filled with water. Trying to pull them off as he stood, he slipped on fish slime, fell hard on his back. The two men cleaning fish snickered and spit. Stunned by the fall, Ezekiel's world slowed, turned clear and precise. Through a small tear in one of the quilted sails he saw torn sky, a momentary glimpse of the golden Network beyond; the wind whistled loud in his ears, but there was dead quiet inside his skull; tingling beneath his skin, he breathed and tasted salt. The sun, a signalman's lantern, swung back and forth from one side of the main mast to the other. There was no reckoning in time's pocket: when he closed his eyes, the world came back orange, loud, and in motion. The frozen-winged gulls rode the air directly above him, shrieking for fish.

Ezekiel watched Wong Fu Gee's face change places with the sun. Looking down at the stunned Irishman, the fishing boss shouted to one of the men at the salting barrel, then continued forward. The bridge builder sat up, tugged off boots and socks, pulled himself to his feet again. Taking a jackknife from his pocket, he opened it, smiled at the fish cleaners, made sawing motions in the air.

Ezekiel worked the fish pile through the afternoon. The cleaners had reduced it to a couple of finless sharks (dorsals already bagged for aphrodisiac soup) and the eel-like creature. Ezekiel stared at the wolf fish, a long finned tube of monstrous guts. It puffed a lumpy, spotted face as it tried to catch its breath. The agony of the bulging human eyes wrenched his heart with pain.

The lines were hauled in again. Ezekiel turned and saw he was surrounded by another population of deck-slapping fish. The Irishman contemplated a four-foot shark on the deck: whipping its tail, gills opening and shutting like louvers, water shooting out at each lash. He felt seawater moving through the shark's heart and through his own. A crack in the pump, stumbled rhythms, a bell tower full of angels and griffins, the grief of both the damned and saved in a language of rainbows on all frequencies, the earthround grid of polyprismatic light. Meanwhile, pumping in the dark garden alone, tangled in thorns, the blood-filled rose of the Sacred Heart.

Around sunset the wind died and the ocean calmed. Ezekiel had forgotten how to hear without shouting against the wind; his ears ached, words circled his teeth without knowing where to go. Just as he began to feel hunger worming its way up into his mouth, the Irishman noticed the man with the red bandanna setting out the evening meal: a wooden tub of cold rice, dishes of pickled greens, jerked meat, and a dried, toasted, fishy-smelling substance with tentacles. The rescued bridge builder was given a set of chopsticks. He fumbled in his rice, unable to pick up pieces of meat or vegetable from the dishes laid out on the deck. As the fast-consuming circle of eaters left Ezekiel far behind, Wong Fu Gee offered a spoon, but the newcomer declined, continued his struggle. It was only when he saw them hold bowl to lower lip, shovel rice into their mouths with chopsticks, that he succeeded by imitating them.

Later that night, Ezekiel joined Wong Fu Gee at the stern.

"Lost our wind, didn't we?" The Irishman had trouble focusing on his rescuer, who appeared to be a walking blur.

"No matter. We can't put in at night. We'll be in Monterey tomorrow morning."

"Monterey! Monterey where?"

"California."

Ezekiel's tongue went numb, so he grabbed for the fishing boss with his eyes, tried to pull some detail from the blur that would explain the impossible. Wong Fu Gee, having shed the rubberized sou'wester and rain hat he'd worn earlier in the day, presented a bony head barely covered by short-cropped gray hair. A rumpled flannel shirt and denim pants covered his lean body down to midcalf. Lower down, Ezekiel stared at toes that were almost as long and big-jointed as fingers.

Being unable to accept his new placement in the universe, the Irishman reverted to smaller questions. "Some things have been troubling my mind."

The fishing boss nodded, squatted with his back against the railing. Ezekiel still struggled to get a clear look at Wong Fu Gee's facial features.

"I thought all Chinamen wore queues."

Wong Fu Gee looked hard at the Irishman, trying to decide if he were worth the trouble of an answer. "Most Chinese men do."

Ezekiel waited for an elaboration, but it never came. He tried again. "What does 'Bocky' mean? All day the mates were calling me that."

Wong Fu Gee looked away from Ezekiel and smiled. "That's *bok kuei*, 'white ghost.' Chinese have difficulty locating people with light skin; they're always disappearing before our eyes."

Ezekiel looked over the stern railing, then back at Wong Fu Gee. There was no moon, but his rescuer glowed a shimmering aqua in the dark. When the junk lurched slightly, Ezekiel felt his brain turn to seawater, drain as a warm trickle out his right ear.

When he opened his eyes into morning, Ezekiel threw off his tarp, catapulted head over heels into the bay. Eastern mists burned orange along the hills, flashed into thunderous dawn as dolphins cast watery arcs, looped into kinetic bridges around the expanding Irishman. He stood waist deep, Wong Fu Gee's junk a child's toy two arm's lengths away— shouted to the fishing boss, called for a hawser to tow them ashore. Ezekiel was a mountain in the sea, a new island, and every breath a celebration of miraculous deliverance: bells and the clatter of organ, incense, Latin incantations. Waves washed against his waist, pulsed through his heart, hymns in praise of the rose hidden in all suffering. Tunnels beneath the floor of the bay rumbled at his feet, and the Network

grid above his head shot sparks of sound and light across a trolley maze
of electromagnetic lines.

A disoriented Ezekiel drew himself slowly from covered sleep,
stretched, noticed how he'd shrunk. The tarp shuddered, moaned,
deformed with spastic kicks and lurches. Then choking laughter,
a hand reaching from beneath the edge. Even after pulling himself
to his feet and spitting out his bilge mouth, Ezekiel was still small,
smaller than the woman who'd steered alongside the junk, working
a single long oar at the stern of her sampan. Wong Fu Gee, the
crew, and the two reborn Irishmen slid down ropes into the boat,
and it rode low through the water as she leaned and pulled them
into shore. Boat woman, hidden tiger, her fierce cheekbones
covered by a mushroom-shaped cane hat and a scarf anchoring it
to her chin; taut shoulders, arms and breasts, with dark full-
budded nipples that promised both pleasure and life, crouching
under her high-collared smock, hue of pearl at morning; iron-
corded legs beneath loose pants, bare feet hinting at the fearful
symmetry above. Only Ezekiel, with his transformed eye, could
actually see the woman, feel her bitter strength in his sinews and
heart. He felt her tidal pull as the crew left the beached sampan
with others scattered over the sand. Overturned boats and shack
encrustations covered the whale's hulk of a hill, driftwood racks
lashed with drying fish, mounds of abalone shells in every direction, internal rainbows emptied of swollen hearts. The crew dispersed—fell into shacks, ducked behind shell piles, into pillars of
fog—but the glowing couple moved up the rocky hillside, beckoned
the bridge builders to follow. In the blur of his rescued eyesight,
Ezekiel saw the man and woman melt into one striding figure,
then divide again, like the yolk and albumen of an egg.

Wong Fu Gee and the woman entered a small structure of
weathered pine. While Jimmy hesitated outside, scanning the hill
for alternative shelter, the lanky sailor poked his nose right into the
boss's door, took in a room where walls sang forth a chorus of
earthenware crocks and jars, unglazed around the rims but caramel
drooling down their bulging sides, and the wooden lid on each
vessel leaking sour, sweet, medicinal, or aromatic spice. The
Irishman walked through the door and breathed the incense of
heaven and earth. He had no idea what he was seeing, but his

eyes moved beyond the crocks, embraced jumbles of shelved bottles with red, yellow, brown, and black sauces and pastes; dried tangerine and orange peel; chunks of melon preserved in sugar, dried red dates or jujubes; dried lotus root, star anise, seaweed in a half dozen colors and configurations. The rafters were hung with flattened dried fish and squid; dried oysters, scallops, and clams in strings; dark red cured sausages tied together in bundles; clusters of dried herbs, seed pods, and bark.

A black lacquer altar squatted in a corner, its three sticks of incense whispering sandalwood smoke out of a sand-filled brass urn. Ezekiel watched orange carp swim around the rim of a plate mounded with tangerines, cut into waves of fragrant air. This new music had captured him: his right foot kicked and lifted into a little step. Above two scrolls, calligraphing the dragon's spine in a world of light, there was a framed silk embroidery of the Taoist hexagrams. Stitched red and black bars shuffled and linked in the sacred puzzle that defines the Path. Ezekiel danced to the atonal symphony, let monkey fancies show him all the steps. As he stared at the Taoist hexagrams, they pulled him even farther into their first and last song: the white light of dawn that moves like a crane, legs kicking red and free in the bamboo grove's black clutter. Ezekiel turned head and hands, danced with all limbs and senses, until his eyes rested on the flourish in the opposite corner, a flapping rainbow perched on a bamboo trapeze.

At the doorstoop, Wong Fu Gee rolled down denim trousers, brushed sand off his feet, pulled on shoes of coarse black cloth. Ezekiel watched the fishing boss perform his rituals, tried to guess why his body moved in contrary directions beneath his clothes.

"Use the bar of soap on the board." Wong Fu Gee pointed his chin at an improvised bench next to the clothesline. "Give her your gear."

As Ezekiel joined Jimmy outside the door of the shack, he came to life again in another sunlight, another reach of the world. Both stripped, and the tall man stretched up under the joyful sky. As they handed their outer clothes to the woman of bitter fragrance, sugar-preserved peel of orange, she pulled fire from beneath a kettle on the shack's lee side. After they'd washed, the woman steered the sailors toward straw-filled mattresses laid end-to-end against the wall, a folded blanket on each. Jimmy chose the mattress away from the parrot, but Ezekiel didn't mind; he watched the bird expand to a forest of color as he fell asleep.

Wong Fu Gee walked past the woman as she hoed beneath pea, bean, and squash vines in her garden. He worked his way uphill to an even smaller, windowless shack—patched and plugged with canvas scraps, hung with floats and torn nets—circled the structure three times, opened the padlock, entered and relocked from within. When he threw a brass and porcelain circuit breaker on the wall, current rushed from a wet cell to an incandescent bulb of his own manufacture, with a filament even Thomas Edison could never imagine. The bulb illuminated his treasury, only slightly more modest than the lost library of Babylon. Each shelved wall was jammed, floor to ceiling, with volumes bound in cloth, leather, and vellum. And hundreds of scrolls—some housed in elaborate painted cases and others simply tied with ribbons. The *Nei p'ien* of Ko Hung was a stacked triangle of ten scrolls lodged in cedar tubes. But that wasn't what he needed. Reaching up to a high shelf on the south wall, he ran a finger along the smudged vellum spines of *The Hunting of the Green Lyon* by the Vicar of Malden, Gerber's *Sum of Perfection* and Ripley's *Compound of Alchemy*, the *Rosarium philosophorum* and *Auroraconsurgensus*, Heinrich Khunrath's *Amphitheatre of the Eternal*, the *Museum hermeticum*, Jabir's *Chest of Wisdom* and *Turba philosophorum* in Spanish versions, *The New Pearl of Great Price* by Petrus Bonus, and *The Golden Calf* by Helvetius, George Ripley's *Twelve Gates of Alchemy*, the Kabbala, and paused on a slender volume blackened with soot. Flamel, Aristotle, Plato, Roger Bacon, Albertus Magnus, Aquinas, Janus Lacinius, Abu'l-Qasim al-Iraqi, Elias Ashmole, Paracelsus, Thomas Norton, Bolos of Mendes, Zosimos, and Cleopatra stood around him, approved his choice as Wong Fu Gee pulled out the text, nameless even to him, and began to clear a spot on his table of Great Works. He pushed a salamander against the octangular furnace, gently lifted a tripod holding an alchemist's egg and put it to one side. The crystalline sediment at the bottom whirled in its blue solution. He shifted sextants, an astrolabe with Arabic calibrations, drafting tools, jars full of pens and brushes, until he could reach a bronze helmet covered with pictographs leaning against the wall. Steering around a golden box that hovered in midair just above the surface of the shelf, he set the helmet by the sooty volume, opened to a diagram that covered two pages with a spider web of lines and symbols.

The golden cube rose through a trap door on the roof and hovered just above the shack. As Wong Fu Gee put the hieroglyphed bronze hemicycle on his head, it gave off an intense blue flash, and the floating cube began to crackle orange against the sky. The force of the discharge threw him back against the table, jingling beakers, retorts, and alembics. Controlling his *chi* was still difficult, even after years of studying the Tao. If untested humans had been within range, the helmet's blue flash might have killed, or stunned at the very least. Wong Fu Gee now focused his meditative powers on transmission and change; there was important information to send, subtle metamorphosis to effect through fire, light, and the direction of *chi* along the branching Network pathways. It was a tricky time to work. The Network's circuits had opened fully during the last few days, and they were just as likely to deliver evil as good. As its axis aligned with the electromagnetic grid lines that ran through Big Sur, the floating cube began to crackle more loudly. Then he smelled it: burning crude oil and rubber. What he suspected was true; they were here, or at least on their way. Laughter bounced from wall to wall inside the shack. Touching a jade wand to the side of the helmet, Wong Fu Gee turned and turned, trying to pick up direction and angle. Then the screams of a hoarse-voiced woman. It was Bjarni and Freydis again, locked in their endless tussle.

The alchemist wondered just who was closing in. It might be Veranius, or Jonathan Edwards—maybe even J. P. Morgan himself. Or an emissary, like J. Edgar Hoover, that bastard son—as yet unborn—of the Supreme Counselor's most splendid perversities. Everyone in the Death Squad's hierarchy, from bottom to top, gnashed teeth at the idea of the Great Millennial Shift. They knew it was coming, could not be prevented, but they'd do anything to frustrate or delay it, delivering as much torture and suffering as possible. Wong Fu Gee, at this crucial nexus, stood guard over the lines and transmission points, receiving and redirecting power and information, but knowing attacks were sure to come. He laid his hand on the green bicycle that leaned against one wall: a mesh of sprockets and gears at its center, handlebars shaped like wings.

Cooking smells: the crackling and sputtering of hot sesame and peanut oil. Jimmy's restless thrashing awakened Ezekiel; the disoriented bridge builder sat up on his mattress, saw the woman squatting in the angled light as garlic smoke and licorice steam dragons rose from twin steel hemispheres on terra-cotta stoves. She had assumed a power squat, with erect back, her bunched calf muscles visible beneath the hems of her pants, black cloth shoes turned out, locking into the floor. The shoes had red circles on each toe, lucky constellations made from perfectly embroidered drops of blood. Now that the scarf was gone, he could see the woman's hair: dark brown with a red cast, cut straight across, baring a taut ridgeline of bone beneath skin. Ezekiel had an urge to lay his hand on that warm tan. She never turned.

Wong Fu Gee walked through the door carrying a black wooden box girdled with a red band, set it down in front of the altar, moved to the table in the center of the room, and gestured an invitation to the two men. Wong Fu Gee and the woman sat on chairs; sections of sawn log served as stools for Jimmy and Ezekiel. As she leaned to serve them rice, turning her head and brushing hair aside, Ezekiel caught his first clear glimpse of her face. She was fine-featured, younger than he'd first thought. A Milky Way of freckles passed from cheek to cheek over the bridge of her nose. The irises of her eyes were ambiguously edged, spreading like iridescent fish scales into the whites. And while those eyes may have spoken, their language made no sense to the Irishman. He noticed a light blue vein snake across her temple, then saw the gold-centered jade disk pinned to the lobe of her ear. As Ezekiel stared, the disk began to spin, pulling him outside of himself into a tunnel of wiry light. Unaware of the passage of time, he started, almost fell off his log, moved back into waking, eyes still fixed to her ear, a numb tingle playing over the back of his neck. The ear now glowed with waxy translucence: it was gnarled and clumped into the shape of extreme age.

A white porcelain spoon floated in the air before Ezekiel's face; its hollow traveled all the way to the tip of its handle. He took the spoon from the woman's hand and looked down, trying to focus on his bowl of food. When he began to eat, he shoveled such huge amounts of rice and oyster into his mouth that he could barely chew or draw a breath. Jimmy growled a prayer for deliverance, but no one at the table paid notice, so he began to slurp from his own bowl.

Burning putrescence violated the good smells of the table. Ezekiel sniffed his bowl, but it still smelled delicious. He discreetly sniffed his undershirt and armpit. They weren't the source of the smell either.

"Beg pardon, but do you . . . ?"

Their host had already disappeared through the shack's open door. Outside a loud clanging rang out, like an iron bar slamming against an empty steel drum. Ezekiel half rose from his chair, holding the edge of the table. The woman reached out her hand, shook her head no, as he eased back onto his log. Her opalescent eyes, the color of air, showed complete composure, mixed with a hint of amusement. Ezekiel stared at Wong Fu Gee's half-empty rice bowl. A flying dragon splayed its toes and disappeared around its edge. Five minutes passed in silence before the fishing boss walked back through the door, seated himself, took up his bowl, tapped his ivory chopsticks even on the table, and shoveled his rice again.

Dinner finished, Wong Fu Gee sat back on his chair and gave the woman a look. Ezekiel glanced at his mate, and when he'd turned back to the woman, she was squatting at the stoves preparing tea. He had not seen her move. In fact, he'd never actually seen her in motion since she'd rowed the sampan and walked up the hill. Wong Fu Gee moved as quickly and deftly as a swallow, but wherever the woman was, she appeared to be stationary.

The fishing boss looked hard at Ezekiel and Jimmy as the woman poured a flowery liquid into the four small cups. He smiled—for the first time since plucking Jimmy and Ezekiel out of the bay by the seats of their pants. The two bridge-building sailors had found their way through the matrix, the Mother's womb, the *vagina materna*, the crosswise passage that runs from east to west, or west to east, since it's vulvic at both ends. It hadn't taken the Europeans long to find the other one, the north-south vagina: De Soto slept with the Mississippi Mother and died. She was easy to find, lying on Her back with Her knees up and Her legs spread open to the hot rhythmic currents of the Caribbean. After the

Spanish had warmed Her up, the French built their pudendal town right on Her *mons veneris* and called it New Orleans. Everyone understood that sweet opening, but the other was hidden, esoteric. Wong Fu Gee had heard of its existence but knew of no case where anyone had made a voyage through it, not even Travelers. Of course, all men intuitively knew of Her secret passage. They even mimicked it on the surface, with the Hudson passage to the Erie Canal, and the steamers from the canal's Buffalo end to Lake Superior. And later the railroads. But that was not it. White men had dreamed of the Northwest Passage, and when they couldn't find it, they invented Manifest Destiny. They desperately wanted to have Her in that special way, from east to west. The Mississippi was too easy, like a streetwalker in the *vieux carré*. But She never gave Herself to them the way they wanted Her. The bones of Her suitors lay scattered from the Appalachians to the Rockies and beyond the Sierras. Wong Fu Gee smiled that She should have offered Her favors to these two Irishmen, and they had no idea what they had experienced.

"Wong Fu Gee, I smell that burning again."

The boss was off his stool and out the door before Ezekiel could offer assistance, so the Irishman sank back into the yellow-and-green flower pattern on the side of his rice bowl. Although the woman seemed to be listening to everything that went on, she had not yet uttered a sound in any language. Ezekiel was surprised when a voice whizzed by his left ear. He glanced at the woman but saw that her lips were not moving. Then a swarm of voices swooped through the door, flew in circles around the table, speaking different tongues, not one of them intelligible to Ezekiel. They droned like furious bees.

Jimmy lurched out of his after-dinner stupor, turned his head in an attempt to follow the blurred motion. "This is bad business, the devil's bad business. We're in mortal danger of our souls if we stay here."

There was little time for the big Irishman to reply. The table began to vibrate, then kicked into a massive jolt that dropped the whole shack a foot. Ezekiel looked at the woman. Her smile pulled a crease from the corner of her eye, pointed straight at her temple. The whirlwind of voices directly above them increased in pitch and volume until it had become a chorus of the damned. When the sounds whizzed out the door, they left a powerful silence behind. There was sweat on the brows of the two sailors as they held fast to the table. Wong Fu Gee walked in and both men jumped. He sat down to his cup of jasmine tea, tossed a small book on the table in front of Ezekiel. The spine said FUSANG in gold letters.

Turning the book over in his hands, the nervous bridge builder looked to the fishing boss for explanation. "Do you mean me to read this? What's the subject of it?"

Wong Fu Gee lifted his dragon cup to his lips, drained it. "Another voyage."

Travelers come in all colors. They came, in fact, before there were colors, or when there was only one, and it contained all the hues that play through the rainbow's reach—riding, walking, flying, and traveling by modes that dissolve in the act of trying to explain them. So we speak blue language, at other times green, red, or violet, the tongues implicit in the pure light that contains them all. Speakers as diverse and consistent as the stars. Considering the chances of truth, what kind of discourse is history? If your head rests on the dream pillow you discovered in memory's hidden room, will the frequency of its power touch you to transforming speech, will the flashing Network lines curl into the calligraphy you need to free the dark riders? They turn restlessly in a night without magic, fueled only by the absence of light. Some will rise, some will seem to be lost in the descent. But no one is ever lost. It is evolution, not erosion, that leads us to our destined encounter with the changes, pulling us from the depths up the mountain-side. It is the promise that has always penetrated every one of our dimensions and incarnations: the Great Millennial Shift.

The lanky Irishman held out the book to Jimmy, his finger pointing to a paragraph in the middle of the page. "It's here, just read it. Fourteen hundred years ago, a thousand years before Columbus, a Chinese monk named Hui Shen sailed here in a junk."

"Whatever the book says, Columbus discovered America, and that's the long and short of it." Jimmy dug the heels of his ruined cowboy boots into the shack's floorboards.

The irises of Wong Fu Gee's eyes darkened. He could have told the Irishmen about the Pacific corridors, the currents that carried Chinese ships from the area southeast of Japan straight to the Gold Mountain, and west from the coast of Mexico straight to Manila. The Chinese had known about them, traveled them, long before

Hui Shen, whose voyage was noteworthy simply because it was the first recorded on paper. And he could have told them about the Empress Wu Ti sending Chang Ch'ien to explore the West long before the birth of Christ. That Traveler reported back on westerners who had gathered enormous amounts of gold, silver, and precious jewels, but were otherwise total barbarians. He suggested merchants be dispatched to sell them some civilization. On a more personal level, the fishing boss could have told his guests other things: that he was an organizer in a revolutionary society in Kwangtung, the land of thieves and heroes, pirates and explorers; that he fled China when he was betrayed by his brother-in-law; that the name he had chosen for himself meant "powerful struggling yellow man"; that he wore layers of tough psychic armor and at the center there was a hollow space containing his real name, the one his grandmother had given him; that he endured harassment in his trade, being forbidden to fish with drift or fyke nets like everyone else, and paid a tax levied exclusively on Chinese immigrant fishermen, so he could be close to the dizzying cliffs and healing forests of Big Sur, where the sun drew the fragrance of sage into the air, incense in the face of heaven; that Big Sur was one of the chief connecting and transmitting points on the Network grid, and especially important in the process of recuperation; that he had already set up the most important single line of projected information in history, aimed at a group of Travelers who lived in Los Angeles over a hundred years in the future, among them Jerry Martinez, Carla Abruzzese, and Wilbur Lum, all activists in the Great Millennial Shift; that he restrained his great pride, endured the injustice and brutality of American whites, because he could foresee the ethnic blending, the demographic and political metamorphosis, the arrival of New America, for which he now acted as midwife; that when his elixirs made feathers split through fingertips and the webs of his hands, he could fly as a white pigeon or black crow, crying out with the sacred crows in the desert language of Fusang; that he could wear sunshine or the antic face of death, rumors of laughter careening off the coastal mountains; that while he knew Ezekiel himself was no Traveler, one of his descendants would join the Los Angeles group. Wong Fu Gee could have said all these things, but he only showed one Irishman a book that told the story of Hui Shen.

If that bridge builder could learn how to use those wings, someday he might fly.

Ezekiel was inside a room of thought, staring at the woman. He couldn't understand when she'd had time to change them, but her disk earrings were gone. She now wore large jade earrings in the shape of monkeys. He watched the creatures dance merrily around her neck. When his attention moved to the ears again, he found them shapely, the fire of life glowing beneath their tan; they were now the ears of a young girl. Ezekiel could feel himself shrinking again.

Then the woman actually moved. She stood up and unbuttoned her shirt, loosened the drawstring of her pants and dropped them to the floor. But when the shirt fell away, all the flesh was gone as well. A heart jumped and shuddered behind the ivory blades of her chest. And below, where a naked womb lay open and visible through her split belly, a gray-haired fetus twisted and turned as it rose through the gash, covered with grease the color of unbleached lard. It held a robin's egg in its hand. The woman spoke to Ezekiel, sang like a mockingbird, with all the sounds of the world. He reached out to touch her, to touch the child who was squirming to life. He reached out to take the egg.

Jimmy delivered a long burp, then a proclamation. "I've a powerful thirst on me, lads. Is there a saloon hereabouts?" He put his hand on Ezekiel's shoulder and shook his mate. "Liven up, man! A bit of grog would do us no harm."

Wong Fu Gee leaped to his feet and held his head as if listening to a distant sound. The shack was filled with the smell of a steam engine belt burned to the point of snapping, or overheated wiring that would in the future be known as electrical. It was the smell of Edison's charnel house, dismembered children, the stench of lost generations, the patterns of work clothes scorched through flesh and written across their lungs and guts. The parrot beat its wings in the corner, screeching "Morgan! Morgan!" Wong Fu Gee had a hand on each of the sailors' backs as he directed them through the door. "Gentlemen, there's a saloon in town called the Cantina Rosarita. Tell Joaquín Quintero that Wong Fu Gee asked him the favor of looking after you."

The fishing boss hurried the two sky sailors to the top of the rise, then directed them toward town. Jimmy never looked back but walked briskly toward a good time. A dazed Ezekiel turned to watch Wong Fu Gee descend the path. There was no sign of the woman. For the first time he noticed where the smaller shack perched higher on the hill. It glowed in waves that alternated blue, yellow, and orange. The sailor started to call out to his host but thought better of it, turned, and took long strides to catch up with his mate.

Wong Fu Gee did not pause to see if the Irishmen had found their way but walked quickly along the path to his alchemical storehouse. As he walked, he jumped high in the air several times, each time landing in a different stance, with his arms and hands turned in odd positions. One time he resembled a crane, another a tiger. He entered his temple of the Great Work with the hunched-over skipping step of the monkey.

CHAPTER III

THE BASKET WEAVER
AND THE SONG

The upright splints snapped back and forth as the horizontals twilled through: over two, under two. Nancy wove the confusion of splayed cane into loops and circles, a coming together to make the holding place that defines a basket. As she mirrored ancestral gestures, Walkingstick's daughter listened to all the voices, grew into a woman from the inside out, keeping an eye on the words that tied together fingers and breath. Mabel Dickson was teaching Nancy double chief's daughter, the most esoteric pattern of all. But the Old Raccoon, as the villagers called Walkingstick, had his nose in the works, danced around the seated women to peek at what his daughter could make. When Mabel scolded him, tried to chase him away from the mysteries she chose to protect, he hissed and chattered, rolled his eyes, scampered the path of the cabin's inner walls with his mockery of woman's law. On one of his passes by Mabel's chair, she stood up, caught him with a hip thrust, bounced him out the open door.

Under the full charge of musky summer, his animal eyes lifted to a canopy of white oak, leaves and branches woven into inverted protection, guarding summer cabin and winter shelter from the contraries of sunlight. Raised raccoon eyes penetrated foliage and beyond to the makings of the sky basket, the Network weave that held everything together, even the pieces that had chipped away from their lives and seemed to disappear. The future of the Cherokee nation was a double-weave basket, rough cane sides turned against each other so only the dazzle of color and pattern showed. That such beauty would continue in the world had to be taken on faith. The sky continued to fill the baskets of the Raccoon's eyes as he contemplated the miserable politics of retreat, and the state of his immediate family wasn't making him any more optimistic. His two sons were tall and strong enough, but they didn't have the heads to take on white talkers and intruders. They could attend to strategy and issues just long enough to carry out a raid or fight a skirmish, but not beyond. Nancy was different. She was short and stringy like him, a honeysuckle vine tough enough to make baskets for carrying firewood, unhusked corn, pumpkins, and dressed game. Yet even though she was in the best of health, quick to see, a stickball player as willing to accept wounds as inflict them, when the light caught her eyes at certain angles, Walkingstick could hear an animal's strangled call, a menacing laughter that haunted him.

Finger flowers, finger spiders were traveling quickly through the bush of split river cane and light. He scanned the frequencies inside the cabin and outside in the late afternoon, when sun tries its hardest to worm past leaves and branches. He knew the full circle of the clearing was ready to bounce into a new pattern for the world. The Old Raccoon watched a woodpecker hammer at a high limb of the south-branching walnut. He scuffled dirt with his feet, calculating how many pulls, twists, and foldbacks there were to the story of the chief's daughter who was really two: sun and moon, earth and water, stone and air. How many variations in the weave of his own daughter's story? He knew these things could be told a thousand ways, every telling a new texture to reawaken spirit through the fingertips, declare another version of the universal shape.

Seven dead in the last month, sudden explosions along the treeline that hid the Buncombe raiders. Women in the roundhouse counseled both war and negotiation with equal persuasiveness, equal despair. Official treaties and reparations, but all the whites ever paid for losses of land and blood were a few shattering coins. Appropriate compensation, because the Tsalagi felt the danger of breaking into pieces too. They listened to their voices diminish into small stories; they ceased to recognize husband, wife, an unknown child. Even the clans were turning to dust. Baskets could gather and hold truth; they pulled scattered pieces into stories large enough to suggest everything there is to know. But these were different times: in this crisis there would have to be new kinds of containers. Nancy dreamed she saw the healing plants hold hands in a circle. They told her a basket woven of green arms and brown legs, the brothers and sisters that grew from the clay or carried fur on their backs, was the only cure for the encroaching disease, a sickness much worse than any the bears had invented to get even with their human enemies.

People needed to live within a song that would continue to sing and play itself: a song in river cane, a song in long strips of white oak, bleached, or dyed with bloodroot and walnut. Some folks were frightened when they heard diminished fifths bend around mountains and split through trees, but Thelonious would help them riff inside that sound, calm themselves up through it. They heard the syncopated patterns, endlessly various, played by sky and water—multiplying, turning back on themselves like the beautiful drumming black people did, the runaways they'd taken into the villages. The black men knew about the Network too, played out their demonstration model on drums and clapping sticks, invoked the weave and celebrated it at the same time. The Tsalagi knew Thelonious too, knew he'd be coming down the road in this same state of North Carolina, but they learned from the black men to call him Damballah.

To pull the dead into light-framing shadow, dark edges that define space and dimension, that can be seen only from the corner of your eye: a way to hold the place of expired breath like a finger in a book, so it can come back into the world, enrapture even the white man eating his pork and beans; a turtle called America, where prophets walk across every street and into every house, as common as air; tattoos to leave a map of the human future, a flower all nectar—no petals, roots, or stem—that encircles our days and nights; a rainbow, a pillow to comfort the unjustly dispatched to darkness, more off the ground than on, a pillow that becomes a tree; a meal brought home on the ferry, food brought back from the place beyond death; freestanding, independent stretches of time that could be used to make alternative endings to stories, to histories, until they all conjoin with the telling that brings the Great Millennial Shift.

As he walked around and around his cabin, the codes began to pull together in Walkingstick's mind. Peace pipes, chief's daughter, unbroken friendship, double chief's daughter, cross on the hill, chief's daughters in diamonds, chief's coffin. All variations and combinations were stories, patterns that blossomed into people—all the people who were, or had been, or would be. Wilbert Smith, the stickball champion, with his 〰〰〰〰〰〰 , and the teeth of ⊐ ⊐ ⊐ ⊐ ⊐ ⊐ ⊐ into the box. Mental compilations, the weaving of ⊓⊔⊓⊔⊓⊔ , the \\\\\\\\\ of it, happily turned into ▬▬▬▬▬ or ⟩⟩⟩⟩⟩⟩⟩ . Walkingstick held himself by the elbow because he could feel his own fading, his lightness and transparency. ⟩⟩⟩⟩⟩⟩⟩ , 〰〰〰 , ▦▦▦▦▦ . He could write it all down. ◇◇◇◇◇ bent trees ▭▭▭▭▭ and ≪≪≪≪≪ . The greatest genealogy ever written: ◇◇◇◇◇ , ▬▬▬▬▬ , and ⬇⬇⬇⬇⬇ . A book about the making of Americans, and a way to keep them from disappearing into the smoke of the blind American night.

"Nancy!" John Walkingstick pushed through the cabin door. The late afternoon light had set up fine patterns against the wattled interior. A finished double-weave basket sat on the table. Mabel and Nancy were gone.

CHAPTER IV | **EXPEDITIONS**

On a bench in the Santa Ana jail, Carla Abruzzese gathered stones together. She looked at her jeans: dirty and bagged out at the knees—and below, raised left foot, wiggling toes resonant with red violet polish. OK, everything was working, but where was the other sandal? And how did both pockets on her coarsecloth Guatemalan vest get torn? Little stones gathering on the bench to improvise a scenario, dance her up to the line where spectator becomes Traveler. She remembered driving to Santa Ana from Irvine, where she lived and taught anthropology at the UC campus, looking to pinstripe her BMW. It was an indulgence, a consolation for the loss of her lover, a graduate teaching assistant named Debra. Carla had come in search of Jerry Martinez and Chaco's Custom Auto Shop. Some-where in the process she was rerouted, traveling first to Mongolia, then

*to Aztlan (where she found the best taquería in the world), and finally
ending up here, in the Santa Ana jail.*

*It was an eclectic party: hookers, drunks, crack heads and ice heads,
assorted street people, and the angry woman on the other end of the bench
who was trying to crush her ribs with her own arms.*

Back to the beginning: the trip to the crossroads starts with an
orange tabby named Balboa gliding down the south side of Fourth
Street, Santa Ana, exploring, opening up new territory, marking
it, claiming it for the queen. A fearless cat, he ignored traffic,
sidewalkers with angry shoes, cat-hating kids on bikes and skate-
boards, a world beyond the reach of law and order. He navigated
through crushed styrofoam boxes leaking salsa, then stopped
briefly beside Francisco Torres, down and out, cuddling the wall,
leaking sardines and airplane glue. The cat laid claim to this small
island of a man, marking the crumpled figure in two spots.
Cruising farther along the cracked cement, he swung into Chaco's
Custom Auto Shop, arched his back, stretched, flashed sharp teeth
and a curling tongue, yawned up acetone, banana oil, the hiss and
rattle of compressors. Nosed around the edge of his milk bowl.

Carla saw the cat turn into the garage as she locked up her
BMW across the street. When she entered the mist of spray paint
and drying agents, the four men were laughing and taunting each
other. One, crouching with an airbrush over the door of a mini-
pickup, shouted out, "Manuel, you are total bullshit. Balboa can
outfuck you any day of the week." Another pushed his round
body against the wall, let loose a staccato soprano laugh, gray
undershirt riding over navel, jeans slipping below the place where
his hips were buried. But when he saw Carla, he wheezed to a
stop, pulled himself erect and wiped his hand across his face. Two
other men, working a '57 Chevy, looked up and stared. The fourth,
still leaning over the pickup door, brushed tawny wisps of paint
into a mountain lion's body, did not turn around.

Unwelcome attention from these garage guys had provoked
Carla into calling them "dickless *cabrónes*." There was no excuse
for their nastiness, even if she hadn't known Spanish—and she
did. "*Gallincita*," "*puta*," grunting, whispering obscenities, and
that one jerk wiggling his tongue at her. They were so impressed
by the power of her curse, three of them reached down inside their

jeans just to be sure. Jerry negotiated a truce, guided Carla into La Estrella across the street to show her his album of design jobs. Alva's *taquería* was no fast food place. A pot of *menudo* on the stove every morning, homemade tamales to take away in sackfuls every Saturday and Sunday, fresh-cooked chili sauces so rich and piquant they brought tears of joy and recognition to the eyes of strangers lucky enough to happen in. But La Estrella was a local hang, the gathering place for neighbors and working folks in this part of Santa Ana, the spiritual reservoir for centuries of Californios, mission Indians, and Chicanos. In the domain of Alva the Compassionate, you could always count more people than you could see. She was Our Lady of the Sorrows and Triple Redemptions, who took care of people, mediated disputes, distributed free herbal remedies in little triangular envelopes, passed old clothes out the kitchen's back door. And Alva made the best *tacos al carbón* in the world.

Laying down the menu, Carla studied Jerry closely for the first time: a child's chubby cheeks, a widow's peak that falsely suggested a receding hairline. His almond eyes remained amused, never changed to match the volatile moods that swept across his face—dancing lines that displayed contraries in transparent overlays. Carla looked up, wondered how a blue veil had dropped between them. But when her eyes returned to the shape-shifting painter, she saw the veil was on him, not in the air: a light blue haze of minute paint drops spread over cheeks, forehead, and hair—his whole face, except for the brown mask of clean skin around nose and mouth.

She leaned forward, tried to get a better fix on Jerry's face, sort out her sense of recognition. What turn in the hallways of her dreams, what pull in the obliqueness of these eyes, an attraction like the moon's, only partly felt? Friend, lover, revolutionary—the secret design of their connection hidden within the landscape of the Night Bird's lunar smile. Jerry never admitted it, but when she said she thought she knew him, or had seen him before, he was sure he recognized her, or at least those gorgeous feet, with high curved arches that suggested flight, mercurial wing bones asserting subtle tension beneath the skin, the second toe significantly longer than the big one: a signing of aspiration and delight. Her serpentine black hair, big teeth, the dark eyes that narrowed slightly when she looked at him. He wondered if she were in one of his art books—maybe that relief of the Mayan noblewoman on her knees, drawing a rope of thorns across her tongue.

Jerry looked at Carla, tracing the prominent line of her nose bridge. "What kind of name is Abruzzese?"

It was Italian, meant her ancestors had lived in the Abruzzi, the mountains east of Rome. She said her father claimed all their relations were Italian hillbillies. Jerry laughed as he lifted the photo album from his lap and dropped it on the table. He turned it sideways and opened it. Carla twisted in her chair, leaned over the blood zodiac's jagged lines, the jazz of monkeys sailing over and through a canopy of treetops, a rain of golden scales, bifurcated parrots calling the kingdom into prayer and celebration, mountain-toothed snakes rising to heaven on the wings of the sun. Jerry and Carla had come together in the magic domain of Alva's taquería, and they almost touched shoulders.

When Carla looked at Jerry's designs, she saw ancient Siberian and Mongolian pottery, the geometric patterns of the shaman's pulse. But when she uttered the word "Mongolian," he pulled the photo album from beneath her eyes, slammed it shut, called the land bridge a white man's fantasy. He said the people of Aztlan came from beneath their own native earth, not from China. Then Jerry's manic talk: monkey gestures to illuminate Aztecs, Toltecs, Mayans, la raza. He told the story of occupying Catalina Island with David Sanchez and the Brown Berets in 1972. They were all set up in Campo Tecolote, armed and ready to defend rights set out in the Treaty of Guadalupe Hidalgo, when the supplies they'd forgotten began to come to light. They had water, cigarettes, and flashlights, but no can opener or toilet paper. Just fields of wild fennel for anyone imaginative enough to put it to use. Luckily, Jerry could always see possibilities. Carla remarked that she'd never heard about any of this. Jerry responded that her lapse was acceptable, since she was an anthropologist, not a historian.

He pushed his portfolio back toward Carla, flipped back and forth through the pages, showed her the elongated lines of his own temple frieze work, Santa Ana's version of Chichén Itzá's courtyard of the sun. It was time out of time, rings stripped from the circular calendar Travelers fashioned to recall the Network, elevating and consecrating the lost streets of his city. He pressed his blue speckled finger on a long calligraphic line, suggested he might run it the length of her BMW, just over the trim, with *las serpientes emplumadas* over headlights and on the trunk. Carla grabbed a handful of her hair, stared down at the album, stuttering retreat.

The gray-haired woman put a hand on Jerry's shoulder, shook it gently, and said, "Que pasa, Geraldo, mi hijo?" It was Alva— waitress, cook, sole proprietor of La Estrella. She complimented Jerry on the beauty of his *querida*, and in his embarrassment and confusion, the painter ordered three *tacos al carbón* instead of two. Alva nodded, tears in her eyes in spite of her smiling.

When Carla shook her head to clear it, she could see reflections shimmering above the gathered stones, pieces of shredded cheese and dried lettuce on her lap, and the cement of the jailhouse floor beneath her feet.

Jerry watched the anthropologist as she lost sour cream and guacamole out the back of her rolled tortilla. When she looked up, the entire contents of her taco slipped away from her, fell into a mass at the center of her plate. She dropped the tortilla, wiped fingers with a napkin, picked up fork and knife.

One of La Estrella's customers, who'd been sitting at a table near the storefront window, jumped up and sprinted toward the kitchen. Then half the patrons scrambled, tipped chairs, sent tables skidding through the *taquería*, shouting "La migra! La migra!" A blond man with a Marine haircut ducked in the front door, shouted orders, flashed a badge pinned to the inside of his wallet.

Carla was still sitting in her chair, but her back was flat on the floor, her knees up under her chin. She'd been thrown over during the stampede to the rear. Rolling to one side, brushing off the puddles of Coke that covered her vest, she pulled herself to her feet, screamed at the man in charge, the pitch of her voice rising as she worked her way around chairs and tables toward the front door. She pointed out that she was not impressed by the INS—and who the hell do you think you are? The man in charge told her to shut up and eat her tamales. She pointed out that there was no excuse for such a rude interruption to what had been a pleasant meal. He told her to get the hell out of the place before he got mad.

As Carla closed in on the man with the Marine haircut, Jerry maintained the same position he had taken when the raid began: his back to the wall next to the jukebox. Now toe to toe with the agent in charge, Carla stretched up to her full length, trying to get her face into his, but she couldn't make it past his chest. When the big man grabbed her by the shoulders and tried to push her out the door, she lifted her knee into his groin with such force that he dropped to the floor. His eyes were wide open and his face was frozen, open-mouthed. The scalp over his ears, visible through his minimal haircut, had turned bright red. The agent's mouth was moving, but no sound came out.

Two other agents jumped Carla. She thrashed back and forth, tried to throw them off, but each clung to one of her arms, and they finally succeeded in handcuffing her wrists behind her back. She wrenched and kicked, trying to break the manacle chain. When the man in green overalls kicked the back of her knee, she fell to the floor. Carla lay on her side, clenching her teeth, in furious tears.

The man with the crew cut was up again, tucking in his shirt, straightening his tie. Jerry walked to the door, tried to put himself between the agent and Carla. "Officer, you don't want to bother with this lady, do you?"

"The hell I don't. She's under arrest. And what's that to you, Paco? Let's see your green card."

Jerry raised his hands in mock surrender. "I don't have one, do you?"

"What are you talking about? I don't need a green card—I'm a citizen of the United States."

Jerry offered his hand in congratulation. "How about that! So am I. Born on Fraser Avenue. Actually, born in L.A. General, then my parents took me home to Fraser Avenue."

"Get out of here. You give me any more trouble, I'm running you in with the bitch on the floor."

Two agents pulled Carla to her feet by the elbows and pushed her outside, hustled her down the sidewalk to one of the unmarked vehicles double-parked in the street. As an invisible crowd of Aztlan ancestors watched the proceedings from the empty restaurant, Jerry stuck his head out the door, shouted encouragement to the vanquished snake woman. But the agent in green overalls pushed Carla's head down, shoved her into the back seat, and slammed the door.

Stones and pieces of shattered glass, the stuff on sidewalks that leaks into your life, then coagulates into an oblong piece of time, like this, with bars around it: a gathering of stones and discarded people, fellow travelers in the Santa Ana Jail.

Handsome Bear stood on the butte, looked around him in the planar directions: blue, yellow, red, and black. Signal towers still held their flames in dark cages as sun spoke light on the stone shoulders of roads. In answer, a bright spiderweb, a Network of dazzling chance. The man stretched his body above the butte, cocked his ear for the canyon's deflected language, bowed to the music that he saw. He looked east and sagebrush flashed into fire; he turned north and watched the plain race away, the last rays of sun salting its retreat with shadows. He watched pieces of sky fall into rocks all along the rim of the world, leaving puddles of turquoise. What the Night Bird didn't drink, the sun people would find and carve with their changing hands:

> Heh heh ah na weh, ah na weh,
> heh heh punariki, wuti na weh . . .

Handsome Bear stopped chanting, clutched his temples, and dropped to his knees. A whistling light beam shot through the hole in the top of his head, straight up through cirrus clouds and into the heart of the sky. The beam detached, spread out, sowed itself where star fields would grow. A stalk of corn eased itself through the same hole in his head, took root where the beam had been launched. Unfolding green—bright hands in all directions. Fattening ears sent out tassels, not corn silk but black-tipped plumes. And when the husks split open, each released an eagle. They rose, like the light, to join star sisters in singing the Song of Creation.

He got up from his knees. There was no longer blood on the top of his head; long black strands of hair had closed over the hole. The Creator had originally given such holes to all sun people. That was so they could talk with him directly—back before prayer sticks of eagle feathers and cotton yarn, back in the days when kachinas danced across the earth and sun people didn't have to impersonate their healing craziness at celebrations: holding the sky in place, calling down rain, making village men and women lock into blossom. Those were the days when gods sat down, ate and drank with them. In these bad times, only babies still had the hole; most grown people had not only lost it but had even forgotten where it was once located. Bone had never sealed over Handsome Bear's soft opening. That's why they called him "Hole in the Head"—or "Baby Mountain," because he was so tall. His other name was "Bear Caller," since he'd once fast-talked a she bear out of killing Blue Stick, after the boy took one of her cubs.

As he climbed down the solstice path, Handsome Bear felt his moccasin soles tingle, wondered if Sun Girl were playing footsie as she walked inverted on the other side of the boundary between earth and air. He took a tender jump, a skip, a little two-step dance. But there was no response. Probably just the otherworld feet of some ancestral sky reader, or wind watcher. His wife had crossed over the winter before, gone ahead of him to the other place. The sun was rising for her, and those others down there, just as it set for him. Staring into the hard-toothed darkness of grief, Handsome Bear momentarily lost his way, tripped on a stone, began a headlong tumble down the butte's stony flank. He reached out his arms, tucked chin, turned a handspring, and landed on his feet. It was a gift; his darkness was gone. Laughter bounced off the butte's shoulders, a laughter so loud and raucous it gathered crows. "Haw . . . haw! haw! Haw . . . haw! haw!" Reaching level ground, he jogged along the dry wash. He'd once been a champion runner, winning so many prizes (polished abalone shell, parrots, pretty women) for Beautiful Village that the gambling elders of rival villages plotted to kill him by witchcraft. Handsome Bear could still make a fast run from the butte back to his home, the sun-soaked earth humming under his feet. There was such power in that earth, lightning exploded up from it to meet the strokes that snaked down from the clouds. Running, and the land trembling with power. He sang encouragement for his daughter's work on her mother's clay cookstove: squash stew, sweetened with the rabbit he'd killed that morning.

His wife, Sun Girl, spoke to him in his night trips, but the words were sand through his fingers. By morning the sounds of her voice had become wind and sunlight. In the daytime, Sun Girl's brown face was a painted stone, cheekbones sharp deerhide smoothing tools. In her white buckskin wedding dress, magic breath feathers sewn into the shoulders and arms, she was a painting on the wall night built behind his eyes.

Handsome Bear was a memory hero, but the assortment of word stones he'd once possessed, making up the village inside his head, had shifted out of position, and the buildings—like parts of Beautiful Village itself—were crumbling. He was more than the head of the Snake clan, he was the village itself. Handsome Bear carried its entire history, from founding to the present moment: all clans, families, lineages, and events, from the three boys who fought the Death Ogre to grasshopper plagues and the birth of twins. He also knew the histories of neighboring villages in the canyon, even the outliers. Or once did, because now his ability to call back and read those dream stones was in question. Sometimes he could, but more often walls collapsed as he reached out to touch them.

A rabbit leaped from its hiding place and raced along through sagebrush and juniper, paralleling Handsome Bear for a dozen paces, then speeding off to the right. Five clans had already left. Some parts of Beautiful Village, stone walls and rooms in the sunlit world of tongue and teeth, had already been abandoned. Some had become burial chambers. There were new migrations. The Crow clan left in the spring to join the others who'd traveled to the southeast, out near High Ground River.

> Spider Grandmother, who gave us
> spider milk and blue corn meal,
> who sheltered us underground
> when the punishing floods came . . .

The fires in Beautiful Village lit the air above its huge enclosed hemicycle, reflected off the cliff that thrust up behind it. Outsiders called them "turquoise people," because the turquoise trade had made them into dream story or vision for others, just as the Red City of the South was for Handsome Bear. The turquoise figurines, earrings, and necklaces sun people made were pieces of sky snatched from the top of the world; wearing them was an eagle ride up to the sun. But the villagers had forgotten they were sun people, not turquoise people; counting and recounting their wealth, they had forgotten how to sing the Song of Creation.

> Grandmother, plan good things
> for us. Scheme with your two eyes,
> give me power to see threads
> of sunlight, weave them into
> hewn rock, feathers, and cotton;
> teach us to sing a good song,
> be worthy to live . . .

Spider Grandmother could see the architectural beauty of a hard life. She'd shown the sun people how to build canals to carry rainwater from sudden thunderstorms, and reservoirs to hold it, so they could irrigate and grow corn, beans, squash, melons, and peppers. Sun people had made an art of living well on the driest of lands. The clans weren't leaving because of a lack of rain—there'd been drier years in the old prosperous times—or because of the marauding outsiders from the north who'd shown up in their territory. It was because the rocks, people, and animals had misplaced their spirits; the web of their world was falling apart.

The memory hero had other worries too. When he got that peculiar feeling in his gut, traveling down his cock and into his knees, Handsome Bear couldn't walk away from any attractive woman. When the urge came, his thoughts, memories, and emotions boiled into dream stew, swept the sun off course, erased all six cardinal directions. There was nothing to sight or navigate by. He'd even broken his vows of celibacy during purification for festival time. How could all the parts of the world hold together when that sacred mating of sky and earth was jinxed by his bad craziness? This was not inspired madness, like the time Sun Girl gave him a necklace of turquoise magpies and he ran into the plaza wearing nothing but her gift, holding a feather in each hand. He'd danced for hours, whistling and chattering fluent magpie to anyone who'd listen. The sun people loved him for the way he made his odd happinesses into stories. At least, most of the time they did.

But the real problem for Handsome Bear wasn't women in general. He worried most over his doings with just one: Red Swallow. She'd always hated Sun Girl, from the time they were children. Handsome Bear knew that but couldn't stay away from the woman, even before Sun Girl's death. He'd wondered if Red

Swallow had something to do with his wife's unexpected trip to the other place: her sudden fainting one morning and the end of breath at sunset. Without ever directing his steps there, he always found himself at Red Swallow's door, looking around, surprised and embarrassed, to see if anyone had noticed him, then going inside.

"Where is that spindle I lost from my basket?"

Slipping her hand inside his breechcloth, Red Swallow laughed. His face was unmoved as he fought the little groan that always passed between his teeth, and his legs tensed, stretched straight over the yucca mat that covered the floor in her room. Knees itched, toes tingled. It always started this way. He'd never been able to get up and leave. She loosened his thong belt and pulled down the cloth, rolled from a sitting position onto her knees, leaned over his crotch.

"Look at this stubborn purple baby, sticking straight up in the air. I wonder what he'd look like if I chewed on him."

Handsome Bear's knees flinched and Red Swallow laughed her asthmatic laugh. "No, no, don't be afraid. I have good plans for you. When I eat you, I have the power to make you grow again. It doesn't take long . . ."

She leaned over, pulled yellow shirt over her head, sheathed his naked spindle with her lips and tongue, working it, leaving it glistening with moisture. Humming, smacking. Handsome Bear watched her heavy breasts swing with the bobbing motion and groaned again.

"Hello up there, Handsome Bear. I've been talking to little Handsome Bear." Red Swallow had released his cock from her mouth, after licking and sucking it in slow pulses until his whole body vibrated to the edge. She turned her head, sighting up the spindle's length to his face. "The sun in my room must be very hot, you beautiful man. You're sweating. But where's the sun? Isn't it a dark world now?"

Red Swallow got up on her knees, turned her back to Handsome Bear, began to tease her buckskin skirt up her thighs. She had the delicate neck of a girl, deeply tanned with a red underglow, and it was framed by braids that ended in clubbed knots; the lines of her neck matched her pretty face, with its high cheek bones and pointed chin. Her feet were delicate too, and high-arched, like a spoiled girl who'd never done field work. Even if they were calloused, they finished out her slender calves with a sensuous curve. But between neck and calves, she was heavy and heavily traveled.

"You're so hot Handsome Bear, put out your fire in my wet place."

Laughing, she jerked the skirt from the tops of her thighs into a band around her waist, wiggled her ass, rolled on her back, raised hips off the mat, thrust out legs and pointed toes, doing splits in midair. As she threw her arms out, palm up, on the mat, Red Swallow presented an irresistible triad of hairy crotches. Her fingers dug roughly between her outer lips, opened them into a wet pink blossom.

"See what you've done to me, my beautiful hard man? Stick it in now, Handsome Bear!"

He eased into the blossom carefully, afraid it might disintegrate—or afraid the blossom might chew him off at the pubic bone and devour him. Red Swallow laughed loudly, and as she laughed he could feel the walls of her vagina vibrate, contracting and relaxing.

When the rage hit him, his slow, measured strokes became uncontrolled thrashing. He ground his pubic bone against hers, trying to get deeper inside her. The oblong cougar pupils of Red Swallow's eyes made him even more frantic. His vision dimmed and the baskets strewn around her room took on a yellow cast, then a red, then a purple. Energy came to him in bursts, like the surges of a thunderstorm. As Handsome Bear rode one of these surges, he leaned down and bit her hard on the shoulder. She laughed.

"Give it to me now, tall boy! Pump your long legs. Pump it into me. Red Swallow wants it now!"

He was sure someone had come into the room and hit him across the back with a log. The stroke made his body arch and convulse until the fire drained out of him. He sank down on her body, sweating and gasping for breath. She was still laughing.

"Handsome Bear, you get tired too fast. So I'll keep you in my hole until you get strong again. Maybe Red Swallow's hairy hole will never let you go."

She pushed up his limp body at the shoulders, licked and sucked his nipples, then settled him back down again. The cold toughness of her breasts and nipples shocked his burning, tingling skin. She rubbed them back and forth under his sweaty chest. Her body sucked the heat out of his, and his hands and arms began to go numb. It was like being tied tightly to a tree. She reached up to the top of his head, but he jerked it to one side.

"My big baby, my very sweet big baby. Let me wash your hair. I want to touch the hole in your head."

"Don't touch me! Red Swallow, let me up. I've got to go."

"I won't let you up until I touch your hole. You've been poking in mine, now I'm going to put my fingers in yours."

She reached up with her left hand as she held Handsome Bear's neck wedged in the crook of her other arm. He clenched his teeth and strained to pull away, exerting so much energy his eyes rolled back in his head. When she saw the whites of his eyes, Red Swallow laughed sweetly, as if he'd whispered endearments in her ear. She tried to touch his spot again and again, but he twisted and turned his head from side to side.

"I'm going to have your hole. Just give it to me. I'm going to have you any way I want you. Do you understand crow feather and blood paint?"

"Don't touch me! Don't touch my head, you witch!"

He knocked his forehead into her mouth and jaw, but all these frantic efforts only made her laugh more loudly. Handsome Bear remembered how pressing ghosts sometimes jumped him as he fell asleep. This had happened to him since childhood. It took all of his strength to fight them off, prevent them from smothering him. Red Swallow was a pressing ghost too—underneath him, but exerting the same force.

A word stone of memory exploded into fire. He looked beneath him and saw Red Swallow was no longer a woman, but an undulating mound of putrid brown slime. He felt death sinking into the dilated pores of his sweaty skin. A stink of decay singed his lungs. He cried out to the pathfinders, snakes and bears, and to Spider Grandmother.

"Fire! Fire! Give me fire!"

He heaved, and with all his remaining strength managed to roll off Red Swallow's body onto the mat. Living blood and sensation began to tingle back into his limbs.

"Stay with me tonight, Handsome Bear. I won't hurt you."

"You'd hurt me if you could. There's a spirit in you that makes bad plans for me. I just saw you. You're the walking death that's killing this village. You've got a power that makes me forget, but I'll never forget what I know about you again."

She laughed in delight at his threats, threw a basket of yarn at him. He batted it away, rose from the mat, and tied his breechcloth. Her easy laughter made him grit his teeth. Never sure of the source of her power, he'd once put his ear to her chest as she lay sprawled in sleep on her mat, listened for two hearts, the sure sign of a witch. Her heartbeat was a strange melody, full of pauses and double beats, but he couldn't be sure. Red Swallow held secrets impossible to penetrate.

Handsome Bear, still running hard, was so close to the village he could see the ladders against the outside wall, and those joining one terrace to another, from the courtyard all the way up to the fourth level. He shouted at two young boys and a girl who were sprinting back and forth along the closed arch stonework.

"Who's the fastest? Which of you is going to double the stick and win everything for Beautiful Village? Two good women, I hear, and a whole new batch of parrots from the South are waiting in the circle. Don't know about our side of the stakes yet."

Rabbit, the taller of the two boys, answered. "My sister is the fastest. But if she gets sick or hurt, I'll be the fastest when we run against Chetro Ketl. Don't worry, Handsome Bear, I can win too."

"Watch out, I hear there's a witch over in Chetro Ketl trying to figure out how to make your right leg fall off. Better hope he doesn't miss and catch hold of your middle one instead."

"Where'd you hear that? What witch? Wait, you're joking with me, aren't you?"

"Haw . . . Haw! Haw! No, no—when it comes to races, I never joke. Anyway, Cold Moon Fire is faster. It won't matter if all your legs fall off. She'll win for Beautiful Village."

The sister raced off along the wall. Stumbling, the two boys set after her. Handsome Bear turned and climbed one ladder to the top of the outside wall, then another down into the courtyard, dotted with the circular roofs of thirty-two kivas. Small children whirled in shrieking spirals, dodging, tagging one another, dogs barking and stalking their heels. Women held babies and chatted with one another. Potters fired their work under stacks of brush and juniper, having waited for the cool of the evening. As he climbed up to his apartment on the third level, everyone he passed greeted him with a word or bow of the head.

Handsome Bear ducked into his door. Bird Grass had heard her father calling out to neighbors as he came up the ladders, his unmistakable laughter, and had already dished out the stew. It was almost as good as Sun Girl's cooking, and he told her so, but received no reply. They ate in silence.

Handsome Bear put down his empty bowl and spoke again. "I smell death."

Bird Grass looked up at him and touched her forehead. "You shouldn't say that."

"You know what I mean: the smell from Lizard's old place. Why did he leave his mother in there when they walled up the doorway and set out for High Ground River? Just tell me, I'd like to know. Are we all buried around here? Or on a night trip, only thinking we walk on top of the ground? There's no difference between Beautiful Village and the other place, except your mother isn't with us here."

His daughter picked up her bowl, placed it on his, and removed them to the storage room behind. But she didn't come back.

"What are you doing back there? Why don't you come out and tell me what you think?"

Bird Grass's voice came from the storage room. "Don't talk about Mother like that. I don't want to talk about the other place. Things will be all right around here again. Why can't you leave it alone?"

Handsome Bear shifted his sitting position, tried to look through the storage room door. "Nothing's all right. I smell death whichever way I turn my head. When your mother watches us, she probably wonders why we aren't upside down with her."

Bird Grass walked back into the living room, hands on hips, face wet with tears. "Don't do this anymore! You just keep making trouble. They wouldn't let anybody else get away with what you've done. Some people are mad about your bad words and the things you do."

Handsome Bear got up on one knee, then sat down again. "Who's mad? Just tell me who's got a right to be mad?"

"Crow Path and his men, for the time you dressed up like an outsider and ran shouting up and down the outside wall."

"Well, they needed to see how unprepared they were. What if it had been a real raid?"

Bird Grass turned her back, kneeled, and pushed the lid back onto the corn bin. Laughter still rattled around the courtyard below. "You make fun of them, and they hate you for it."

Handsome Bear chuckled. "They're mad? Crow Path was such an asshole, shooting that arrow at me. He knew it was me, but he shot anyway. Remember how I reached out and caught it in midair, then threw it back at him?"

Bird Grass was back in the storage room. "I don't want to talk about it. Please, Father, don't do these things anymore."

Handsome Bear turned and looked out the doorway into the darkness. There were no more words with Bird Grass that night, nor the next day.

Two days after his vision on the butte, Handsome Bear woke up before dawn, lay on his bed mat sweating. He didn't know where he was or who he was. The dark inside his skull was blacker than the darkness of the room. His lips moved, began a prayer to Spider Grandmother. When Handsome Bear recognized his own voice, the language of the sun people, he began to remember who he was.

> Grandmother, carry building stones
> into my skull on your spider back:
> old words, the word stones, pictures
> that make their own light;
> map stones and road-marking stones
> to point my way out of otherworld
> darkness, night stones beyond counting . . .

Still lying on the mat, he tried to see the ceiling through the apartment's darkness, recall every figure he'd painted there. First, there were chains of yellow suns and white moons zigzagging across a dark blue ground. There was also a web, a network of interlocking circles, ellipses, and arrows that held all the golden stars together. The great Night Bird, on the window side of the sky ceiling, was barely visible, a shade of dark blue just one step toward purple. He had produced the pigment by mixing prickly pear flowers and juniper root into crushed slate. On the wall opposite the window, there were three concentric circles: black, light blue, and yellow, from the outside in. They vibrated on an earthen red muted ground. The circles were linked together in asymmetrical patterns by lines that were, if you looked more closely, outstretched animals and human body parts. The wall surrounding the window was painted a yellow ochre with birds of various colors on it, and some birds of several colors: parrots from the South, Sun Girl's favorites. The back wall, the one that separated the living space from the storeroom, was the masterpiece. It was Handsome Bear's most telling contribution to the Great Work. In the daytime, and even when there was a dying fire at night, the white wall illuminated the room. On it was a grid of perpendicular and diagonal lines. In the interstices of the grid were many figures, some rendered realistically and others abstract symbols. Handsome Bear had filled the spaces with things he'd seen in visions and dreams, and sometimes painted under the direct supervision of the ancient ones. There was a man with ears of corn growing out of the front and sides of his chest, arms and hands held high overhead. There was the cone with flames rising from its apex. A sphere with wings, and a circle surrounded by extended snake tongues that sang with celestial voices, the one Handsome Bear had seen and heard after being bitten by a rattlesnake at the snake dance. There was also a flower with human legs as petals and a dark hole in its center. A cloud raining arrows. A stag with a small man standing between the antlers, grasping one in each hand. An eagle with the legs of a man, and a cougar with a hawk's head and wings attached to its neck. There was a circle that enclosed swirling spiral lines, representing the sun people's migrations through the four worlds; and a circle with a cross inside it, a large dot in each of its four segments, representing the first pattern of life. On the opposite side, a naked spiral, the sign of all human entry. There was a man with a large penis who stood naked over reflecting water, but the inverted image below was a woman, with a spread and swollen vulva. Their legs touched at the soles of their feet, and their coming together made a diamond shape. The chain down the right side of the wall was made up of interlocking snakes, each swallowing its tail. He still possessed every detail of the Work; Handsome Bear's memory, at least for the moment, was intact.

Pulling himself up from the bed mat, he walked quietly past his sleeping daughter, squatted in darkness by the water jar, brushed cold water on his face. He was a big man, with extraordinarily long legs, so when he squatted down he looked like a giant grasshopper.

Those long legs had made him the fastest runner in the village, and were the first thing Sun Girl had noticed about him, or so she told him later, after she became his wife. He stood up, walked to the front door of the apartment and ducked through it to the bigger room of the moon and stars outside, then climbed down two ladders to the courtyard, walked to the entrance of the Snake clan kiva. The snake festival was only a few days away, and it was Eagle Claw's night to watch the fire and holy things. That was good, because he was a dream signer, read night trips like the taste of rain on the wind.

"Light on your face and hands, Eagle Claw."

"Light."

"Handsome Bear on the edge, I'm coming down now." He waited until he heard Eagle Claw's whistle, then climbed down the ladder through the hole in the kiva's roof, the window that separated the two worlds of earth and sky. It was just before dawn; the sun watcher was still waiting. But the brightening eastern horizon said the link that joined the two worlds would make its appearance at least one more time.

A man kneeled on the sand floor of the kiva, facing a shrine of feathers, wood, and fabric; it was a futurist machine man with organic trappings. At the foot of the shrine was an elaborate abstract painting made of colored sand, and near the stone bench that hugged the entire circumference of the kiva wall was the sipapuni, the womb and navel of the universe. Eagle Claw rubbed blood back into his wrinkled legs and arms.

Without seeming to have reached anywhere, Eagle Claw made a pipe appear and offered it to Handsome Bear. They smoked for a long while.

"Eagle Claw, listen. I took a trip tonight. My hands and feet were pictures, and those pictures are still burning in my head."

The old man knocked the ashes out of the pipe, put it into a decorated deerhide sheath, then put the sheath into a juniper box with abalone inlay. "Lay out the night trip findings. I'll try to see which way the word stones point."

"The stones live in a place that drips sunlight, honey for the eyes."

"Go ahead, put them around the fire. We'll see if they hold light." Eagle Claw tossed a small bough of green piñon on the flames. The sap and resin flared, lighting up the kiva's interior.

Handsome Bear ran his hand over the flames, touched his fore-head, then began. "Three bearded men walked into the village. The hair on their heads was the same as the hair on their faces: yellow-red like dried corn stalks. And they wore bright metal bracelets on their arms. I looked at the men and wondered what they were doing in Beautiful Village. When I turned to see what the sun people thought of them, I found no living people there, only bones scattered over the ground."

At this point Handsome Bear fell silent, looking thoughtful and somewhat embarrassed. Handsome Bear hadn't told Eagle Claw that Sun Girl was standing next to him throughout his dream. She didn't speak, but she was there.

"You've got to tell it all, Handsome Bear. You know I can feel the pull in your heart."

Handsome Bear took a quick look at the brightening sky through the kiva's entrance, then continued. "You're my uncle and my tea-cher; I'll tell you what I can. Listen. I asked the bearded men where they were from, and they said they sailed in long dragon boats and lived on great open waters. I was going to talk with them more and ask them questions, but they handed me two shining metal axes. The metal they were made of wasn't orange, like the copper bells from the North Lake people; it was more like gold, but was harder than gold. It had a bright yellow shine like the sun. Knotted up snakes on the sides of each blade. It was hard to tell how many snakes there were, or if they were fucking. A beautiful web of snakes. I started to ask about the power of the snake axes when the sun flashed on each blade. The snakes came alive, slid off the blades and onto the ground. Snake chant words started to fly out of my mouth. I reached down and picked up one of the snakes, put it between my teeth. I could feel it talking in my head, saying, 'Come away and find me where all the colors live.' I put the snake down, still holding the two axes in my left hand. Then I heard voices and laughter behind me. When I turned, I saw Beautiful Village was full of living people and animals again. My heart kicked me hard and I wanted to laugh. Then the axes disappeared. When I turned back to talk with the strangers, I saw them walking down the road. I wanted to shout, ask them where the axes were, but someone behind me called my name, and I looked over my shoulder. When I searched for the bearded men again, they were gone."

"Which road did the strangers come into the village on?"

"Had to be the western road."

"Right, because that's where the great sea is, to the west."

"The Western Sea, where the abalone shell traders come from."

"Did these men leave on the same road?"

"No, I've never seen the road they left on. It's not part of the canyon. Not in this world."

Eagle Claw spit on each palm and held the backs of his hands against his eyes. He didn't move or speak for a long time. "There are tricky things here, and they worry me. What do you think your night trip is telling us to do?"

"We've already heard about these men and their long dragon boats. My grandfather told me stories about them when I was little. Now we've got to find them and get the snake axes. If we use those axes in our snake dance, the spirits will come back to the canyon, if the Creator sees fit. Snake clan people have to travel west and find these men."

"How?"

"Later this morning we'll call for a meeting of the whole clan, and I'll tell them about my night trip and what it means. If they agree, we'll leave after the snake dance festival is over. When we dance, we can ask the snakes how to start, and how we should travel." Handsome Bear pushed his fingertips into the sand at the edge of the kiva fire.

Eagle Claw shook his head. "I think we should ask the snake spirits now—my teeth are itching for them already—and every day before the festival. We've got to start asking them now, because if we really do this, it'll be the hardest expedition anyone's undertaken since the ancient ones came up into the fourth world."

"We'll do it as it should be done." Handsome Bear looked into the heart of the fire. Tiny silver snakes twisted furiously in the flames, looping themselves into knots. When the knots opened, they darted back and forth like schools of anchovies, began to seize one another—mouth to tail, mouth to tail—until they formed an arch over the fire. It was a rainbow. It was also a bridge.

| CHAPTER V | **THE CANTINA**
ROSARITA BLUES |

Robert Leroy Johnson cries out for women, both evil and kindhearted: he's got mean things on his mind. Cocked hat, brim pulled down on one side, his killer smile. But women give him the lowdown shaking chills, make hair rise up on his head. The only kindhearted one he knows, the one he left sitting on an evening porch back in Rosedale, Mississippi, studies evil all the time. She knows cockroach, weevil, dead man's moth; at night she turns her back on sheep and cow when the hants ride them sore; she's got her mouth all stuck out and devilment on her mind. *Loup-garou* . . . Open hand, closed hand—black cat's paw with six claws. Jump back! Good Lord have mercy.

I got stones in my passway
    and my road seem dark as night
I got stones in my passway
    and my road seem dark as night
I have pains in my heart
    they have taken my appetite

Who rides that same old fire-eyed sheep back across the delta and down toward the bayou? Must be the raspy spirit from underground, come forth the speaking hole yawning in red earth. Riding beasts with cloven hooves, riding women, and riding old R. L. nearly to death as the morning fire arrives. Snake on the road—he touches his cat bone for good luck. Snake at his heel—it's going to take some deep medicine, some deep power medicine. Jump back! White snake, black snake: the two entwined, drawn back to strike from beneath his snakeskin shoe. Lord have mercy.

I have a bird to whistle
    and I have a bird to sing
I have a bird to whistle
    and I have a bird to sing
I got a woman that I'm lovin', boy
    but she don't mean a thing

He cries out for shame when his West Helena friend-girl flicks her tongue, pants and moans, lets loose with Mr. So-and-So's name. When he looks inside her ear, the anhelical fold coils into a baby snake. There's a bone-handled knife with a broken point lying on her sink board. She says, "I gotta cut me some blood." Look away! That girl's going to slice into her arm! Turn around, spit three times, toss salt out the door. It's time to pick up and go, time to dust his broom. Time to grab his guitar and ramble. He bows to the painted lizard and to the directions that slide over sea, mountain, morning fire. But it's only a matter of time. Every branch in that dusty crossroads takes him back to Wolf, the gilded splinters, a hot brownskin woman with three gold teeth and her stuff squeezed into a red snakeskin dress. She lurks in the street, sidling up to every downtown man she meets.

My enemies have betrayed me
    have overtaken poor Bob at last

My enemies have betrayed me
    have overtaken poor Bob at last
And there's one thing certainly
    they have stones all in my pass

She's got a lock of his hair and a piece of fingernail. She's got a lock of hair and a little bit of fingernail. He left cornmeal, two fingers of whiskey on the doorstoop last night. Dry wheat shattered beneath the flail. Lowdown doney, she slipped a blood stone in his pocket as he slept. Then it came in thunder: slow talk, dizzy talk, the holy stutter. "What're you that's riding me? Call out your true name through my mouth! Come into my knowledge!" She's a no-good doney; she studies numbers and she studies the rain. A shame, a crying shame; it's shameless love. He's seen her in his whiskey dreams, standing with her three upturned faces at the crossroads—the haunted forking place, the sacred coming together place—under the horned light of the moon.

Now you tryin' to take my life
    and all my lovin' too
You laid a passway for me
    now what are you trying to do

You got to pick up and go to Ethiopia or Chicago, China or Detroit, and hope she doesn't beat you there, laying for you in the dark street outside your boardinghouse door. One of her faces is a high yellow mama with a sweet pause between her two front teeth. Another is a small blackskin woman with tight teeth, colliding white and gold, who smiles her ice so carelessly. Her skin is cold leather and she sucks you hard. The third, who waits each night outside the juke joint, is the girl who'll someday put her speaking dagger through your heart and end the song.

I'm cryin' please
    please let us be friends
And when you hear me howlin' in my passway, rider
    please open your door and let me in

You got to pick up and go, join that pack of slick troubadours: diddling guitar strings, washing road dust out of their teeth with pint flasks of whiskey. Duded out in pin-striped city suit and city black shoes. "Jump back! Don't you touch my smooth black skin, mama, 'cause I got the powers. I'm gonna burn you."

I got three legs to truck home
　　boys, please don't block my road
I got three legs to truck home
　　boys, please don't block my road
I've been feelin' ashamed about my rider
　　babe, I'm booked and I got to go

You got to pick up and go, Jack, to Chicago or Ethiopia, Detroit or China, Jersey or New York City, or to the land of California that is everywhere under your feet. That land shines in whiskey dreams, rides slung under the mail train or in the back of a Greyhound bus, because snakes are the spokes of the wheel that moves these blues, but nobody sees the hub, nobody knows what holds the whole thing together. California's a place where a man don't need shelter from the rain—that snaky old lightning and rain—and the wind there won't howl your bad name. It's lonesome in the land of California too, but the moaning sounds out there, those howling riders, turn sweet like oranges, burn in the evening light that blossoms when you sit on the porch and pick your song. Waves beat time, a slow rambling time. The three-faced woman is waiting at the crossroads, and she'll only make love with a two-faced man.

In 1929 orishas walked heaven and earth, wrote love letters to the world in the sky and dust of Commerce, Mississippi. Papa Legba, Ogún, Shangó, Damballah, sassy Erzuli: they picked cotton with R. L. and his folks. Now those same spirits amble through the streets of New Orleans, celebrate the Feast of the Ultimate Meat, feign masks, show charming teeth to the chosen in their final hour. Red-sequined woman bumps her hips and turns, wears bones on the outside of her face. Erzuli's back in town, that three-faced water woman, laughter of the crying virgin, love knot resewn a thousand times, letting the tears of her coming propel the boats she steals from the sea. She's back in town, walking Crescent City streets with the other orishas, along with Ethel Wright, her husband, Thomas, and their friends the Rolands, down from Michigan to catch this mad joy firsthand. Two glittering female clowns mime a dance around Ethel as she passes under the marquee of the Hotel Meridien on Canal Street, just back from lunch at Brennan's.

As she stumbled on the carpet edge and into the doorman, Thomas caught Ethel by the elbow. She let out a sloppy giggle, swiveled the heel of her right shoe to see if it had come loose. Thomas tightened his grip. "When you have two glasses of wine at lunch, seems like everything gets in your way."

Ethel pulled away from Thomas and coasted solo toward the reception area. She understood New Orleans was a Network hotspot, but she hadn't come expecting to see Damballah. Nonetheless, there he was, right behind the desk. His Mardi Gras disguise: Creole fast-talker; dark, curled hair; light skin silky as his suit. He splayed manicured fingers over the marble, showed elegant French cuffs. In the smoked mirrors behind him, two uncoiling snakes—one with red eyes, the other green. He talked gumbo, beignets that sugar your mouth, pralines, blackened red fish, red beans and rice, fried mudbugs, alligator meat, alligator women, dangerous streets, and special drinks in secret bars, but the language of his eyes and invisible tongue sent rolling shocks through Ethel's hips, made her toes itch, lofted her into a street above the other streets, rich with dust and sweat. Could feel it: forehead, neck, trickling down her sides and circling her waist. *She had a bird to whistle, and she had a bird to sing.*

Smiling, loose but distant, the shadows on his face lighting up cheekbones and jaw, Creole deskman at the gate, the gathering point, the crossover. Since all souls and flesh eventually come together here at the Terminus, where America stands knee deep in the Great Mother's muddy discharge, Ethel had no trouble tuning in: the sensual pull and the stones in her passway too. Her husband, Thomas, could also sense the possibilities, wondered how to program satellites using the city's wet sex for one coordinate, and interfacing maternal links between plants, animals, and stars. There were ecological implications in the cross-phyla of complex variables; they required a constant scan for what he called key word readers, the glitches in his programs that often evolved into superior software, even before he had a chance to launch them into orbit. Having seen the eddies that exist in the fabric of the universe, Thomas intuited the existence of Travelers but never imagined he slept next to one every night.

With her star-connected husband waiting by the elevator, Ethel continued to fix her eyes on the deskman, saw Damballah's low forehead and high snake brows beneath the Creole's skin. She could feel his squirming seed, dawn and generation. The notion grabbed her from the inside out. He returned the stare, appreciative of the lacy bra pressing against her dampened blouse, the way her belt cinched tight from beneath. Ethel smiled the sweet pause between her teeth, the open gate, Papa Legba's starting place. Can Damballah make love to the same woman more than once? Could such a woman ever come back from that dream? *I got a woman that I'm loving, boy, but she don't mean a thing.*

The golden deskman directed Ethel and her party to Shakespeare Park on a quest for Mardi Gras Indians, servants of the feathered serpent, the southside gangs that shook their plumed trousers, sang prayers into clouds rolling up from the Caribbean. Those boys used to do some serious cutting: fingers, ears, arms, and legs offered up as carnival sacrifice. Coffins the next day. But now they were singing New Orleans, dancing the changes, doing nothing less than create new heaven, new earth.

"Blackhawk the Savior!" The dancer pranced out ahead of his tribe, his roving gang, shifted hips so outrageously Ethel thought he might come apart in the middle. A mass of white feathers head to foot, trimmed with plumes dyed black, rose, and chartreuse, clusters of peacock feathers, bottletops, medallions fused from broken colored glass. Downy feathers in a tall frenzy of motion. He jumped high in the air and did a half turn before landing, squatting so deeply it seemed impossible his legs could support him. When the dancer got to the intersection, he leaped and twisted, looked left and right, pointed down the cross street and shouted "Woo! Woo! Woo! Woo!," launched into a war dance, kicking the pavement hard in a furious syncopated beat. Another picked up the signal, waved the banner of the Wild Magnolias, braided with gold, encrusted sequins at its center, turned and called out to the leader behind him—a large man, and the most elegantly feathered—midway back in the procession. Words shot back and forth, but Ethel couldn't understand either one. When she looked back to the intersection, she saw fifteen or twenty Black Indians from a rival gang, watching and beating rhythm as the two banner carriers stomped a challenge at one another, raising and lowering their flagpoles like spears. The Magnolia began to signify.

Hey-an dan dalu wild maboula!
Handa wanda o mambo
Said uptown ruler and downtown too!
Handa wanda o mambo!

Crouched as if ready to spring, the other danced to the Magnolia and sang back.

We the Wild Tchoupitoulas!
We the uptown rulers!
Big Chief got mighty cooty fiyo
He gone run you down the bayou!

Ethel's stomach jumped: in all the screaming and dancing, the Indians in their traveling costumes, the clatter of cow bells, drums, and tambourines in the second line behind the Wild Magnolias, she could feel the edgy static of potential bloodshed. Mardi Gras was crazy, but these Indians were crazier. Even though she had been cautious and circumspect as a union picket, she now felt a fierce attraction to this confusion, forced her way through sidewalk onlookers and into the street, where she lost balance, caught herself with a hand on the curb before hitting the pavement. Something lying in the gutter pulled at her eye. A small brass ornament, crudely made: it was a spotted snake with green glass eyes. As she picked it up, got bumped from behind, Ethel became part of the Wild Magnolia second line: the mobile choir, a congregation chanting out its call and response. The pace of circling rhythms escalated as the Indians moved down the street, and she found herself jumping up and down, shouting along, even though she knew none of the songs being sung.

The processions from both directions formed a ring around the intersection, and now the two leaders circled one another. The Magnolia spun around on one foot, crouched down, reached into the leg of his feathered suit and pulled out a tomahawk. He held it high in the air. Shouts went up from both gangs and their second lines. When the other leader shrieked and leaped high in the air, the Magnolia hollered, "Bow wow! Bow wow!" and pointed to the pavement, demanding surrender. His rival answered, "Only time Tchoupitoulas kneel and pray is when they burned out the holiday!" The Magnolia jumped in the air, lunged at his adversary with the tomahawk. Shrieks went up from both sides. The Tchoupitoulas leader raised both arms, danced in circles, released a high-pitched war cry, then dashed down the street, his procession in pursuit.

Ethel, shouting and laughing with all the rest of the Wild Magnolias, followed as they ran and danced down the street to the next intersection. The Magnolia leader whistled an order, and the gang began to sing a song she recognized.

> My grandma and your grandma
> sittin' by the fiyo
> My grandma say to your grandma
> "Gonna set you flag on fiyo!"
> Talkin' 'bout hey now! Hey now!
> Iko, iko un-day
> Jock-a-mo fee-no ai na-ne
> Jock-a-mo fee na-ne . . .

Ethel joined in. A popular song from the sixties, but she'd forgotten who sang it.

The procession slowed down, bunched up, filed from the narrow street into a wood-fronted building, WHITE ROSE INN on its window in unlit neon. Wild Magnolias and their entourage of banging, chanting holy fools sliding across oiled hardwood into the inn's cool must. Ethel took a deep breath of the place. Walls phosphoresced with mother of pearl. There was dancing in the back, a long bar down one side, and a pulse throughout the room—in the walls, as if something were straining from the other side. A huge egg ready to collapse inward, a reverse birth. White feathers, white walls in darkness, and with every new step Ethel took, the room expanded at impossible angles: walls, floor, and ceiling overlapping like the petals of a night flower. She felt the ceiling's vibration against her forehead, heard its low buzz and felt the tug. This was a Network crossing, a gathering point, a spirit membrane between the two worlds. She looked at the flurry of dancing feathers around her. Her intuition made sense. Music from heart to sinews, stretched in all the sacred directions. Ethel pushed her palm toward the south, noticed two white-cloaked women in the back corner. They stood under a miniature ship suspended from the ceiling, ladling seafood gumbo into styrofoam bowls for the Indians who sidled by. The rich and spicy smell made her remember lunch, look behind her for Thomas and the Rolands, but they were gone. She'd lost them chasing Black Indians through the back streets.

For a moment Ethel worried about her star-bound husband, but then turned toward the bar and saw Magnolia Big Chief, hip against brass rail, bottle of beer and a plate of yellow rice cakes before him. Indians and supporters filed by, each one touching him lightly on both shoulders, but he didn't seem to notice. Ethel decided to do the same, but as she touched his shoulder he turned.

"George Johnson, Big Chief of the Wild Magnolias, at your service, ma'am." He looked down and smiled the gap between his teeth, breathing audibly through his nose.

"OK, who am I and where am I from?" She reached out and pinched a feather on his arm, but looked nowhere except into his eyes. One was much larger than the other, and that strange mark of beauty disrupted the density of air and light, reconfigured his electromagnetic domain.

"You were born up North, but your folks is from somewhere down here, probably. And you want to know something about us Indians. That's who you are, pretty lady. Your name is White Buffalo Calf Woman."

Ethel looked into the bigger eye: all pupil, a black moon. She knew only Travelers could witness the dilation of the Network's rose of light. "Close enough."

He laughed, resting his hand on her shoulder. "Like the Nevilles say, 'Wild injuns down in New Orleans, they the prettiest thing you ever seen.' And damn good, those musical boys, even if they be on the part of the Wild Tchoupitoulas, the ones we just run off."

Ethel studied his bottle glass medallion. "Were you really going to hit that other chief with your hatchet?"

"Don't worry, sugar." George gave Ethel a quick hug. "We don't do that stuff no more. Used to be killing and cutting and such. It's all peace and justice now—Queen Leaf and the Blackhawk teach us how. Listen, sugar, I got to leave for a bit, but don't you slip away."

As George headed for the restroom, Ethel turned and scanned the inn, noticed a tall, husky woman at the center of a bouquet of

Magnolias. The woman wore a leotard brief with tiger stripes and a coating of red glitter, black chiffon pulled around her waist like a tutu. A silver crescent moon hung on the front of her Marie Antoinette wig. Gold and silver streaks down neck, shoulders, and thighs. Ethel studied the masquer, then penetrated the disguise and recognized her. It was Dierdra McDonald, an English professor at her school—native of Trinidad, the one she'd slyly dubbed the Voodoo Queen of Midwestern State. Recovering from the astonishment of this chance meeting in a New Orleans backstreet bar, Ethel moved closer to the queen and her retinue so she could listen in.

Dierdra laughed a long laugh, starting low and working up to a squeal. Her musically inflected Caribbean English enchanted admirers. She stretched even taller when she laughed, and looked at every man around her. "Oh, my, you boys slangin' each other out there—it was marvelous!"

Magnolia Spy Boy smiled and put his hand on her arm. "Sure we do, baby. You know how it is—you keep talkin' till you get cut. And we the uptown rulers. Downtown rulers too. Ain't nobody gonna touch our gang."

"Just because I've never seen New Orleans Carnival before . . . You boys don't fool me with your flags and mambo and all that jazz. Phooey on you Black Indians; this is voodoom!"

The group burst into shouting laughter, rushed to hug Dierdra, take a few whirls with her around the jammed floor space. She raised two clenched fists and shook her hips with the loose-jointed Indian Ethel had seen on the street. Someone started to slap a tambourine and both held hands over their heads, shoulders pitched back, hips thrust out like limbo dancers.

Ethel decided to join the party, called out to her colleague. The tiger dancer looked up. "Ethel, is that you? What in the world are you doing down here?"

The Detroit Traveler caught Dierdra by the elbow, and the circle of admiring Magnolias tightened, checked out the newcomer. "I wish I could wear something like that."

Dierdra fluffed out her tutu and laughed. "Who's to stop you?"

As the two women and their entourage moved toward the gumbo table, Dierdra pointed to a small gallery of framed photographs and engravings on the wall. "Look, Muddy Waters and

Howlin' Wolf and Bessie Smith and Robert Johnson. These sure are bluesy Indians. What a handsome dude that Robert Johnson was. 'You better come on in my kitchen, it's goin' to be rainin' outdoors.' They don't make men like him anymore."

Ethel looked at the photograph of Johnson, his cocked hat and pinstriped suit. She noticed that his right eye was disconnected from the left, pointing in another direction, focusing on a different world. "Yeah, a handsome rascal. They've got pictures of Indians here too: Blackhawk, and I guess that's supposed to be Crazy Horse, but who's the woman? There's no name on that one."

Ethel looked back toward the door, hoping Thomas had caught up with her. Instead, there was a small boy, dressed only in an oversized dirty white T-shirt and shorts. He leaned into the door-jamb and cried. She was about to go to the boy's assistance when the Magnolia banner carrier charged in through the doorway, holding his right hand as if it were a dangerous animal. He stumbled, skidded on his knees across the dance floor. There was a rush of Magnolias, and some crouched at his side. The touched man shouted, cried out in pain, said his hand had been taken from him by the Tchoupitoulas. But Ethel, moving closer, could see no signs of a wound. She looked around her, tried to guess whether or not this was part of the show. Looked at the door again, saw a light-skinned woman in a red dress, zebra mask over her eyes. She was trying to pull the crying child into the street, but he would not let go of the door jamb. One of the Magnolias at the banner carrier's side pointed at the woman, shouted out that Queen Matilda was there. She disappeared into the street, a number of Magnolias in pursuit.

Dierdra was pulling people away from the wounded Magnolia. She kneeled, grabbed his hand, and stretched out its clawed fingers. As he shrieked, she slapped his open hand, leaned over and bit him on the palm. He shook in his white feathered outfit, tried to get up, but Dierdra hit his forehead with the heel of her hand, pushed him down on the floor, and covered his body with her own. The touched man convulsed for a few moments, then was still.

Ethel watched the healing until the crowd hid the two Mardi Gras celebrants from view. She suddenly felt a desperate need for fresh air and squeezed through the inn's vibrating crowd, most of whom seemed unmoved by the crisis, continuing their whirlwind singing and tapping and jumping. Ethel made it almost to the door before she felt someone grip her wrist. It was Big Chief. He raised her palm, placed one of his yellow rice cakes in it, and closed her fingers over the offering. With a smile he disappeared back into the surging crowd. When Ethel stepped out into the sunlight, it hurt her eyes. Head throbbing, as if she'd been holding her breath underwater, she drew in the thinner air. Thomas stood in the deserted street, looking at the sky, imagining laser angles of incidence.

That night Ethel lay in bed and stared at the high ceiling of her Hotel Meridien room, tasting a great sweetness in her mouth. In her left hand she held the brass snake. On her extended right palm she studied the red gridwork the Chief's rice cake had imprinted there. She closed her hands and then her eyes. Standing at the crossroads, the haunted forking place, she saw bones all around her: bones with fur, bones growing sweet grass, and hollow bones with snakes crawling through them. Good Lord have mercy.

When Monterey bounced orange and rose twilight off adobe, it shot straight lines in all directions, and not one of those lines intersected its neighbor at any point. There was a strange, atonal symphony rising from exploding California light—the light that grows everywhere under your feet, puts a spin on the compass inside you, makes you ramble into holy fire. Jimmy and Ezekiel had been setting out and coming back on themselves for nearly an hour. The eaves of verandas drew brown shadows across their pathways on the streets. As the two bridge builders skirted those barriers of muddy light, they picked up and laid down the curled toes of their salt-caked boots with care.

A washbasin of soapy water flew from a doorway and slapped the dust behind their heels. They were heading down a passway off the Calle Principal. "Señorita, donde esta la Cantina Rosarita?" was the extent of Ezekiel's knowledge of conversational Spanish, so when the woman he addressed pulled at her apron and gave him her back, he tried to think of alternative plans. He and Jimmy continued several more yards into the town's underglow of darkness, turned left into another alley, and saw a stucco rainbow of painted flowers and the cantina's name painted over the doorway in gothic script. The lanky sailor ducked his head to clear the lintel. Jimmy followed, took a look around the room, and muttered that he'd forgotten what it was like to be in the company of white men.

The two Irishmen had just begun to get their bearings when a bustling and scraping arose in the doorway behind them. A child's voice called out, "Perdon, Señores." Ezekiel pulled his eyes from the rough-timbered rafters of the cantina, turned, and saw the girl, face covered with tattoos: obscure animals and totems, blurred at the edges, drawn in bumpy lines even darker than her skin. She led a silver guitarist who hugged the painted instrument to his chest with one hand, poised the fingertips of his other on her cranium—delicately, as though he could read impulses directly from her retinas, his own long since ruptured and decayed. Silver hair and beard, white cotton shirt and pants smudged by the same tawny patina that sweeps over silver plate, hinting at gold. Knots of filigreed silver studded his belt and boots. As Ezekiel stared, the old man's wrinkled lids flashed open: angry basilisks, luminous whites with silver running through what had once circled into pupil and iris. Hair straight to the shoulders, red gold skin glowing in its golden dance, drawing light into the room. Men at nearby tables turned and greeted Don Antonio but avoided looking at the girl.

As she guided the silver man, the tattooed assistant watched Ezekiel from beneath her eyebrows. He didn't look like any gringo she'd seen before—not a ranch hand, farmer, merchant, or fisherman. And she wondered why the strange creature couldn't shift his eyes from her as she led Don Antonio to a stool in the corner. It was obvious he didn't know who she was, didn't understand that no one in the cantina was allowed to see her. The patriarch took his seat, balanced the guitar on one knee, and began to play. Don Antonio, blind, child-led, pulling single notes from strings and then strumming, singing "The Guadalupe Hidalgo Blues," the Yankee-Jack-refuse-to-understand-my-language blues, the call-me-lazy blues, the call-my-religion-witchcraft blues, the forgot-who-taught-you-how-to-ride-horses-and-raise-cattle blues. "The Guadalupe Hidalgo Blues." As she tended the silver man, the tattooed girl felt the push of his old angers and joys, and remembered all of her own—pain she shared with the old man and pain that had been caused by him. He sang about loss, and the brilliant fandango that would come before the end, the great shaking and collapse along the ridgeline of the world.

Signed at Guadalupe Hidalgo, February 2, 1848.

A truce, a document, but the peace it brought could only simmer, just beyond the range of Yankee hearing. Sometimes bandidos got their attention, but those gringo vigilantes couldn't put together words like "Joaquín" and "Tiburcio" to make any sense. They could loop rope into nooses, but they forgot the language of signs. They couldn't see how, taken together, those signs would always make a song.

in the name of Almighty God

It was an unwritten song of sweet grass, sage, bears, and long-horned cattle, mountains caressing both ocean and dawn, holding much more than gold. That song, "The Guadalupe Hidalgo Blues," had been sung day and night for thirty years but sounded only as low sibilance in gringo ears.

Mexicans now established in territories previously belonging to Mexico

Manifest Destiny, moral order, Protestantism, frugality, and industry. Dana had laughed at the comic-opera military of the Californios in *Two Years before the Mast*, but when the fighting came the Yanks got their noses bloodied a few times, even with the odds overwhelmingly in their favor.

and which remain for the future within the limits of the United States, as defined by the present Treaty

Joaquín Quintero's hands were square rocks. Good Lord have mercy. The tattooed girl watched the cantina's owner bring a bottle and sit with the tall man and his small, red-faced friend. In a few minutes he pushed back his chair, turned, and strode away.

shall be free to continue where they now reside, or to remove at any time— retaining the property which they possess in the said territories

Don Antonio had stopped singing "The Guadalupe Hidalgo Blues" and was now playing his guitar in rapid, percussive clusters of notes. He was playing a dance of joy, intersecting memories of high-stepping, hat-snatching women he'd known from fandangos in the years before darkness. Don Antonio wove an invisible cloak of eros to protect himself from the evening fog that crept in from the bay. It protected him and it protected the tattooed girl. His notes flew across the room like a barrage of bullets.

Mescal y vino y jerez. Spigot-tapped barrels mounted on joined pairs of wooden Xs at the back of the cantina. The tattooed girl watched as Ezekiel turned more somber and Jimmy flushed until his backlit freckles looked as if they might jump off his face and bounce away. The little man stood up and tried to dance, whirling a lame jig step. But when Consuela and Rosalva came to join his celebration, he pushed them away, shouting and gesticulating. When he stumbled against his table, the empty bottle fell, rolled off, shattered against the tiles. Consuela held up her little finger, pointed at Jimmy's crotch, then planted a left hook on his pug nose. His knees gave out and he collapsed onto the fragmented glass. Ezekiel rushed to help, but the red-haired bridge builder was already struggling to his feet. He was shouting again, but his eyes seemed detached, loose in his head. Consuela lunged at Jimmy, and nearly everyone in the cantina was up and encircling the knot of struggle, cheering Consuela on. Both Jimmy and Ezekiel were on the floor, boots striking their bodies like rattlesnakes. They tried to protect themselves by grabbing table legs but took a relentless pummeling nonetheless.

A single gunshot and thick white smoke filled the room. The crowd moved back. Joaquín approached what had been the center of the melee with a long-barreled saddle pistol in his hand. He signaled a bearded man to help him drag the subterranean sky sailors by their heels out the door and into the street. When Joaquín closed the cantina several hours later, Jimmy and Ezekiel were still lying in the gutter, semiconscious, groaning, but unable to move. The last patrons filed out of the Rosarita, spitting on the two in farewell. Leading the silver man out the door, the tattooed girl passed, bent over, emptied a handful of street dust on Jimmy's chest.

Jimmy and Ezekiel groaned to each other, as much as the pain in their bruised ribs allowed. They wondered how they might get back to Wong Fu Gee's shack, but such worries were completely unnecessary. The fishing boss and his woman companion had just turned the corner, he carrying a kerosene lamp, she leading a burro on a rope down the alleyway. Neither said a word to the Northwest Passage pioneers but draped each one, stomach down, over the burro's back. As the disabled revelers were hauled back to Wong Fu Gee's shack, Ezekiel tried to apologize. Jimmy let loose with frequent shrieks and moans, occasionally mustered the strength to curse his host.

Neither of the rescuers paid any attention to the battered men. When they got back to the shack, they unloaded the sailors at the base of a fish-drying rig. After dousing the two with several buckets of cold water, the woman pulled off Ezekiel's boots and rotated his big toes in both directions to relieve the pain in his shoulders and neck. The silent nurse did not offer the remedies of Chinese reflexology to Jimmy. She removed their shirts and trousers, applied a brown liquid from an old whiskey bottle to the bruises of both men, and forced each one to take a drink from the bottle too.

Jimmy and Ezekiel were surprised to find they could walk unassisted by noon the next day. Wong Fu Gee led them to the San Francisco steamer, saw them on board, and paid their fares. Jimmy limped inside the passenger compartment without looking back. Ezekiel glanced down at his crusty boots and began to stutter.

"Wong Fu Gee . . ."

"Ezekiel, I'd suggest you look into alchemy." The fishing boss turned, walked down the boarding plank and back toward Point Alones.

The two bridge builders arrived in San Francisco the next morning. But in the seamen's taverns of the Barbary Coast they got the same reception as in the Cantina Rosarita. Sailors who listened to Jimmy tell his tale laughed and jeered, saying the only way to go cross-country from New York to Monterey was the transcontinental railroad. When Jimmy cursed them for their ignorance, they'd beat him senseless. Ezekiel often shared in the treatment, though he seldom spoke himself. After a number of beatings Jimmy found the memory of his heroic underground voyage began to fade. By the beginning of October he'd allowed himself to forget the passage entirely, suspecting it had something to do with the drunken stupor in which he'd spent most of his life. Ezekiel, on the other hand, continued to ponder the significance of the experience but kept such meditation to himself. As a reading and a writing man, whenever possible he pursued stories and scraps of information on the early Chinese explorers, keeping a detailed journal of his research.

Ezekiel Smith decided not to return to New York City, or try to contact any of his family or friends there. He settled in San Francisco, joined the labor movement that had been started by fellow Irishmen. A little over a month after his passage, he sought out Wong Fu Gee in Monterey. The fishing boss's shack had new occupants, and the people in Point Alones village said they'd never heard of Wong Fu Gee. On October 13, 1878, Jimmy McMullen shipped as an able-bodied seaman on the SS *Lorna Doone*, bound for Jakarta.

Galactic spinning and swerving, stars in their lazy curl, electro-magnetic snakes of power and light that undulate into possible music. Those songs are up there, out there, in there, waiting for you to hear them. You roll the FM dial behind your eyes until it rests on a flashing number. The dream gate opens and you pass through. You've found the number for your shining, as it slides out from beneath the map we call the world: molten lines of latitude and longitude burnt down through crust toward the magma core, joining where all directions merge into one. Such a number can revive an ancient song, a dance to honor blood and the lines drawn through it, our kinship to everything that moves on micro-stellar planes. The rhythm of this dance sweeps new music across tongues that have forgotten how to roll an *r*, sound a holy name, utter lost vocables to recall thunder and wind. When the wind of the song sings us into being, it sets up a humming on the cosmic harp that is greater than the sum of all its parts. It's the Song of Creation, and it's waiting for us to pick up the tune.

Jerry parked his van on the Boulevard, removed his car stereo, cut through the Santa Ana Civic Center to the county jail. California was shining under the face of heaven, in Santa Ana and next door where the 5 and 55 freeways collided, snarled into the colossus of concrete and rebar locals call the Orange Crush. That deformed monument was also the line of demarcation between brown and white. Pale-skinned Tustin sat snug on the east side, where valencias hang by one finger to boughs in surviving groves, lost garrisons of orange flesh edged by Pop Tart condos with Spanish names: Miramonte, Montecito, Mandevilla, Serrano. But no one who lived in Tustin spoke Spanish, only the visiting maids and gardeners, who lived on the west side of the rising ramps and overpasses in Jerry's hometown. Santa Ana was brown—just about pure *español*—but that suited him fine. As he walked through the Civic Center smelling smoke, he thought about oranges, how he'd picked them with his family when he was a kid, about Tía Lena reaching too far and falling off her ladder. The foreman said he couldn't take responsibility, so they drove her to the hospital in his dad's old pickup. That was around the time Senator George Murphy said God had intended *braceros* for stoop labor because they were built so close to the ground. Jerry thought he and his folks were built to rise like birds into trees, yet no one could see their wings but him. Orange County's remaining groves burned silently in the hazy sun. It's lonesome in the land of California, and all those moaning sounds—from the ghosts of mission forced labor camps and the pastel barrios of cities—those howling riders turn sweet like oranges and burn in the sun. But not in Santa Ana. There were no oranges in the Civic Center, where Jerry slipped between government buildings pushed tight together, repositories of clerks, files, judges, lawyers, and angled toward the jail.

It took over an hour to post bail, buy Carla's passage out the door, get her moving toward his van. No sage in this canyon of worn concrete and glass, but a cluster of homesteaders, an officially tolerated enclave, their supermarket carts loaded, contents held together with tied-down garbage bags, broken produce boxes from the land of plenty. Dozens of carts chained to benches, trees, each other. Jerry half-carried Carla past the angry bench of cart herders as she did her hobbled, one-sandal dance. She was confused, still trying to gather stones together. The Santa Ana homesteaders were not much interested; she looked like any drunk or coked-out mama from the neighborhood, just not as dirty. A man in a torn raincoat stood a few feet away, gripping a bicycle rack, his arms and legs shaking—in his pockets the jingling fragments of Thunderbird dreams. The man looked over his shoulder as Jerry and Carla passed, lost balance, released the steel, and toppled over. When Lucky Jane, the double-sweatered woman on the end of the bench, jumped up to help, one of her bench mates snatched Jane's paper bag from the empty spot, retreated around the corner of the courthouse. Burning uprooted orange trees in the canyons of Tustin, burning light bouncing off the glass walls of the Civic Center. This time of year in Southern California, all it takes is one match and a good Santa Ana wind to turn earth and sky into a brilliant show of wildfire light.

When Jerry got to where he'd parked the van, slicked-back hair and sunglasses squatted on the sidewalk. A slamming syncopation knocked out on an old guitar: "the twilight's last gleaming . . ." He'd seen the guy when he parked but had paid no attention. Now he watched the street musician drum fingertips against the body of his guitar like a flamenco player: "the bombs bur-ursting in air . . ." Red, white, and blues: anyway you sang it, always those same old Guadalupe Hidalgo Blues. There was a felt pen sign leaning against the open guitar case: PARA CARIDAD. Without releasing his hold on Carla, Jerry reached into his right pocket with his left hand, tossed all his change on the scuffed purple velvet in the case. He helped her into his van, looked back, asked Carla if she didn't think the man looked like José Feliciano, who was supposed to be dead. And what was the year he sang the national anthem at the World Series, got booed down before he finished? If Carla heard Jerry, she made no sign. She stared ahead without blinking, had not yet uttered a sound.

Starting the engine, Jerry put both hands on his leather-wrapped steering wheel, told Carla he'd take her back to the garage to pick up her BMW. But she continued to stare straight into the dashboard, trembling, lips moving slightly, still without audible speech.

It was only when he told her not to worry, he was in no rush, eased back in his seat, and turned off the ignition, that she announced that she wanted to be taken straight home: Amalfi Drive in Turtle Rock. Jerry got on the 55, worked his way over to the car pool lane, reached down to turn on his favorite salsa tape, but looked at Carla and decided against it. He felt sorry for the woman, but her sullenness was beginning to irritate him. When the fast-moving traffic slowed suddenly, he hit the brakes, and she lurched into the dashboard. Jerry grumbled about bumper-to-bumper traffic in the car pool lane, as clogged as the rest of the freeway, then noticed Carla pulling herself back into the seat. He told her to buckle up.

She tossed her hair from side to side, smoothed it with her fingers, gazed straight out the windshield. "I've never been arrested before."

Jerry laughed. "Oh, yeah? Never would have guessed it. I've been there a couple of times. Once a long time ago when I was marching. Resisting arrest—which is legal language for getting beat up by the cops. The other was for improving the looks of my own money."

The anthropologist tried to laugh, but it came out a groan. She put her hands over her face and began to sob. When she stopped, her body shook. "Do you realize I'll never get a grant or fellowship again?"

Santa Ana's most eccentric custom painter got out of the car pool corridor, jumped in front of cars lane after lane until he reached the right shoulder, then drove the van over exploded tires and car fragments at full speed, the veins on his forehead standing in high relief. "Shit, because of what happened today? How're they going to know if you don't tell them?"

"Don't they have a record? Hey, it's not legal to drive over here, is it?" Carla looked over her shoulder.

Jerry spoke in a gravelly voice. "Let me know if you see a cop."

"It's just that I've been trying to get money for an expedition to Mongolia. Jerry, aren't they going to catch you doing this?"

As his van whizzed down the shoulder, the artist hummed and chuckled. Carla seized the hand grip on the door. Jerry checked her fearful expression, careened to the next exit ramp, took surface streets across town until he delivered the frazzled woman to her door.

They'd been stationary long enough for the van's engine to stop whirring, but she'd made no move to get out. Jerry, still vibrating with manic energy, threw up his hands. She turned and spoke. "Listen, I really appreciate what you've done, but I don't want to be alone right now. Why don't you come in, sit down for a few minutes and have a beer?"

Jerry looked away. "I got to get back to the garage. Maybe some other time." He tried to rest his eyes everywhere in the van except on Carla, but they finally slid back to her. Even with a face puffy from crying, running mascara and eye shadow, she was still beautiful. And her feet—dirty, chipped polish on the nails, one sandal missing—were the sexiest he'd ever seen. Jerry rubbed his eyes and released a sigh. "I've got a real backlog at the shop. You know, the kind of work I do takes a lot of time."

She touched his arm as they climbed the steps. Jerry was pretty sure he should be doing something else. Recognizing that old crossroads feeling, he looked down at his shoes; there was no hesitation in them as they crossed Carla's threshold. The only problem was that carping, skeptical voice in the back of his brain. It sounded like his mother. Or maybe Leslie, his girlfriend.

Carla kicked off her lone sandal and headed into the back of the house. "Sit down. What kind of beer do you want?" She called from the kitchen as Jerry sat on the edge of the long white leather couch that took up the center of the living room. He splayed his fingers over the freeform glass coffee table, studying the patterns of a Persian carpet that lay beneath. The surrounding cluttered walls reminded him of a museum of ethnology. African and Eskimo masks, pre-Columbian sculptures—or pretty good forgeries—brass objects with geometric patterns and Asian characters he did not recognize, all these artifacts covered walls, shelves, and display stands. A cane, formed by two intertwining snakes carved in dark wood, leaned against the magazine rack. On the wall next to the front door hung a feathered Indian medicine shield.

"Jerry, what kind of beer do you want?"

He noticed his smeared fingerprints on the coffee table, tried to erase them by pushing a shirtsleeve back and forth over the glass. The van painter looked at his hands as if they were strange artifacts too, with a history of their own.

"What kind you got?" He followed his hands as they moved through the air, comparing them to one displayed object after another.

"We've got either Heineken or Budweiser. Which one?"

"What kind of folks you give the Budweiser to?" His hands lit briefly on the glass table.

"Is that what you want, a Budweiser?" Carla spoke from the distance of the kitchen as if she were only partially listening.

"No, I'll take the other." Hands retreated to lap, and he listened hard because her voice was moving out of range.

Minutes later, his head jerked around as Carla came into the living room with green bottles of beer and lager glasses on a serving tray. She had rematerialized suddenly and somehow looked much better put together. Carla set the tray on the coffee table and poured beer into his glass. Without pausing to pour her own, she threw herself against the back of the couch, so close to Jerry she was partially behind him.

He looked up at the wall again. "You've sure been a lot of places I don't even know about."

Carla readjusted herself, throwing her bare shoulders forward. "Not as many as you'd think. Some of these things I got myself, over the years. Most of them my parents brought back to me when they took trips. Like those wooden masks and the walking stick they got me in Nigeria."

"What about that leather thing on the wall?" He pointed to a scepter resembling a limp-handled broom, but when her hand touched his elbow, he forgot what he was trying to say, and turned to look at her again. "What is that wild basket thing hanging over there in the corner?"

Carla got up and walked to the woven tube suspended from a high hook. "I got this myself in New Guinea. It's a full body mask they use to represent a messenger from the fertility god. Nice piece, isn't it?"

"Yeah, I don't think I've ever seen one like that before. With a hat attached—a hat with an open top. Wouldn't do much to keep the rain off your head."

Carla laughed for the first time. "Oh no, that's not a hat. It's supposed to be the foreskin of a penis. They use it for the fertility dance that comes before the flood season in New Guinea. You want to try it on?" She reached up to lift the grimacing body mask off its hook.

"No, no, thanks. Listen, I've really got to go." Jerry was off the couch, nearing the front door. "Don't worry about your car. I'll keep an eye on it until you get over to pick it up."

She crossed the room, pulled at his arm. "Come on, sit down and finish your beer. You don't have to be nervous around me. Frankly, I'm not interested in men. And since you showed me *tacos al carbón* at La Estrella, you're going to have to let me turn you on to something before you leave—Tuvan throat singing."

He reseated himself behind the glass coffee table, drained his glass while she put a CD on her stereo, recorded in a small country near Mongolia, Carla explained. The first song began with careening strikes on an instrument that sounded like a banjo, then a deep, otherworldly voice blasted from the speakers, an octave or two below anything possible. Jerry was in a vibrating state of transition when the man's voice split into three separate parts: two drone notes, low and middle range, and the high flutelike whistle of the melody, a Celtic bagpipe jig. It was the Tuvan blues, the stuck-in-central-Asia blues, the lost-my-beautiful-horses-to-Russian-cars-and-tractors blues. Listening to the voice and its ambiguous message sent a charge of electricity through Jerry's limbs. The sound was too familiar, like a thing that could come back and seal up the open spaces in your life. Such a realization was all it took to lift him from the couch, push him through the door and down Carla's front steps. She watched him from the porch until he got into his van. The anthropologist on the verge of travel, navigable memory, waved good-bye to her rescuer, walked back inside without closing the door.

As he backed out the driveway, Jerry patted his shirt pocket for his sunglasses. Damn! He'd left them on Carla's coffee table, but there was no way he was going back to get them.

CHAPTER VI | # THE TEMPLE OF REMEMBERING

Memory is a channel of riprap stones teasing script from the water's flow: a conduit for dreams, the promise of fullness between heaven and earth. When light whispers in air, or over the spillway that pools the collective flood, all our stories arrive in merciless collision. As subtle as ribbon embracing a parchment scroll, or brash as the weathered mantle that lies beneath our feet, memory's pattern of deceit hiding in our full view. A certain insistence, the myth of loss to conjure a point of departure, but the real map is always there, bannered across the sheer face of the mountain. Nothing is ever lost; mutations are not comings and goings but the roll of ballast from one side to the other in heavy seas, the voyage that always ends where it began. Language and code, the call to temple and sacrifice, the source of our covenant. In the dance of all universes, a bouquet of mystic roses we call the Mind of God, memory is totality—all that is, was, or could ever be.

The branches moved, projected their shifting patterns on the two log sitters: hieroglyphics, a weave of light outside time. The man and boy, nearly the same size, sat on a recently chopped white oak. Someone would be back to peel its bark and strip its flesh for basketmaking. As the elder whittled a locust sapling in silence, Washington Muskrat fidgeted, his dark thick bangs completely covering the boy's eyes, making it almost impossible for him to see through the blind. Occasionally he'd try to blow his hair out of the way by directing a shot of air upward with his lower lip, other times he'd sweep it back with his hand, but it always returned to the original position. John Walkingstick continued to carve, registering the codes of light that embraced them.

"When the Night Bird finished sowing stars in the new moon's dark field, he got hungry, was sorry he hadn't kept back any seed. So he took one long scoop out of the darkness with each wing. The only thing left was what he'd missed in the middle, the star river. Inside his stomach the star seeds began to burn, and got hotter until the whole boiling mess erupted through his mouth. He vomited stars all that night, mixed with pieces of half-digested food. The combinations of stars and food landed on forest and field, gave birth to every plant we have. A red star and a squirrel leg made honeysuckle, a yellow star and lizard guts made the cowslip."

Washington reached down between his legs, pulled up a handful of grass. "I know that story. It's about where disease came from, and why the plants are our allies."

"Why did your mother send you to me? There are six or seven others who could teach you better. I don't have the time, and I don't need your chickens." Two hens, legs bound, feathers mussed, lay by the log. Terror had fixed their eyes into bright pebbles.

"My mother says Old Raccoon is best for plant medicine."

A flurry of shavings came from Walkingstick's attack on the locust sapling. "I have no raccoon medicine. They only call me that because my eyes are buried in dark circles."

The elder looked up from his carving, waved the knife. "You think you know the stories I tell, but you've never heard any of them before. If you only pay attention to what a story says with its eyes and mouth, you'll miss it entirely. The true story is the rhythm of its telling, the way it pulls bones and muscles back and forth until it's planted in you and you can call it back when you need it, walking or hunting or dancing. The use of the story is what it does in the air before your eyes."

"John Walkingstick, do you know why Nancy always runs faster than me?"

"Because you're so small?"

"No, she said it was because I was born backwards and so I'm always trying to run in two directions at once. I asked my mother about being born backwards, and she said she thought I was born in the usual way but wasn't sure. She couldn't exactly remember." Washington poked with his own stick at beetles rousted from beneath the tree trunk. Walkingstick spit through his front teeth with a *tick* sound and hit a daisy three or four paces away. This was the third time he hit the same daisy the same way. Washington watched the daisy sway from the impact; he wondered if this were part of his first lesson.

Washington took another breath shot at his hair. "Nancy told me she left the village under a full moon one time. She said she met bear people and they gave her two eagle feathers."

In a clear place close by their settlement on the Swannanoa River, John Walkingstick and Washington Muskrat talked through the first part of a summer evening in 1832. Daylight sky rivers exchanged colors, reflected the way the Blue Ridge Mountains guided three great valleys to a point of intersection at Gray Eagle, an hour's walk away. That directional coming together set up a crossing point in the Network. Walkingstick nudged the bottom of the carved sapling against the instep of his moccasin, bent it over his knee, pulled it down to see how evenly it would bow.

"Have you heard about memory tea?"

"Yes, my mother makes it out of blue thistles."

"That's the usual kind. There are others that bring back memories you never had before."

It would be difficult to accept the notion of spontaneous protein synthesis, in this case of polypeptides, if it weren't for the attractive and completely verifiable feature of the feedback loop. When neural activity increases, so does the stimulus regulation function of intracellular synthesis, as well as the alternating metabolic function of genetically deter-

mined cytoplasms and concentrations of homeostatic regenerative tissue in the primary-sensory areas of the brain. The end result is an almost simultaneous firing of the relay nuclei and the axosomatic intralaminar nuclei, providing the speed necessary for the successful transfer of highly encoded material. Effective registration of these codes is the best-known characteristic of the complex of functions we call "memory."

"White Bear called the tribe to council. They prayed to the eagle spirits in the common language of humans, animals, and plants, threw tobacco on the fire. That was before we forgot how to speak that language and creatures split into a thousand tribes. In those days humans were new to the world of sky and sunshine. We'd just come out of the caves. When the squirrels first saw us, they couldn't decide whether we were strange animals or moving plants. They guessed we were a new kind of mushroom."

"Walkingstick, do you know mushrooms for eating and the ones for walking dreams?"

John Walkingstick held the bow he was carving at arm's length, sighted down it. Although it was heavy, his arm never wavered. Washington Muskrat could feel the tug of the stick's weight in his own right shoulder. But he was startled as the Old Raccoon jumped to his feet, whirled the carved wood around his head. It roared like a sudden gust of wind on a mountaintop.

"The reason animals were so mad was humans ate everything. In the caves we didn't need to eat; we drew power through a necklace of crystals. When we first came out of the caves, we learned to live on roots, berries, and honey, which the plants and bees were happy to give us. But humans wanted new things to taste, so they imagined weapons and tools to bring those things into their mouths. They made hoes and digging tools to plant corn, squash, and beans; they made spears, knives, blowguns, traps, bows and arrows to kill birds and animals; and they made small hooks to pull fish from rivers."

The boy was beginning to be unnerved by the change of timbre in Walkingstick's voice, as well as the quick darting moves his head was making. "Is this story about plants or bears?"

"This is a story about bears, who one time almost forgot their claws, who one time began to remember they were human. It's also a story about humans, who sometimes remember being bears, and other kinds of music they once sang.

"White Bear had the strongest medicine. He could call down thunder. But Long Tooth Brown Bear was the first to speak at council.

" 'A man killed my brother. He cut the flesh from his lovely bones and now wears my brother's skin to taunt me and my clan. This is a blood debt, and the man has made no attempt to ask forgiveness or offer compensation.' Long Tooth Brown Bear turned his head from side to side." The boy jerked around as he heard these last words. They weren't spoken in Walkingstick's voice at all, and the storyteller didn't seem to be moving his lips. When the elder mimicked the heavy lolling sway of the bear's head, Washington laughed with relief. The storyteller laughed too, but it was almost a snarl, and when Washington turned again he caught a glimpse of long curved bear teeth in Walkingstick's mouth.

There has been some difficulty demonstrating the connection between the cortifugal discharge response patterns and the Hofstadler-Reese configuration. In his studies of higher primates, Miller has found no significant evidence of any connection at all, disputing Steinbrandt's findings in his research with dogs at Stanford. Of course, postulates about the connection between cell response codes and electrostatic potential in those same cells go back as far as Jung. In fact, Jung's studies of the functions of memory have provided the basis of modern electroencephalic therapy. Jung pioneered theories about the connection between heat-electrical patterns in the brain and schizophrenia. But what he really remembered, as he made clear in Memories, Dreams, Reflections, *was alchemy. It is perhaps less well known that in Jung's later work he rediscovered the risk of spontaneous combustion in psychotherapy subjects when phlogiston is present in the anterior cortex areas, especially in the temporal lobes themselves.*

" 'Humans killed everyone in my family.' Scratching Black Bear and the council house growled." Walkingstick leaped to his feet and began to roar. He turned violently in a circle, as if he'd been cornered by men or dogs. Each time Old Raccoon turned, Washington thought he saw another bear.

"White Bear stood up. 'Why should we act surprised? It would be hard to count all the seats in this council roundhouse that have been emptied by humans. Now what are we going to do about it?' "

Washington could see White Bear, hear his scratchy voice. He noticed his left ear was torn and scarred. Walkingstick sat on the log, hands on knees, looking at the grass between his feet. The story seemed to be going on without his help.

" 'We should make war on the humans!' The council was almost unanimous.

"White Bear spit. 'And how do these humans kill us? Aren't we bigger and more ferocious than they are?'

" 'They use bows and arrows!' This time the bears were unanimous.

"Scar Mark Black Bear shook his head. 'We could easily destroy them all in one day if it weren't for their bows and arrows.'

"White Bear waved one paw. 'Do bears have bows and arrows?'

" 'Of course not. Bears don't have bows and arrows.'

" 'Then how do you plan to make war on the humans? With their bows and arrows they'll kill us all.' White Bear was getting angrier.

"There was nothing but silence. The council had no answers. White Bear called for refreshments before returning home. Small bears brought in baskets of fresh, dripping honeycomb and huckleberries and set them around the fire. Normally they would have had boiled squirrels, chipmunks, rabbits, and such, but since the other animals were having councils on the problem with humans at the same time, the bears were afraid of offending their allies. They began to heave great paws full of honeycomb and berries into their mouths. When the bears were ready to go home, they sang out with growls, groans, and burps."

Walkingstick paused for a moment, or the story paused, because Washington was sure the storytelling voice was coming from above his head. Now each bear spoke for itself. He could hear them and smell their musk. The boy could see mange on the fur of one, flies around the open wound of another, and the yellow encrusted eyes of still another. Washington shook with fear but stayed seated and continued to listen.

"The next evening they met again.

" 'Why don't we make bows and arrows of our own?' Long Tooth Brown Bear's wife, Red Crest Bear, had a new idea.

"Small Foot Black Bear scratched behind his ear. 'How do you make bows and arrows?'

" 'You cut, bend, and smooth a strong sapling for the bow.' Falling Down Black Bear spoke with authority. 'While I was hiding up in a tree, I watched them do this in their village.'

" 'That's how they make the bow, but how do they make the twanging string for the bow?' Small Foot Black Bear was still scratching behind his ear.

" 'I was hoping you wouldn't ask that.' Falling Down Black Bear's voice fell. 'They take bear guts and stretch them, twisting them as they dry into a hard, taut string.'

" 'These humans have no heart!' Red Crest Bear cried out. 'They kill us with pieces of ourselves!' "

"I'm human, and I've never killed a bear!" Washington jumped up and begged forgiveness of the bears he saw around him.

John Walkingstick reached down to the ground and picked up a long, even sliver of white wood. "What does this look like?" His voice sounded calm, proceeding as usual from his own lips.

Washington was terrified by the sudden return to the ordinary. He tried to refocus his attention. "It looks like oak strips people cut to make baskets."

"The shapes of baskets and the patterns on their sides carry all of our stories, everything we know about the world. If you know their signs, you'll know and remember the medicine of everyone who has come before."

"Are you going to teach me about baskets?"

"Haven't you seen baskets every day of your life? What can I teach you about them?" Walkingstick threw the wood sliver back on the ground.

"I want to learn the secret of your medicine."

"First you have to know about bears. Plants and bears. Do you remember when Falling Down Black Bear got up from his seat and took the council into the trees? He picked a young locust and shook it back and forth the way man bears do when they want to attract woman bears, until the tree came out of the ground. Then he dragged it across sharp rocks until he'd barked the locust and smoothed it into a fine bow. The bears saw the weapon he'd made and gave a great cheer. But when someone asked how they would string it, there was silence. All the bears looked at each other. How could they war on humans with a stringless bow?"

Washington listened to words spoken by an ordinary story-teller, just like the ones he'd heard all his life. But he could still hear his own heart beating in his ears and wouldn't lower his guard.

"Scar Mark Black Bear called out from where he was leaning against a big fir tree, scratching his back against the bark. He looked sad. 'I'll give my body to you so you can string the bow. I'm too old to fight; this is my revenge against the humans.'

"The other bears cried out at their brother's offer, but knew it was the only way. Scar Mark Black Bear bared his throat to White Bear, and the chief tore it open with one bite. The other bears pulled out his intestines with their claws. After the proper drying and twisting, under the expert eye of Falling Down Black Bear, they were ready to string the bow with what was left of their friend.

"White Bear set up a target, then walked back to take the first try with the bow. He pulled back the string, but when he released the arrow his claws snagged the string and the arrow tumbled to the ground. All the other bears tried the bow and the same thing happened.

"'It's clear we won't be able to shoot our bows at the humans with our long bear claws.' Falling Down Black Bear thought, then solved the problem. 'We'll have to trim them. I'll volunteer. Let me sacrifice my claws.'

"When he'd done this, Falling Down Black Bear pulled back the bow string and shot his arrow into the center of the target. A cheer went up from the bears. They all wanted to trim their claws so they could prepare for an attack on the human villages. Only White Bear wasn't happy. He climbed part way up a tree and shouted at the excited bears. 'How can we climb trees without claws? If we can't climb trees, we can't hunt. The possums will laugh at us. If we can't hunt, then we'll starve. Bears are not bears without claws. Scar Mark Black Bear has already died for this foolishness. I won't let another one of us die for nothing. We are bears. We fight with our teeth and claws. If we try to fight with human weapons, we'll only make fools of ourselves. Or even worse, we'll become humans. We'll become our own enemies, and there will be a council of the creatures to decide how to get rid of bears.'

"The bears were ashamed to be reminded of Scar Mark Black Bear's sacrifice. They unstrung the bow and buried the string with the rest of their brother.

"If the bears had found a good plan, we'd be at war with them now, like Catawbas and Muskogees. Their hatred toward us is why we never ask pardon of a bear's spirit when we kill one, as we do with every other animal."

Since Walkingstick's storytelling voice had seemed normal for some time now, Washington was getting his old confidence back. He wanted to ask questions again. "I don't think bears are evil. I feel sorry for bears when we kill them." Washington knew Walkingstick's hatred came from grief over the loss of his wife to the bears, but didn't dare say so.

"Did I say bears were evil? How can you remember if you don't hear? We throw these stories like nets, out into the world and up into the sky. We also send them deep into ourselves, like the lines we drop to the lake bottom to catch buffalo fish. All the stories ever told are out there. So are all the stories that will be told. When you feel another line cross your line, or if you feel a tug on it, you've found the Network. If you aren't careful, you'll be lost in the gaps or burned by energy and memory lines, which run straight as true directions. And if you learn to travel the Network, you'll find enemies far more dangerous than bears."

"What's the Network?"

"Someday I may show you White Bear's motions, his thunder chants. But now listen to these memory chants Old Katalasta taught me. They're my own versions; if you don't make changes, they'll lose power every time you use them until they're worthless." Walkingstick reached into his deerskin bag and pulled out a gourd. "Shake the rattle and listen."

The Old Raccoon got up from the log and began to dance, turning in a circle, first one way, then the other, chanting sounds that had not yet resolved into words. One of his feet always hit the ground harder than the other. Washington shook the gourd in time to Walkingstick's dancing and chanting, tried to open himself to all the things he'd have to remember. Then Walkingstick's words came.

"Remember that teeth are small stones, the tongue in a rock's crack is fallow dirt, but a promise. When you shit out your heart, it's a green river. You will rise up clean of all mistaken battles. Your chanting boat will carry you beyond the cliffs and their tender trees."

The words began to buzz around Washington's head like bees. They wouldn't stay in a line; they swarmed wildly, and he was beginning to lose the ability to hold them. As he tried to remember what Walkingstick had just chanted, the elder started up once again. The boy could hear the crackle of the Old Raccoon's synapses firing, all at once and in all directions.

"Remember to hit the earth with fire sticks, harvest the stars, find the two-hearted bear who sleeps in your village as a child. When you plug mud into the oak's hole, and feel lightning in its wet shaking, you walk away without fear of death, your stone feet speaking to you in the language of blue valleys."

Washington was getting so dizzy he was sure his shaking rattle was out of rhythm with the chanting, and he expected Walking-stick to attack him for his lack of concentration. But the elder seemed to be moving away from him quickly, even though he continued to dance on the same spot.

"Remember the flower that never leaves the earth, a rock seed daisy, eye waters turning to fire. When you stand beneath the wet mother, your ears are the eggs of the redbird's whistling, and all your heaviness falls away. Your moon eyes lift the petals, mix them with light, make them rain over leaping dogs."

The best-documented case of this phenomenon appears in Irving's Child Psychiatry, *where it is recounted that a boy in therapy for gnashing his teeth simply exploded in the psychotherapist's office. Irving speculates on the presence of quicksilver as well as phlogiston, if not in the cortex, then at least in the rhinencephalon peripheral areas. This would explain the prevalence of the feminine, a primary source of spiritus vitalis, in the boy's personality. In such a situation the volatility of mutable* materia prima, *the failure to effect a therapeutic copulation between the volatile* materia *and incombustible sulfur in order to produce a fixation of the spirit, would necessarily lead to the combustive marriage of ether and the child's* forma, *his substantial manifestation. This, in turn, would result in the child's being extinguished and illumined at the same time. Unfortunate as this case may be, it has brought Irving and the rest of modern science one step closer to achieving the Great Work. And the Great Work, of course, is the infinite extension of memory, an overlay of all the circuitry in the universal Network.*

By this time Washington's legs had become so weak he just sat down where he stood. The boy was doing his best to avoid passing out. His face was wet with sweat and tears from the extraordinary effort he had made to memorize John Walkingstick's chants and his sense of total failure in the attempt. At this point he had no idea what he'd heard. Even worse, he seemed to have forgotten everything that had happened to him all day. His mind was completely empty. When Walkingstick finally stopped dancing, the boy confessed.

"Walkingstick, I'm not good enough to follow you. I heard what you chanted but didn't understand or remember a thing. My mind feels open, but it feels empty too, like a deerskin bag of beans dumped on the ground. I'm the empty bag."

It is said that Saint Thomas Aquinas composed and dictated three works at a time. This feat of memory, concentration, and focus would be beyond belief if it were not for our knowledge of the artificial mechanisms for storage and recall available to the scholars of that time. They practiced forming a chain of hooks, and a chain in turn hanging from every hook, and from each link of those chains, another hook and chain. Every abbey stone a hook, each bee in the garden a link in the chain. The world itself a hierarchy of memory that recalled itself merely by glowing in the hot afternoon. Aquinas and Dante were memory heroes, without doubt, but so was Kantu the Yoruba, thousands of years before them. He and other griots remember all history, all time, and see in the structure of trees, dirt, immutable suns, moons, and stars that there is no time, that syllables come from the Network and return to the Network in a perpetually energized permanent feedback loop. So call on Erzuli and Shangó, sweat and sing, dance out the world as it is! She will make you remember your life as an animal hunting in the dark, a bird flying over mountains and impossible forests. She will ride you, fuck your soul, and ride you again until your memory cries out for the dust of Africa. Speak to Erzuli, pray to her and she will make the sea cough up hidden and conspiratorial files of memories, memories . . . our oldest kin . . . the stuff that always was and always will be . . . the humid land rotting and producing in undulant cycles, thrashing into a frenzy of fire. Shangó is thunder. The immutable spirit. The Great Work. The materia prima. *Let the orgasm of the world split through its reluctant crust; Erzuli has gone down to the sea. She has pulled up her dress around her waist. Erzuli has thrown herself into the waves; she is purity itself. Let Robert Johnson strike his*

beat-up guitar and sing of Shangó and Erzuli forever, as he always has.
Let him ride the spirits of memory. Let Ethel Wright bring her Great Work
from Detroit into the half sunshine of the mobile and discursive world.
Let Dierdra bring us news from Trinidad, dancing in Erzuli's red dress,
deliver memories from our timid, exploding hearts.

Walkingstick looked at the ground between the boy's feet, as if
he were looking for Washington's intellectual beans. He held his
silence for a number of minutes, leaving the student in anguish as
he waited for a response. Finally, the Old Raccoon spoke. "You've
learned enough for one day. Come back tomorrow at noon. And
don't bring your beans with you."

Handsome Bear climbed down the ladder into the circle of the
lotus temple. The black lacquer steps had been attached to the wall
and the temple pronounced done over two months ago. Kublai
Khan declared it the heart and jewel of his Pleasure Garden.
Handsome Bear had been present at the ceremony for the temple's
consecration, and had visited several times since, but never alone,
as he was this morning.

"This is where the colors live." That the voice resonated in a
temple devoid of any corporeal presence but him didn't frighten
Handsome Bear. He accepted wonders. But this reminder of the
speaking snake in his axe dream made him angry; he still had no
idea what the words meant. Hearing words he couldn't grasp was
as frustrating as grasping for things he couldn't remember, and it
had been a long time since the objects and spirits of the various
worlds had connected properly for him. They had once meshed
together like the warp and weft of a beautiful rug, but that now
seemed another man's life. The Chinese and their confusing ideas
were not relieving his frustrations. The aesthetic principles Ch'ien
Shih-ch'ang, Khan's chief architect, had tried to explain to Handsome Bear were more like tears in fabric than a woven rug. They
almost pulled together and made sense, but not quite. It was a
miracle that the collaboration of the two men in building the
temple had come to fruition. Both were stubborn, but Handsome
Bear knew that Ch'ien Shih-ch'ang had more to lose. Khan's
disapproval would have meant the end of the architect's career, but
Handsome Bear was only a visitor and still intended to return to
Beautiful Village.

He put his hand on the wall, something he wouldn't dare do with Khan's officials there. This new world had too many rules—including where and how you could spit—and people never took the time to explain them to you. They only let you know when you violated them. As he put his hand on the gold walls, continuous and without visible seam, Handsome Bear let his eyes wander over the peach orchard and monkeys embroidered on the sleeve of his silk coat. It was an amazing piece of work, a gift from Kublai Khan. But when Handsome Bear looked at the hand attached to the end of the sleeve, he couldn't remember ever seeing it before.

Khan's people and other visitors to the capital had a madness for gold and silver that was hard for Handsome Bear to understand, but he admired the burnished metal wall that ran around the inside of the cylindrical temple. He was glad he'd won out over Ch'ien Shih-ch'ang, who suggested covering the wall with gold-plated reliefs of Christian crosses, stars of David, Buddhas, and the moon and star of Islam. The architect wanted to indulge the Khan's notorious ecumenism, but Handsome Bear had insisted upon simplicity, a total lack of ornament. He had argued that the kiva form was sacred to his people and their religious beliefs, and that he didn't feel those beliefs were in any way inferior to the four religions Khan practiced. Ch'ien Shih-ch'ang's concession to Handsome Bear was more out of fear than understanding. He knew Kublai Khan was interested in the religion of the sun people and had discussed it at length with their chief representative, the "Big Baby," the man with the hole in his head. To risk the ruler's anger over a mere question of ornamentation seemed foolish to the architect. It was dangerous to underestimate Khan. His mind was as large as the endless domain he ruled. Khan's elaborate gestures toward those four great religions might seem to be simple shrewdness, an insurance policy in both spiritual and temporal matters, but his enthusiasms were hard to predict. With his own eyes Ch'ien Shih-ch'ang had seen the Great Khan crying as he listened to the exhortations of an outlandish, big-nosed Christian monk from the West.

The interior of the lotus temple was unornamented, except for a kneeling configuration of flesh and blood called Handsome Bear, and the sipapuni sunk into the floor at his left. For Handsome Bear the temple's floor was even more dazzling than its walls. Blood red glimmering brightly, the porcelain tiles had been fitted together so carefully that no seams were visible, unless you put your nose nearly to the floor. Handsome Bear glanced at the sipapuni, a sign to recall the mother's womb, and the navel to remind the sun people of their journey from the previous world. He thought about traveling and wandering, and he'd done a lot of both in recent years. He'd seen so many marvels since his expedition departed from Beautiful Village. But he knew there were ways to travel still unknown to him. For instance, could the sipapuni be used to enter into the Network directly?

"Pray for colors. Ask Spider Grandmother, because they are all here at her disposal." It was the same voice again. As Handsome Bear looked cautiously around him, without turning his head, he began to notice the transformation out of the corner of his eye. The walls and floor were turning a creamy pink, and everything around him resolved into graceful, sensual petals rising to sharp points. When he realized he was inside the lotus, Handsome Bear felt peace, a subtle pleasure. The hair on his crotch tingled, but then a wave of doubt swept over him. It was his old fear of losing himself permanently. He'd seen so many axes in the last year, most of them more spectacular than the ones the bearded men handed to him in his famous dream. Why hadn't he taken the axes and returned to Beautiful Village? He was seized by nostalgia as an image of the village rose before him, then disintegrated with the pink petals into the hard sheen of the temple's walls. When the gold shrank to slivers, needles of light, and dispersed over a tawny color that turned increasingly green, Handsome Bear noticed a scattering of blossoms and buttons, and knew he was now within the cactus. Familiar territory, but not here in Khan's kingdom. Then he saw Sun Girl, for the first time since he'd crossed the icy waters with the salmon people. She smiled, spread her arms, and with her right hand pulled an icicle dagger from midair. Driving it into her chest, she exploded into blood. His scream was suffocated by the new skin that coated him. Blood had also covered the walls of the temple, turning them a rich, deep red. The surrounding petals, sensual as skin, told him he was now within the rose. He closed his eyes and called on Spider Grandmother to relieve his pain and loneliness, tried to remember the Song of Creation, but could neither pray nor sing. The songs were gone, but the pain was too. Maybe Spider Grandmother had heard his request after all, even over here on the other side of the world. He felt large and expansive, insubstantial, saw the lotus temple inside his own head, and his kneeling figure within that tiny temple. It changed from lotus to flowering cactus to red rose in such quick succession that everything blurred. Then he saw nothing at all, neither darkness nor light.

After long silence in that void, the voice returned and surrounded him, came into him and at the same time spoke out of him through every pore and orifice of his body. Handsome Bear felt his heart growing too large to hold within his chest. He tried to cry out, but instead of his own voice he heard the other. It was Eagle Claw. The old man spoke in different languages but always said the same thing. Handsome Bear, even without the magpie necklace he'd given to Kublai Khan, knew what the words meant: "This is the temple of remembering. This is the temple of remembering. This is the temple of remembering."

A column of sunlight shot through the entrance in the temple's ceiling and tore through Handsome Bear. It blasted straight through his head and splintered into a rainbow. He wanted words, and now they began to form in his mouth:

"Help me remember how to weave the spider's web, how to find the nest and stream where I was born, the taste of red dirt and salt, and the hard lump they make in my stomach.

"Help me remember the life of fingernails inside the flesh, the secret passage where moonshine is darkness; that rocks are the true ancient ones. They can live anywhere and know more than we do.

"Help me remember cloud mountains where the cactus god lives, and the places you travel when you taste her; the Night Bird, who sings so loud in his joy we can't hear him; being a man and a woman, having all the sacred places, and being a tall bear for healing.

"Help me remember the food that animals bring to us, squash flowers and long beans, and their prayer that we not eat them all; the mesas and buttes in my muscles and bones, how to strain up their sides and play their music; the voice of the canyon, where the wind grows feathers and cries out in warning.

"O Grandmother, help me remember holding bone tools in my hand, how they make the bones in my fingers stretch a little farther; the sun where it shines strong on the sun people, before it wanders away to other worlds; that the sea is my other brain, and the sky my dream spirit that flies in itself; smoke from the kiva fire, how it rises into the world with the words and breath of people from the other side.

"Help me remember who I was before I fell asleep."

There was a flash of blue fire around Handsome Bear's shoulders. It looked like the light that dances along a ship's rigging at night and sailors call Saint Elmo's fire. It pulsed and crackled, traveled over every part of his head and body. When Handsome Bear spoke again, his voice was different. It came from the far end of an unseen passageway.

"I remember the road of crisscrossed metal and wood, how it cut the land into pieces; the flying places where people ride, with thunder and fire, and a smell that stops your breathing.

"I remember when flowers rained over the earth.

"I remember giant metal kachinas carrying black ropes over the mountains and across the world; paper places where they keep as many pictures as there are stones in the desert. Each picture is an ant or bee, and they all think together with one mind.

"I remember the coming of the prophet, with his spirit shirt and buffalo dance; and great fat animals with horns, who die in the desert, swell up, and explode.

"I remember big pipes made of sandy stone, and crawling through them as a child.

"I remember light coming from a place between his eyes, and it turned the dark world into day. The people brought offerings and the earth trembled.

"I remember picking up small metal circles on the street, and as I put each one in my mouth, it gave me a different picture; shreds and strips of hard black hide scattered at the side of a smooth road, and how they pointed in no direction; the villages beside the smooth road, and the big places for riding that traveled on black circles.

"I remember at the heart of the sutra there is nothing; the promised word from the prophet is never spoken.

"I remember the bees dying in the sand at the edge of the sea, how they warned me not to forget."

Walkingstick squatted by the fire outside his summer cabin, tempering the wood of his finished bow. He heard a volley of shots, looked up, and saw puffs of smoke along the treeline. There was screaming and confusion, canine as well as human, throughout the village. Someone was banging a kettle as an alarm but stopped after the second volley. Nancy and Washington Muskrat ran out of the trees behind him, grabbed his arms, pulled the Old Raccoon into their escape. There was no standing and fighting the Buncombe raiders; they gave no quarter to Cherokee man, woman, child, or dog when they'd sighted in on them. The three returned from the cave later that afternoon, found the bodies of Oo Loo Chi, Polly Miller, Toosa Walker, Tu Nah Na Lah, and little Jinney Soldier laid out in the high place at the center of the village. Deerskin-wrapped remembrances rested on their chests. When the sun left that evening, Chewconas Tutley, his head wound unable to be healed, joined the other five who waited for him by the night river.

In the Winter Palace, across the capital from the Pleasure Garden, Marco Polo sat with Kublai Khan, playing a game of chess, each game piece holding a different kind of jewel on its head.

"I remember," said the Great Khan, as his Italian friend and informant told him another city.

CHAPTER VII | # JOURNEYS TO THE WEST

The knot of snakes snarled over, around, and through itself: green sand boxed by piñon planks against the kiva wall. There were whipsnakes, bullsnakes, sidewinders, and long fat rattlers. A boy held a feathered wand, tickled coiling snakes to slackness: genetic memory of talons from a sudden sky. Eagle Claw lifted another snake from the box, carried it to a large bowl with white zigzag patterns fracturing its dark sides, bathed it in scented water.

Handsome Bear kneeled in the sand next to the box, watched his uncle's sacred work, listened to the lone flute in the corner. The Big Baby was already moving in the paired line of snake men—mouth carriers and wand bearers—that would appear the next day. That ceremony was his last hope for assistance. Since receiving his axe dream, there had been no new communications from the other side. All that had come from his memory stones was the familiar story of Snake Boy, the father of the clan, who burned a log hollow, plugged himself inside, rode the wild Otherworld Canyon River to an island far out in an empty sea. With the help of Spider Grandmother, he defeated his enemies and came home with a snake woman as his wife. But how could Handsome Bear compare himself to Snake Boy? The purity of spirit that brought the clan hero success had never existed in his life, or if it had he couldn't remember when. There was too much ugliness in his personal history, and not all of it could be blamed on Red Swallow. The Bear Caller stared at the snake box. Somewhere in the winding knot, a shifting pattern of scales and color, was the language he was seeking: a map that was breath on air, and would bring redemption for himself and his village.

Freydis stood over the body of Snorri's son. Her men were still chasing the *skraelings* as they scrambled to their canoes. Face down in the autumn leaves, the corpse stumbled straight into the underworld. Freydis could see the boy had been running away when the *skraeling*'s tethered stone hit him in the back of the head. She drew back her leg to kick the corpse for that act of cowardice, but stopped herself, fixed eyes on what had been the back of his skull. It was now bloody mush, spreading a crimson as dazzling as the leaves scattered over this place they called Vinland. To Erik's daughter the rivulets running through the mesh of blond hair were an autumn blossom: a sudden, unexpected beauty. She knelt by the side of Snorri's son and cut off his right hand with her borrowed sword, wrapped the hand in fallen leaves, and hid it in an oak tree hole, fixing the location in her mind. She wiped the sword with more fallen leaves, returned to stand over the corpse and scream at her men.

"Come back! You fools, why are you standing there when the wretched *skraelings* are in their boats and can't be chased? You are fools and cowards! Look what they've done to Snorri's son. They've cut off his sword hand. This is a blood debt that will require ten of their heads with lovely split tongues in payment!"

The men walked back quietly and stood in a circle, looked down at their dead friend. They didn't want to meet Freydis's eyes straight on.

"You're all useless. How could I have chosen such useless men?"

Asvald studied Freydis out of the corner of his eye, noticing a light spattering of blood at the bottom of her buff-colored tunic. He didn't remember Freydis actually fighting hand to hand with the *skraelings*. He hated and mistrusted the woman, as did all the other men. No one was deceived by her girlish face. "You freckle-faced ice demon," he mumbled to himself, but was afraid to say anything back. If she decided to be angry with him, she'd happily sneak into the cabin where he slept and cut his throat. Even if he could sleep with open eyes, guarding himself against such an attack, how could he stop her dark powers? Asvald and the men from Helgi and Finnbogi's camp, the expedition's former partners she'd now declared rivals, called Freydis "Blood Woman," but only in whispers, and their eyes shifted with terror if an animal or bird came into view when they gossiped. They had no idea how far her powers reached. Asvald was disgusted by what she'd done to Snorri's son. He turned, walked back toward his camp.

"Asvald! Where do you think you're going? Coward! Does a little blood bother you so much? Dying is the best thing this boy ever did. Come back here. Help bury him and mound up his grave!"

Asvald kept walking as though he'd heard nothing. He looked around him at the colors of the leaves in the trees and those on the ground. There was nothing like this in Greenland, not even in Iceland. He drew in a deep breath and tasted the drunken smell of grapes fermenting on the network of wild vines that covered the trees around him. Asvald stopped, looked back over his shoulder, and for a moment watched men from the two camps digging the grave under Freydis's command. He spit hard on the ground. "If someone could kill that witch, this would be paradise."

"The ends of your arms, from the elbows down, and the bottoms of your legs, from the knees down, are white clouds. The green and black of your faces are the growing corn and the darkness of water when it's a cloud-rider."

Handsome Bear, half-listening as someone instructed two young initiates, continued to stare at the kiva fire. He jerked a clump of long black hair from his head and threw it into the flames. It flared and smoked, sending up the odor of burnt flesh.

"Be my witness, Eagle Claw. And hear me, Grandmother. I'll give myself completely to the snakes tomorrow. If they choose to carry our prayers and requests to the spirits, good. If they choose to ignore us, let them bite me too. If I live through tomorrow, I know Grandmother has blessed our expedition to the Western Sea."

Eagle Claw leaned forward and held his hand over the fire without flinching. "I witness for Handsome Bear. When we put the snakes in our mouths tomorrow, let the words travel inside our heads and into our ears. Tell us how to hold our spirits within us when we're far from our world."

"These are our houses, whether Leif wants to give them to us or not." When Freydis smiled, the down-turned corners of her mouth always made it into a sneer.

Thorvard leaned his shoulder against the cow carcass he'd strung by its hind legs from a tree limb. He directed the flow of blood from the gash in the cow's throat to the center of a wooden tub, listening to his wife curse her brother, Helgi, Finnbogi, and anyone else who dared cross her. She invoked the Vinland spirits, spit three times to seal the doom of her enemies. Since the tortured hulk screened her from Thorvard, he didn't notice that she dipped her right hand into the tub, licked the blood from her fingers.

When the cow was drained dry, the husband and wife lugged the tub back to the cookhouse, where the women were preparing to make blood puddings. Thorvard turned and walked out, but Freydis stayed with the women, making them watchful and nervous. She took a bronze cup from the hand of a braided young girl, dipped it into the tub, then drank it down before them. The women looked away.

"You're fools. If you drink blood and let me teach you, you'll be far stronger than men. That cow has eaten Vinland grass for months now and has taken in the spirits of this land. They're in the blood I'm drinking. That's the only way you can draw the strength of the Vinland gods."

Freydis dipped the cup into the tub again and offered it to Hekja. "Here! Drink it down. Drink all of it. This is your chance."

Hekja took a step backward but kept her eyes fixed on Freydis. Her mistress and expedition leader snorted, laughed with all her teeth, and drained the cup. Freydis threw the empty cup at Hekja, ducked out the cookhouse door, walked quickly into the forest.

The late afternoon light mellowed the colors of turning leaves, and every tree trunk was washed with ochre. Freydis stopped at an old oak tree with a large squirrel hole, reached in, and pulled out a buckskin bag. When she loosened the thong, grains of dirty rock salt spilled to the ground. Digging deep into the bag, she pulled out a wizened hand, dropped the bag in a root crotch at the base of the tree. Freydis kneeled and brushed leaves aside until she'd cleared a small circle of uncluttered green grass. She lay the severed hand on the grass, palm up, and poured water from a leather flask over it. From under her tunic she pulled a piece of carved wood that looked like a cob of dried corn, each kernel in clear relief. Blood Woman had carved it herself, after observing the dried corncobs the *skraelings* traded with her expedition. She sat on the ground, pulled tunic up over child-swollen belly, her split legs forming tangents on both sides of the circle. The green grass reached up into the hair of her crotch.

"Gods of dark places, come inside me." She picked up the hand, kissed it, then rubbed her clitoris with the wrinkled fingers. Freydis worked herself until she began to breathe hard, then groan, sometimes grunting like a wounded animal. As she opened and moistened, she thrust the fingers hard into her vagina.

"Reach through this hand and fuck me, Vinland spirits! I want all of you inside me! Pour yourselves into my child!" She lay back on the ground, shaking with the approaching orgasm, the distended navel on her swollen belly vibrating as she gasped for breath. When she got as close to coming as she could stand without letting go, she dropped the hand, picked up the wooden corncob and plunged it inside herself. After releasing a long, spasmodic shriek, her head fell back on the leaves.

Veranius appeared, sudden in the twilight, a ferociously beaked nose cutting his smile in two. He was there to collect the red-haired demon as one of his own, lure her with the promise of power beyond her fiercest imaginings, claim her for the Death Squad. Freydis was curious but cool in her response. As the confidant to Tiberius Caesar stood before the oak tree in the cold fall evening, dressed only in light sandals and a sheer tunic with purple hem, she asked if he were a Vinland god. His lids snapped open when he laughed. They revealed eyes so dark, she could see neither white nor color in them. Rising as he laughed, Veranius turned slowly in midair before her, as if he and his brilliant white tunic were lighter than wind. His manner was urbane and effortless as he described a whole world of weaker beings in bondage, to torment or kill as the Death Squad saw fit. When Freydis resisted the idea of taking orders, he added that if she served the Death Squad, darkness would fuck her better than any man.

Freydis lay in the grass, legs splayed. "Are you a *skraeling*?"

A surge of light ripped through the oak tree, left a ruins of overwhelming darkness: palpable, liquid, and strong with the sweetness of flesh rotting against bone. Freydis awoke to a moonlit night sky pushing through the branches of the oak tree. Her skirts were still above her waist, crotch hair moist with dew. She rolled over, drew herself up, pushed the hem of her tunic down over her hips. She felt in the dark for the buckskin bag she'd left against the tree roots, jammed the hand deep into the salt, replaced the bag in the hole, tucked the wooden corn cob away, and walked back to her camp. Her heart was mad with new power; her crotch still throbbed with the memory of a new and devastating lover.

Almost all of Beautiful Village had gathered outside the eastern wall, waiting for the expedition to set out. Handsome Bear stood, looked across the canyon without appearing to see anything. It was near light, the sun ready to pounce, promise of water riding through air and filling everything as if it were light. He began to walk, his moccasins tracing a snarl of small circles. There were twelve of them: Handsome Bear, Eagle Claw, six young men, and four young women, including Cold Moon Fire and Rabbit, the sister and brother who were the village's fastest runners. All the travelers but Handsome Bear had strapped thick rolls of strung-together reeds on their backs, each containing a blanket, dried food, and other provisions. Some had spears in their hands, others bows, with quivers slung crosswise on their backs below the reed bundles. Each one had a skin of water strapped around the waist, so it tucked into the small of the back. Handsome Bear's kit was still on the ground.

The expedition looked east for the starting signal, the sunrise over the rim of the canyon. Everyone but Handsome Bear. They watched him out of the corners of their eyes but tried not to embarrass him by staring.

Eagle Claw walked up behind the circling leader, reached up to put his hand on his nephew's shoulder. "Come back now. We have to pray for good signs and blessings. It's time for you to come back now."

Handsome Bear stopped pacing but didn't respond. He was inside a cloud of stars that constantly shifted and warped into different formations. He tried to read the signs offered to him. All night long—in fact, for almost four days now, since the end of the snake dance, when he'd watched the purifying black water of otherworld darkness pour out of his mouth—he'd been reading signs. Feathered serpents in flight everywhere. There were more in the air around him than the rattlers and sidewinders gathered for the dance. Fire lizards streaked over the ground before his eyes, and he could see them darting in all directions along the horizon, like earthbound shooting stars. Last night he'd spoken to Rainwater Ram, the beast with lightning horns, god of crossing paths, whose face is a triple cross within a circle. Ancestors had been there too, including his grandmother's grandmother, Sun Bird, who was young and beautiful in her white buckskin marriage dress and boots, and who had black circles for eyes.

"Handsome Bear, please come back now. The sun is coming up. You have to say the words and sing the song before we leave. People have given the lives of their children to you to keep and protect." Eagle Claw spoke quietly. His words were meant only for Handsome Bear, and no one else seemed to hear them.

Curling smoke weaving through the Network of flashing lines, a huge yucca mat in blue flames stretching across the sky. The landscape was empty: no Beautiful Village, no cornfields, no canals, no piñon, sage, or yucca, just the fire pollen that continued to settle on his skin. Then everything came back: cloud panthers, leaping deer with their heavy tails, bear, fox, coyote, and nervy squirrels. The world was green again, and he knew this would last forever. All the snakes had taken the messages of the sun people to the spirit world, delivered their true language. The healer felt happiness in his long legs, and his feet began to move in a dance. He turned slowly to the left, then to the right, as his feet kicked syncopated time. He was back in the cornfields again, touching the tasseled ears. His arms and chest turned dark blue like corn. He had become the corn goddess, felt the sacredness of her female places. His head snapped to the right, then to the left, like an eagle's, and his arms spread out as tasseled wings. Knees bent, he began to squat and kick into the dance. He flew over the irrigation grid of Beautiful Village: catchment basins, channels leading thunderstorm waters into the main canals and down into fields at the base of the canyon. The panther would come and go, appear and disappear, sometimes taking the shape of water, sometimes flesh sprouting claws. Once the panther turned and spoke to him with a black woman's face. "Remember the people you pass as you travel. Some are enemies, some will be family. Their colors are the four directions: red, yellow, black, and white."

The panther turned to water again, raced downhill through the canals. There was a flash of lightning that lingered, rolled itself into a column, then crested in a fiery cloud. Handsome Bear stopped dancing and stared at the cloud; there were faces in the column, a multitude—red, brown, black, yellow, and white—and a multitude of voices singing and screaming around it. Then quiet. There was only one man, squatting in a bright room before a shiny gray metal house that sat on two black disks, and each disk contained a bright silver disk within it. The man had short dark hair, and some of the same grew on his upper lip. He wore unusual clothes. The squatting stranger ran his hand over the shaped and undulant gray metal, touching the picture he had painted there. It was a picture of the canyon where Beautiful Village lay, surrounded by clouds pierced with lightning. There was a feathered serpent, fire lizards, the water panther, and all creation suggested in delicate strokes of color. In the middle of the painting there was a man's face. Handsome Bear recognized it; it was his own.

"It's time to remember the circle." The leader stood still, hands raised over his head. All the other expedition members watched but waited for more words before they dared move toward him. "The circle will mend only if we break it first, make it into an arrow, and shoot it into a new world across the sea."

Eagle Claw and the others came closer now, stepping quietly as Handsome Bear continued to speak.

"Snake Boy has shown us how to travel in water. By land to the water, and by water to land. We'll start when the sun shows us its full circle."

Rabbit's heart beat fast in anticipation, and he scuffled the sand with his moccasins. When Red Swallow's hand touched his shoulder, he jumped and spun around.

"Don't say anything, Rabbit. I have something for Handsome Bear, but he's been touched by spirits and I don't dare speak to him now. I have special medicine to protect all of you while you travel. Here, tuck it inside your belt and make sure you don't lose it as you run along."

Rabbit looked down as Red Swallow pushed the buckskin medicine bag behind his breechcloth thong. There was a red feather sewn into it. "I'll give it to Handsome Bear as soon as we're on our way."

"No, I want you to keep it. You're young, but if you carry this you'll be as important as anyone. You'll protect everyone along the way." Red Swallow smiled and hugged the boy, but his attention was directed at his leader.

Handsome Bear stooped down, picked up his roll of reeds, slipped his arms through the buckskin straps that held it on his back. Rabbit and all the others shifted their rolls to make sure they were secure. Big Baby looked toward the east again. The upper tip of the sun flared over the rim of the world, but the crowd remained silent. When the bottom of the sun's circle had barely cleared the rim, the crowd burst into a cheer, and the twelve started down the west road at a quick jog.

The cheering diminished as the villagers watched the expedition mix into the haze of the distance. Most returned to their apartments or to the fields to begin the day's work. A few stragglers were startled as Red Swallow gave out a cry and started to dance alone. She chanted under her breath.

"I've planted the seed, I've planted the seed. My handsome man, my Big Baby, you'll carry my mark and my blood-dark medicine wherever you go—a dried baby's paw and an old man's nose, wrapped in sage. With my bag on you like a tick, I will follow you and dog you, my lover, wherever you go, wherever you go. Handsome Bear, wherever you go, like blood on your forehead and lips."

Freydis held her salted hand and prayed to Veranius, demanded not just the gift of foresight but of omnipresence as well. She wanted the power to throw blood into future generations through her icy gates of flesh. She wanted daughters, granddaughters, an endless posterity capable of seizing Vinland in their teeth—dominating forest, lake, plain, and mountain, everything they saw. Freydis's fire rips blood up through your skin, freezes it to salt, red spines that spring out and glow like blue death. Jagged icebergs of time float down the coast from a true north only lazy men, reluctant travelers, could have invented. North in reality is a spiritual state, where the Freydis wind rises, wild like the gods of the New World: blue, blue-green, musty with moss and lichen, the indelible stain of permafrost. She makes us into icebergs, lost beyond recognition, to ourselves or any others. But there is fire in the veins of her swollen breasts, blue mixed with the cream of blood that curdles on her teeth. Salt in blood, in fire, on her teeth, tracing maps of conquest across the coming time. Those maps can be read only in winter, a transparent skull held up to a starving candle, a bitter night when even death seems a blessing. But the maps will lead where Freydis least expects, to a girl more kin to a Dwamish earth child than the Blood Woman, a girl who can see everything without wanting to possess it. She will rise up, heir to a lost race that has run through human veins for millennia. Returning for the Shift, a child of promise stands in light, takes the mutilated hand, and grows it into a bodhi tree.

Handsome Bear, Eagle Claw, Cold Moon Fire, Rabbit, Two Bucks, Magpie Girl, Descending Cloud, Dancer, Crow, Little Ram, Red Stone, and Broken Hand ran at a good pace across desert and brushland until sunset the first day. The next morning they were already running when the sunrise hit their backs, heading due west, with occasional detours around buttes and mountains. When they began to enter the high Kachina Mountains on the fourth day, their pace slowed. In the dark of that evening, exhausted, Handsome Bear looked for an open and level place to camp. He spotted a ridge that offered protection from the strong westerly wind that had been pushing against them all day, and he shouted for his runners to stop. Moments after his voice rang out and echoes began to return, there was a sudden and much stronger gust in their faces, pelting the whole expedition with a fine sand that stung their skin like bees. Eagle Claw was pointing toward the ridge when an arrow grazed his shoulder and buried itself in the reed-wrapped blanket of his roll. More arrows whizzed in, all missing their mark except for the one Crow took in the calf. Large stones bounced off the rocks around them. The young ones ran away—Cold Moon Fire straight up, as fast as she could, others scrambling on all fours. They gathered again behind a formation, dropped their reed packs, and strung their bows.

Handsome Bear and Eagle Claw stood their ground, trying to locate the enemies. Arrows and rocks continued to fly, missing both narrowly, until a large rebounding rock hit Handsome Bear in the thigh and knocked him down. Pain flashed lightning into his eyes, and at that precise moment a jagged inverted tree of lightning exploded in the cloudless evening sky. He picked himself up, shouted toward the holding illumination of precious colors, demanding to know if he were facing men or gods. The delayed thunder echoed and rumbled off the mountain peaks; the arrows and rocks ceased to fly. There were a few moments of motionless silence, then the sky ignited with another flash, and arrows rained down again. Handsome Bear and Eagle Claw ran to join the expedition behind the rocks where they were crouching.

The Big Baby directed the men and women to draw their bows and aim toward the ridge, choose a silhouette with the next lightning flash, and shoot. They all rushed for position against the upper edge of the rock, but Cold Moon Fire lingered by the leader's side, asking what if they were being tricked and another group was moving to attack their rear. A bolt of fractured light tore up the sky, and a volley was released. The expedition leader caught a glimpse of the girl's face, calm and ferocious. Handsome Bear ordered his group to release another volley with the next stroke of lightning, then drop back, slipping along the ridge to the treeline. They looked over their shoulders to check the direction he was pointing. Lightning flashed, and arrows tore into the wind. One of the creatures on the ridge above let out a high-pitched sound, like an eagle shrieking.

Gunwales icing, the sail and lines threw sleet as they snapped in the wind. Freydis lay in the bottom of the dragon boat, surrounded by her women. When a surge of pain hit, she cursed everyone on board: their ancestors, their gods, and the lives they all hoped to live. Hekja rested her hand on Freydis's pulsing belly. The water had broken, and the cursing sprees were now getting closer together. Hekja kept her eyes on Freydis's swollen labia, looking for a tuft of wet hair to make its appearance at the center of the small dilation between pink folds. Thorvard had put his cloak under his wife's back and legs, to protect the arriving child from the icy slime of the planks below Freydis's crotch. The cloak too was soaked and icy, from the sea spray, Freydis's amniotic discharge, and her raging sweat.

"Thorvard, you bastard! Pull her around and run before the wind. I told you to do that. I'm going to get sick down here if we keep pitching this way!"

"Freydis, we can't do it. We'll lose our way and miss Greenland." He stepped over a bench and reached his hand down to touch her forehead, but she slapped it away.

"Don't touch me, you cowardly pig! I still command this expedition! Run before the wind or I'll kill you when I get through down here. No daughter of Erik has ever lost her way on these seas. They belong to us. The salt water is mine to travel as I please! Do it now!"

The men hadn't dared let their eyes rest on Freydis, for fear one of her curses would stop their hearts, kill them where they stood or sat. They looked at Thorvard and he nodded, signaling them to reef the sail. He nodded again at Ketil, and the giant steersman leaned the rudder to starboard, set the ship running before the powerful northwesterlies.

"It's coming!" Hekja shouted and reached between the labia to grip the child's head. It was slipping through steadily now, as Freydis groaned and pushed: the head, the compressed shoulders, then the whole child and afterbirth, which settled with a smack on Thorvard's cloak.

Freydis had been clenching the bone handle of a knife between her teeth. Now she removed the knife and held it in her hand. "Give it to me! What is it, a boy child or a girl?"

Hekja had cut the umbilical cord with her own small knife and was holding the baby by the ankles, shaking it upside down. "It's a boy child! A great large boy child!" She handed the screaming and gasping child to the mother, who nestled it between her swollen breasts. The child was wet with blood, salt water, and the gray-white grease that allows a fetus to grow and thrive submerged.

Freydis stared at the spasming child on her breast. "You were fathered by a god of Vinland, not this pig who calls himself my husband. You'll be the most powerful man alive. The two of us will seize all the houses and lands in Brathalid, all the stock, prizes, and trophies of those lame Greenlanders. We'll rent them back to the cowards."

Thorvard leaned over his wife and held out his hands for the child, but she ignored him. He stared at the strange oblong head, with its shock of red hair. The creature suddenly ceased squalling, snapped open its squinting eyes. Thorvard's heart sickened within him. The child's eyes were a deathly opaque green, as green as the eyes of a snake or lizard, as green as the icy sea they traveled.

Two hawks sat motionless on air, above the edge of a cliff that looked into the canyon. They watched ten dusty, sun-darkened figures jog along the trail as it snaked its way to their destiny. Handsome Bear looked over his shoulder, trained his eyes on the hawks as he ran. He knew he was close to the sea; the birds were the first appearance Eagle Claw and Red Stone had made since crossing to the other side.

Running behind Handsome Bear, Cold Moon Fire shouted, "I think I smell the sea. Is it cool and damp?"

The ten runners bunched closer, believing they were nearing their goal. They'd traveled hard for twenty-eight days, and there had been casualties. None of them had ever seen the ocean before, so their dream eyes threw probable colors on every turn of the trail. Running hard now, they were heading into a long curve around a steep hill covered with tawny grass. It was the color of sand, or a mountain lion. Handsome Bear thought of stopping, climbing to the top in an attempt to sight water. He'd just turned his head to shout an order when a group of sixty or seventy bare-chested men and women, armed with spears, their hair bristling with feathers and leaves, faces whitened with clay, closed around them from both sides of the canyon trail.

Handsome Bear hoped to talk his way out of a fight; the numbers were impossible. He tried to identify a leader in the reception party. To his right there was a heavy-set man with a crown of redtail hawk feathers. The Bear Caller held up both hands, palm outward, in a gesture of peace. He unstrapped the bow from his back and laid it at his feet. When the man in the feathered crown stepped forward, Handsome Bear began to cut the air with his hands, signing a greeting. The man nodded acknowledgment. Handsome Bear untied one of the turquoise necklaces he wore around his neck and held it stretched between his hands. As the crowned man reached out to accept the gift, one of his men jumped forward to help him tie the buckskin thong at the back of his neck. Another one of his troop, a small gray-haired man, came forward and spoke quietly in his ear. The leader gestured to the man to approach the newcomers.

"Is turquoise person? Think word you say." The man bowed his head slightly, intimidated by the size of Handsome Bear, who stood over a head taller than anyone else in the canyon.

"We're sun people from Beautiful Village. Do you know our language?"

The gray-haired man laughed with delight that he had guessed correctly, tapping the butt of his spear on the ground. He turned to look back at his leader, who nodded that he should continue.

"Name Blue Dogs of Sea. Trade abalone shell to turquoise for you persons long time ago."

"Are you the abalone people?" Handsome Bear tried to restrain his excitement at the possibility.

"Yes, abalone people outside person name us. Trade?"

"Is the man with the crown of feathers your chief?"

"Yes, Acorn Teeth chief. Happy persons for abalone people."

"Tell him I am Handsome Bear, a chief of the sun people, and that I have important business with him."

The gray-haired man turned to his leader and translated the message. Acorn Teeth gave out a long ululating shout that made Handsome Bear flinch in spite of himself. Then the interpreter turned and spoke to the sun people's memory hero.

"Acorn Teeth welcome turquoise chief in village."

The chief was now motioning enthusiastically to the sun people that they should follow him. When his troop of warriors saw this, they sent up ululating howls of joy. There'd be feasting, not bloodshed.

"When we got to the Kachina Mountains . . ." Handsome Bear lost his balance again, would have fallen over into his bowl of acorn mush if the woman serving him mussels and scallops hadn't caught him and propped him up.

The abalone people looked at each other, wondering how the huge stranger could be so drastically affected by their toloache tea, prepared by boiling jimson weed. Hawk Fingers had adjusted its strength to the estimated height and weight of the guest, and he seldom made mistakes. This tea was made from the white flower, and if the strength were miscalculated it would only make a person sick. If an error were made with the root, it could be fatal.

Blue Sea Dog walked around the central fire, leaving the place where he'd been standing at Chief Acorn Teeth's side. The little man was now cleansed of his clay warpaint and free of leaves and feathers. Like the rest of the abalone people, he wore only a short grass skirt and a necklace of cowrie shells. When he went to one knee and put a hand on Handsome Bear's shoulder, the memory hero's eyes were watching sparks fly up through the vent in the vaulted roof, inside the large roundhouse that swelled out of the ground at the center of the village. He didn't seem to notice the friendly touch. Blue Sea Dog wondered where the spirit of the guest of honor had wandered. "Too far away? Have rest."

"No. You were telling me about the . . . I feel very well. I was telling you how Night Bird people attacked us in the Kachina Mountains. We never saw them. The only time I saw one was when the ancestors helped me paint it on my ceiling in Beautiful Village."

After passing around the fire to his leader and attempting to translate the memory hero's slurred words, Blue Sea Dog stared back at Handsome Bear. It would be impolite to say anything more about his behavior, and the sun people runners who had come with him said nothing. Anything was possible. Maybe this was normal behavior when these strange people feasted. In the old days he had only dealt with them as a trader, not as a friend.

"We saw sand people—plain daylight when they attacked— killed three of them before they ran away into the sand."

Chief Acorn Teeth sat on a mattress of fronds covered by a blanket. They were the same kind of fronds used as roofing material for the ramadas that made up the majority of the structures in the village. Acorn Teeth listened to Blue Sea Dog's translation of the guest's words. Then he motioned his assistant to lean down, spoke softly to him. The interpreter nodded and directed another question at Handsome Bear. "How sand persons go? Dig lizards, go in?"

Handsome Bear struggled up on his knees, leaning his hands on his thighs. Cold Moon Fire sat just behind him, ready to come to his assistance if he began to fall again. Handsome Bear stretched, then rested his hands on his hips.

"Sand people not as dangerous as the dream river. Might not have come back in any form, to any human place. All lost in our dreams for days. Fire lizards and water panthers! Water panthers with red and yellow feathers on their shoulders. Eagle wings! Followed us through the desert into this canyon. Waiting outside . . ."

His legs went slack and he fell back over his heels into Cold Moon Fire's arms. He shivered, eyes open, looking intently at things in another world no one else in the festival roundhouse could see. Acorn Teeth rose from his mattress and walked over to his guest of honor, who was now grinding his teeth, kicking his heels into the reed mat beneath him. The young running champion looked into the abalone chief's eyes, to see if her leader's vulnerability would inspire understanding or malice.

Blue Sea Dog spoke to the girl. "Acorn Teeth think turquoise chief got bad spirit from sweat. Not think how." Blue Sea Dog shrugged his shoulders.

Handsome Bear began to shout. "They killed Red Stone. Coyote women killed him when they sang their songs and made love noises. They lured him away from camp and he tried to fuck one out in the brush. They ate his head that night." Handsome Bear screamed and the entire tribal meetinghouse went silent. He flailed with his arms, pawed his back as if reaching for an arrow from his quiver. It took all of Cold Moon Fire's strength to keep her arms around the big man's chest.

Hawk Fingers moved slowly and quietly along the periphery of the circular wattle-and-adobe wall until he was directly behind the struggling guest and the girl who was trying to restrain him. As he took each step, he cut the air with his extended hands, first on his left side, then on his right. When he was right behind them,

Cold Moon Fire twisted her neck and looked over her shoulder. The medicine man reached out and placed his palms on the top of Handsome Bear's head.

Hawk Fingers jumped back, as if touching the holy man and memory hero had given him an electrical shock. The abalone medicine man spoke quickly to Acorn Teeth and the chief in turn directed his words through Blue Sea Dog.

"Hawk Fingers speak turquoise chief hole in head. Know that? Sorry. No touch, touch." The translator was miming an apology, since the crisis had drained what little knowledge of the sun people language he possessed.

Cold Moon Fire looked down into Handsome Bear's face. He was wrenching his head back and forth, whipping his hair against her breasts. But the memory warrior was on the other side of the darkness, looking into a circle of light. He saw Sun Girl's face in that circle, but she was frowning. Then he saw two huge eagles descend on his daughter as she climbed the ladder to their apartment on the third level of Beautiful Village. They grasped her buckskin dress in their claws, pulled her high into the air, then turned west and glided into the setting sun. Handsome Bear heard Sun Girl screaming, "Bird Grass! Bird Grass!" He was grinding his teeth so loudly, Cold Moon Fire was afraid they'd pop out of his mouth. The rest of the expedition had now left their places at the feast and gathered around their leader. Rabbit told his sister he wanted to help, but she ignored the offer.

Handsome Bear let out a long, deep groan. It ended as a rattle in his throat. "Eagle Claw! They took you at the Otherworld River. It was Red Swallow—a dead child's hand, and a nose. We burned the medicine bag and sent you on a raft to meet our snake kins-people. Eagle Claw! The whole world's burning up, and you don't talk to me anymore!"

Acorn Teeth's daughter, who'd been sitting behind the chief, rose, walked to the ring of people who'd come to Handsome Bear's assistance. She pushed through it, kneeled at the memory hero's side, leaned over as if she were going to kiss him, but lingered above, dropping tears from her face into his. Handsome Bear felt the drops hit his forehead and cheeks, then tasted them. He came back to this world, to the roundhouse, and looked at the girl.

There was a halo of light around her face. And within that circle was a halo of darkness; her shock of black hair looked like one of the abalone people's thatched huts. It surrounded the high ridges of her cheekbones and the reaching sadness of her eyes. As he lifted his hand to touch her shoulder, convulsions ran through his body, one after another. His face contorted and relaxed several times, then he began to cry. He moaned, looking at the chief's daughter as if he were about to speak. Cold Moon Fire moved away as the abalone woman slid behind his shoulders and held him. Acorn Teeth's daughter murmured to him in her own language, but he only heard the piercing war shrieks of some other woman, shouting words that were entirely unfamiliar—and then Red Sparrow's taunting laughter.

"Eagle Claw, you left too soon. I haven't found the axes."

Blue Sea Dog stumbled, and Handsome Bear caught him by the arm. A diamondback rattler wound itself across the path a few paces ahead. The memory hero wondered if the snake were Eagle Claw, or an omen that he was close to finding the snake axes of his dream. Stopping short and waiting, the translator paused even after the snake had disappeared into the brush, then signaled Handsome Bear on. As the only speaker of sun people language in the village, he'd been given the privilege of showing the visitor the ocean close up. The rest of Handsome Bear's expedition had been led down earlier in the morning, while he was still lying on his sleeping mat indisposed. Still muddled and dizzy, having lost a clear sense of what had happened during the last day or so, it occurred to the memory hero that his spirit might never have left the land of the dream river.

"Metal axe." The interpreter chopped at the air with his right hand.

Handsome Bear snapped his head around, wondered if Blue Sea Dog could understand mind language as well as the smattering of sun people language. He looked down and tried to read the small man's eyes, determine what powers he held. "How did you know I was looking for the men with metal axes?"

"Said night, sick for tea."

Handsome Bear grimaced. It was the first time anyone had alluded to what had happened the night before. He touched his hand to his bare chest; the skin was still tender and sweaty. Could he have humiliated himself and not remembered? "Are there any dragon boats here now?"

"Dragon boat? Dragon?"

Handsome Bear tried to pantomime a dragon, feathering his fingers, shadowing the creature's sinuous loops through the air. "I'm talking about men with orange hair and beards who ride in long boats that look like dragons." Handsome Bear gestured around his chin to demonstrate the length and fullness of the axe men's beards.

"No dragon boat." Then the translator smiled, chopped his hand through the air again. "Axe boat!"

Handsome Bear wondered if he had misremembered the dream that had set his expedition in motion. "Are you saying there are other kinds of boats carrying men with metal axes?"

Blue Sea Dog looked up into Handsome Bear's eyes and smiled. The expedition leader took that as an affirmative, pressed his questioning. "Where are they from? How do I find where they live?"

As the two men walked around the edge of a cypress grove, Handsome Bear looked up and saw the ocean. It was deep blue, with reflected light sizzling across its surface. Handsome Bear held his hand over his eyes to see better, but the water still dazzled him. He didn't notice Blue Sea Dog pointing north to indicate the direction Chinese traders came from. As they walked further, he could see an expanse of sand the same color as the low desert they'd passed on their journey west. At the edge of the water the sand inclined steeply. There were children and dogs squealing and barking, running in and out of the water, playing tag with it, beating at the waves with sticks, then running from them. Handsome Bear had seen big waves of water flowing down the canals into catchment basins during the most violent thunderstorms, and he had seen the rough water in the river at the bottom of the Otherworld Canyon, but he'd never seen anything like ocean waves before.

Blue Sea Dog swept his arm across the expanse of beach, water, and horizon. He turned and smiled at Handsome Bear, shrugging his shoulders, gesturing, "What do you think?"

Handsome Bear didn't answer. He looked to his left. Children were jumping rope with a long strand of bristling seaweed. He couldn't understand their language, but he understood they were counting and chanting. To his right he saw his expedition and some of the young abalone people playing in the waves. He turned a full circle in the sand. Everything he saw was miraculous. The air was filled with bright white birds that cried in ear-piercing shrieks. Some kind of water hawk, he thought. The beach itself was covered with glistening, strong-smelling seaweed, small flies hovering above the mounds. There were strange large birds, graceful as they stretched out in flight, but ugly as paunchy old men when they floated on the swells.

"Blue Sea Dog, I want to sit here by myself and look at this for a while. Come back later, when we need to return to the village."

Bowing his head, the translator backed away from Handsome Bear. The memory hero sat on the sand. In fact, his legs gave out and he landed hard. He was feeling dizzy and weak, incapable of cogent speech, and that was the main reason he sent the interpreter away. After the previous night, he wanted no further embarrassment. The abalone people had been generous hosts, but he was afraid of showing any further signs of weakness; the Big Baby always believed vulnerability encouraged attack.

He looked out over the ocean in search of the boats suggested by Blue Sea Dog's oblique allusions. Suddenly the bright seascape, the din of surf and playing children, flashed to darkness and silence. Handsome Bear caught a glimpse of a sleeping man, then the noise of a crashing wave brought him back to the light. He was dizzy, even sitting down, and was trying hard to hold himself upright. Darkness and silence returned; the man was there again. He lay face down on an elevated mat, with a blue blanket draped over the lower half of his body. Moonlight fell on his brown back through large transparent sheets of water or crystal. Handsome Bear knew the man's name was Dream Painter. When the sleeper's ear began to glow with a powerful light, Handsome Bear knew it was time to speak.

"Dream Painter, listen to what I have to say to you. You don't know who your people are, but you need to find out. When you paint, what is your medicine? Travel the circles, the hidden paths, lead your people to the Rainbow Bridge. If you paint the map, their faces will come to you. You'll see your invisible kin. My powers are yours: my hand inside your hand, my eyes inside your eyes."

The light and noise of the ocean returned. But to Handsome Bear, the thundering water sounded like a gentle flute playing Snake Boy's lost music. Handsome Bear rested a palm on each knee. The expanse of the ocean began to fill his chest; he felt a joyful fullness, and love for a world that could shine as brightly as this one.

Startled by a hand on his shoulder, Handsome Bear turned, expecting to see Blue Sea Dog, but it was Acorn Teeth's daughter who stood next to him. Her skin and hair glistened with water. Sidelit by the sun, the hair that covered her woman's place was on fire. Handsome Bear's eyes moved up to her nipples, flat and big, so dark they were almost black. Drops of water had collected around them, and there were a few grains of sand clinging to her breasts. She kneeled by his side and kissed him on the neck. He leaned forward and sucked the seawater from each nipple.

Jerry Martinez awoke sweating, his arms wrapped tightly around his chest. Something had burst inside him. He wondered if he were having a heart attack like his father had two years before. When he threw his legs over the side of the bed and sat up, he felt better, more lucid, but still sick.

"Shit! What a dream. Rainbows and medicine. Shit."

But when Jerry spoke, his tongue caught fire. It itched and throbbed. He heard the voice that had spoken to him in his dream—but this time it was inside his room, not mixed with the sound of collapsing waves. Handsome Bear stood in front of Jerry's chest of drawers, identified himself by name, then walked out the bedroom door.

The sweats returned, along with the wild bouncing energy inside his chest. In panic, the van painter wondered how he could have fallen back into his dream again, still sitting on the edge of the bed. Dream or not, the energy inside his body pushed him to his feet and into his shirt, pants, and shoes. He walked out the apartment door, down the stairs to his parking space in the car-port. Jerry fired up the van, headed out onto the streets, hoping that a drive around the neighborhood would clear his head and settle him down. It was still dark, only a few cars on the street. He glanced at the clock on the dashboard.

"Three-thirty in the morning! Shit, what am I doing out here?" As an answer to his question, Carla's face appeared for a moment in the windshield. "Bitch patrol again. When am I ever going to learn my lesson? I must be crazy."

Jerry drove up and down the streets of Santa Ana. Since La Estrella was closed, he went to an all-night taco drive-through. He cruised hookers' row, sizing up the girls and their pimps. Linda Cristobal took the prize for best outfit: black vinyl boots that rose almost to her hips, a G-string that didn't begin to cover the hair on her crotch, and a slender belt across her enormous breasts. She was there on the street for a guy who needed some serious play-time, but Jerry only waved and drove on. He cruised for another half hour, unaware of location, thinking about Carla and Hand-some Bear. When he focused on the street again and took a bearing, he found himself in front of Chaco's Auto Shop, chewing a soggy taco. He let himself in, drove the van into a work bay, went into Chaco's office to heat up water for instant coffee.

"How am I gonna get through the day, starting at three-thirty A.M.?"

Not being able to shake the manic energy, he paced back and forth beside his van, then leaned against a steel post and looked at the wide blank expanse of gray on the side of the vehicle. He went to his tool drawer, rummaged through it, pulled out a roll of paper tape. After masking off a large rectangular area on the left side of the van, he began sketching with a fine black grease pencil. Usually a deliberate and methodical craftsman, his hand was now working much faster than either his eyes or mind could move.

Jerry put on his spray mask and was airbrushing quickly, weaving shapes together. There was a tawny mountain lion with huge eagle wings attached to its shoulders. Behind it was a swatch of brilliant turquoise, covered with scallop shells, iridescent pol-ished abalone shells, a parrot. Lightning zigzagged through the painting, and the black of night was lit up here and there with bursts of yellow, red, and light green, a kind of flaming night rainbow. At the vortex of this swirl was the face of a man with straight dark hair draped over his left shoulder and a strangely contemplative bear thrusting its snout over the right. The man had high cheekbones that pushed up hard beneath his intense eyes, moving them slightly out of kilter, as if each eye were looking at a different thing. At the top of the man's head was a ring of blood, and from it grew a corn plant, covered with fat, ripe ears. The husk of an ear at the heart of the plant was torn away to reveal the kernels. They were a dazzling turquoise.

The Coalition

| CHAPTER VIII | # FIRE OF DARKNESS, FIRE OF LIGHT |

Bjarni took his after-supper stroll, berry and venison on tongue, expansive evening gold filling his eye. He wound through the oak scatter around Karlsefni's Vinland palisade, approached a wall of forest no European two-legged could penetrate. The adventurer noticed field mice scampering along the boundary between the low grass where he walked and a gloomy world that refused entry, offering a dark edge to define the light. Mice leaped into the air, frolicked with cream-colored moths that looped and swarmed above. Bjarni stopped, hands on hips, to admire this world of wonders: food without planting and husbandry, animals playing games together. As he threw his beard-snarled face back in laughter, an explosion of birds in the forest, another at the treeline, and a lone creature burst from nothingness into life. Squealing in pleasure, paw spinning—first one way, then the other—cavorting light on its feet as a mouse. As it raced toward Bjarni, he saw a thing the size of a bear: dark, shaggy, but sleek and lithe as a lion, baring a set of teeth the match for either animal. The creature fixed on Bjarni's head and neck with lustful eyes. He'd left his shield at camp, had no time to draw sword from scabbard before the Vinland creature launched into air. Bjarni's only defense was to raise a bronze-covered forearm. His attacker ripped away a chunk of flesh near Bjarni's elbow, just above the armor, and the force nearly tumbled him over. Snorting, frothing, clawing the ground a few paces away, chewing its trophy—iceberg green eyes raised to Bjarni's over a beastly smile. He drew his sword before the second attack. It leaped again, stretched out in midair, baring four sets of nipples on its hairless belly. Bjarni stepped sideways, lopped off a foreleg that dropped at his feet. A scream, human enough to make Bjarni look over his shoulder, tore through the clearing. But there were neither Vikings nor *skraelings* nearby. The sound had come from the beast, now lying on its side, separated from one of its legs, glowering rage and betrayal. Bjarni picked up the limb from the grass, held the talisman high, its twitching claws fully exposed. He took a step back, noticed mice and moths still frolicking along the treeline, at the margins of his vision. The beast, up again on three legs, limped toward him at unlikely speed, seized the limb in its teeth and ambled to the forest wall. At the last moment, before breaking the barrier, it turned and eyed him, screamed a woman's scream. The scatter of oaks, still bathed in pure Vinland twilight, echoed with the weight of a millennium of sorrow.

Arm torn to the bone, Bjarni blew pain through clenched teeth, pressed a hand against his blossoming raw meat. A place of marvels! Not only did food grow itself in this new place, stories wrote themselves before your eyes, words grew on trees and leaped from the mouths of animals. As he ran back to the palisade, he joined the ecstatic dance of Vinland creatures, stronger than any pain, laughed out loud at his blessing: fragments of sacred stories the gods had allowed him to see and hear. His own travels had interleaved with theirs, and he'd come away alive.

Bjarni stumbled through the palisade gate, fell to his knees. Hrothgar ran to his side, seized him by the shoulders, dragged him to a log, then entered the north wall dwelling, returning with strips of linen to bind the wound. He wadded his own neckscarf, pressed it into Bjarni's armpit to slow the bleeding. Hrothgar, a seer as well as the expedition's only barber and surgeon, sniffed the air, looked all around him, kneeled, and smelled the blood on the wounded man's tunic. Bjarni knew another story was coming to life. The old man touched the blood-covered sword still clenched in Bjarni's hand. "Who were you fighting out there? What outrage have you done?"

"A beast attacked me, a strange one. I cut off its leg but it ran away on the other three, then came back to take the one I cut!" Bjarni laughed at the scene still floating before his eyes.

"But the blood on your sword's not animal blood. It's Viking blood, surely Red Erik's, or the line of Red Erik. And he's home in Greenland, at Brathalid." Hrothgar tasted again, held his head to one side, pulled at a braid of gray hair. "This blood belongs to Freydis, his daughter. She won't come for another five years, but her night form has already arrived."

Bjarni's eyes rolled back in his head. He was beginning to feel pain bite into his naked bone.

Hrothgar caught the adventurer by the shoulders as he began to slip off the log. "When she comes in the flesh she'll commit a deed so sorrowful, it can never be known beyond circling stories Icelanders will tell—words that will carry us all forever, like double-cargoed ships into the dark lands. But for now, Bjarni, she only wants to talk with you."

The next evening a much stronger Bjarni returned to the treeline, hunted along the lit border that stands against darkness. There was no patch of blood, no weeds or grass twisted in struggle, and no mice or moths. He stopped, scanned the treetops, saw little pieces of disappearing day trapped among the leaves, then continued along the margin.

"Freydis, it's Bjarni Grimolfsson again. I'm here to talk. What do you want from me, woman? My share of the takings: wine, rice, and skins? You're hungrier, greedier by far than your father and famous brothers. Have you watched me when I walk out here to settle my stomach? Do you want to lay with me?" He stopped, listened hard for a rustle in the brush. "I know your husband, Thorvard, isn't here with you yet. Come out and I'll fuck you as much as you please, if that'll satisfy this anger of yours."

A crash in the brush to his left: the beast rushed onto open grass, all four legs intact. It raced around Bjarni three times, backed slowly to the margin, raised its snout for a long scream, then plunged into the dark undergrowth. Mice crept out and moths descended, resumed their acrobatic delineation of earth and sky.

"Freydis, I don't know how you got to this beautiful land before coming on a ship, but I don't blame you. I was such a stupid man; the first time I saw these shores I didn't even beach the boat. Wild red woman, let's share the banquet. When you took that piece of Bjarni's sweet flesh in your mouth, did it taste good? Play with me, Freydis. I've never fucked an animal before, but I'm willing to try. I'll ride you or you can ride me, but you've got to promise not to bite, or at least not bite as hard as you did before."

Bjarni stood at the treeline, called out his version of the story until darkness fell. There were moans and growls in response, from different parts of the forest, but no creature showed itself.

Joey traveled over the intersection of Broadway and Pacific Coast Highway in Laguna Beach. Not a street person, more of a streetless person: his true domain the sky and sea. He held a wool blanket around his shoulders, balanced a styrofoam cup of gas station coffee in his palm. Nine-thirty A.M., air wet and heavy with fog after a night of healing and adventure, Joey Patchouli (as he was known at the Western Edge) was ready to try for a morning snooze on the crescent of grass that fronted the boardwalk. He lay there, face and spirit spread open to sky, pigeons circling a halo around him, gulls squawking sarcastic greetings from adjacent pilings. Birds knew Joey, could see the light that poured from his hands, forehead, and ears, the light that danced onto the ground from the soles of his feet, leaving a trail as bright as suicidal grunions streaming to a moonlit shore.

Later that morning, sun out and heating the air, Joey walked down to the beach, flopped on the sand, watched pelicans in war-plane formations overfly imploding waves. He popped the carrot-shaped air sacs in the kelp, mounds of it dragged in by last night's tide, and dreamed about Egypt, New York, again. Rich land-locked scent of mildew and roses, the taste of rusty iron, the speech of every rabbit, stone, or trilobite that had ever lived by that cold loop of Lake Ontario shore. Groaning sunsets, moss on the north side of trees, dogs and squirrels in their seasonal dances, burying the sunrise for months at a time. Corporeally he had not been in Egypt for twenty-three years, 1969 to be exact. His mother had kept him close to the heart of her flour-dusted apron—in the house and mostly out of trouble—until he turned twenty-four. Three days after the cake (turtle-shaped, with strawberries for eyes) and the lonely chorus, just his mother and himself, Mrs. Malone transmuted into the element of air. She discovered herself, a spirit flying over wetlands and birch scrub to an old home she'd never imagined. But the Pinto that contained her more drossy remains, earth and water, stayed lodged at the bottom of Pilcher's pond for nearly a year before the ascent of engine oil attracted attention. Joey was still waiting for his mother's return when his sister, Audrey, picked him up. She was now Mrs. Bob Herzberger, and had seen little of Joey and her mother since the marriage. Bob told her he didn't have much use for extended families, or godforsaken genes—bent, broken, or arriving in the wrong color. His problem was not bigotry, he explained; it was a matter of science. Darwin had set it out in clear terms. The weak and inferior were meant to be cut from the herd and taken by wolves. It was part of the divine plan, and he had no inclination to commit blasphemy by challenging it, not even for the sake of a brother-in-law. So there was no missing person report filed when Joey wandered out of the Herzberger basement bedroom next April. He sniffed the wind, headed due south until he hit the New York Thruway. Joey climbed the fence, made his way across the westbound lane and onto the wooded divider strip, sat down, and contemplated movements of the sun. He had no plans.

The next day passengers from a psychedelic school bus, bound from Boston to San Francisco, out on the median for an unauthorized rest stop, found Joey under a budding maple. When invited to join them, he laughed, made trilling noises, skipped up the stairs into a long compartment draped with paisley and tie-dye. It was the first time Joey had ever been picked up by a school bus, and he liked it.

His metamorphosis into Joey Patchouli took place on that bus. He couldn't resist sniffing the clothes of girls who wore it, and that was eight out of nine. To keep him from their scented parts, they saturated a red bandanna and tied it around his neck. But this didn't satisfy him. He still sought out the aroma, savored the way it mixed with warm female skin. Later, after watching Joey lick ice cream off the bottom of his chin, the girls changed their minds, would put a drop on their panties and a drop or two beneath, a kind of non-verbal request. Joey homed in on patchouli like radar. And the girls found that for a man of few words, his linguistic ability was extraordinarily developed. In fact, Sweetwater, a lanky redhead from Brookline, rechristened him "Joey the Tongue." Other girls said that made him sound like a hood. But Joey didn't mind; he drank Sweetwater with the same enthusiasm he had for all the natural wonders of the world.

The purple and aqua bus was highballing through Iowa corn-fields into the setting sun when Joey's fellow travelers first offered him a toke on a joint. Previously he'd been demonstrative about his enjoyment of the weed's aroma, drawing it in with deep breaths, but when they placed a joint in his mouth, he'd smile, open his lips, and let it drop to the floor. Not satisfied with this refusal, Allie the Alligator decided to slip a tab of acid into Joey's glass of Tang one morning as they trundled through construction detours on the Nebraska panhandle. When word spread, the driver, Rich Callahan during this particular leg, pulled the bus into a rest stop so they could watch the sunshine take effect. After waiting two or three hours as Joey moved from one picnic table to another, comparing his view of the sky from each one, they gave up. Back into the bus. His comparative sky viewing was nothing special; he grooved like that every day. There were no changes in his behavior at all. Even the Alligator was impressed. For the rest of the trip, they called him Stone Patchouli.

After arriving in San Francisco, Joey took up residence on the corner of Page and Ashbury. True, various communes in the area traded him around every few nights, but during the day that was where he lived, sitting cross-legged on a piece of dirty blue vel-veteen, blessing all animate and inanimate spirits that came his way. People would leave coins, beads, parts of sandwiches, and the occasional joint on his cloth, but he was no collector. He gave everything away. For Joey, the air itself was enough to eat, drink, and smoke, although someone usually had the motherly instinct to see he downed a hot dog or bag of fries. Joey seldom thought about eating but never forgot to stay high. He tapped fingers and toes on the sidewalk, kicked out funky counterrhythms—always heard the Song of Creation and hummed along.

Phalaenopsis took him to Venice when she headed south for a Doors concert. She'd planned to bring him back to the Haight, but somehow he stuck there in the warmer currents. Even in Sin City he had no trouble maintaining his reputation as Joey the Tongue, and that kept him in brown rice, lentils, and generally a place to crash. One day on the beach he healed a gull's broken wing by a simple laying on of hands. Credible witnesses claimed there was a hole in the air for more than an hour above the miracle. They described the colored mist that rose from the bird and spread like a palm tree. Word got around. Over the next few days and weeks he helped a lot of hurt and lonely animals, people, plants; Joey redefined the energy of hip and mellow, enough to attract the attention of the straight world, in particular a social worker named Penny Caruthers. After a single interview on the street, remarkably one-sided, she was convinced he'd been traumatized, needed the security of institutional care. Venice locals moved him around their underground railway of crash pads, snatched him off the street if anyone spotted Penny. But when she put the police on his trail, the Venetians decided to move him south to the care of fellow travelers in Laguna Beach. And Joey remained there, generally unharrassed, for nearly twenty years. Like the official greeter, a graybeard hipster waving at cars along the Pacific Coast Highway—a gesture dating back to stagecoach days—Joey Patchouli became a Laguna institution.

Who knew where Joey got the tattoos on the backs of his hands? On the right a snake coiling around a cracking egg, on the left a red horse with leathery wings. He himself didn't know the meaning of tattoo, nor could he see his hands, even when healing. Sometimes when the magic happened he'd witness a bird alighting on the hurt thing, or the arrival of a rat or lizard. But everyone else saw hands and glowing tattoos. Hands weren't the only Patchouli anomaly; Joey couldn't see his face in mirrors, or in the reflection of shop windows—but everywhere he looked there was sky, sea, and a long circular chant of creatures.

Joey yawned, moaned, sneezed, and shook his head and shoulders, whipping his long hair. He told jokes to dogs as they sidewalked past on leash. He told them liberation stories, in sounds beyond human hearing. One time he grabbed the leash on a yellow Lab, looped it around his own neck, and began to gag. The master, having no sense of humor, jerked the dog, undid the leash, and strode away. Joey kept moving during the day, catching naps here and there. In between he watched chess games at boardwalk tables, counted birds on Pelican Rock. He sat and grooved by conga players when they jammed through the ebbing light, blessed accidents of eyesight and earshot wherever he went. The hurt and lonely seekers came only late at night, searched for him in the parking lots that were the stations of his nocturnal pilgrimage. The silver gray man in Armani slacks and cashmere sweater caught up with Joey in the Wells Fargo lot. Joey knew what was wrong; the snake between the gentleman's legs had lost its coil and bite. So he kneeled before him as the man dropped his pants, lay his snake hand on the hurt animal. Officer Jerome Redding, a rookie with the Laguna police, caught the pair in his headlights. He cuffed them hand to hand and brought them in. Apparently Jerome didn't watch television, because he was the only one in the station who didn't recognize the silver man. Both he and Joey were released back into the night. The gentleman, unfortunately not entirely healed, found his Jaguar and drove back to Beverly Hills. Joey bumped through the rest of his stations until dawn, then stopped for his morning cup of coffee. Seven A.M. Birds sweeping and swirling in all directions. Another beautiful day.

"J. W.? Let's do up some more of that spicy tobacco grass of yours— a walk in spring rain."

"I'll load it in my pipe if you're game for the trip."

The darker man replied by raising hand to chest, palm down, and letting his fingers drift away from him. John Walkingstick and Thelonious Monk on an evening porch in Rocky Mount, North Carolina. Those lonesome riders howling in the bush. Homecoming at the Edge, a crack, a vein of purest quartz running through Dixie and its heart of shame. Thelonious pulled rabbit skin down around his ears, watched his partner fire up their vehicle of flight.

"Back to the caves, ain't that right, John W.?"

"Could be the caves, might be the gate. Who can tell? The gate swings both ways; one time you'll hit it going out, the next you come back in. I once got trapped inside the wall, and that cost me more than a lifetime."

"What kind of skin we gonna wear this time?"

"Could be fur or feathers or fins."

The bebop master pulled at his nose, shook his head. "Yeah, I can dig it. Another Saturday night and Sunday morning, the longest of afterhours."

The fire was still burning. Sometimes you see it, sometimes not. Like those West Virginia towns with grass so hot it can't hold snow; coal smoke rising from fissures in the schoolyard, behind the drugstore; acres of unsalable real estate caving into the mines as fire eats them out from below. Fire burning for decades, lifetimes. Not like the wildfire that tore down the six miles of Laguna Canyon in less than half an hour. That one took what it wanted and didn't linger. But it left power in the ground, and the scorched slopes were green and strewn with flaming orange poppies the next April. Fire of darkness, fire of light. Always there, whether you see it or not. It singes the hair on your knuckles, keeps you quick and loose, traveling light, open to Network hotlines that let you rise like stars and smoke.

Thelonious held the red clay bowl of the pipe in one hand, steadied the stem with a finger from the other. He drew down hard, lit his face with the sudden glow. Staring through the porch's bellied-out screens, he waited for the first sound of voices and song at the treeline, then remembered himself, passed the pipe back to Walkingstick. "Yeah, it's a crepuscule, just as wild as that. They're starting to come in now, all the riders out there in the oaks."

"Not talking music. Besides, this time the tune is playing us." Walkingstick drew hard on his pipe and passed it back to Thelonious, holding it by mouthpiece and bowl.

It was the caves all right. Feathers and encumbered flight among leathery wings and fur squealing night flyers, the moon children. The two smokers flew farther into the narrowing cave until it burst wide open—a crystal prairie, ionic grasshoppers, the light of sky surging from below and drifting back down through high-vaulted holes into the well. Stories thick as sunfish under a dock.

"Sometimes snakes are born from the mother alive and ready to strike. Sometimes they bide their time in eggs." Walkingstick turned his beak to Thelonious, then preened the blue and white feathers on his chest. The bebopper in red, twitching his head with fixed eyes. Walkingstick spoke again. "Right now we're inside the serpent's egg. Come time for it to crack, we'd better be ready to travel."

"Strangers at the gate. Shaking bars of hard water and still wanting in." The redbird sang.

"It's the shape that's hard to guess, being here on the inside. If we ever get out and fly over this thing, it's going to steal us out of the heart of laughter." Blue jay with all its mocking calls.

"Yeah, we can pick up some creatures, carry them by the shoulders or the seat of the pants, keep the thing moving."

"You know that's the reason I called you. Testimony for the cracking shell, the beginning of the Shift. Make music so holy it can't just settle back into soot and dust. Strike sparks from their sleeping prophesies, send wildfire words from their own book into the ears of villains and hypocrites."

"There was a rainy night in New York, an orchid that opened up and asked me in. I was a bird then too, but different—green and orange. Drinking whiskey, scratching claws against windowsill stone. Then the five visions of Saint Mark's Place, opening their eggs one after another: wings over face, heart, cock, hands, and feet. Death Squad hoods in front of the pizza parlor, me on the roofline, looking down from a nighthawk neon sky."

"Not just music, but the Song of Creation. I want those eggs in the tree that lifts the chamber of heavens, leans and arches over mountain and sea, takes on the five holy colors of sky, becomes the final bridge."

Horsemen, empty glasses, ladies of pleasure in feathers and beads, the dance. It was a Network session, laying the musical weave, pushing and pulling, drawing in golden wires and looping them around the rope that rises like glass.

Walkingstick flew up on the ledge, looked beyond the end of things—light below trembling between radiance and implosion. He turned to his companion. "What you say, Mr. Sphere, should we head on back?"

The redbird looked down into the burning light. "Not yet, man. No need."

"Dizzy spells." Ezekiel Smith rolled his eyes, tipped his head back. The proprietor of the herb shop and his assistant tipped their heads back and laughed, waited for their new client's next trick. "Dizzy. Vertigo." The tall Irishman touched a forefinger to the top of his head and danced in circles beneath it. The herbalists laughed again, staggered comically. They wondered why this crazy white ghost wanted to make himself dizzy, but were willing to watch what he'd do for a few minutes. The stranger was the most amusing thing that had ever happened into their shop, and unlike other white ghosts, didn't seem particularly hostile or threatening.

"That's right, dizzy!" Ezekiel smiled, waved his head from side to side, then held it between his palms. "I want herbs, medicine, to make my dizzy spells go away. They've been plaguing me since the passage." He pointed to the shelves that lined the shop and their jars filled with seeds, dried roots, and animal parts, but the Chinese herbalists weren't interested in following his finger. They smiled, looked him in the eye, and waited for the next trick. He paused, looked at them expectantly. They smiled and waited.

"Good Lord, they haven't a notion of what I mean to say." As Ezekiel turned and looked through the shop's open door, hoping a translator might be somewhere in sight, she walked by. He recognized her face and hair, but didn't quite trust his eyes. Rushing out the door, looking up Stockton Street, he knew that sure-footed stride: it was Wong Fu Gee's woman, dressed in a black coat with a high red collar. He walked after her, closing quickly, but hesitated before overtaking. Looking down at his own tingling hand, he could see bones shine through his skin, remembered the burning white of her rib cage in Monterey.

She took a left turn off the street before he could decide what to do. He trotted past open boxes of squash and leafy vegetables, cages filled with ducks and chickens, until he reached the corner, peeked around it. Looking down an alley, Ezekiel's chest tightened. There was no one to be seen, except an old man and a small boy squatting on the cobblestones, pulling clay jars out of a straw-filled box. He'd had a chance to find Wong Fu Gee again, and now it was gone.

A door swung open to his left, and a man wearing a blood-stained apron stepped out, stretched, shouted the music of Cantonese over his shoulder into the shop. He turned, caught Ezekiel's eye, jumped back inside the door and slammed it. Looking back toward Stockton, he saw the old man and boy dragging their box around the corner. Then Ezekiel heard shuffling footsteps, turned, saw a young woman walk toward him. She was dressed in a dark blue cotton jacket and baggy trousers, a quilted vest—wrapped around her like a story—to keep out the morning damp. Astonishingly tall: not his height, but he was a giant compared to the men in the herbal shop and the people he passed in the street. She turned to enter a doorway, and he saw the long single braid of hair touch the back of one thigh.

Ezekiel looked up and down the alley. He was alone again. Keeping close to the wall, he moved quietly to the place where the tall woman disappeared. He looked inside an open window; the darkness of the alleyway made the room, its tables, and occupants glow. Patrons drank tea from small cups, used chopsticks to pick up dumplings and white buns from stacked wooden hoops, diced meat and vegetables from little bowls and saucers. Ezekiel looked for the tall woman and found her sitting in the far corner, between a chubby woman and Wong Fu Gee's silent marvel. His knees locked, trembled under the wave of dizziness that washed over him. Ezekiel touched the wall to steady himself.

Wong Fu Gee's woman saw him hunched in the alleyway, dodging his gray shock of hair back and forth at the open window. The eyes of the ageless woman fixed on his: free smiles for the stunned Irishman—one from the tall woman too. She was so attractive, she momentarily diverted him from his obsessive pursuit of Wong Fu Gee. The woman was a concerto of high cheekbones, pronounced dimples that echoed the exclamation of her lips, a luminous face finely scattered with freckles, a long shapely forehead beneath her drawn back hair. It was a kind of music he'd never heard, and its effect was a jolt that fired up the filament of his illumination.

He was lost in that ecstatic other world again. Numbed teeth and fingernails urged him to dance on the cobblestones. A lapse in time fused the stillness of air around him; the expanse of direction and chance shrank to a forgotten moment. He felt himself pull away from the senses that had gotten him there: an urge for a new place and vision. Ezekiel mumbled as he jigged in the alley, paused in his antics, looked into the teahouse window once more. Patrons were scrambling to their feet, staring and pointing at him. Wong Fu Gee's woman walked out the door, the tall beauty behind her, and touched his sleeve. He felt a surge of power enter his arm, lift him slightly off the pavement. Looking into his eyes, she began to speak, although her lips didn't move.

The Irishman again lost concentration, turned and stared at the tall woman, whose eyes, teeth, hair, and skin were a conspiracy against his power of speech. As he began to stutter syllables, several cooks and the old woman who ran the teahouse bustled through the doorway and pressed Ezekiel to the wall, as if crowding into the back of a trolley. They turned him and tripped him into dizziness again, as the patrons scurried through the door and down the alley. He held his head in agony, shouted at the fleeing women, "Where's Wong Fu Gee? What's the tall woman's name?" The cooks and old lady backed away, disappeared into another doorway. Ezekiel stood alone in the alley, peering into an empty teahouse.

He walked quickly back to Stockton Street, scanned in both directions, but could see no sign of the women. Leaning back against the corner, his breath snatched away by grief, his saw a tiny tea cup nestled between cobblestones at the mouth of the alley. It was Chinese, a perfect circle with a handle, topped by a curved lid that made it look like an egg. He picked up the fragile porcelain, lifted the lid. The walls of the cup were so delicate, daylight penetrated its sides. It sang in his pocket as he walked toward the labor hall on Montgomery Street.

Whale's Hand held the totem high above his head, pointed its nose due west. He blessed the three long cedar boats, their crews and passengers—Handsome Bear and his expedition. Cutting through waves on the arm power of paddlers, the boats pushed through surf into morning mist.

"Whale Spirit, Supreme Counselor to all fish and underwater creatures, give safe passage to Handsome Bear, a worthy man. Hear me, Whale Spirit, as I tell you the five great things Handsome Bear did when he left the abalone people and came north to find us, searching for wind boat people and their axes.

"One. He left Acorn Teeth's daughter and continued his journey, even though the plump girl, the girl with the sensitive knees, made him happy, both cock and heart, and he'd rather have stayed in the warm land by the water.

"Two. He traveled north until he stood on the great sky cliffs, saw the ocean far below turn to blue stone. He saw pathways crack through that stone, all leading to the setting sun, the place he had to go. Handsome Bear will go there, and return from the direction of death, if you so will it.

"Three. He spoke to Wong Fu Gee, a wind boat trading man who will live in a southern bay rich with fish in years to come. This man warned Handsome Bear of other men who'd come riding on wind boats, riding large dogs—other kinds of men, touched by death and without blood, sorrow bringers, who will take earth people prisoner, make them live in boxes, put them to work skinning creatures with long horns, scraping their hides, as many hides as stars.

"Four. He traveled farther north and danced with the bird people so he could fly to the top of a red sky tree, see across the ocean. When he slept that night he saw a bridge run across tree-tops, saw it arch over the ocean like a rainbow. Then he saw a net of golden strands floating in the sky, holding together the six directions and all things possible. Bear people whispered useful things to him that night, and in the morning he saw their huge prints at the door of his lodge.

"Five. He talked to Seattle, a chief of our salmon-eating land in years to come, who blessed him and sent him to us, so we could carry him west across the sea to the wind boat people, where Handsome Bear will find his shining axes.

"Whale Spirit, Handsome Bear is a worthy man. Let him find what he's looking for, and direct the currents to carry our boats and men safely back to us."

Whale's Hand passed the totem to his memory apprentice, smoothed the sand with the soles of his moccasins, and squatted. He drew three circles with his forefinger, side by side. In the first he traced a spiral, working from the outer edge in. In the second circle he pushed an impression of his fist into the center. He passed his palm over the third circle seven times before leaning over it and shouting words no one could understand. He paused, leaned back, then pushed his face nearly to the sand and shouted again. He looked from one circle to another, then stood, addressed the people gathered around him. "The underwater ones have heard us."

The Wizard of Menlo Park and the Death Squad's Supreme Counselor sit holding hands over a table. The electricity that sizzles within its glass is stolen power, filaments made from the eyes and tongues of every disposable child in the world. Coal mines, steel mills, tire factories, oil refineries, railroads. Steamrollered streets paved with knuckle bones, knee joints, cranial and mandibular fragments, lead to the House of Morgan. But the game goes on in this room where there is no darkness, where no fire gives warmth, even if you think you see the light. The mockery of a flame between their locked hands and arms is the expanding prison that might circumscribe the globe. They organize General Electric, Disneyland, the Chase Manhattan Bank. The Supreme Counselor's blindness donates art treasures to the Metropolitan Museum of Art, the Wizard's deafness is frozen into the disks of a phonograph. In this imagined light, as they hold hands around the game that will bring us nuclear fission, the oil from their palms corrodes the chance of life. All that remains are clumps of scorched grass, the final stands of trees. They plot a vigorous blasphemy against the human spirits who've endured through the bloody history of this game, spirits who rest in water, trees, and rocks, or fly through clouds strung into the Network. Spirits holding in their patterns, waiting for instructions from the tower, the moment of the promised Shift. Thomas Alva and John Pierpont, conspiring to remove our eyes and replace them with virtual reality, dark marbles filled with the vacuum of their image. They've planned movies that will lead us to their cavern, the catacombs of the unredeemable dead. They fight against time, even though it's their invention, even though they've always known that in the end they'll lose.

CHAPTER IX | **CRUISING THE PCH**

Californio Harley: maroon tank and trim, raised chrome handlebars, high-stepping fandango in long, sweet motion. Jerry reached up and out to hold the grips, creased a dip between his shoulder-blades, a kind of double antenna, so he'd never lose the sun's location, or magnetic force lines that define direction. He chose the Harley, because after the *L.A. Times* feature on the "visionary van painter of Santa Ana," his Chacoan Dodge van had become so famous it froze traffic into gridlock wherever he tried to drive. For an anonymous run to Laguna Niguel (to check out Francisco Torres, his claim to rancho ancestry) two wheels were better than four. Of course, down here in Southern California there was grid-lock even without the special van, since the guys who stole the water and locked up real estate also designed the freeways: an endless turning back on yourself, a cruel parody of the Network Travelers use. Racist talk shows on the radio bands overhead, ribbons of concrete below—colliding, sideswiping, biting into each other. Even after his encounter with Handsome Bear, Jerry still couldn't navigate the Network that arched its harmonious rainbow of invisible wavelengths over all this confusion, but he was doing a pretty good job on the freeway.

Freeway mysteries: exit ramps, interchanges, gates to the car-poolers' open road. Where else but in this crazy world could two-wheeled chopper pilots ride the diamond lane alone? Bridges, an underpass, a gallery of funky beachtown structures—including an *Arabian Nights* onion dome rising from the Sunshine Hotel—peeking down into a trough that channeled flash floods of freeway traffic. Cruising into Costa Mesa, his motorcycle backed off with tonal authority. Breathing easy, sun on helmet and T-shirt, air blowing armpits dry, releasing accumulations of car shop acetone, throwing incarcerated light from his heart and liver up into the community of sunshine, where the Network—the blue engine of the sky—pulls it all together. In the midst of lay lines, on fre-quencies congenial to the resonant bounce of fiery laughter, he smelled power leakage around the edges of two o'clock.

Jerry shook his head as he drove. Carla had a smug offhanded-ness that always pissed him but teased him back for more. And Leslie, long gone Leslie. In the midst of an internal debate over the relative merits of his girlfriends, current and ex, he heard the siren behind him, pulled to the right. An ambulance wheeled by, paused briefly at a red light, then kicked up dust as it accelerated into the ultraviolet. Jerry arrived at the same stoplight, dropped right boot to the asphalt for balance, looked up at the billboard behind the chicken shack. There were pictures of six kids—Hispanic, white, Black—all killed by drunk drivers. Jerry clenched his teeth; those kids had lost the lives that were waiting for them. Francisco Torres, wired to a bed at Western Medical, was also a child of this same California earth—now barely alive as a delicate binding of skull and jaw fragments, reconstructed collarbones, a gauze-defined pulp of soft tissue still clinging to strands of gray sideburn. Nightsticks from cops instead of a drunken car, but how could the painter mourn any less, divert his anger? Not yet ready for the help of Travelers in his daily life, Jerry couldn't hear the sound of celestial voices through his helmet, or see Handsome Bear, who always stood at his side when he took a long look at the edges of absence. It was blockage. And not just the Death Squad jamming signals; the artist simply wasn't tuned in yet. When he and Carla got back to his apartment after a visit to the hospital, he threw one of his kitchen chairs against the wall, knocking two prismacolor Aztec designs to the floor. The fall of Tenochtitlan. Bent metal frames, broken glass.

Carla leaned against a doorjamb, arms folded, her mouth in its trademark twist. She'd been giving Jerry what she thought were helpful suggestions, but he hadn't listened to any of them. "Let me know how it all works out." The woman was gone before Jerry could turn around. He started toward the door, then squatted on his heels, fell back, planted the seat of his jeans into the rug, and felt sorry for himself.

The visionary van painter leaned into the curve as his Harley pulled him around the loop that would send him southward on the Pacific Coast Highway. He couldn't help laughing. OK, it was true, Carla still read "beautiful" no matter what language you spoke—and the powerful legs, knocking the wind out of you in the midst of fucking, the wild foliage of pubic hair that reached almost to her belly button. When he dropped his jeans the first time they made love, stood there in his red BVDs, she called them "Noriegas." It was enough to make even her hard-edged anthropologist routine endearing. But what really had him was her feet. In sandals they traced the lineaments of ecstasy. Even in other kinds of shoes, the pleasure of reimagining her supple arches and sensual toes threatened serious mental derangement. So why would the woman seldom or never cut him any slack? As he passed the Ardell Yacht Brokerage House in Newport Beach, his mental gears slipped from Carla to Leslie, who'd moved to Albuquerque to live with a maiden aunt after she and Jerry broke up. Leslie, with the strong shoulders and startled eyes. She was more of an adventurer than any of these rich turkeys who bought million-dollar boats to sail to Catalina or Dana Point. He remembered years ago, riding the jeep up the Sierra trail to retrieve Leslie from the final exam of her survival course. Three days before, the instructors had dropped her in the wilderness with nothing but a Swiss army knife. There she was, sitting on a log by the trail, tired, hair and clothes greasy, stuck to her body, but still looking good. Even more intense than usual. She was always tough and determined, for herself and for all of his causes, jawline hard as a fist. She was the only one who believed Jerry's talk, that a purity of ideas could make a better life, and she was still waiting. The hard pressure in his chest blew out his mouth as a sigh, fogged the helmet's visor.

Traffic started to jam up just past the Rolls Royce dealership, so he rode the line, whizzing between cars until he arrived at the accident that had been waiting for him. A scatter of broken glass, green and glacial in the sunlight. Cops directing traffic, various emergency vehicles with their flashing lights sending a secret code. Things were still cooking. A VW convertible caved into a small crescent from the passenger side, and a Mercedes station wagon with a broken nose. Two blue uniforms slid a girl, head and shoulders strapped to a stretcher, into the ambulance that had passed him in Costa Mesa. Jerry could smell the blood, taste it: Newport Beach and its usual white bread had suddenly turned into a vision of feathers, gold thread, a cloak to embrace the dance. Second sight had come without warning to the cruising biker: a descent into earth and blood—and a simultaneous lifting up, an ascent by means of balconies, bridges, causeways over Lake Texcoco, all miracles of human invention. Jerry looked above highway and the buildings that ran alongside, saw a light so delicate it held the tracings of bird flight for a moment in midair, long enough to construct a memory network of webs and convergences.

An unusual taste lingered in his mouth, the subtle spice of fear and lost knowledge, as he pulled away from the accident. He could feel Francisco's presence, a sacrifice and redemption written in blood. A cacique, a king. It was starting to make sense. When the Great City fell to Cortez, who was just another brutal cop, the dream moved north and became Aztlan. A gathering up and miraculous transfer of pearls, cloaks woven of cotton and bird down, tapestries, painted statuary, tables and chairs tattooed with inlay of precious woods and stones. It was an ornate life of aerial dreaming, and the feathers that lifted us up were tipped with blood—the blood of animals, nectar from the springs within our deepest selves, and all provided to speed the passage. A deep tunnel carried us from darkness into light, and back into the darkness that held the light, a journey that taught us to build bridges and causeways, frame canals for pleasure and commerce, that taught us sudden darkness most often comes at midday. Balconies, corridors, galleries as elaborate and whimsical as the calligraphy of diving swallows against twilight's muted orange. Gold filigree, gemwork in turquoise and abalone shell to accent the cages of aviaries, their confinement so exquisitely refined it transcended naked freedom. The Red City of the South was carried north in memory and dreamwork: an invisible kingdom that survived the bearded strangers and their clumsy destruction— encased in unimaginative steel, dragging cannons. Zagging north- ward through deserts, over mountains, canyons, tree-choked valleys, a kingdom carried not on backs but between the temples of memory heroes, the new priests and kings. Dream gardens and alchemical fire. No matter how many were battered or left for dead, the survivors carried a treasure so large the conquistadors overlooked it: an invention of dazzling light called Aztlan.

Jerry rode into Corona del Mar, where every street was named for a flower or plant—Acacia, Carnation, Dahlia, Fernleaf, Golden- rod, Heliotrope, Iris, Jasmine, Larkspur, Margarite, Marigold, Narcissus, Orchid, Poinsettia, Poppy—and above the post for every street sign an illustrated banner. When his eyes dropped back into traffic, he saw Francisco floating above the highway, holding a prickly pear cactus in one hand and a cluster of wild artichokes in the other: a dual crown of thorns. The sun ancestors had brought knowledge of the edible cactus north. Nostalgic Spanish priests brought the gift of the fat edible thistle. But having slipped out of mission gardens and across the Californian desert expanse, it had grown scrawny and hard, now as inextricably native as the rocks along the shoreline. Thorns in food, and thorns as food: grinding it all together to make the bread that is the body and sustenance of the world. Floating above the street, the king now held out his hands, and from their wounds grew the lotus, the cactus, and the crimson rose.

What did it matter whether he could find corroboration for Francisco's claims in the Laguna Niguel library, or in the library at the San Juan Capistrano mission? Jerry gripped the handlebars hard as the idea arrived. Of course the cacique was an heir to the rancho families. All of us are, because we've survived. The elab- orate stories and dreams we keep weaving, spreading beneath the sun: murals on freeway dividers and flood channel walls, the sides of markets, churches, museums, and even the polished sides of vans. Francisco Torres is the King of Laguna Niguel. And if Montezuma's memory, bleeding and yet miraculously alive, chooses to declare this the center of his magic kingdom—ignoring the gated enclave of whitebread darkness in Anaheim, the Death Squad's version of an amusement park—who's going to stop him? Let all those plastic condos transform into palaces, markets full of the pure products of cultivated earth and human ingenuity, with a hundred aviaries, the open nests and flight ramps for creatures feathered, furred, and traveling on two legs.

As a car pulled in front of him, cutting him off, Jerry squeezed his brakes and emerged from his frenzy. He was almost through the town of Corona del Mar but remembered nothing of the passage. On his right he noticed an establishment called the Five Crowns, a "fully licensed public house, est. 1965." Tudor facade, geraniums in long boxes. What the hell is this, a pub in a town named Corona del Mar? And these white folks say Chicanos are confused about national identity? Jerry was so amused, at the pub and at himself, all the circling loops of his dream, that he snorted into the visor of his motorcycle helmet, steamed it up. Stopping at the last light in town, he flipped up the transparent shield, felt the wind on his face as he roared down the highway.

Looking to the right again he saw his first clear view of ocean. It was the Pacific at full sweep, swallowing all the light of the sun into a blue dazzle. He knew if he wore his hair in dreadlocks and the state didn't require him to wear a helmet, this would be the moment God would surely choose for rapture—lifting him from the seat of his Harley and drawing him up into heaven. His eyes pushed out toward Catalina, the island he'd helped occupy over twenty years before as a teenage Brown Beret. He knew it was there, hidden by mist along the horizon. Jerry rode up and down the hills and across the low washes that intersected the coast highway: a Sunday cruise, even if it was on Tuesday. He passed Crystal Cove, where his mother and father brought him as a child. He'd walked the beach there, picking up sea-tumbled eggs of pure quartz. When he asked his father what kind of bird could lay such eggs, and what was inside them, Reynaldo told him a story about flying turtles.

By the time Jerry coasted down the hill to the Broadway inter-section in Laguna Beach, he was no longer on a fact-finding mis-sion. An angry world had reopened itself to pregnant chance. Stopping at a light in the center of town, he looked past park and boardwalk to the beach volleyball nets. Beyond that, large tubular waves spoke hollow thunder as they collapsed. Checked his gas gauge, but when he raised his eyes and let them wander the crescent beach south toward Dana Point, an electric shock passed through neck and arms into his hands. Steep hills and cliffs pooling into rock formations and expanses of sand as they hit the sea—he'd seen the place many times in his life, but now was a moment of true recognition. This was the beach Handsome Bear had stood on when he spoke to him: Laguna, or whatever those other people called it in that distant time.

When a horn honked behind him, Jerry pulled to the side of the highway but kept his eyes on the beach. Driving another half block, he parked the Harley, put all his quarters in the meter, and headed for the waves. As Jerry descended a wooden staircase to the beach, Joey Patchouli left his spot on the grass, dropped over the edge of the boardwalk onto the sand. After crawling for a distance, he shed his raincoat, stood up, and walked into the waves. When the silent healer held his hands high over his head, invoking all the Network powers, the sky tore itself open, revealed a sizzling grid. Energy poured down out of the hole in the air—like water, or lightning—and Joey drew it into himself. Iridescence pooled around his waist, a purifying spillage of light. When the moment was over, the sky closed, and Joey walked back up on the beach, fell backward into delirious exhaustion.

Boots off, pant legs up, water surging around Jerry's ankles, cool at first, then warming up. The flowered hillsides, punctuated by clumps of sweet green prickly pear cactus; half-submerged rocks tumbling down the hillside and scattering into the surf, carved by wind and water into unreadable petroglyphs, the language destined to save the world; arrangements of stone, weed, and sand that sur-passed a Noguchi garden. It was the edges, the collision of water, dream, and light, that drew Jerry along. Handsome Bear was there too, held him by the hand, directed his attention to strewn seaweed, children playing in the surf, diving birds, the same things the Bear Caller had seen himself on his introduction to the great ocean.

Jerry was unaware of his company, thought himself alone when he arrived at the rocky point, a natural arch worn through its center. Handsome Bear released the apprentice Traveler's hand, let him walk through the gate, a foamy wash caressing all four of their ankles. The Chacoan lingered to watch the wave recede, while on the other side Jerry hoisted himself onto a ledge, climbed the rippled sandstone ship until he stood on its prow, bound forever for Catalina. He looked out past yachts, fishing charters, and commercial ships, flung his arms into the air. "Come back, Handsome Bear, I need some help here!" The memory hero laughed as the invocation reached his ears somewhere between the canyons called Grand and Chaco. Lowering eyes, the Santa Ana painter noticed the faint outline of the Canaleño dream island, spread along the horizon like a smile.

"You talking to me?"

Jerry turned to face a man tucked into the rock, windblown blond hair suppressed by Walkman earphones and distant music. Sun flashing from dark planes that covered his eyes, notebook on lap, pen in a gesture of pause above the page, but forget conversation. Jerry said he thought he was alone, and clearly wanted to stay that way when he gave the man his back, took in the open sea again, eyes wandering left, where three kids fished with Coke can rigs near a blow hole. He grooved on the throat sounds of their Zapotecan dialect.

The blond man chattered, noodled around the eloquent sound of Handsome Bear's name, but got no response from Jerry, who conversed only with crossing wave patterns, ears open to the wind. When the Santa Ana visionary heard faint bebop, horns and saxes tugging at a complex melody, he tried to locate the source. Sitting Man's earphones were looped around his neck, but still at full volume. It was Mingus, the greatest bassist who ever lived. That's where the two rock creatures found talk in a common language.

Sitting Man bebopped jazz and told bear stories, handsome and otherwise: dirty dancers in a pit on the outskirts of Bern, Switzerland, doing tricks for carrots; the little bear standing by an open storm drain in Michigan, no more than a foot and a half in height. He'd eliminated muskrats, moles, woodchucks, and possums, but had never found a picture of the animal that had stared him down.

Jerry took a good look at the upturned face, most of which was covered with hair, except for the dark glasses. Sitting Man looked like a bear himself, so the painter reminded him that bears come in all sizes, that millions once lived in California, long before Anglos made it into a state, and that old rancheros caught bears with lariats, threw them into pens with bulls, bet on the outcome of the fight.

The man looked down, wrote something in the margin of his notebook page, then mentioned that a woman friend showed him a set of medicine cards after he told her the story of the little bear. She'd said bears used to chat with Indian medicine men. When he insisted the bear hadn't said a thing to him, she replied it was because he didn't know how to listen.

Jerry walked over to the niche, leaned his back against the rock. "Not being an Indian, I can't help you with that sort of thing."

The bearish man checked out the van painter over the rim of his sunglasses. "Don't get me wrong, now, about the possibility of the supernatural. I once met Duke Ellington—at the La Guardia Airport coffee shop in 1989. You know, with the Russian Cossack hat in black curly sheepskin."

Jerry reminded him that Ellington died in 1974, but Sitting Bear said he knew that, and wondered if the guy was a lookalike until he caught that smooth trickster smile. Nobody could imitate it. Had to be Ellington. Anyway, since he preferred straight-ahead bebop to big band, if he were going to imagine someone whole cloth, it would more likely be Thelonious Monk or Charlie Mingus.

"My grandmother put in a few appearances after she died." The painter shaped air with hands, described messages left in odd arrangements of furniture, china, and silverware, how the family knew it all meant something but they weren't sure what.

Jumping up from his niche into laughter, the writer pointed toward the tourists who'd just been soaked by the blowhole. Jerry ignored the small catastrophe, held his hand up to the sun, asked the bearish man if he'd ever felt his palm burn when there was no reason for it. "My mother said it means a spirit is standing next to you and wants to shake your hand."

Protesting that he was pretty sure he was still alive, the blond man reached over and grabbed Jerry's hand, shook it, asked if it burned.

"Man, it's been burning for almost an hour. Always the same one too—my painting hand." He gave his companion a new lookover. "Do you have a name, other than Little Bear?"

"Larry Smith, and I'll bet you're Mark Rothko."

"I'm no abstract expressionist. Name is Jerry Martinez; I do cars, vans, pickups, hotrods . . . and sometimes money." He took out his wallet, made a gift of a fuschia beaver.

The two men watched the swirl of gulls above the three boys, who were throwing broken shells from the mussels they'd used as bait, taunting the aerial messengers. Smith asked Martinez where he was from, admitting he was only a temporary resident himself, in Laguna with his son, Justin, on sabbatical from a teaching job, trying to finish his book. When Jerry asked what the book was about, the bearish man talked about a long poem set in Rome, derived from his experience as a Fulbright scholar at the university there, in the middle of the cholera epidemic of 1973.

The van painter shook his head. "How can you write about Rome when you're living in Laguna? Just look around you, man. This area was sacred territory to the people who lived here, a sanctuary for all the tribes. It's a power place. And you're telling me you're the type of guy that talks to bears?"

"But that's the whole point. That little bear never said shit to me. Anyway, how do you know all this—you an amateur anthropologist or something?"

Martinez and Smith walked back to Main Beach together, skirting the waterline, scampering to the right when maverick waves washed in. They watched a little dog retrieving a large stick from the waves, nearly drowning in the backwash every time. It was a fated and auspicious encounter: Jerry found a sea penny, corroded green beyond recognition, Larry found a quarter dated 1969. They walked past double-D silicon girls in thong bikinis, an artist painting a bad seascape on an expensive easel, a guy with a bagpipe playing "Amazing Grace." If either the writer or van painter had looked at just the right angle, he'd have seen Handsome Bear there too, frolicking up to his waist in the waves they avoided. He mimicked the swagger of Jerry's walk, did his impression of Smith's head-down loping stroll. He pointed and snapped his fingers when one of the men said something that jingled ankle bells, turned a feather on his cloak, imperceptibly lifted the two mortals on their separate paths of flight, brought them closer to hearing the Song of Creation. He danced most when their political discussion stopped and the two men set their eyes on the horizon, the long reach of the Pacific, their dilated pupils subliminally sighting the Rainbow Bridge. Handsome Bear looked at the Evian umbrellas and roped-off area in front of the Hotel Laguna. He put hands on hips and laughed, took one last look at the pasty white skins roasting under the ferocious sun, and was gone.

The two strollers left the waterline, passed Joey Patchouli spread-eagled on the sand—arms stretched out, chin tilted up as if he were inhaling the sunshine. They climbed the stairs to the boardwalk, sat on a bench with a brass placard dedicated to a Laguna resident who'd officially joined the spirit world. Smith pointed at Joey down on the beach, said people in Laguna claimed he had healing powers. The writer liked the idea, because it meant that instead of living high on the hill, healing lonesome New Agers in a million-dollar house, he'd chosen instead to live on the streets. Jerry responded by grumping about all the talk of homeless people, mostly bullshit, since everybody is homeless, sooner or later, and street people have as much magic as anybody else, probably more. He talked about a friend living in the streets, a glue sniffer who got along reasonably well until the Santa Ana cops nearly beat him to death.

Smith said he was sorry, but not surprised, remarking that Laguna Niguel was a pretty nasty place too: rows and rows of pre-fab condos, like a huge columbarium, a place that would be happy to sell you your death. Jerry smiled and shook his head, watched a woman jog by with a terrier on a leash. He began to riff with the writer's image: grass, parks, the Crown Valley Parkway as a cemetery, or a golf course, and it didn't matter which since they're both finally the same thing. Smith was beginning to get excited with the possibilities, suggested sneaking in at night and building driftwood sculptures. Jerry thought a quick shanty town would be even more appropriate, then arrived at his ultimate groove: call the homeless together, ride them over, and set up camp. Cardboard houses and campfires, a national convention for street people on the grounds of the Crown Valley Parkway. Jerry threw his head back and cackled, then noticed the startled look on Smith's face.

The writer turned the vision slowly before his eyes. "I think that's a great idea."

"What idea?"

"To have a national conference for the homeless in Laguna Niguel." Smith looked at Jerry, who was staring out toward Catalina. "When you get ready to do it, let me know. I'll be there." The writer tore a page from his notebook, ripped it in half, and the two men exchanged phone numbers, shook hands, moved in different directions.

Jerry walked from the bench to the public phones next to the Hotel Laguna garbage bins. Two men stood a few feet away with their backs turned to him, arguing, one with a yellow Lab straining its tether to the point of strangulation. As Jerry was punching up his number, Joey Patchouli walked by and spoke a few low sounds to the blond dog. It settled back on its haunches, smiled, let its tongue droop out one side of its mouth.

"Hello, Carla? It's me. I just wanted to let you know how it all turned out."

CHAPTER X | # THE JOURNEY OF ONE HUNDRED STEPS

Beneath layered skins, under a dark bowl of sky leaking starlight, Handsome Bear startled awake in the midst of heavy-breathing bodies. A hand slid under the covers, prowled up his thigh, and closed around his cock. His back pressing against a cedar plank, the memory hero lay in the stern of the Salmon Eye. It was just after midnight; he'd been moving in and out of sleep, waiting for another rendezvous with the dragon, the one that swam under the painted belly of the boat, followed him in dreams more than half-way across the Pacific. The adventuresome grasp snatched Handsome Bear's breath away. He hadn't been touched down there by any hand but his for months, not since the expedition headed north from the land of the abalone people, where he'd reluctantly left Acorn Teeth's daughter, the girl with the sensitive knees.

They were a day's journey west of the 174th parallel, near what is now called Attu Island. The year, as we currently measure time, was 1181. In that period, however, crossing the International Dateline pushed you forward a century, rather than a day. When he broke the blue beam that snaked over the water, made his lurch into the next century, Handsome Bear had seen the sky split in two. The hand lightly squeezed his cock, coaxing throbs and tingles out of the neglected organ as all his other muscles tightened. But he didn't speak, continued to draw the long loud breaths of a sleeper. The hand worked him up and down into stiffness, then retreated, leaving the Bear Caller to wonder who it belonged to. He thought it was a woman, but wasn't sure. Maybe it was a lonely salmon person; their rowers were all men and they had smaller hands than sun people.

The other boats in the joint venture to deliver sun people to the kingdom of snake axes and other marvels presumably lay within sighting range, but who could tell in this dark of the moon? Three painted boats and sixty-three people. Handsome Bear could never have carried enough turquoise to finance this voyage; the salmon people who volunteered were young men wanting to see the jade kingdom, return home with potlatch wealth and the aura of sophistication world travel affords.

Just as he was putting together a scheme to determine who that midnight caller might have been, the skin lying over his hips lifted. A cold shot of night air blew against his thighs and abdomen, then the thrust of slippery buttocks against his erection. He smelled something strong, reminding him of Red Swallow. The hand reached back, grabbed him, and guided his cock into a hole. He thought it was a woman's front one, but wasn't sure. As he slid in, it felt so good he stopped worrying about discovery by the sleepers around him, or the ridicule that would follow. He thrust into tightness, his left hand falling lightly on the bare thigh of his partner, hard with strain. Could this be part of a dragon dream? That creature transformed into so many shapes and genders, anything was possible. Yet dreams concentrate on one sense, and in this dark experience, all senses but sight were at play. Besides, the one thing you could count on from the dragon was flamboyance. His silent partner was nervy, but not flamboyant. He or she hadn't moaned, not even drawn a loud breath. Still, Handsome Bear could see the dragon's spinning eyes and fiery mane as he pumped into his companion, so hard he knocked a cedar bracing plank loose from the stern. There was a loud slap of balls into hair and wet; but he could no longer control the tempo, no matter who might hear. As he approached climax, the hole closed down tighter around his cock—went rigid, then spasmed several times when he shot into darkness. The buttocks slipped away and the cover was replaced over Handsome Bear's legs. Big Baby sensed a body moving toward the prow but couldn't determine an exact location. He felt his cock, wet with his own juices and his partner's, smelled the hand. Still not sure, he considered how different salmon people were from sun people. They had a fishiness that came out of every pore.

The only salmon person who'd ever completed the round trip along the island ladder, the journey of one hundred steps, was Round Hand. He knew signs and currents, how to travel the outer sea, read the stars that guide you from one rung to the next. His main task, other than navigating west across the Aleutian chain and south along the Kurils, was keeping his sailors and seasick passengers from panic, a tumble into despair. He knew how long and hard the voyage was, so cajoled the disheartened, constantly misrepresented time and distance to head off the mutiny that was always about to break out. Only Handsome Bear refused to complain. Round Hand was now asleep; his second in command and two other men steered the Salmon Eye into wind and wave until dawn, when paddles would be in all hands, propelling them through green swells to their destiny.

When gray clarified into enough light to see the horizon, everyone was up and pulling a paddle, including Handsome Bear. Two people at a time, in rotation, ate a small portion of pressed salmon and berry cake. It had tasted good to Handsome Bear when the voyage began, but now he was sick of it. He hadn't seen corn, beans, squash, or chilies for as long as he could remember, nor a piece of meat since they took to the sea. The two women on the Salmon Eye were paddling forward of Handsome Bear. He studied their gestures, trying to connect any movements with the experience he'd had the night before. Descending Cloud was broad in the shoulders and strong; she pulled her paddle through the water with as much energy as the more expert men. But when he glanced at her heavy thighs, he knew she couldn't be the one he fucked. That left Cold Moon Fire, the young running champion who was always angry at him. She'd complained almost every day since the voyage began, although the first week of the trip she'd said little, being so seasick Handsome Bear was afraid she was going to die. He looked at her wiry figure. Her paddling was choppy, not quite synchronized with the salmon people. He had the desire to touch her neck and ears, smell them, then laughed at himself. Her ears turned back into her head, rather than standing out, a sure sign of stubbornness he'd never noticed. There was a smile on his face when Cold Moon Fire looked over her shoulder. She first wore a startled expression, then glared at him. Handsome Bear turned his head to the other side of the boat, eyes falling on the rower across from him. It was the young salmon person with streaks of red running through his long hair. He had large perfectly straight teeth and showed them to Handsome Bear in a sly smile. Was the young seaman laughing at Cold Moon Fire's rebuff, or was he the companion from last night?

The dark clouds rolling across the horizon took a sudden turn and were now approaching as fast as the sea was churning. Round Hand called out orders and the crew spread slick tanned skins across the open parts of the boat. When the downpour began, the water beaded and ran into strategically placed water gourds. Handsome Bear tipped his head back and let the rain fall into his throat. He closed his eyes and imagined a rain panther passing over the sun people's canyon, filling runoffs and catchments, sending water to grow good things in their fields. When he opened his eyes again, all he could see was gray.

Freydis's men glanced down or out to sea, but refused to look at her. Heading back to Greenland and Erik, her outlaw father, the crew's memories of the massacre made the witch even more impossible to accept. She'd screamed at them, promised rewards, and threatened punishments, but nothing would make them reaccept her into the human community. Her red hair was a bloodstain. How did the men and women they'd killed, fellow Greenlanders, deserve that fate? Not that these men were beyond a ruthless shedding of blood if there were promise of some gain. But their leader had so disgusted them in the needlessness and excess of the carnage that she'd changed the way they saw themselves. Thorvard sat brooding in the stern by the pilot, not wanting to be acknowledged or disturbed, and even his relentless wife left him alone.

Orm watched the sail billow and tug slightly to port. If these winds held, they might reach Brathalid in a week. But how could they return with this cargo of shame? He knew what the men would do, including Thorvard, if they dared: throw Freydis overboard to the fish. Or even better, tow her behind their dragon boat tied by one ankle. Who'd dare present such a plan? Most of the men were afraid even to think about it. They knew she had the power to read both dreaming and waking minds, to hear the spoken word before it passed the portals of the teeth. If they executed justice on the open sea, it would have to be quicker than thought, so she'd have no chance to conjure a defense. And if she went down, wouldn't she bring the whole ship with her, pull it into a maelstrom she'd create in the center of the sea? Her command of death and darkness was beyond question. Supposing they could bring about her end and somehow survive, then who would spin a likely tale for Eric? As old as he was, his enmity was still fatal to anyone who chose to live in Greenland.

Orm clenched the hilt of an imaginary sword in his hand. Unfortunately, his real one was stowed, along with shield, war axe and other fighting gear, in the hold of the boat. It would be difficult to get it without being noticed. But he still imagined the pleasure of seeing Freydis's head fly off with one clean blow, land in the waves, float for a moment, roll until he could see the surprised look in her eyes, then sink to the bottom of the sea. They'd drag the bleeding trunk, wait for sharks to arrive, spread her across the world in poison mouthfuls. Then the men could forget, go on living in what remained of the sunshine.

A paralyzing pain tore through his right hand, made Orm drop his imaginary sword. As the pain traveled up his arm into his shoulder, then his heart, he tried to cry out for help, but the sound was stuck in his throat. Freydis stood alone at the prow, jaw set eastward toward Greenland. There was light coming from the back of her sheepskin vest, a small burning sun. As it pulsed, Orm could feel her power throb in his head, the pain in his arm and chest increase. Above Freydis's blazing hair was a small glowing cloud. He heard her baby scream, back in the stern of the boat, tended by Thorvard. With every scream, every pulse of the light implanted in her back, the cloud clarified, solidified, until it finally stared back at Orm—a green lidless eye. It burned at the edges of his memory, fire catching dry leaves. Then it was all smoke, the tumbling of the soul without path or direction. Sudden darkness.

Dragon dream, Handsome Bear's hard reach for light. High-frequency undulations along brain waves, dream waves: loops of energy as teeth, scales, and claws. Each scale, centered with a red searching eye, rolled in laughter and menace. This dragon breathes water as well as fire, and the results are clouds, storms, the sea itself. Sometimes scales turn to feathers, and the dragon rises on the motion of its plumed legs, whips its tail to propel it high into the reaches of blood and darkness: a drop of each in the Tao of its spinning eyes. The dragon rose through the first three worlds this way—shot out the sipapu, the navel of the world, as a quick string of fire. Handsome Bear drew in a painful breath, found himself running through lost otherworld corridors in the land of shadow people. Those long halls reminded him of the tunnel to the snake kiva in Beautiful Village, but they had no end. If he could only fly like the dragon, he'd have more faith in the chance of reaching some kind of light. Light is a dragon: feathered god, a messenger from the king of heaven, a crust of sunshine running in a banner down its zigzag spine, its tongue a snapping pennant on the end of a spear. The dragon had adamantine scales and barbed spikes; the emerging hairs of its inner light could cut a man in half. If you glimpsed the belly, a side it never displayed, you'd see the dragon smile through all openings and protrusions, as it possessed the mysteries of both seed and egg. The dragon circled Handsome Bear, embraced him with the whirlwind wake it kicked up. He felt invited, lured farther on the journey that leads to annihilation and eternal presence, a refusal to be boxed by time.

Handsome Bear's eyes fluttered open, saw the stars above the boat, their lopsided movement, a low lumbering circle around his dream. He felt sweat slip over his temples and down his neck. Chanting a song for light and power, a distillation of sky, water, and rock, enough to open his way, illuminate signs for him to navigate by, he asked for the memory of sacred things. He wanted it burned into the map he'd carried since the day he was born. It was a prayer for a language strong enough to conjure flight. Then he saw dragon streamers so long and colorful they rivaled the striations in the canyon wall behind Beautiful Village. The snakes who'd spoken to him there, leaving divine messages as he held their slack bodies between his teeth, were cousins of this dragon. They were also cousins of Quetzalcoatl, the changing one who lived near the Red City of the South. He was the eternal coupling of eagle and snake, the marriage of heaven and earth. Handsome Bear rode the back of the ocean dragon high over its domain, watched the loss of claws, teeth, and scales as large as boulders. They fell with lazy motion into the water, lodged in its fluted emerald as shining islands. The dragon flew over the new pieces of land it had created, dropping shreds of its hair, and they bent into rainbows stepping from stone to stone. The dragon swooped lower until the Snake clan chief could see people cross arches making up the Great Rainbow Bridge. They were sun people! But unable to steady their feet on that rainbow light, they fell in bunches to the sea. Handsome Bear grieved, but as he looked below the arches he saw cavorting creatures. His people had become dolphins, flying over and through the waves.

Transformation didn't surprise Handsome Bear. He knew a dragon could turn into a butterfly, or dissipate into a cloud. Such a creature could embrace you, or abandon you like a heartless parent. Through the sinews of the dragon, lightning turned to stone, and the rocky guts of earth lifted as mist into sky. Islands or memories, the dragon showed steppingstones, a ladder to be climbed. This was what traveling meant, and the dragon was a bridge to take us there. Handsome Bear envisioned Bird Grass in his sister-in-law's apartment. His daughter was kneeling on the floor, grinding blue corn and singing. He called for her to look up, take a step into the sky and join him, but she continued her task as if she hadn't heard him. He could hear the dragon's laughter as it whirled around him, eyes spinning like moons. Handsome Bear held out his hands to the elusive creature, agreed to accept the pain.

The dragon answered, but it spoke with Eagle Claw's voice, one Handsome Bear hadn't heard since he'd left his uncle under a pile of rocks on the east bank of the Otherworld Canyon River. "My nephew, snake man, this is a good journey you're taking. Have you reached the land of the axe men? Are you returning, or have you just set out?"

Wind, water, and fire passed through Handsome Bear as he flew parallel with the dragon. Forest bird, sea bird, no place to land and find rest. Then the power of winged movement left him and he began to fall, flying backward so fast he could barely keep his eyes in his head. He was being pulled by one ankle into a horrific void. Then he stopped in midair, felt absence congeal into water around his body. Flying through this new medium, sometimes as the painted cedar boat, with its silver salmon face nosing through the waves, sometimes as the dolphins who played alongside, or even whales, monsters he viewed from the beach before leaving the salmon people's land. But when his flight through the water's surface came to end, a force from below grasped an ankle, pulled him deep into a sea that darkened into a starless sky. Lit by demon light, he watched another kind of creature circle him: wicked teeth, a long misshapen body, poisoned skin that dislodged in large flakes—beyond loathing, a curse on creation. The memory hero finally recognized the creature: it was Handsome Bear.

Rising through the sea and himself, he broke the surface, was greeted by the dragon's shaking head. It lingered over the waves—laughing, spinning its eyes—then was gone. Hole in the Head tread water and waited for an approaching wave to break over him, but it melted into a swell that lifted and lowered him gently. Before the next wave arrived, Sun Girl and Red Swallow walked down its angled face into the trough, regarded the helpless man bobbing at their feet. They held hands, wore the white buckskin dresses reserved for brides. Smiling together, they leaned over as if to kiss the memory hero, but as their lips brushed his ears they shrieked, rolled their eyes like the dragon. When Handsome Bear cried out to them, they exploded into pieces of colored light that sizzled and sank into the sea.

It was late in the afternoon; the setting sun lit the westward route before them as blue skies at their backs closed to darkness. The wind had settled; the whitewater that shot over their prows all day was gone. Swells lifted the boats and rolled them gently, but Handsome Bear was brooding. One of the sun people on the Sea Hawk had been swept away the night before. Or had fallen in. Or had jumped. Whatever the circumstances, Crow was gone, and the rest of his people were terrified. The dread and loneliness of the open sea was far worse than the dangers they'd encountered crossing the desert on the way to the abalone people, or the difficulties they'd experienced on the long push north to the land of the salmon people.

Handsome Bear leaned his paddle against the plank seat, moved by crouching along the bottom of the boat until he arrived at the stern. He wanted Round Hand to pull the Salmon Eye, Sea Hawk, and Turtle Glider together so he could address his people. Round Hand's wrinkled face barely revealed his eyes, so it was difficult to gauge his response. Most of the time his whole face was smiling: so many lines pointing in so many directions you were sure he was amused. Handsome Bear had already asked many times, struggling with salmon people language, how much longer the voyage would last. Would they arrive before winter set in? He'd noticed the days getting colder, and the storms were now more severe than the rains of midsummer.

Speaking quietly in the stern, Round Hand signed to Handsome Bear as he explained that the journey of one hundred steps was longer than anyone on board could guess, even those who'd heard about it since childhood. He said they were more than halfway there, but still faced the longest and most dangerous open sea of the voyage before arriving in the jade kingdom. The Bear Caller noticed seamen taking quick glances over their shoulders as they paddled, trying to string together the conversation by catching stray words and signs. Speaking in a low tone, without signing, Handsome Bear asked if the voyage was as hard for the bearded axe men as it was for them. Round Hand laughed, his scatter of teeth catching the light of the setting sun, and began to describe their boats, the huge pieces of cloth that made them go much faster than salmon people boats.

The snake clan chief looked down, tried to imagine how a piece of cloth could propel a boat, wondered if some of his own conjuring could help their painted boats move faster. He hadn't thought to offer before, since ocean travel was entirely beyond his expertise. Round Hand interrupted his thoughts to remind him that he'd made the trip to the jade kingdom once before, and then returned home. He said the chief who led that earlier voyage had chanted the way to him, and it was in his head and heart forever.

The old mariner added a last bit of reassurance. "I could navigate by dead reckoning, never looking up, and still deliver us safely to the jade kingdom. But you know I can read the stars as well."

It had never occurred to Handsome Bear before, but now he realized Round Hand was a memory hero like himself. Leaning closer to the old man, he asked him why he decided to take the second trip. The voyage leader smiled and shook his head, scattered his expressive wrinkles through the air. "Sky dogs. I want to ride one again myself, before I die." Handsome Bear searched the chief's eyes, to determine the reliability of the sky dog story, but the old man looked away. Then the Bear Caller maneuvered his lanky body back to the plank seat that served as his paddling position. Round Hand shouted at the second in command, who raised a paddle and waved signs to the other boats. They answered the signal and drew closer. As the seamen looped rope around the pikes in the gunwales, Handsome Bear crawled his way back to the stern and touched the old navigator's arm. "Can I mention the sky dogs?"

The leader of the sun people stood with spread legs, balanced himself as swells passed under the boat. He said good words about Crow, assured everyone the young man would find his way back to the sun people otherworld. Cold Moon Fire made a harsh noise, between laughter and sobbing, but when the leader looked her way she'd put hands over face. Handsome Bear could see the signs of anger and disbelief in the eyes of his people. It was like the time he told everyone in Beautiful Village he'd found a city of rabbit people hidden in a nearby canyon. Many had rushed out to look, but when they returned they were in an ugly mood, unable to see any humor in the prank. He was known by the sun people for such episodes of imaginative extravagance, and many of those who had bad plans for him had given him the kind of looks he was getting from his expedition now.

Handsome Bear raised his hands and uttered the name Eagle Claw. Feeling a shift in their mood, he described his uncle's appearance in a dream, said the old dream reader had proclaimed the journey a good journey and had decided to become their guardian spirit. As he watched for signs of acceptance in the faces, Hole in the Head thought of the ambiguity in Eagle Claw's dream message, and Round Hand's systematic misrepresentation of the length and difficulty of the trip, things he didn't dare speak about. Just before the seamen cast off, freeing the ropes and pushing the butts of their paddles against the neighboring boat, he shouted about the jade kingdom, where there were sky dogs men could ride. As the boats drew away, there was new energy in the strokes of the paddles into calm seas, and the sun people talked to each other, signing excitedly to the salmon people beside them.

That night, as he lay under skins in the stern of the boat, the dragon returned. Handsome Bear could smell the ravishing monster before he saw her. Like Venus, a dragon is born again and again from the sea: a snake fish, a mermaid, a gorgeous bundle of fury that cruises just under the waves. But when the dragon reared, sent up an exploding fountain of water and light off the starboard of the Salmon Eye, a flash of his tasseled light streaked out beyond the crescent moon. Handsome Bear recognized his lost brother, Quetzalcoatl, god of the arts and wind. Coming to him in a vision from the Red City of the South, that brother had given him power as a child of six. Eagle Claw blessed that dream, and Handsome Bear's father did too, as all the men of the Snake clan gathered in the kiva to smoke and sing. Quetzalcoatl had flown to him on reversible winds, left him a map of all the arts, the grid-work of the sacred directions, then abandoned him, a child to himself. When he departed, he laughed like a woman, trailed a diminished chord so light and seductive that the Bear Caller carried it in his bones for the rest of his life. This dragon that teased and played with him along the night sea, like the feathered Quetzalcoatl, was here and gone at the same time, held together by a green-and-red web of light strong enough to obliterate the stars. When the stars disappeared, she became another set of stars, remapped chances for this and other worlds. The extended curls of her mane, the iron sinews of his shoulders, carrying the burden of both seed and egg, the dazzling pulsations along the creature's side, reflected the frequencies that drew it into unity. A list of things that can be a dragon: every man and woman; all creatures of the air, land, and sea; the sky, mountains, or sea itself. Everything is on the threshold of spectacular transformation—edging along the boundary of male and female, dark and light, laughter and screaming, then suddenly transgressing that border. The dragon's supple lines configure the Network, its power to suspend spirits and transfer them across the illusion of time, piggyback them onto the unsuspecting creatures of this world. John Walking-stick harnessed that power to prepare for the Great Millennial Shift. The Cherokee healer knew laughter and spinning eyes as well, knew that all creation comprises one huge dragon, on a dream flight home to the place where we all began.

When he awoke, Handsome Bear was happy. The self-doubt that had sounded a low, continuous flatted note through the song of his life was gone. He sat up, looked to the east, saw the preamble to the rising sun, then heard an even better music: flutes, stringed instruments, and things that made sounds beyond imagination. Hundreds of instruments together, their notes and chords circling one another, rising and falling, with the slow, majestic beat of full breathing, the pulsing heart. He watched an orange sliver of sun rise above the horizon, expecting another dimension of music from the play of light. Handsome Bear shifted his attention back inside the boat, noticed Cold Moon Fire hunching on her plank seat, a cloak of skins over her shoulders. He asked if she heard the music. When she pointed west, Handsome Bear looked up and saw a cluster of deep black clouds he hadn't noticed before. An enormous bolt of lightning cut through one of them. Cold Moon Fire smiled with a twisted mouth. "You call that music?"

After a long struggle to keep the boats afloat through this storm, spinning all six directions out of sight and mind, the sea began to calm and the crew of the Salmon Eye renewed their energetic paddling. Round Hand had announced that by his calculation they were close to Sea Egg Island, the next step in the ladder. He said they'd reach it in a day or so, or maybe that very day. Everyone fixed eyes on the western horizon as they paddled, looking for a shadow or a sign. They'd seen more than the usual number of sea birds for two days, but such things had happened before far from any land.

When one of the salmon people cried out, everyone thought he'd sighted the island. Instead he was pointing to the taut fish line they'd been trawling. Round Hand jumped to his post in the stern, supervised the hauling in. When the sun people put down their paddles and moved to starboard to watch, they threw the boat out of balance, so the chief ordered them back to their positions. He had the line pulled in and let out several times, played the catch as his seamen groaned and cursed through their fight with the unseen creature. Round Hand called for Handsome Bear to witness the victory, and the memory hero saw a long shadow just under the surface when he looked over the side of the boat. The old mariner whispered that he thought it was a shark, a big one. They'd have to bring it aboard carefully, or it would chew off someone's arm or leg. When the seamen finally wrestled the creature into the Salmon Eye, it stretched a quarter of the length of the boat. Everyone stared at the long tube: discolored and lumpy flesh packed inside scaleless skin, crenelated frills behind its head where gills should have been, green streamers hanging from every part of its slack body, eyes larger than extended hands, with flat, gold-streaked irises. When a seaman pulled open its jaws, he revealed a double row of needles, all slanted inward. Handsome Bear was horrified. He'd seen something like it before, but didn't know where.

Round Hand studied the creature, poked at its side, then pulled out his whalebone knife and cut a slash along its belly. Guts spilled across the bottom of the boat. He reached inside the fish, searched tentatively, then shouted that the creature had been sent to give them strength. He said he'd never seen anything like it before, so it had to be a gift from the sea gods. The old navigator peeled back some of the skin and cut out a large fillet of pink flesh. Setting it on a plank seat, he cut portions for each of the crew. He told his second in command to signal a rendezvous with the other two boats so they could all share the gift.

Round Hand gave Handsome Bear the first portion, but the snake clan chief waited with the soft mass in his hand until everyone had been served. It was hard to hold, as if it were still alive. When the rest of the crew bit into their portions, they laughed at the sweetness of the flesh. They proclaimed it excellent luck, a sign they'd complete the journey quickly. Handsome Bear stared at his piece, studying the small capillaries that ran through the ooze. It slipped through his fingers, as if struggling to return to the sea. Picking it up, he reluctantly took a bite, chewed, and swallowed. He was surprised at the taste. It was sweet as fruit, and a pleasurable sensation passed from his stomach to the extremities of his body. He ate another bite and observed how pulsations of euphoria passed over him. When he finished his portion, he returned to his position and began to paddle furiously, even before Round Hand had given the order. The whole crew laughed at his odd behavior, which they interpreted as holy clowning in honor of the blessing. But as they laughed, Handsome Bear stopped paddling, stood up on his plank seat, swayed momentarily and fell overboard.

Four seamen jumped to his rescue, but when they pulled the lanky man aboard he was unconscious. Round Hand ordered them to wrap him in skins and place him in the stern. But neither he nor anyone else who spoke to Handsome Bear could get a response. The afternoon brought fever. Round Hand chanted a whale spell, splashed cold seawater on the sun chief's contorted face, but there was no improvement.

Freydis greeted Handsome Bear with a laugh, holding an elaborately carved axe in her hands. "Now you're on my side of the line, *skraeling*. On your way to fulfill a proud destiny, you took the wrong branch at the crossroads. I've been waiting for you."

Handsome Bear stared at the fire-haired woman; she looked like the bearded men in the Beautiful Village dream that had inspired the expedition, but her face showed a ferocity he hadn't seen in theirs. How could she be standing over him like this? Her hair, face, and hands gave off light, but it illuminated only her. He knew he was either kneeling or lying down, but couldn't see his own body to be sure, to know if there were any hope for defense.

The Viking seer opened her vest, pulled it from her shoulders, and dropped it by her side. Her bracelets clanked as she continued to strip layers of clothing from her upper body. "Do you *skraelings* believe in hell? That's where you're going, weasel. Do you like the idea of dragging all your followers down to hell?"

Handsome Bear breathed in her scent, a muskiness as strong as a bear, or stag. Her breasts were heavy and full, with flat pink nipples the size of a palm. They pointed straight at the earth, the otherworld beneath, reinforcing her threats. "We must be meeting in the spirit world, woman, or I couldn't understand your language."

Freydis swept her tongue over her lips, unbuckled her belt, and began to untie the drawstring at the top of her long skirt. "I'll bet you'd like to suck my tits, *skraeling*. They're full enough for a man like you. When else will you be able to drink milk again? When else will you be able to feel home and comfort? To think they call you Handsome Bear! You're so weak and malformed. If I gave birth to a child like you, I'd split him from skull to navel with my axe before he gave his first cry."

Handsome Bear felt for his own bone and flesh in the dark: cold skin and spasms of shivering. "Woman, how could you know me?"

The warrior and explorer laughed. "How could I not know you? Do you think women don't talk to one another?" She dropped her skirt, thrust forward a round belly, powerful thighs, and a triangle of red hair that indicated the point of entry. "If you won't drink my milk, then eat my woman's juice. Crawl over here and put your mouth on my lips right now!"

The clan chief looked at the woman in fascination. Her language was repulsive, but he found something in her fierceness attractive. She was ferocious as a cornered animal, but he was the one who appeared to have no route of escape. A response to her invitation was not possible; as far as he knew, he had neither corporeal tongue nor cock to answer her taunts.

Freydis squatted and spread her knees, leaning back on her hands. "You're so small now, *skraeling*, you could never please me. If you got any smaller, your whole body would fit inside my cunt. And to think they call you Tall Boy!"

Handsome Bear couldn't remember the origin of the tears on his face. "Witch, I've smelled your smell before. Stay out of the light that falls on my path. You can't stop me from reaching the kingdom of marvels, returning with my two snake axes."

Freydis picked up the axe she'd dropped by her side. "Like this one, you fool? Do you think you can pick it up without being bitten?" She laughed and drew the blade across the top of her left forearm. Blood jumped out of the gash, ran in a stream over her fingertips and onto the ground. She laughed. "You can take the next cut, *skraeling*. Cut me any place you choose, as deep as you wish. But the cut after that is mine, and it will be on your body this time, if I can find the scrawny thing."

The Bear Caller began to chant to Spider Grandmother for light and vision, for a return of feeling to his body. The Viking woman took a step toward him, lifting the axe. He shouted at her, "Get away from me, witch! I understand your bad plans for me; you want to make me disappear."

Freydis laughed again, and threw the axe down in front of her. It was close enough for Handsome Bear to see the entwined snakes carved into the bronze. "And if any of you pathetic wanderers return home to Beautiful Village, who would it be but you, Handsome Bear—an outcast just like me. You, a thing with a bloody hole in your head, more worthless than a stillborn child." She shrieked, held her arms to either side until they feathered into wings. With the sound of warped thunder she rose, spraying Handsome Bear with blood. He could taste it as it trickled down his face and into his mouth.

As the bird woman rose, she carried all the light with her. The glow receded, became smaller and weaker until it went out, the last ember in a dying fire. Handsome Bear's darkness surrounded him: total, solid as flesh, an absence of light both rich and comforting. The darkness held him closely, so he didn't need to move. It pressed him so tightly, he forgot how to breathe.

A hand grasped his shoulder, shook him gently. "We're about to land on Demon Island, but we'll leave as soon as we can find water. The two-leggeds here will kill us if they catch us."

It was Round Hand's voice. Handsome Bear took a long breath of pungent sea air. His ribs hurt. The inside of his mouth was stuck to his teeth, with a strong taste of salt, grief, and darkness. He lifted himself on one elbow, looked over the gunwale and saw a heavily forested land rising out of the sea. The memory hero ran his hand over his face, refamiliarizing himself with its features, then through his crusty hair. Round Hand leaned over and looked into Handsome Bear's eyes, then shook his head. Listening to the drone of the navigator's words to the others, which he couldn't yet register as language, the Snake clan chief realized Round Hand had been talking to him for a very long time, but it had only now accumulated into partial consciousness. When the Salmon Eye wedged itself into sand, and the seamen leaped overboard to beach it, he lost his surge of energy and settled back. This time he rested not in darkness but in a gray zone, where he could observe sounds and smells and pieces of light, but they were stars too far away to grasp.

When he felt the hand on his shoulder again, Handsome Bear's eyes opened fully and he sat up. He looked around him in panic. The crew members were all laughing, but not at him. They threw their arms in the air and sang. Round Hand kissed Handsome Bear on the cheek. "We've crossed from Demon Island to the jade kingdom."

The Bear Caller looked at the approaching shore, with its scattered trees bent inland by fierce coastal winds. There was no sign of humans, or that they'd ever lived or hunted there. "Where are the axe people? I can't see any marvels in this land."

Round Hand laughed, said that in a week or so of coasting south they'd arrive at the outer reaches of the kingdom. And he was right. Eight days later, they paddled around a rocky point and found a sea outpost of the Great Khan's empire. It was a village that specialized in the hunting of seals, a pelt Kublai Khan demanded for his military officers' winter coats. When the three painted boats entered the harbor, surrounded by much larger junks, the amazement of the Manchus was even greater than that of the salmon and sun people. The villagers cried out, running up and down the log pier.

The old navigator pulled his whale helmet out of the cedar locker in the stern of the Salmon Eye, put it on his head, and pulled himself up onto the pier, followed by the rest of his crew. The Sea Hawk and Turtle Glider hung back, waiting to see what the Salmon Eye's reception would be. Handsome Bear began to move in the stern, shedding the skins that had wrapped him for months, but this wonder went unnoticed. The Bear Caller threw a leg onto the pier, hoisted himself up, joined his fellow paddlers. He stood more than a head taller than the largest of the assembled people, his plastered hair and twisted face making him look like a human raised by wild animals.

When a contingent of Manchus, headed by three officials, came to the end of the pier to greet them, Round Hand signed his good wishes. But as the Manchu officials looked at one another, it was clear they didn't understand. The old mariner couldn't remember any such difficulties on his first trip, was wondering how to proceed when Handsome Bear pushed himself to the front, raised opened hands, and clapped them together. His fellow travelers pulled away from him amazed, both at his wild appearance and sudden reemergence into light and life. One official walked up to him, bowed, delivered a short speech. The clan chief, with the help of his magpie necklace, recognized a few of the sounds he heard.

The Manchu welcoming contingent signaled for the Sea Hawk and Turtle Glider to land. When all three boats had been made fast, the crews were walked to a large wooden building in the center of the village, given bowls of a rice barley mix, topped with grilled beef, and a cup of tea. The head official displayed a brushed proclamation he'd just completed. It announced the extraordinary meeting to Kublai Khan. As he displayed and read the scroll, the salmon and sun people smiled politely, thinking he was showing them artwork. To them a painting without color was hopelessly primitive. The village headman rolled the message, tied it, and ceremoniously handed it to a long-cloaked messenger. Some of the salmon people followed him outside, where he mounted his horse and galloped off in a southwesterly direction. They ran back into the courtyard, shouting that they'd seen a sky dog, that it was as fast as the stories they'd heard, and would let a man ride on its back. During this agitated discussion, watched closely by the Manchu hosts, Handsome Bear and Round Hand observed the nature of the building, guards, relative numbers. The old navigator caught his friend's eye, shrugged his shoulders, but the Snake clan chief was listening to the officials speaking Chinese. He tried to categorize and memorize every sound, reading its music, intonation—the inflection of eyes, hands, and body movements too. Handsome Bear was startled when the hosts guided Round Hand and the others outside but left him in the courtyard. He was looking for paths of escape when two young women appeared, bowed, and led him to another room in the building, where a hot bath in a cast bronze tub awaited him. They scrubbed off the accumulated salt and grime of the voyage. After drying him, they worked perfumed oil into his hair and combed it straight. Handsome Bear was surprised that he was allowing strange women the intimacy of washing his hair, but he was exhausted and didn't think they had bad plans for him. They led him, already drowsy, to a smaller room with a bed and tucked him into it. There was a brazier of hot coals in the middle of the room. It was so warm, he began to imagine the painted figures in his Beautiful Village apartment and fell back into darkness.

During the next two weeks he was kept in separate quarters, and met continually with curious officials from this village and those nearby. In chairs and tables assembled in the courtyard they inspected and discussed the newcomer, his size, features, and apparent intelligence. They spoke slowly to him, and he began to understand some references to objects and his fellow travelers. He tried to convey to them the tremendous distance the expedition had traveled. Three days after his arrival, Handsome Bear began to string together some of their words. They laughed, gestured for him to continue. The next morning he was awakened by a tutor, a young man with a short black beard, equipped with paper, ink stone, and brushes. He demonstrated calligraphy to the newcomer, who mimicked the tutor's strokes so well, the young man was astonished. Later, when the Bear Caller laid brush to paper, he painted a picture of Round Hand with his whale helmet, then pointed to the floor, indicating that he wanted the navigator to join him there. The tutor left the room, returned with two officials, who smiled and bowed, and led him across the village to where the sun people and salmon people were being housed. Rabbit and the crewman with the red streaks in his hair were getting lessons in horsemanship, and the crowd laughed and cheered when Rabbit fell from his mount onto the flat pavement stones. Handsome Bear signaled to Round Hand, who smiled from across the street, but the Manchu officials never left the expedition leader's side, and he could exchange only a few remarks with sun people who stood nearby before he was guided back to the central building. That night, lying on his bed, he stared at the rafters that had been painted red and green. He felt his body rushing forward, still caught in the whirl of his journey.

When Khan's soldiers arrived with huge wheeled carts and elephants to transport the visitors and their three boats to the emperor's palace in Khan-Balik, Handsome Bear was the only one who wasn't intimidated by the huge animals and heavily armed soldiers. He bowed and said good-bye in Chinese to the Manchu officials. He greeted Khan's officer-in-charge, who eyed him malevolently. The officer was nearly as tall as Handsome Bear and wore a black beard that pointed in all directions at once. He brushed aside the Manchus' attempts at ceremony, went to the pier, set up block and tackle, hoisted the three boats. His soldiers carried them to the elephant carts, fastened them with chains and ropes. The officer gestured his contempt for the size of the boats; it was clear he thought the equipment and personnel he'd been told to bring were far more than what was necessary for the job. A cheer went up. Handsome Bear and the officer turned to see Cold Moon Fire in a footrace with one of the soldiers. She beat him badly. The officer shouted, and his soldiers fell back into ranks, closing around the salmon and sun people. A palanquin was brought forward, and the officer signaled for Handsome Bear to get in. The Snake clan chief paused briefly to inspect the halberd of one his personal guards, then pulled the curtain and seated himself on the cushions. As the palanquin was hoisted, Handsome Bear touched the green-and-red silk brocade of the interior. It was a luxurious traveling egg. He remembered the ocean dragon and wondered where it had gone; he held up his hand in the filtered light, saw his feathered fingertips extend into long crystalline claws.

THE SAN FRANCISCO

CHAPTER XI

PUBLIC LIBRARY

Ezekiel Smith spread flame under the retort, saw energy pass through the glass and into the bubbling mixture. His shack was dark, except for a lone kerosene lantern and the fiery glow generated by various alchemical experiments. Beyond a lightless window the moaning foghorn danced with itself. He waved his left hand in blessing over the homemade apparatus that branched in all directions from a spouted globular vessel, producing steam, sea smell, creatures coming into being and then dying within it, smoke at the margins, seepage around corks and rubberized fittings. The Irishman was in pursuit of the White Orchid. If he could only discover its true nature, he might delineate the highest path of philosophy, find the Network, join in the Great Work undertaken by all Travelers. But such a leap was unlikely. Although

Ezekiel could sustain himself in a world of dreams, and although he'd suspected there was a pattern to the marvels he'd experienced since his transcontinental passage through the underground river, the world of immanence had not yet presented itself to him. If he had known what it meant to be one, Ezekiel would certainly have wanted to be a Traveler—but he had no idea.

As he shifted a table loaded with snarled glass apparatus, something slipped to the floor. He stooped to pick it up, a flat piece of polished picture agate a little larger than a twenty-dollar gold piece, its receding panorama of hills and mountains in sienna, tan, and rusty red. She'd laid it on top of *Gulliver's Travels* after tucking in her last letter and reshelving the book. Ezekiel reached out his hand into that painful dream: the whole smoldering library, too many words to breathe, surrounded by smoking margins, the familiar Swift volume lying on a table, bloated with repressed flame. The letter said no more Saturday afternoons; Siu Lan Eng would no longer be available to retrieve his penned expressions of current interests, experiences, interpretations of various readings, dreams, circumspect lyrical admirations of her beauty and intelligence. Since his first encounter with the tall woman outside the teahouse, Ezekiel had trimmed his face up with a San Francisco-style beard, moustaches swept up in jaunty semicircles on both sides of his nose, and had bought himself a bowler hat. After getting off work from the foundry on Saturday and cleaning up at his Howard Street room, he was off to old Pacific Hall, recently converted to the new San Francisco Public Library. It was everywhere: memory smoke, partially burned gas, the by-products of contained literary combustion that hazed over his vision. But he could still see her reaching fingers as she was about to retrieve the book and one of his earlier letters. He hadn't waited at the table as previously agreed but stood behind the stack, reached through, and touched her. Siu Lan had lingered for a moment before withdrawing, looked at her hand as if she'd never seen it before.

Denis Kearny, with all his debates on the merits of the Workingmen's Party of California in the sandlots by City Hall; a merchant husband with a bad temper and bodyguards, old but vigilant; the pungent seepage of an array of experiments, an acrid metallic smoke biting into his lungs; her beautiful tan skin, freckles, a high forehead, cheekbones to be kissed in dreams; the betrayal of a proposed voyage to Fusang when he broke his promise and followed her to the apartment in Chinatown. Ezekiel fell to his knees, saw that the pavement was gone. There was the kind of terrible smoke that came after explosions pushed through walls and scattered them over the streets. She raised one hand, said good-bye, turned, and walked away. When Ezekiel finally gathered enough courage to lift his eyes from the pavement, look down Bush Street, she was gone.

The wounded Irishman held out for two weeks before going back to Stockton Street, lurking at the entrance to Siu Lan's building. But the stares of early morning shoppers who brushed by made him move down a few doors. Lingering by the open boxes of a vegetable market, he ran his hands over Chinese eggplants, bunches of bok choy, small bound sheaves of gow choy, stacks of fuzzy squash, gai choy, the rippled jade skin of bitter melons, large sections of winter melon with white dust over the rind, clumps of fresh ginger root, until the storekeeper and his wife glared him away. He crossed the street and took a position at the mouth of an alley, where he found a perfect vantage point for his vigil. But he was jostled so many times by people entering and exiting the alley, he gave up and moved on. The Irishman decided to stay in motion, several dozen paces down one side of the street, then back the other side. After making a few of these circuits, he had attracted the attention of every storekeeper in the area. Fearing he might be a Kearny arsonist or thug, casing the street for a likely target, they gathered and confronted him as he ambled by, eyeing huge jars of dried black mushrooms. A spokesman asked if he were lost, and could they help him find his way, or would he like to buy a steamed chicken or roast duck. Ezekiel smiled as he was surrounded, but when he politely declined their offers, the storekeepers tightened their circle until he felt elbows and shoulders in his ribs. Ezekiel pushed over the vegetable man, began to run down the street. Something whizzed past his ear. As he turned and looked over his shoulder, he was hit in the forehead by an orange. He saw a flash of light, then a swarm of colored stars, stumbled backward.

Produce continued to hit the wall and splatter at his feet, so he stumbled on as fast he could. It was almost a comfort when the hand reached out and pulled him to one side. He looked down.

It was Wong Fu Gee's woman, shaking her head and smiling. As he began to ask her a question, she put an envelope into his hand, turned, and disappeared into an explosion of pigeons. The only pedestrian he could see looking south on Stockton was a small gray-haired man in a flannel shirt, turning into an alley a half block away. After this moment of comfort had escaped him, Ezekiel continued to run, didn't slow his pace until he'd reached Market Street. Leaning a shoulder against the wall, he opened the envelope and read.

> Ezekiel,
>   Siu Lan Eng is far beyond you now, traveling somewhere overseas. The pursuit you have planned is completely useless. Your only hope is taking my advice. Study alchemy and the Tao.
>   Wong Fu Gee

The word "overseas" was a more violent assault on Ezekiel than the treatment he'd received at the hands of the Chinatown merchants. He thought of trying to follow her, shipping out as a sailor again. But what route had she taken? And if she'd returned to China, which province, town, or village? A message from Wong Fu Gee, a man he'd sought without success for so long, should have made him ecstatic. But this note burned his fingers, sent up the sickening smoke of betrayal. The fishing boss had apparently joined the conspiracy to deprive him of the source of all light. It was an act of cruelty beyond his understanding.

Good Lord have mercy! Robert Johnson went to the crossroads, walked to its bonfire and dark night, turned his back on the laughing moon that had conjured his wrongs. Lost his city woman, while hants caught at shirtsleeves and the cuffs of his pinstriped pants. It's darkness, child, and the moon's possessed the sky. A city woman feeding words as sweet as sweet potato pie. Then she packed the words and left him to himself. She'll come back when rocks grow out of trees. Gold tooth, silver tooth, mouth of lead, skin sparkling diamonds in the morning. Quicksilver on the loose, trying to flag a ride. Dark bird lighting on the arm of night: she's playing his whole life backwards, sinking him back into the birthing swamp. A city woman drains you down to grief and pitifulness, walks you to the margins, then back to the crossroads, where the rising sun's going down. Crying, "Mercy! Mercy, if you please." Walking on the earth, the place that holds directions and carries the rain—wind trapped in his pockets, shoes without a shine. Clean as a knife sliding against steel guitar strings, she brought him down. He could smell the smoke and sulfur coming from under her door. Four-fingered child, don't call me on the phone, and when you wave your hand up over my head, don't steal my eyes. Snake eggs, clear-skinned as a diamond and full of fire. Her water-drawing touch, the one that stills both bruise and cramps, takes soft sung notes that drive the sun down its course, blood through the arm of a tree and into its fruit. Good Lord have mercy.

Ezekiel returned to his room on Howard Street, took out paper and pen and began to write an angry reply to Wong Fu Gee. After a few lines he paused, realizing the note would be impossible to deliver. He might as well put it in a corked bottle and cast it into the bay. The next moment he was out on the street again, walking toward the Ferry Building. He had dreamed of living with Siu Lan in Berkeley, since he considered the people who lived there more civilized than San Franciscans. It wasn't until he was halfway across the bay that the true purpose of the trip took shape before his eyes. There was no reason to continue the struggle. If he could just slip over the railing, drop, breathe in enough water to fill his lungs, it would all be finished quickly. The old sailors, fearing the agony of days of treading water after being lost overboard, had told him how to do it. When he gripped the railing with both hands, preparing to vault over, he looked up into the sky. It was blue, free of fog, as clear and bright as the sky that had bounced with light the day he surfaced in Monterey Bay. Then he heard the same fractured octave that had accompanied his second birth. He pulled back, let go of the railing, and smiled. The totality of the sky had written a word he could finally read. All these experiences were part of a test. His journey through the underground river, his rescue, the sojourn with Wong Fu Gee and his woman, his chance meeting with Siu Lan Eng in the library, and the relationship that developed from it. But, of course, it could not have been a chance meeting. "Study alchemy and the Tao." Siu Lan would be his when he'd mastered these obstacles. Whatever the cost in money and effort, he was now prepared to undertake it.

When he arrived in Berkeley, he couldn't decide what to do first: try to find the texts necessary for the quest or search for a room where he could set up a laboratory. He knew alchemy involved fire, odd combinations of mineral and vegetable essences, and that it required tables full of beakers, retorts, salamanders, and distillation coils. Within a week he had rented a shed in the warehouse district near the bay. He'd found three books on the subject of alchemy in a used bookstore near the university campus, and copied out in longhand passages from several others in the library. He'd purchased a supply of sulfur, quicksilver, antimony, spirits of alcohol, tinctures of silver and arsenic, and other elements necessary for the practice of this mystery. The process of his redemption had begun.

But what about Siu Lan? Her name translated as White Orchid, but what did that mean? It had to be the key, and knowledge of its meaning would necessarily lead to possession. Feminine, yin to be sure. Probably moist. Whether nocturnal or diurnal, that was a much harder question. Antimony, quicksilver, one of the sulfates, or maybe a vegetable distillation, the essence of some variety of white orchid? He knew better than to ignore the obvious. What about the beautiful crystalline eggs he'd seen in his passage? They were surely a clue. He moved from table to table, glanced at the philosopher's egg he'd been trying to assemble. Glass within glass within glass—he had heated, twisted, shaped, but with few encouraging results. In the meantime, he was simultaneously pursuing a number of hypotheses on other tables in the shack. Gas fires burned under beakers and retorts, sending vapors into labyrinthine corridors of distillation tubing, which he had learned to soften, bend, and assemble himself. In the process, he had singed the hair off his knuckles, hands, and forearms—and scorched the lower part of his beard.

Just before noon, exactly a month after the revelation of a new life had come to him on the ferry, Ezekiel was in a state of high agitation. All morning he felt that he stood at the gate; knowledge and Siu Lan stood just on the other side. He could sense power in the air, like the electrified yellow light that precedes a thunderstorm. The neophyte alchemist, eager to complete his quest and fulfill his destiny, turned up the fire under the distillation of kelp and arsenic, with tincture of antimony as a catalyst. Metamorphosis. The moon taking wing and landing on earth. It was clearly outlined in one of his books. The retort bubbled so vigorously that it shook on its brass tripod. Ezekiel had turned his back to the apparatus, was looking at the white bird peering in his window, when the thickening mass began to spatter into the tubing, jamming its passage, and the explosion occurred.

The bird came closer, bowed, divided itself into a high bony forehead, a hank of straight black hair, teeth, a slender hand with white fingernails. The moon was a dance of silver snakes around the room. First the movement of the bird, then the muffled music of the underground river and its treasure-filled eggs, the low deliberate voice of Siu Lan, one he'd heard only once before in his life. She gestured, formed letters and symbols with her fingers. She spoke in the poetry of fiery decay, the sacred directions, lunar transformations, black heat, and the Trismegistus phoenix of hermaphroditic flux. Wong Fu Gee and his woman rested their chins on each of her shoulders. Their faces were grim, like the pictures of the dead carried before Chinese funeral processions, or the stern ancestors above family altars. Siu Lan spoke in formulas, philosophical propositions, sweet distillations of light. But as Ezekiel reached out and touched her face, passed the lightest touch over her lips and cheekbones, feathers reappeared, the sound of fractured organ notes and the mighty beating of wings. The roof of the shack dissolved to sky as the morning's haze burned off, and she rose, once again pulling beyond his sight.

Ezekiel lay on the floor in a rubble of table splinters, glass fragments, twisted metal rods and wire. His smoldering coat haloed his body. Cross-currents of smoke rolled along the floor, up the walls, and swirled under the shack's ceiling. He mumbled the word "wings," attempted to lift one shoulder, then fell back moaning. The sole of one boot bore a large red stain. It took the exact shape of the island of Maui, the place where Siu Lan and generations of her progeny would reside.

CHAPTER XII | # THE FALL OF LAGUNA NIGUEL

CAR PAINTER PLANS HOMELESS CONFERENCE

A Santa Ana man known for his van and truck illustrations has announced plans to hold a national conference for the homeless in Lions Park, Costa Mesa, on the 4th of July weekend. Gerald Martinez, an employee of Chaco's Custom Auto Shop, said the conference will feature a number of activities, including nutrition seminars, free health clinics, instruction on how to find and maintain alternative housing in urban areas, and a "plenary discussion" of the philosophy of Emiliano Zapata as it applies to urban and suburban land reform in the United States. Mr. Martinez said the Zapata roundtable was a response to the recent political enthusiasm for privatization.

Martinez claims to have chosen Costa Mesa for this as yet unauthorized event because of the pressure local merchants have put on area shelters and soup kitchens to shut down their operations. The organizer said he had originally considered an economic boycott in response, but felt that giving the merchants a chance to meet a wide spectrum of homeless people might better enable them to overcome their stereotypical thinking.

Robert "Bud" Wilkins, Chairman of the Costa Mesa Chamber of Commerce, was unavailable for comment. Mayor Stephen Tobias said he had heard nothing about a homeless conference, that no permits had been applied for, and without city permission such a gathering would be illegal and not tolerated. He said he had no specific plan of action in case large numbers of people arrived without the proper arrangements, but appropriate measures would be taken if the circumstance arose.

In response to Mayor Tobias' comments, Martinez said all duly constituted authorities had been consulted, and permission to proceed had been granted.

Martinez claims that he has received indications of interest from as far away as New York City, Washington, D.C., and New Orleans. He said he had also received queries from Haiti, Cuba and Brazil, but the money required to transport participants from those locations was beyond his budget.

Of course, Jerry had no intention of holding his National Conference for the Homeless in Costa Mesa. The anxiety experienced by the city fathers after reading that May 3 article in the Orange County edition of the *L.A. Times* was a nicely measured punishment for their collective meanspiritedness. It also guaranteed there'd be a large show of force by police and the Orange County sheriff in that area, making it a perfect decoy. July 3, the day before the conference was to begin, the authorities erected barricades around Lions Park, set up checkpoints on various streets throughout the area. When Jerry heard that his decoy had drawn over a thousand uniforms, and the usual media show as authorities bussed undesirables out of town, dropping them at the Santa Ana Civic Center, he knew there'd be adequate breathing room if he could act quickly enough.

Merchants and politicos in Costa Mesa were congratulating one another on their handling of the situation as the visionary van painter airbrushed the last strokes on his master plan. He was a student and admirer of Garibaldi, the great Italian liberator and guerilla strategist. Quick night marches to flank and surprise the enemy were a Garibaldi specialty, and Jerry reached his hand into that bag. With contributions from sympathetic liberals who'd been impressed by the plans described in the *Times* article, he rented a dozen dilapidated charter buses, gathered over one hundred vans and pickups in a call to the magic revolutionaries of the Santa Ana area. They spread out and gathered the people who'd been massing for days in Santa Ana, Orange, Fullerton, and especially in Anaheim, near the Disneyland entrance on Harbor Boulevard. Two chartered boats moved two thousand souls from Long Beach to Dana Point, constituting, as far as Jerry knew, the first successful marine invasion of California territory since the Mexican War of 1848. He calculated that even if he were prevented from returning for a second load, he could deliver five thousand people to the Crown Valley Parkway in Laguna Niguel before dawn. In fact, his charter buses and the van and truck convoys made three runs before the police and highway patrol set up effective blockades. He'd transported over ten thousand people to a mile-long stretch of the green manicured areas surrounding the parkway, spilling over onto the El Niguel golf course. Those who were still waiting at the various pickup points around the county were signaled by cellular phones, told to follow their maps and instructions, try to reach the area on foot.

When the gray dawn broke on the Fourth of July, news and police helicopters dropped down for a closer look. There were ground cloths and tents scattered over the area, and even a few lean-tos already set up against trees. A great number of Americans of all kinds—reclining, squatting, standing, sitting—transfigured the suburban white bread landscape into a reenactment of the morning before the Battle of Gettysburg. Alternatively, if the Washington Monument had suddenly sprouted out of the Crown Valley Parkway, you'd have thought you were witnessing a reenactment of the Poverty March tent city of 1963, righteous protestors waiting for another Martin Luther King Jr. to emerge and rally the crowd. The rolling greenery could also recall a stretch of Woodstock real estate in 1969, except that this scene had no mud. Dry conditions, variable patchy fog night and morning, generally sunny, with highs in the upper seventies to low eighties.

Jerry's Chacoan van, parked up on a green near Club House Drive, was command center. Set up outside the vehicle: TVs, computers, fax machines, and a bank of cellular phones with encoders, all powered by a single gasoline generator. Up to this point, Jerry had succeeded beyond his expectations. Now, as he sat on the curb, he experienced a moment of crisis and self-doubt. Here was where the master plan ended and inspiration needed to kick in. How could he shape this disorganized mass of humanity into a coherent protest? Although he could describe the evils of the contemporary world, and although he had a vision of what might transform it, he was a painter, not a political organizer or an orator. As he watched the people around him laughing, trading jokes, exuberant with the power of their numbers, sharing trucked-in day-old doughnuts, Jerry hoped nobody would get killed. He prayed to the muses of Aztlan, the gods of fire and blood, that they would infuse him with the genius to complete this painting, even more ambitious than his fantasy of turning a Greyhound into the Bridge to Aztlan.

Travelers run on memory, the pure energy that lights up the Network, but where are Southern California's memory heroes? If there are any here, they've gone underground, moles in the system. Hard to locate. The rest of us continue to trust in computers bloated with data, meaningless garbage, and consider ourselves relieved from the obligations of memory. Will Mnemosyne help? Better to call on the ancestors, that Rainbow Bridge of black, brown, and beige. They're listening to Jerry now, keeping tabs on the moaning and grinding of the earth, the music that is a seismic prelude to the Great Millennial Shift. John Walkingstick is about to make dimensional contact, release spirits that have been stored in the Network's star system for over 150 years. The channels are about to be thrown open, energy and power rushing beyond anyone's control. Travelers are materializing out of earth, air, and water: memory's transubstantiation into flesh and blood. They're arriving for the Battle of Laguna Niguel.

By noon Jerry had given a crash course in crowd control, distributed red arm bands, and sent the monitors to various sections of the encampment. His strategy was to keep everything cool and sit tight, wait for authorities to move first. Helicopters, both news and police, were circling, hovering, driving everyone crazy. That kind of psychological intimidation needed to be neutralized by the volunteers. Larry Smith and Carla had been moving through the crowd, reassuring, mediating disputes, keeping up morale. The crowd had grown visibly larger all morning. Since all access roads had been blocked by the police, Jerry assumed people were leaking through the rows of identical pink condos and over the walls of gated enclaves that encrusted the ridges on both sides of the parkway. The Aliso/Woods Canyon Regional Park on the north side, toward Laguna Beach, was another likely route on the underground railway. Jerry had already advised folks who'd missed earlier transportation that this would be their easiest access. Some of those making it through were people who'd hitchhiked in from all over the country, but a lot of them were Southern Californians who'd been watching the coverage all morning on TV and didn't want to miss out on the excitement. It looked like a better bet than any Fourth of July parade. Morning radio and television traffic programs had issued traffic advisories, warning motorists to avoid the PCH south of Laguna Beach and to avoid the Crown Valley Parkway entirely.

Carmen Noguchi from KTVL got around the police lines with an assistant shouldering a minicam. As she worked her way through the crowd, she did quick bites from random doughnut munchers, asking each to describe the leaders and the purpose of the demonstration. There seemed to be a lot of uncertainty, but one of the monitors finally pointed the newspeople toward the painted van and its nest of paraphernalia. Carmen caught up with Jerry by a cluster of trees where two groups were in a turf dispute.

The reporter reached her microphone over an anonymous shoulder. "Who are you, sir? Is it true you're in charge here?"

"Jerry Martinez. Tell me what you'd like to know."

Carmen looked to be sure her assistant's minicam was running, then pushed past demonstrators until she stood face to face with the visionary van painter. "Why are all these people here? Does this have anything to do with the homeless riot that was threatened in Costa Mesa?"

Jerry laughed, gestured with one hand. "Do you see anybody threatening or rioting?"

Carmen tried to maintain her smile. "Not at this moment, no. But why are you people holding this demonstration? I understand there was no permit. Is it a protest against government policies?"

"Which ones? Almost anything interesting you do in life is a protest against some government policy. Do you see that man over there?" Jerry pointed to Francisco Torres, sunning himself in his wheelchair. "He's the King of Laguna Niguel, descended from the rancheros. He decided to take back his land and invited us along to share in the fun."

Carmen scanned the faces in the crowd, signaled her cameraman to do the same. "Are you people Indians? Do you plan on occupying Laguna Niguel to make some kind of territorial claim? Is there some casino connection here?"

"Do I look like an Indian?"

"Tell me, Mr. Martinez, how many people do you think you've gathered here today?"

Jerry looked up and down the parkway. "People used to say ask the organizers for a figure, then subtract twenty or twenty-five percent."

"But aren't you the organizer?"

"I don't have the slightest idea how many people are here. What do the cops say?"

"Twenty thousand."

"Then it's easy: just double a police estimate, and you'll be close. I'd say maybe fifty thousand. That's a pretty good bunch of people—better than I'd expected."

Jerry turned his back and walked down the slope to the van, ignoring the questions Carmen asked as she trailed along, sticking to his shoulder. He peeled her off as he stepped into the back of the van and closed the door. Outside he heard her put together her signoff.

"Well, there you have it. Carmen Noguchi, here at the nerve center of the demonstration on the Crown Valley Parkway in Laguna Niguel. A lot of restless people, not much direction or organization. Apparently no clear idea of what they're doing here. KTVL will keep you up to date as events develop. Back to you, Jennifer."

Memory. Mnemosyne, and her bastard daughter Catastrophe. Thousands of partisans gathered to liberate Laguna Niguel, and thousands of others sworn to protect order and property arriving to oppose them, all carrying the stories that propel their lives. The maps have been drawn, surveyed, and registered, but are about to be reimagined. There are signs of directional change on these hills overlooking the Pacific, and it will result in a new version of the map of who we are. While the Laguna Niguel and Dana Point police, the sheriff's deputies, the California Highway Patrol, and security guard contingents of different stripes struggle for a plan of action, we have time to name and conjure.

There's Derwood "Woody" Wall, former Los Angeles Chief of Police. He caught up with the situation the afternoon of Day 1, driving a camouflaged Humvee to the combined forces command center at PCH and Crown Valley Parkway, in the parking lot of the Ritz Carlton Hotel. Reporters immediately recognized the "Berlin Wall," as he was known to them, and asked why he was there. Volunteering intellectual resources and expertise derived from his experience during two L.A. riots was his reply. Woody's favorite line was "Good walls make good neighbors," which he attributed to Carl Sandburg. "You can quote us on that."

There's Annie O'Rourke, a ninety-two-year-old retired Irish nurse who has been feeding the homeless for fifteen years in Anaheim. When only two men showed up for lunch, instead of seventy-five, she found out about the conference and had a volunteer drive her to Laguna Niguel. Annie was not fond of cops: bad memories went back as far as the Irish Revolution. So when Sheriff's Deputy Jim Dillon grabbed her by the shoulder as she tried to cross police lines, she gave him an Irish scrub, drawing the attention of minicams and reporters. She pushed through into the crowd of demonstrators, looking from side to side, sighing, asking the Lord to help her feed all her boys.

There's Chester Long, Orange County District Attorney. His hero from boyhood, when he imagined himself a junior G-man, was J. Edgar Hoover. After reading Gentry's biography, Chester bought himself a red sheath, tried it on in his walk-in closet, just to feel closer to his mentor. His wife, Pam, always spoke about the need for men to get in touch with their feminine side. Maybe the dress would help him channel Hoover's spirit. He slipped the sheath back into place at the bottom of a drawer full of jockey shorts, didn't make it on location in Laguna Niguel until Day 2, wearing a helmet and a flack jacket, a nice pair of cutaway black lace panties under his pin-striped pants. He insisted on personally coordinating strategy for the impending bust.

There's Malathion Girl and her partner, Johnny Medfly. This team of performance artists, who lived in an abandoned building in East Hollywood, made it over the ridge on the afternoon of Day 1. When she spotted a minicam, Malathion Girl broke into a shortened version of her burnt sugar massage. On her shaved head was a tattooed crown of thorns, blood trickling over the temples. She'd also shaved her pubic hair, and finished her act by pulling her black tights around her knees, swiveling her hips, and massaging her burnt sugar.

There's Charlie Beckwith, an officer with the Dana Point Police Department. He had the cleanest teeth in the department. Flossing after every meal, then a trip to the men's room with his Water Pik. Charlie would never pick his teeth with wood because of the possibility of gum damage. He tried to explain these dangers to fellow officers, but they laughed and called him obsessed. Charlie was cursed with prophetic vision. As people around him smiled, no matter how young, he saw the final state of their teeth and gums, the dues they'd pay for bad oral hygiene: bridges, gingivitis and gum surgery, full dentures. It was a terror impossible to articulate, and difficult to live with.

There's Wilbur Lum, an ethnic studies professor from UCLA. Carla met him when he came down to UC Irvine to help organize the Asian and Asian-American students, who made up about one half of the student population but still had no official status as a group. Lum's mother was an activist in the Republican party, but he never mentioned that. He's written two novels and five books of poetry, the last entitled *The Fu Manchu Taxi Service*.

There's INS agent Harold Kinsolver, who was dispatched to the scene as soon as television pictures from the demonstration verified that Hispanics, possibly illegal aliens, were involved. Kinsolver was in the business of collecting and redistributing people. He also had an extensive collection of matchbooks, miniature bottles of liquor, and presidential signatures.

There's Carmen Noguchi, "On the Spot" reporter for KTVL, and anchor backup for Jennifer Choy. Although she had no blood ties to the famous Japanese sculptor and designer, she considered herself related by creativity. She'd pieced together facsimile Byzantine mosaics on the walls of two bathrooms in her Brentwood home. Talent ran in the family: her ten-year-old son, Amadeus, had already played solo violin with the Los Angeles County Youth Orchestra.

There's Laguna Niguel police officer Charlotte "Charlie" Ranier. She worked for seven years as a waitress in Mission Viejo before applying for police training. Her fellow officers called her "Pussy" Ranier behind her back, but in her presence or over the radio only dared meow. Jim Dillon made the mistake of a crude commentary on her physical endowments, without realizing she stood behind him. She swept his legs with one foot, took him down with her club across his throat, then gave him a big kiss on his cheek. Around the station, it was pretty much "Charlie" from then on.

There's a man who looks an awful lot like Thelonious Monk. He wore a silver-colored suit jacket several sizes too small, a leopard-spotted hat of fake fur. He carried a medicine bundle like the one Walkingstick found when he and the bebopper made a quick backdoor exit from a circle dream.

There's Imperfecto Ruiz, who came all the way from Silverlake to tell the authorities Jerry Martinez is the head of a New Age satanic cult. He'd studied the van pictures in the previously published L.A. Times article and was convinced they were the work of the devil. He found Christine Worthington on site and told his story. After hearing him describe his Church of the Awakening in Silverlake, she asked if he'd taken the name Imperfecto as an act of humility. He said no, his mother had been a grammar teacher, showed the reporter pictures of his sister, Presente, and brother, Pluscuamperfecto.

There's Christine Worthington herself, a specialist in the journalism of homelessness, welfare, and illegal immigrants. She'd called up the Jerry Martinez file on her computer, found the van painting article, and pretty much nailed him down—tired old activist, perpetuating the persistent but ridiculous myth that anything worth noting happened in the sixties. In other words, he was a scam artist. She was a Stanford alumna, her favorite magazine *Vanity Fair*, and since she had secret ambitions to political office, she'd hired a Jamaican nanny instead of a Hispanic one.

There's Reggie Fournier and his sidekick Nathan Sampson, Wild Tchoupitoulas from New Orleans. They'd brought along, not full regalia, but traveling kits that consisted of single eagle feathers attached to white headbands of artificial rabbit fur, wristlets of the same material with colored streamers. They'd traveled light, dodging rednecks and the devil moon. When they found the coast with its millennial blues and bloody water, they knew there was conjuring afoot.

Jerry didn't want to stand on top of his van and speak to the multitudes. You don't stand on a work of art. But when several partisans rigged boards crosswise over the utility rack, he carefully crawled up and pulled the microphone after him. As he began to speak, the crowd pushed toward the van, until people stood shoulder to shoulder as far as a minicam could see in all directions.

"My name's Jerry Martinez, one of the people who sent out a call for the tribes to come together. I'm glad you heard and came."

Cheers and whistles; the partisans began to feel the power of the dragon they'd become. Heads turned and swayed, pulses rolled over the scales of an animal made of human hair in a hundred colors.

"A television reporter just asked me to explain what all of this means. I have no idea. Let me be straight with you: I don't have any plan or a set of demands. Nothing like that. Look around you. We all came together here, and that more than anything else is the plan. I just hope something beautiful happens here today. Well, something beautiful has already happened. Let's just hope the power of it carries for a while, and some good comes from it."

Whoops went up as inflated beach balls spun over hands, rolled in bent spirals across the top of the crowd. Shirts had begun to come off as the sun burned away the last shreds of fog. A woman to Jerry's left stripped and had a man hoist her on his shoulders. Her flesh, even more abundant than her enthusiasm, first drew cheers, then cackles and whistles.

"I don't know what's going to happen." More raucous laughter. "Hey, you guys, I'm talking about what's going to happen to all the people in this valley. But I'll tell you who got us here, against all odds: Giuseppe Garibaldi. I read about him when I was a kid, and he's been my hero ever since. He was a great liberation fighter, the man who freed and unified Italy, freed slaves in Latin America too. When the American Civil War broke out, Abraham Lincoln wrote to him and asked him to be a general in the Union Army. He wrote back and said, 'First free the slaves.' Lincoln never got back to him on that. And don't look at each other and tell me the slaves were freed over a century ago. Think about it. We're all slaves here, every one of us, no matter what color."

A man with scruffy blond hair and a walrus moustache jumped up and down, yelling, "Preach it, brother. Preach it!" The crowd cheered its approval.

"We've forgotten how to live, can't wait to jump into any set of chains the bosses offer us. Let me tell you about the time Garibaldi recruited a thousand college students, put them into a couple of rusty boats, and sailed down to liberate Sicily from the French army. He didn't have any specific plan, but he knew he could improvise. Moving quickly, usually at night like we did, he kept the enemy off balance. They could never predict his strategy. Within a month, he did exactly what he said he would.

"And it's not just strategy. Garibaldi succeeded because he believed in what he did. He hated tyranny. No compromise and no negotiation. And he always knew the first thing you had to do was free the slaves."

There were scattered cheers through the crowd. A few people were chanting, "First free the slaves!"

"He fought the Pope's soldiers near the Vatican in Rome and beat them. That was supposed to be impossible too."

Annie O'Rourke shouted from back in the crowd, "Let's leave the Pope out of this!" The crowd laughed. Jerry asked what she said, then laughed himself when it was repeated.

"OK, OK, we'll leave the Pope out of it, at least for today. Anyway, I'm starting to talk too much. We're going to distribute food as it comes in. So just sit tight, have fun, and share what you've got. There are two medical tents, one down on the west end, the other up on the side of that hill to the north. We'll try to do all we can, but I want you to take care of each other. Be good."

As the cheers rose, there was a bustling in the crowd about fifty yards away from the van. A couple of conga drums were hoisted overhead and an even bigger cheer went up.

"OK, then, looks like you're going to have some fun. For the time being, I'm going to split." Jerry passed the microphone down to Carla, then crawled over the back of his van and dropped to the ground. The congas started up, were joined by the sounds of sticks against empty bottles. A half hour into the rhythm jam, there were five congas, a set of timbales, two cowbells, gourd rattles of various sorts, and a huge circle of active listeners, handclappers, and wood whackers. They played off one another, ran down looping tunnels of syncopation and came back, tested counterrhythm against counterrhythm. A shrill whistle blew a few short bursts in Afro-Cuban time, and the jam swerved down another thunderous rhythm avenue. Annie O'Rourke worked her way through the crowd to the jam, borrowed a cowbell, and beat furious time on it. The man who wore the leopard-spotted fake fur cap took over a conga from one of the men, wrapped his legs around it, threw down an oddly shaped cluster of beats, paused, then came back in on the half beat. He moved in and out but never lost time. In a few minutes he'd pulled the whole jam around to his eccentricities. Bebop, the anthem of democracy, rose so strongly into the Network stretching across the sky that small sparks and flashes shot along the circuits. A number of reclining crusaders noticed the effect but kept the observation to themselves.

Reggie and Nathan got on their traveling outfits, danced with the jam, did some serious hand jive and cross-foot work. When they broke into "Iko Iko," the congas turned and embraced the melody, and the crowd around them sang as much as they knew or could pick up by mimicry. It was all "Hey now!" and "Jock-a-mo fee na-ne" in the California sun.

The Goodyear blimp had joined the helicopters, giving the television audience sweeping aerial shots of the carpet of celebrating demonstrators. Their jam went on for hours. New people came by, traded off on instruments and joined in, or just listened, then went on. The music only stopped when late in the afternoon two Cessnas swooped down into the valley dropping garbage bags full of individually wrapped ham and turkey sandwiches, and boxes of apple juice. There was some damage and breakage, but nothing rendered completely inedible. After the demonstrators rushed to see what had arrived, the monitors took charge, assured fair and orderly distribution. Most got a half sandwich and at least part of a drink. Annie O'Rourke shouted until she got the attention of a large segment of the crowd, told them to take off their hats while she gave thanks to the Lord for the sandwiches from heaven.

All day there were television reports of rumors that a National Guard regiment was being mustered. When reporters asked authorities, they refused to comment. In the twilight, demonstrators looked down the hill toward the PCH, watched trucks and armored personnel carriers unload weekend warriors. They bivouacked on both sides of the parkway. Jerry watched through binoculars and estimated numbers. He figured by the next day they'd have enough to do damage to his crowd, which had nearly doubled in size since morning, in spite of road blocks, dog patrols, and aerial surveillance. When it was completely dark, he told Carla he wanted to get some sleep, because he was pretty sure the uniforms wouldn't undertake any major action at night.

Back inside his traveling masterpiece, Jerry rigged a curtain to block off the front of the van, taped newspaper over the back windows. He stripped down to his red BVDs, and was about to climb into the double sleeping bag with Carla when she flipped on a flashlight.

"I can't believe you've got those Noriegas on again. Did you go back and change into them yesterday?"

Jerry got up on his knees, turned his back and shimmied. "Why not? Something borrowed, something red. Isn't that what they say? Thought about the red Che Guevara T-shirt I got in Barcelona, but figured that might be too distracting."

Carla laughed. "Get into the bag, cowboy. You're going to need your strength for tomorrow." They lay together quietly for a while, listened as troubadours began to play guitars and sing in a grove of trees just downhill. As she heard lines and fragments from "The Guadalupe Hidalgo Blues" and "Last Fair Deal Gone Down," Carla became aroused. She had a weakness for the blues; it electrified muscles throughout her body, but particularly in her powerful legs. When she heard those snaky rhythms, her legs felt an overwhelming urge to wrap themselves around something. An exhausted Jerry had taken her advice and was dropping into deep sleep when he felt the Abruzzese leg lock around his hips. He knew there was no turning back, but cautioned her about the potential audience outside, including television cameras. He wanted to keep it quiet and low key.

They were both grinding their teeth, holding the usual noise down to a musical hum, moving toward that explosive moment when Carla's legs would close down, squeeze out his breath, and Jerry would feel energy surge up from his hips into his head, ready to explode out his ears. Just at that moment, orgasms in the balance, Handsome Bear, dressed in his green-and-blue silk dragon coat, appeared to both of them separately. It was a Chacoan split image in Jerry's Chacoan van. Animals all over the place: creatures Jerry had airbrushed on the exterior of the van were sliding, stepping, and crawling over their legs. An eagle beat its wings against the roof above. The memory hero and his totems had arrived to give Carla and Jerry traveling instructions. He told them a new sipapu had opened, and the power was beginning to rush through, but they both needed to move away from it to gather strength before coming back to finish the work. For Jerry there were visual instructions, starting with a panoramic sweep of the Grand Canyon, then running over the Painted Desert, the Hopi mesas, and Canyon de Chelly until it reached Chaco Canyon. For Carla the instructions were verbal: "Go to the jade kingdom, find a guide who can take you into the mountains of Mongolia. The bear people are waiting for you. They know you're coming."

When the van of visions returned to darkness, Jerry and Carla were still in a confused tangle, their spirits directed away from one another, each wondering if the other had come.

Day 2, July 5, dawned as gray as the Fourth. Hungry people roamed the encampment, trying to barter for food. Jerry and Carla were still tied loosely to one other in their sleeping bag when a crowd monitor rapped the side of the van, announced someone named Guzman was there to see him.

Jerry pulled on jeans and a T-shirt, crawled out the back door, closing it quietly behind him. He'd guessed it was news people looking for an interview, but when he spotted Guzman, with suit and briefcase, he knew he was dealing with some form of cop.

"My name is Oscar Guzman, assistant to Chester Long, Orange County District Attorney. I'm here to see if we can work something out." He smiled as he looked around him, watched news cameras and demonstrators gather.

Jerry shook his head, then rubbed his hands over his face. "What about some food? We're all pretty hungry around here."

Guzman released a small chuckle, straightened his tie. "Food can be arranged. We have plenty of it down at the National Guard encampment. All we need is orderly dispersal."

"OK, Señor Guzman, cut the stuff. Why are you here?"

"First of all, we'd like you to clarify the purpose of this occupation. An article in this morning's *Times* says you are representing
the Juaneño band of Indians and making a tribal claim on this
territory."

"I haven't read the paper, but now that you mention it, sounds
like a good idea. I've been to the mission in San Juan Capistrano,
and it always looked like a forced labor camp to me. Sooner or
later, the bill's got to come due for all that unpaid work."

"You're not a Juaneño?"

"Nope. I'm Jerry Martinez, from Santa Ana, and a good friend
of Francisco Torres, King of Laguna Niguel."

"We've done research on the name Francisco Torres and come
up with nothing."

"Bad research. Listen, I've got things to do."

Guzman squatted, opening his briefcase on the ground. "I'm
going to have to serve you."

"Good deal. You brought us some doughnuts? *Churros*,
maybe?"

Chester Long's assistant held out a subpoena, but Jerry's
bladder pressure was more compelling. He'd turned his back and
was walking away, suggesting the assistant to the district attorney
deal with some of his associates, and that was anybody who was
standing around.

"Yeah, why don't you deal with us?" There was laughter as the
crowd tightened around Guzman. He picked up his brass-
trimmed briefcase and clutched it to his chest.

"Then tell me, why are you people doing this?"

"First free the slaves! First free the slaves! First free the slaves!"

After Oscar Guzman ran the gauntlet, was thoroughly pinched
and groped, he made his way back down the parkway to head-
quarters in the Ritz Carlton parking lot. Chester—in helmet, flack
jacket, and black lace panties—was furious that nothing had been
accomplished.

Later that morning, the Hoover protégé sent a mixed contingent
of ten local police, sheriff's deputies, and highway patrolmen to
arrest Jerry. They were all carrying sidearms, and the deputies
were toting shotguns as well. As they worked their way through
the crowd, they drew jeers and catcalls. But when Laguna Niguel
officer Dan McAfee pulled Jerry out the back of his van, ripping

his T-shirt, there was a tumultuous roar of anger, and the crowd rushed in, pinning the cops to the side of the famous vehicle. When they drew weapons in response, Jerry asked how many shots they thought they'd get off before the crowd took them down. After a five-minute standoff, Jerry talked them into surrendering their weapons, which were emptied of bullets and shells and returned to them. As the contingent made its way back down the hill, the crowd chanted, "First free the slaves! First free the slaves!" The Tchoupitoulas started up a dance to "Iko Iko." Jerry smiled and waved from the top of his van, but knew the next attack from the protectors of property would not be resolved so peacefully.

The crowd had grown so much overnight—by twenty or thirty thousand, according to helicopter surveillance teams—that Chester Long accused Sheriff Robbins of sloppy containment work. But the sheriff said that every possible access point was under heavy guard. The numbers they were reporting were impossible. Of course, neither man knew that the Network channels had been thrown wide open, that the Inspiritation, the transfer of spirits, had begun. No gun or attack dog in the world could cope with that.

There's Wong Fu Gee, who because of his alchemical achievements and study of Tao breathing channels was still alive and in human form. He wore jeans and a flannel shirt, his close-cropped gray hair jutting out over his temples. He moved through the crowd, from east to west, hilltop to golf course. Measurements, calculations, as he gathered energy for the time when it would be needed.

There's Bjarni Grimolfsson, teeth missing, dressed in checked golf pants and a dirty windbreaker. His blond hair swirled over the top of his head like flames. As he watched the marvelous expansion of the crowd, the unchecked energy of this other coast, he couldn't help laughing.

There's Chief Seattle, sitting against a tree, feeling his woman's breasts, stretching out his bare and shapely legs. He looked through the pockets of his shorts, found a wallet, the contents telling him he was Laura Rothman of Laguna Beach, an unemployed real estate agent. He was glad to be alive and breathing the sea air again.

There's Thelonious Monk, sitting under another tree, from which he'd hung his medicine bundle. Humming "Straight, No

Chaser," he knew it was time to fly, reconnoiter. Redbird out the door and back in through the window. He saw Walkingstick on the opposite hill, kneeling, holding the seven-fold wrap in his hands, Nancy kneeling beside him.

There's Joey Patchouli, who had slipped in from Laguna Beach. Holding silent discourse with the hawks who'd been circling from the first day, protecting the crowd, setting up a barrier against helicopters, distorting the satellite photographs being transmitted in from Washington, D.C. Those spy satellites were Edison's babies, with all the energy of dark orbiting eggs, rotten edges on their semiconductor teeth. Thomas Edison & Co., J. P. Morgan, J. Edgar the unholy son, and Walt Disney, the illustrator of the Death Squad's dreams.

There's Emiliano Zapata, chewing a piece of sweet grass, looking over the battlefield. Pancho Villa, at his side, nodding, and Robert Johnson, in tattered fatigues and a black stocking cap. They knew there might be casualties, but the Shift had begun, and this time they were going to win.

There's Freydis, Erik's bloody daughter, raging in the body of Bernadette "Bernie" Parker. A drunk, often cast out of Annie O'Rourke's soup kitchen for gross solicitation. She'd worked for years as a high school receptionist by day, a barfly at night, until she finally fell through the safety net and ended up on the streets. She shouted about cutting a couple of cops. She howled her loathing of every elected official, from the President to Chester Long, District Attorney. Agent provocateur for the Death Squad, she worked the crowd for people crazy or desperate enough to turn.

And there's Handsome Bear. He was in China, he was in Chaco Canyon, he was in Laguna Niguel. His bear heart on the sea, soaring across the Crown Valley Parkway, snaking up through the new sipapu that was as yet unseen. Through that navel of the universe came the seeds of a new world that has always been on the verge of being born. Handsome Bear looked down into the valley. These were his people now. He'd lost everything in trying to save his own, and in the subsequent dispersal he'd become the spiritual warp and woof for the Network's new weaving.

It was around four in the afternoon when Jerry hauled the microphone to the top of his van again. Spirits were high. Three planes flying down the coast, trailing banners that advertised Bacardi mixers, a car dealership, and a phone sex number, upon reaching Dana Point turned and deployed banners declaring, FIRST FREE THE SLAVES! The planes then flew inland, dropping garbage bags full of granola bars. They'd been divided and eaten, but people were beginning to get restless in their hunger. Jerry asked the crowd for ideas, where they might go from here. There were scattered shouts from different parts, and Bernie Parker yelled, "Kill the bastards!" The crowd was beginning to get up a head of steam when someone shouted to look up, and they all watched a parachutist trail red, blue, and white plumes of smoke, pulling his steering lines, finish with a running landing one hundred yards from Jerry's van. There was terrific cheering. They all forgot their anger until a police helicopter dropped down and warned through loudspeakers that the crowd was an illegal assembly, gave it two minutes to disperse.

Jerry looked down at Carla, covered the mike with his hand. "Oh, shit, they're going to gas us." As the helicopter speakers repeated the message, Jerry tried to shout over them and calm the crowd, but out of the corner of his eye he saw it, an army transport helicopter swooping down from the west, trailing CS gas like a crop duster. People were screaming, surging in various directions, many in danger of being trampled, but Wong Fu Gee, who saw it coming, calmly put on his bronze helmet, held out two metal rods that sent a blue charge surging from one end of the valley to the other. The gray, opaque tear gas flashed into flame, cleared, and resolved into a glitter of golden dust drifting like manna down on the crowd. A scatter of black and white feathers fluttered in the air. No one moved. People took tentative breaths, but the air was purer than it had been five minutes before. Wong Fu Gee had bagged his apparatus and was already heading over the hill by the time witnesses began to recount what they'd seen him do.

Unfortunately for the residents on the crest of the hill, Wong Fu Gee's protection extended only to those in the valley, and the gas deployed by the National Guard helicopter had driven them, gagging and spurting tears, from their houses and condos. Several old people were unable to draw breath at all. Those less affected were screaming down into the valley for help. The medical staffers in the tent on the hill ran up with an oxygen tank. When they got through the gate, people were on their knees, coughing, vomiting. But Amanda Sellers, a retiree from Dubuque, Iowa, lay on her back, face turning blue. Since she didn't appear to be breathing at all, the oxygen mask was of no use. Carla and Larry Smith pushed through the ring of onlookers.

Smith dropped to his knees. "Isn't somebody going to give her CPR?"

A medic ran up with a throat tube, and was about push it into her silent mouth, when Joey appeared, kneeled at her side. He pressed his tattooed hands over her temples, rocked back and forth. Amanda gave out a great whoosh and began to gasp for breath. Joey rose and walked from victim to victim, touching and healing.

One of the men, his face burnt bright red by the CS gas, was gesturing with a wet towel. "I can't believe they'd do this to us! I just can't believe it. It's got to be some kind of mistake. The police are here to protect us from people like you."

Carla and Larry helped Amanda to her feet. Her neighbors led the woman to a shaded area by the wall. Carla turned, looking through the crowd for Joey. "Larry, who was that guy who put his hands on the old lady?"

"His name is Joey Patchouli. In Laguna Beach they think he's a healer. You know, laying on the hands. I can introduce you, but I don't think he can talk. At least, that's what I heard."

When they approached Joey, who'd now finished his ministrations, Carla didn't wait for an introduction. She walked up, hugged him, told him she thought he was a beautiful man. Joey and Carla walked down the hill from the gated enclave hand in hand. People were standing in clusters, arguing, exclaiming, describing what they'd seen and experienced: the helicopter, the cloud of gas, the flash, the glitter and feathers drifting slowly to the ground.

Jerry was in his nest of televisions, all buzzing with news about the unsuccessful gassing. Reporters on the scene were claiming miraculous intervention but had been urged by station managers to pursue more factual explanations. Down at the command post, the National Guard commander was being asked what had happened. Was it possible that the demonstrators had deployed a secret antigas weapon? The commander said that was nonsense; it had to have been a bad batch of gas.

When Carla caught up with Jerry, he was surrounded by his own set of reporters demanding an explanation of what they'd just witnessed. He told them he had no more idea than they did, and crawled into the back of his van. Carla pulled the door open and crawled in after him, Joey in tow. "Jerry, you've got to meet this beautiful man. His name is Joey. He healed the people up on the hill who got sick from the gas."

Jerry leaned his back against the interior of the van, legs pulled up to his chest. He took a look at Joey, recognized him as the one Larry Smith had pointed out the day they met in Laguna Beach. "Beautiful, yeah. How you doing, Joey?"

Joey looked down, kept a grip on Carla's hand. She decided to translate for him. "He can't talk, but that doesn't matter. I can tell he likes you. Can you see the light around his head? I think he is the most beautiful man I've ever seen."

Jerry laughed, wiggled his eyebrows at her, in imitation of Joey's excited facial expressions. Carla kicked the van door open, pulled Joey out, and disappeared. That night Jerry spent a good deal of time explaining how he thought she was joking or, even worse, patronizing the retarded. He apologized, promised he'd make it up to Joey, to her, to anyone she might want to choose. Carla wasn't impressed. She slept on top of the bag.

It was the morning of July 6 in Michigan, but still dark on the Crown Valley Parkway in Laguna Niguel, except for the circling spotlights beamed down from the helicopters. Dierdra McDonald walked into her living room, brought coffee for Ethel Wright and herself, sat down in front of CNN. The two of them were planning activities for faculty sympathetic to the impending UAW clerical worker strike at Midwestern State University. But the California news had taken over. They were still running footage of the helicopter gassing and its magical transformation. Over and over: replay, reverse mode, stop and enhance. A panel of experts on tear gas, gas warfare, germ warfare, and crowd control had been assembled. Each one offered an explanation, from freak weather conditions to spontaneous combustion. The National Guard had already given the official position: a faulty batch of CS gas. But nobody was buying that, not even the media. They had all seen the huge flash, and they knew the people on the hill had gotten thoroughly sick.

Dierdra pushed her notebook to one side on the couch. "What do you think of this Jerry Martinez? Nice if we had him on our side. Interesting-looking guy."

Ethel sipped her coffee and stared at the screen. "Crazy stuff happens out there in California. Not that sometimes it doesn't get a little wild around here, but just not as obvious."

"What's going to happen to these people?"

"I've seen it all before: riots in the cities, on the campuses. Guess you were still in Trinidad back when that was going on. Trouble is, just when you think you're winning, people start getting killed."

Dierdra jumped up. "Look! Look at that, now." Wavering on the screen was a fuzzy isolated image of Wong Fu Gee, bronze helmet on his head, reverse polarity rods extending from his hands. The panel of experts was being asked to comment. Meanwhile, in the Pentagon a much more detailed resolution of a similar photograph was being studied. It had been shot from a satellite in the Edison surveillance system, a nexus in the network of the Morgan-Edison artificial intelligence trust, high-tech lingo for the Death Squad.

The Secretary of Defense leaned back in his chair and sighed. "The guy's clearly Oriental. Probably Chinese. If the Chinese have this thing, where does that leave us?"

Jerry woke up to a clear morning. When he lifted the corner of his newspaper shade and looked out, he saw sunlight bouncing over the valley like the echo of cannon fire. His stomach was empty and burning with acid. Looking back at Carla, still asleep, the flap of the bag pulled up under her chin, he knew it was over. Even if the President had given direct orders to stop gassing from the air, it was going to get nasty, one way or another. Although Annie O'Rourke seemed to have a steady supply of snack food, from what source he couldn't imagine, and large numbers had leaked out of the valley overnight, there were still just too many people. And they were too hungry to go on much longer.

He could sense the listlessness in the partisans as Carla passed the microphone to the top of his van. This morning there was no enthusiastic crowding around the leader.

Jerry waved hands over head for attention, but the murmur of the crowd continued. "Hello there. Nice morning, isn't it?

Probably's going to be a great day for the beach. Listen, there's no use me bullshitting you. This thing we've been doing is over. It's been great, but it's over. We've been lucky so far. What happened yesterday was a miracle. Nobody got killed or seriously hurt, and we want to keep that victory. Anyway, I'm hungry, you're hungry.

"Since this is probably the last time I'm going to talk to all of you, I've got something else I want to say. Look around you, look at each other; remember what you see and who we are. We're not outcasts or some kind of marginal mistakes. You wouldn't know it by looking at TV, movies, or magazines, but we are America. We've been here a long time, and no matter how hard the bosses pretend, we're not going away. Just don't forget that.

"I was watching the morning news a few minutes ago. They showed pictures of the cops and guardsmen being fed by the Ritz Carlton staff. The chef was explaining to the reporter what all the goodies were. You know, I remember reading a couple of years back that the Ritz Carlton wouldn't serve people of color, even rich ones. They'd make you wait for a table until you gave up. I think it's time for America to pay the Ritz Carlton a visit—and that means us, folks. Put out a few more tables, Chef Charles, because we're coming down for our free brunch. We've been paying installments on this meal for over five hundred years, now we're going to eat it, and it better be good!

"Pick up your gear, clean up around you. We don't want them to say we were bad house guests. Let's go eat!"

The crowd cheered, pulled in behind Jerry, Larry Smith, Carla, and Joey Patchouli, who still held the anthropologist tightly by the hand. They marched down the parkway at a good pace, at first chanting, "Free brunch! Free brunch!" Later, someone shouted, "First free the slaves, then we want our free brunch!" and the crowd took it up. Thousands streamed down, chanting, cheering, past Camino del Avion, picking up speed. When they took the last bend before descending to the Pacific Coast Highway, they saw what was waiting for them. Over a thousand National Guardsmen in formation, with bayonets fixed, backed up by halftracks, helicopter gunships hovering over the highway.

Jerry marched up to the first line of soldiers. "Are you guys ready to serve our free brunch?" The stern-faced guardsmen refused to crack a smile.

Jerry turned and addressed the partisans. "I guess they're not ready to feed us. Some other time, I'm sure."

As the Santa Ana visionary was speaking, two CHP officers pinned his arms, told him they had a warrant for his arrest. They grabbed Larry Smith and Carla too. The crowd began to shout, surging forward into the first line of soldiers, who retreated a couple of paces. Jerry convinced the highway patrolmen to release him for a moment. He threw his hands above his head and the crowd cheered.

"Look, folks, I told you it was over! You've got to go home now, before it gets any meaner. Don't worry about us, we're going to be OK."

Thousands of people still poured down the Crown Valley Parkway, but the soldiers opened corridors to the PCH, and the partisans divided into two streams, going north and south. In forty-five minutes, they were all gone. The weekend warriors moved up the valley and took possession of the emptiness. Some wandered onto the El Niguel golf course, practiced putting with the butt ends of their carbines.

In the paddy wagon on the way to the Santa Ana lockup, Carla was laughing and crying, clapping her hands together ecstatically. This exploit overshadowed anything her parents had done in Berkeley during the sixties. Her mother's favorite story was that she'd hidden Mario Savio from the police one night in her apartment. Carla had listened to that kind of thing for years, heard her mother tell her how cute she was as a child, being pushed in a stroller on the Sproul Hall picket line in 1964. She'd been embarrassed by the run-in with the INS, and never mentioned it to her parents, but now she had stories of her own.

Larry was happy too. All of his life he'd regretted not staying in Sproul Hall in December 1964, getting arrested with the Free Speech Movement martyrs. Being dragged down the steps by his heels, thrown into a bus and shipped to the Santa Rita prison camp. Not having been there always seemed to him to be a terrible moral flaw. Now he'd redeemed himself.

Smith studied Martinez, who held his head in his hands on the opposite bench. "Come on, Jerry, it can't be all that bad. You told me you've been arrested before."

The disciple of Garibaldi leveled a look of disgust at his compatriots. "Sure. You guys kill me, acting like this is a party or something. Easy for you—you're just small potatoes. You'll probably end up with misdemeanor charges. But what do you think they're going to do with me?"

Smith looked up at the ceiling of the paddy wagon. "Elect you governor of California?"

	MORE JOURNEYS
CHAPTER XIII	**TO THE WEST**

Khan held up his hand, signaled the running translation to silence, leaned toward Handsome Bear. "According to your religion, how many worlds are below us?"

The Bear Caller looked at the interpreter. He'd understood every word Khan had spoken, except "world." Unsure of what his host was asking, he made a sideways motion with his right hand. "The sun people made three passages from a lower land to a higher, but only one place exists beneath the earth we walk on."

Reclined and at ease, Kublai Khan ran his fingers over the mound of tapestries. He and Handsome Bear, who sat astride a low wooden stool, knees pointing in the air, were alone in a dome-shaped tent, skins stretched tightly over its frame of flexible poles. They were alone, except for the interpreter, who was officially nonexistent. Whenever Khan got nostalgic for his wandering days, horseback and conquest, he commanded his personal guards to pitch a Mongolian yurt near the peach orchard in his Pleasure Garden. Usually he retreated there to be alone; Handsome Bear received the extraordinary honor of an invitation to join him on this occasion.

Studying his tall companion, the Great Khan read the way skin stretched over the bones that framed his face. "Handsome Bear, are you in good health?"

The memory hero had heard the phrase so many times, he responded quickly. "Yes, I am."

Khan pulled the fur trim of his hat down to his nose, but kept one eye on the explorer. "Does the girl we sent you still make you happy? If you're tired of her, we'll send you another one."

"Your Excellence, I'm very happy with Ping Shang-lien. I'd never ask for another girl. When I return to my land and people, I want to take her with me."

The Ruler of the World laughed, folding hands over belly. "If you took her back, her father would kill himself. As much as I value your friendship, I also value justice. But if Shang-lien is keeping you here a little while longer, I'm happy."

Handsome Bear dropped his eyes, the sweat and fire of sudden shame covering his face and neck. "She makes me too happy, Your Excellence."

"There's a young woman in your expedition, Cold Moon Fire, who delights some of my people. One of my best generals has asked to have her."

"Great Khan, I promised that girl's father I would protect her and return her safely to Beautiful Village."

Khan traced the raised edges of a tapestry falcon with one finger. He pushed back his hat, stared at the low flame of an oil lamp for several minutes. "You see how complicated these things become."

Handsome Bear checked with the interpreter, repeated the word "complicated." When he was given an explanation, he nodded his head.

The Supreme Potentate lifted hands with fingers interlocked, wiggled them to sign inextricability. "But you've done wonderful service here, my friend. The temple you built with Ch'ien Shih-ch'ang is magnificent. Our mudangs, the spirit-talking women from the Silla Kingdom, have said it's a gate to the other world."

Handsome Bear followed the dim light into his host's eyes; they seemed as distant as the borders of his empire. The Big Baby had no more words to speak. As his attention was drawn down by the bird-patterned carpet spread over the grass, he thought about Shang-lien, the wonders of the jade kingdom, then Beautiful Village. He should have been home with the axes by now. His daughter was already older than Sun Girl had been when they were married. Having certainly taken a husband, he wondered how many children Bird Grass had brought into this world. When Handsome Bear raised his eyes, he found Khan studying him openly.

His host shifted from reclining on one elbow to a sitting position. "I asked you here for a reason other than your good company. I want you to join one of my ambassadors, Marco Polo, a man from the far west, on a trip to the mountains of Mongolia. Your people sometimes call you Bear Caller. That's what made me think of you in this regard. There are people living high in those mountains who look like bears. They are hairy but leave human footprints. I've heard of them but never seen them. They pay me no homage, no tribute. I want you and Marco Polo to find them, present my claims, and bring some of them back to the capital."

Khan leaned on one elbow, rubbing a tapestry of magenta, blue, and gold with the palm of his hand. "I'll see that you're properly equipped for the journey. You'll leave tomorrow." The ruler nudged his fur-trimmed hat over his eyes and reclined. When he started the heavy breathing of a sleeper, Handsome Bear shifted off his stool, went to one knee, bowed, then backed out the flap of the tent, which had been opened by the guards who stood outside.

Who says the development of the written word was a defining moment of human progress? Think of all the memory that was lost when people decided marks on clay tablets, papyrus, or vellum had the power to hold creation together without their direct participation. Dancing and chanting moved from the inner sanctum of the temple to streets outside the palace. But true written culture—

inscribed, printed, microchipped, and digitalized—does not date from ancient times. Humans haven't always been strangled by this thing called information. Ancients chanted their books; their mouths, minds, and memories had not yet stopped working. The fatal pivot came late in the fifteenth century, when Erasmus's colleague watched with horror as the great humanist read a book in silence. Then the progressive slippage: Columbus, colonialism, big capital—all based on the idea that words and things (and people as things) can be controlled, possessed by privileged individuals, rather than held in communal trust. At the precise moment of that loss the Death Squad visualized total victory. When reading went silent, writing lost the potential of sacrament. Previously a book was no more a final product than sheet music. Now we have supercomputers, and anything that calls itself information is impossible to let go. Our voices have abandoned us; only machines speak.

At first, stories were translated into writing and then sung. Afterward, writing was translated into silence, and minds got smaller, lost the ability to embrace totalities. Now the only object of long regard is the self. When memory gets smaller, mind loses the edge and proportion of vision. But patterns still exist all around us. No matter how much it is ignored, the Network will never disappear. Spider Grandmother weaves her asymmetrical model of the universal circuits, square and round at the same time. It's the kind of writing that can be read only with second sight. It is the transcription of a song that sings itself: creation, eternal becoming.

Forces of extinction, cultivated by the Death Squad, try to shrink memory into small drops of blood—a burial inside fear, grief, and self-contemplation. They have created the cult of the gunslinger, a rugged individual with responsibility to no one but himself. Then Walkingstick discovered how to pull the worthy dead from their shadows, hold a place for each one like a finger in a monumental book. There is a marking finger for every spirit chased from the sacred house of its body by injustice as silent, sudden, and astonishing as Erasmus reading without moving his lips. Death Squad executioners have no respect for rituals of the body's death; they erect arrogant monuments to the extinction of memory, like books molding in the library of lost souls. Luckily, Walkingstick held close to mnemonic literacy of both eye and tongue. Reading the star map, he achieved a convergence of power across all frequencies, drove darkness back into light.

The night Handsome Bear received his travel orders from Kublai Khan, he slept with Shang-lien under his arm but dreamed he was in a cave with Cold Moon Fire. It was one of the sacred caves from the canyon of the abalone people, and wildfire blew across its mouth, blocking both entry and escape. As fire crept into the cave, and into their lungs, the man and girl began to sing. Their skin scorched and blew away, their bones pulverized into dust, joined the whirlwind of heat and color. Fragments of the song they sang joined with the fiery dust of their bodies, formed a new song. It was a chant of destruction and a chant of weaving, a deep rhythm of words, a story spun long enough in the telling to heal forever.

Eight centuries later, after the occupation of the Crown Valley Parkway, Jerry Martinez listened for music but could only hear the song of emptiness. This was a blocking darkness, not the choral silence that strums across the spectrum of possibility. Reporters stalked him everywhere he went, shouting questions, mostly rhetorical, that he never answered. His face had been seen so much on television, there was no place he could go anonymously. Others might be flattered, but he was disgusted. The good things had already happened; the rest was going to be *caca*, and he knew it.

When Chester Long charged Martinez, Abruzzese, and Smith with felony conspiracy to commit misdemeanor trespassing, the writer from Laguna Beach was ecstatic. Smith envisioned another trial like the Chicago Eight; some fascist Orange County judge would be assigned, maybe even worse than Julius Hoffman. He thought it was a chance to "put the System on trial," and Carla was delighted at the prospect too. Jerry was skeptical; he had no desire for martyrdom, and he didn't think Larry or Carla would either, if they knew what was at stake. It was fortunate that the county CEO, afraid of bad publicity and the enormous expense the bankrupt county would incur in putting on a nationally publicized trial, convinced Chester Long to reduce charges to misdemeanor trespass. Each of them paid five hundred dollars and it was over.

Chatting in bed one night, Jerry and Carla decided it was time to take a break from Southern California, pursue the dream paths outlined by Handsome Bear. The next morning an Irvine travel agent arranged a China Air flight to Beijing, a train from Beijing to Ulaanbataar, but told the anthropologist she'd have to find transportation further into the interior of the Changajn Nuruu after she arrived.

A week later, after dropping Carla at LAX, Jerry pointed his Harley east and set off on his own quest. He was in disguise, with a looping novelty store Zapata moustache glued to his upper lip, a turquoise bandanna tied over his hair. It was almost midnight as he ran over the high desert on Route 15, approaching Barstow, but he could still feel heat from the pavement percolating in the air. After dueling with a big rig—marked "Covenant, Chattanooga, TN," with a picture of a scroll and an antiabortion message on the back—Jerry pulled off the first Needles exit, ate a very early breakfast of steak and eggs in a truck stop with one wall devoted to a collection of Elvis Presley clocks. When he returned to Route 40, he was glad to see his nemesis wasn't waiting for him, and he traveled alone through the dissipating heat of Yucca Flats, with only the sting of bugs hitting arms and neck to punish him for previous sins. As he ascended into Kingman, Arizona, the sky was beginning to lighten. He could see surrounding mountains pushing up in silhouette, and a crescent moon rose over one of them as he pulled into town. He was hoping the sunrise would wake him up, clear the spaciness in his head, so he could make it to the Grand Canyon without stopping, or falling asleep and spinning out into the brush at the side of the interstate.

Later that morning, standing at the South Rim, Jerry looked out over the canyon. He felt the hugeness of its silence, the power it held to itself in defiance of humanity, and the power it exerted on him, pulling his soul into its space. There was so much energy there, he was afraid to go any closer to the edge. Finally getting up the nerve to sit on a stone outcropping, front row at the drop-off point, he contemplated visual impossibilities: a succession of red and orange towers fading into a distance that sometimes read simply as a wall. Over his right shoulder flew a huge bird of prey, the pinfeathers of its wings separated into dozens of fingers. Jerry had come to an end, a limit, at least temporarily. He retreated into the piñon and juniper, fell asleep on a bench.

When he reentered the fourth world that afternoon, Jerry asked a ranger behind the desk at the information center what kind of bird he'd seen. Bearded and wrinkled, blue eyes that appeared faded from too much sun, the man was a transparent smile. "Those are peregrine falcons. Tough birds, too. Just hell on bats. They catch the little suckers in midair, shear off both wings, and eat 'em in one bite. Down on the lower levels of the canyon, we're sweeping up piles of bat wings all the time."

As he directed his Harley east on 64, heading toward the Hopi mesas recommended by the ranger, Jerry tried to imagine a pile of leathery wings, or the kind of jacket they'd make if sewn together. Turning south on 264, he noticed how narrow the two-lane highway was, and little used, since grass sprouted through its cracks. Clusters of purple flowers shouldered up to the pavement. It pleased him to think they were escorting him to his destiny. The clouds were so unusual they kept pulling his eyes from the winding road: cotton candy diagonal streamers that descended almost to the ground, then curled upward and disappeared. He guessed the desert air that was drying out his eyeballs absorbed the rain before it had a chance to hit the ground. Like rain-absorbing air, Jerry felt he was pulling in strength as he sped over the plateau. He'd been riding across the huge Navajo reservation since leaving Grand Canyon National Park, so when he saw a curious sign by the side of the road as he approached the Hopi mesas—RELOCATION IS GENOCIDE—Jerry remembered hearing about the bitter land disputes between the two tribes. Later, at the Second Mesa Hopi Center and Motel, where he stopped to check out the museum and get a Coke, he saw "Nadine Benaly sucks kachinas" written on a bathroom wall. The same tensions expressed with a little more humor.

It was five-thirty when Jerry parked in the Sichmovi central square, in front of the cultural center, where guided tours of Walpi began. He walked in, stretched, asked the middle-aged woman with kinky permed hair when they were giving the next tour. Counting bills and change from the donation box, she replied she'd just given the last tour. The sign outside and the sign on the table both said "TOURS 9–6." Jerry looked at his watch: it was 5:40. He asked her if he'd come too late. The woman said she'd be happy to accommodate him—the next morning, at about nine-thirty. Jerry had considered the possibility of using his charm to convince her to make an exception, but something in the placid but fierce expression on her face told him there wasn't going to be any mind changing that afternoon.

As he left the cultural center, a disheveled drunk thrust a kachina doll wound in Saran Wrap under his nose. Jerry waved it off. Climbing on his Harley, looking around at the old stone houses and the newer ones built of cinder blocks, the village reminded him a little of Mexico. But there was another presence he didn't recognize. It had something to do with space, distance, a loop hidden in time—the stubborn certainty of a people who knew where they were, and that it was home.

Jerry rented a room at the Keams Canyon Motel, ten miles down the road, walked to the restaurant next to the laundromat. Two little girls were playing with a black puppy, carrying it like a doll. There was a good chance the puppy was the offspring of the mangy dog he'd found sitting in the shadow of his motorcycle, tits hanging from her stretched underbelly like the she wolf that suckled Romulus and Remus. He'd noticed the reservation dogs; even though they had different colors, all seemed to be the same breed. Small, tough, scrawny, with spacy coyote grins that declared the confidence of the survivor. Jerry ordered at the restaurant, pushed back from the table, and looked around. On one wall were a dozen kachinas marching over a hill. Jerry stared at the picture. He knew nothing about kachinas, but the representation of these creatures, with a suggestion of alien and transforming power, made the hair on his neck stand out.

Bringing him back from that kachina otherworld, the waitress put a plate of pork chops and frybread under his nose. The web between her thumb and first finger was tattooed with four dots, three in a line and one above it, forming a small triangle. Jerry wondered if that indicated a secret Hopi society, or maybe a stay in prison like tattoo tears. When she placed his strawberry shake on the table, he could see nothing but pink light. The shake filled a glass nearly as large as a flower vase, twice as big as anything Jerry had ever seen. That turned out to be good luck, since one of the grilled pork chops was so red in the center he didn't dare eat it. He wrapped it in a napkin and took it back to the motel, offered it to the dried-out mother dog, who was still cuddled next to his motorcycle. She enjoyed the meat so much, he suspected collusion between the restaurant and the animal population. "OK, it's all yours, Pork Chop Girl."

Jerry watched TV for a half hour, then lay exhausted on the bed, cool damp air blowing from the air conditioner mounted in the ceiling over his head. It was dark, and he had lost his bearings. His legs trembled from fatigue and road vibration as the room turned slowly counterclockwise. He was thinking about the mural on the front of the building that held the store, restaurant, and crafts shop. It depicted the canyon wall, with the characteristic notch at its center, and sacred figures were shadowed suggestively over the rocky face. If you looked closely, you could see the stores, and to the right another identical mural, and within that an even tinier mural. As he crossed the gray zone into sleep, Jerry looked up at the rim of a canyon burning pink and orange with twilight. A dozen silhouettes—sprouting fur and feathers, heads round, square, and pointed, all possessing two legs but reaching far beyond the human in their challenge to dimension—looked down on him.

Marco Polo raised a gloved hand, signaled for the soldiers and carriers to stay back, turned to Handsome Bear, and posed several semiarticulate questions in Chinese about the twelve creatures who stood before them. Polo was always ready for wonders, could catalogue and describe them, determine their value in European currencies, but at this moment his mind would not translate what his eyes were taking in.

Handsome Bear was signing to the emissaries who had just appeared on the mountain slope. They seemed to have floated down from a higher elevation. "Yes, they're bear people. But if you listen closely to the sounds they're making, you'll hear another kind of language." The Traveler tried to explain how their grunts and growls, the way they danced stories with their hands, could convey history or delight, all the subtle refinements of mind that were so clear in the clothes they wore and the wool cloth they were offering the outsiders, measuring it out hand to elbow. It was undyed, but elegantly woven by gradation of tone. You could get lost in the complex geometries of its patterns, fall through clouds until you landed again on the peak of this little-known mountain. Above the heads of Polo, the Bear Caller, and twelve Neanderthal emissaries, the power lines hummed. They were made of pure energy, layer upon layer of rectangular grids that rose from and descended against the shoulder of the mountain. Since the creatures of this encounter all stood within the web, they were surrounded by diagonal connections that flashed between the layers. Handsome Bear recognized the design: stone fractures on canyon walls back home. Only this time he and the bear people stood in the middle of some airy schematic rock. In a warping and wefting of directions, it was both the otherworld and this one at the same time.

Before the memory hero and his Italian partner stood an illuminated mosaic of heavy pinched jaws, foreheads low enough to disappear behind the orbits that swelled beneath their eyebrows, bunches of reddish brown hair pushing out of woolen collars and sleeves. Handsome Bear signed the happiness and deep honor he felt in being allowed to meet the bear people of the jade kingdom. The shortest of the Neanderthal emissaries stepped forward. She held a bouquet of creamy flowers, each with a drop of purple at its heart, and began to chew off blossoms one or two at a time. She moaned, fell to her knees. Handsome Bear stepped forward, lowered himself to one knee, joined her in feasting on the flowers. The blossoms shot sudden fire through his teeth and lips, ignited the bones of his jaw and skull. Small fiery creatures crawled past tongue and palate, spiraled around the inside of his brain pan. He understood why his new partner's eyes had rolled back in her head. Light fell all around him in chiseled blocks, similar to the ones the ancestors had used to build Beautiful Village. Within each translucent block was the sign of an open hand and an open ear. He knew it was the face of time again, revealing herself as eternal pregnancy, a constant opening into the present from every imaginable direction. Handsome Bear reached out and put his hand on his partner's shoulder, then heard singing in his sinews and veins. It was a music that walked away like water twisting down a mountain stream. Not the Song of Creation, but the song that is creation; not just celebration, but the process of coming into being. He wondered if he could hold such borderless energy within the net of memory, or ever hope to translate it for Kublai Khan.

Jerry arrived at the cultural center 11:15 the next morning. A dozen men, women, and children were trying to find shade in the square, waiting for a tour to begin. Jerry checked with the woman inside—Lorna, their new guide, a small woman with ponytail pulled through the back of her Colorado Rockies cap, wearing a FREE TIBET T-shirt in red and gold—then returned to the square. Spotting a penny in the dusty street, he stooped and picked it up. Curled into a potato chip, it felt like tremendous luck when he dropped the coin in his pocket.

As they crossed the natural bridge that links the ancient fortress of Walpi to Second Village, Lorna gave final warnings about following the rules she had set out. But the group wasn't listening. They were all rushing to a doorway where a woman and her two children displayed kachina dolls and gray piki bread wrapped in cellophane. Jerry watched Lorna as she watched the tourists. He had no inclination to disobey. With her huge, impenetrable eyes, her ambiguous expression somewhere between a smile and a scowl, he'd finally found someone who could go toe to toe with Leslie for quiet but ferocious determination. Jerry turned away from the buying frenzy, glanced up at a stone house perched high on the rocky prow of the mesa. An old man wearing traditional shirt and headband sat on a chair in front of his door. He winked at Jerry and gave him a military salute. Lorna rounded up the group again, pushed them onward, giving assurances that they'd have more chances to buy whatever they wanted. Jerry tagged along, looked down as he walked past a stone step. A penny covered with deep green patina lay in a groove worn in the stone. He reached out to pick it up, as he always did, since the visionary painter believed that failing to pick up a penny was a slap in the face of the god of good fortune. But Jerry stopped his hand in midair, pulled it back, called out to Lorna, "Is this penny part of a ritual, some kind of offering?" She stared at him, brushed swarming gnats away from her face. "No, it's just a penny."

Jerry was embarrassed and laughed at himself. But he didn't pick up the penny. Remembering the sign that warned against photographs, sketches, note taking, or removing anything from the village, he felt the potato chip coin burn inside his pocket. Pulling it out and setting it next to the green one on the step, he figured if there hadn't been any penny-leaving ritual before, maybe it was time for him to start one now.

Separating from the group, Jerry strolled to the western side of the fortress, leaned against the wire fence, and looked down the cliff at the rusted metal refuse scattered below. It was so far down, the identity of the objects was hard to determine.

"Excuse me, you're standing on the roof of a kiva." Lorna's impassive face hovered a few feet away. She pointed at his feet. Jerry looked down and seemed surprised at where they were located. Humiliated by his accidental disrespect, he walked off quickly.

"I'm sorry. It was so gradual coming this way, I didn't notice. It's more obvious on the other side where the ladder is." Jerry pulled the bandanna off his head and mopped his face, even though it was dry. The Zapata moustache was gone. He'd forgotten to put it on that morning, but it didn't matter, since no one had recognized him. Jerry looked across the plain toward the San Francisco Mountains, hoping the omnipresent Lorna would forget him and go back to the group.

"Don't worry. You're OK. It's an easy mistake to make."

Back in the cool of the cultural center, Jerry slipped a twenty into the donation box. He asked Lorna if she knew much about the Indian ruins east of there. When she wanted to know more about which ones interested him, he was unable to offer any names, but said he could draw her a picture. Looking over his shoulder as he sketched a hemicycle with a honeycomb of squares and circles running through the middle and around the circumference, she sniffed with authority.

"With all those kivas, that could only be one place—Pueblo Bonito."

Italo Calvino eased back from his desk. He walked across the room, peeked through shutters at the orange of the Roman sunset, the flicker of swallows and their reckless erotic diving, the dance of flesh into death. The writer lived in the most substantial of all cities, every street corner choked with history, politics, the stonework of millennia. But each evening, especially from certain vantage points, like the Pincio Gardens high above the city, you could witness the whole thing dissolve, a sugar cube in a cup of espresso. Rome was an invisible city too, like the ones he was straining to hear in his book. Marco Polo was telling a string of them to Kublai Khan, but something in the atmosphere—maybe sunspots—had disrupted the transmission. Right in the middle of "Sophronia," Calvino had lost Polo's voice. It was no longer the magic of invisibility, of infinite possibility, but a wall of static and ultimate darkness.

He crossed the room, seated himself before the typewriter, cradled his traveling mind in his hands, elbows pointed into the writing table. What was a benevolent tyrant? Could anyone forgive Khan for his conquests, the legacy of the Mongolian empire? Could anyone forgive Marco Polo for his willing collaboration? Calvino stood, pulled *The Rise and Fall of the Third Reich* from the bookshelf. Opening to the middle, he removed a small folded document, his Italian partisan papers from World War II. He studied the identifying photograph of a young man with a long, unfocused gaze. The cities those eyes once searched for were beyond memory. Authenticated with a red star, half on the paper, half on his shoulder, the photo was from another world. If the war had turned out otherwise, who would have spoken to Hitler about his invisible cities? If the Führer had not self-destructed by breaking with Stalin and pursuing a long fatal reach into Russia, would Calvino himself have woven the stories of an impossible kingdom to the weary, drowsing emperor?

The questing van painter ran through the possibilities as he blitzed down Route 9, his mind so overloaded and his attention so distracted that he put his Harley into a spin when he hit a dip in the road. Dragging both boots, wrestling with the handlebars, he kept the motorcycle upright until he could slow to a stop. Jerry pulled to one side, got off the bike, and beat the dust out of his jeans. His mind had cleared, and it stayed that way until he drove into the Navajo agency town of Crownpoint. Gassing up his Californio Harley, he asked precise directions to the twenty-mile dirt road that would take him to Chaco Canyon. Navajo boy leaning against the pump, biting into his cigarette, rolling both sleeves on his white T-shirt up to the shoulder joint. "Been a big rain yesterday, and there's no getting over that road."

When Jerry asked how long he needed to wait, the boy said it was likely going to rain again, so he couldn't say. Anyway, he wouldn't go into Chaco on anything but a four-wheel drive. You could wreck a good motorcycle on that road.

Jerry screwed on the cap of his maroon gas tank, kick-started the Harley, turned north on Navajo Nine and then east again after a couple of miles. He drove until he found the soggy gash that led to his rendezvous, with a barricade and a National Parks sign declaring it closed. He looked hard but could see no structures from the road. The visit to Handsome Bear was off, and there was not a thing he could do about it. Pulling his motorcycle to the side of the road, he dropped the kick stand and parked it, then squatted in the brush, his back to the canyon. Something strong was working its way through him; it was already on its way, no holding back. In quick succession he saw the battered face of Francisco Torres, the chanting crowd that marched down Crown Valley Parkway to a confrontation with the Guard and police, and Carla in handcuffs, holding them above her head with fists clenched. He dug his fingers into the pastel earth. Jerry knew there were animals all around him, could see them out of the corners of his eyes: prairie dogs, snakes, badgers, rabbits, coyotes, bears—eagles and falcons above. But there was also a darkness that tasted bitter in his mouth, tasted like failure. Even though he was saturated with desert light, the darkness lingered. The van painter fell to his knees, watched large drops fall into the dust. He was astonished at the rapidity of the rainfall, and then groans and sobs wrenched their way like animals through his throat. He dropped his head into the splatter, rode the spasms a few minutes, then gasped, trying to recover his breath. As the convulsions of frustration released him, something far more substantial grabbed him by the ears, hauled him to his knees, then to his feet.

Handsome Bear stood before him, eyes too angry to meet. Jerry looked down, but Handsome Bear grasped him by the chin, tilted his face up. "I asked you to come, and you're here."

Jerry wanted to apologize for his failure to reach Pueblo Bonito, but the words would not pass his teeth. The memory hero stood to one side, aimed Jerry's eyes to the south. "That's where my people live. They're not in this place anymore. They left Beautiful Village years ago, even before I came back from the jade kingdom. Don't cry over ruins. Go to Zuni and talk to the living; don't linger with the dead."

When Jerry lifted his head from the sand, it was late afternoon. His throat and mouth were dry, his neck and arms scorched by the sun. He pulled a water bottle from a saddlebag and drained it, even though it was hot enough to make tea. That evening he arrived in Gallup, checked into a motel, scoured himself in a cold shower, and lay naked on top of the bed, air conditioning blasting on high.

"I'm Sascha Simone Sakeva, and I'm seven. I live in Sichmovi, but I've got some river shells from Flagstaff. Would you like to buy some?"

After a trip to the Zuni pueblo, and a talk with the man who was finishing a kachina mural in the mission church, Jerry drove back to First Mesa in search of more magic. Goading him the whole way was the image of the black-and-white-striped Hano clown. The *koshare* was sitting on a rainbow above the altar, laughing as he watched the universal dance unfold. Jerry looked down at the Hopi girl as she held out a handful of tiny shells.

"Four dollars each." She ran her tongue over her lower lip, peeked at the grinning Californian out of the corner of her eye. "My brother is carving a wind maker right now. He has a mud-head finished but has to put the spray on it. You want to buy a mudhead?"

"What's a mudhead?"

"Their faces are brown mud, and they have a point on their head so they can stick the clowns, and they carry snakes that scare the clowns."

"I didn't know kachina clowns were so bad."

Sascha giggled. "Very bad. They talk with their mouths full, and they eat too much, and do naughty things."

Jerry ambled toward the north end of the First Mesa, Sascha at his side. She pointed to an old stone house with a boarded-up door. "A mean kachina lives there. It's not part of our family, but we leave food for it. When the dance comes it'll give food back to everybody. Do you want your shell now?"

Jerry pulled out his wallet and paid her for two. "Maybe sometime later I'll get a chance to look at your brother's mudhead, but probably not today."

"That's OK. Now we have eleven dollars, before we only had three." Sascha ran around the corner.

He continued along the deserted pathway, past an old house being renovated to look like a Taos adobe. A flicker on the pathway made him drop his eyes and watch a large red-tailed wasp pull itself backward out of a hole and fly away. When he looked up, he noticed the man who'd saluted him on his first trip sitting by his front door again. Jerry waved, walked on, but the man signaled for him to climb up and talk.

His lack of teeth gave him a permanent smile, but his eyes were fierce and satirical. He held both knees as if he were on the verge of bursting into laughter and needed restraint. Looking away as he spoke. "Seen you walking around."

Jerry leaned over, tried to get a fix on what the old man was watching. "Yeah, this is my second visit to First Mesa."

The Hopi turned and tested the clarity of Jerry's eyes. "You writing a book?"

"No, no, I'm a painter, not a writer." The old man's eyebrows jumped up, lifted his headband. Jerry held out his hands, palms stretched open. "Don't get me wrong, I haven't been sketching or painting anything around here. I paint on cars and vans."

Jerry tried to find the target of his host's eyes; they appeared to be scanning the horizon, but he wasn't sure. A couple of stories later, he realized the old man was sighting on World War II, savoring the way the Hopis had once again saved humanity. Stories done, the man leaned back in his chair, touched his headband, and sighed. "You're a painter, eh? I had a car that needed painting, but it's dead now."

Carla pushed down on the saddle, tried to lift herself, relieve the shooting pains that ran from sensitive knees up her inner thighs. Sore back since the sitting marathon on a wooden train bench from Beijing to Ulaanbataar, but this ride was worse. Fur hat, coarse blue Mongolian long coat, pants that tucked into boots— outfitted in the village, with the help of a guide, the only one willing to join her on this quest. Surrounded by high-elevation scrub, steel-colored rock peering down, naked except for teasing wisps of cloud, there were no signs that any two-legged had ever passed this way, let alone a Neanderthal. Not one villager at the base of the mountain had been able to speak English, so she wasn't sure if they knew what she was looking for. Or maybe they did, and the laborious climb was their idea of a joke, a con on the lady from Beautiful Kingdom. The guide's horse kicked over the top of the crumbling slate incline they'd struggled to climb all afternoon, and his string of two packhorses jigged around rocks in an attempt to catch up. Carla was looking up the butt of the dappled gray, a small Mongolian horse like the other three, not much larger than a pony. She shouted, "Stop! Stop!" to the guide. It was the only English word he knew. The rest of their conversation had been pointing and crude sign language.

When Carla finally cleared the ridge, she was surprised to find herself alone. No guide, no packhorses, just a wide, level expanse where neither man nor animal could hide. She dismounted and dropped her saddle-sore butt on cold stone, holding the horse by its reins. A dust-filled gust of wind swept over, and as she raised a hand to protect her eyes, the horse jerked away, ran a few yards and disappeared. Carla raised herself on one knee, surveyed the emptiness, then sat down again. She followed the sound and visible energy of breath as it passed in and out of her mouth, realized she wasn't panicked by the stranding. Mist descended as she watched for some sign to tell her how to continue. Or if not to continue, then how to die.

Several hours passed before the sitting cloud dispersed, let the clear twilight sky rekindle her vision. She recognized the bright planet, Venus, over her left shoulder, but none of the dozen creatures who wove a circle around her, dancing a slow sideways step. Each wore a large inverted fishbowl of terra-cotta with three rimmed holes, one for each eye and another for the mouth. Humming and sonorous groans resonated within the masks. Spherical lumps on the sides made ears, but similar growths were also attached to less obvious parts of the head. Ornaments of feather, horsehair, pine needles, painted geometric symbols of various sorts in red, white, and turquoise—three had cones growing straight up from the top. As they danced, she heard their collective breath, the scramble of murmur and lament, pull into unison. The stranded anthropologist listened to this strange music as it built a powerful hum inside her skull. She heard words—disconnected, ambiguous in meaning, but spoken in perfect American English.

A figure wrapped in a magenta tunic leaped forward from the dancing circle, held a triangle of thumbs and index fingers over his terra-cotta mask. Echoing between Carla's temples: "Snake ears." As the magenta figure rejoined the line, another, bare from the waist up but completely covered with thick reddish body hair, wearing kilt and deerskin boots, danced forward, released his hands, let finger birds fly to the left and right. Alighting on the top of his mask, they formed a circle. "Musk water." The bird handler returned to the line and another mudhead, dressed in a loose, vertically striped cape, stepped forward. Above his mask signing hands formed a square. "Star butterflies, star snakes." When Carla heard these words, she began to cry quietly. Tempo picking up, the masked figures now moved in a clumsy jig, lumbering as bears do on their hind legs. The twelve raised their hands, made the triangle sign together, followed by the circle and square. Carla remembered staring at cards with these symbols as a child, trying to convey "blue circle" or "pink triangle" telepathically to her brother.

"Our voices have traveled a long time, ridden your shoulder since the moment you were born. Ancestral to you—in the mountains, desert, and cells of your body. But we are younger than a child, the cell division that explodes on our heads."

The telepathic spokesman threw his striped cape back over his shoulders, revealed a blue-and-gray feathered serpent wound many times around his torso. The other dancers uncoiled it, shared its tense body hand to hand as they continued their circling. Lazy eyes, fixed on eternity, and the flicker of its tongue sensual lightning. As they deployed the serpent, Carla saw tattoos—red, yellow, or green—gleaming up from beneath the tufted hair on their hands: glyphs that made the shuddering anthropologist burn in her joints and teeth.

"A story to be known, but not told, as invisible as our mountain city. It conjoins star and animal tracks with the great circuitry, up and over, over and under, weaving a web that is gold and diffuse in the daytime, referenced by points of silver at night."

Carla raised her eyes to the inverted bowl of sky and saw that its blue had cooled to darkness, light bleeding through the punctured vessel as stars, even in places she'd never seen them before. The band across the center was a terrible wound in the process of healing, a river that could carry away everything that lived.

"This horse will take you home." The dancers stooped and released the feathered snake. It slid along the rock, rolling, buckling into kinks and stretching out until it reached Carla's feet. Two of the mudheads came forward from the circle, pulled off Carla's boots, coarse cloth trousers, and lace panties. An overwhelming music staggered her breath, made blood itch. The feathered snake darted its tongue up one thigh, then the other. She couldn't move. If she could, where would she go to escape the burning feet, the urge of pleasure that had brought her to the edge of orgasm? Never in her life had she been open to the public like this, but it seemed logical and essential. So did the call she heard in her own voice, but not from her mouth. "Handsome Bear, are we ready to join the line?" She looked down, watched the snake pursue its foreplay, then flash into a bundle of strung light, so bright it seized all the colors and left her in darkness. When Carla could see again, a kneeling kilted figure with gray-haired arms and hands was lifting the mask from his head. It was just what she'd come to find. Before he touched his palm to her forehead and sent her into blackness, Carla turned one gorgeous thought: "I've met Joey's grandfather."

The people of the village at the base of the mountain, the one she'd bussed into four days earlier, found the anthropologist wrapped in several blankets, the outer one a red, green, and yellow design of circles, squares, and triangles interwoven with abstract representations of tongues and penises. She'd been left on a low altar constructed of skins and pine boughs. The rosy-cheeked Mongolian villagers were polite but avoided proximity. When she got on the bus that would take her back to Ulaanbataar, she was enclosed by a circle of empty seats. The bus revved its engine and careened through the bumpy village street and out onto the main road, kicking clouds of dust over dogs and sagging clotheslines. Carla leaned back in the uncomfortable seat, plastic tape and vinyl over broken springs, shut her eyes. Without moving head or opening eyelids, she looked up. Even in the middle of the day she could see the Milky Way reach its magnificent arch over her, and over every other creature that walked the earth or flew through the air. She could see each star clearly, and the vertical bands of power and light that make the sky into aurora. A tiny figure sat astride the pulsating band of stars as if it were a horse. Unruly hair everywhere, sprouting from its face and covering its body like a jumpsuit, except for the bottoms of the feet. Protruding lips and teeth in a smile that mimicked the crescent moon. The figure waved its arms, held out winged hands for balance. Carla filled her lungs with galaxies of atoms and exhaled joyous breath. She was already home.

CHAPTER XIV | **COALITION**

Triangulation: swimming through crosswinds of light, kneeling in hope and trust at the crossroads, looking for a sail. Or a dead tree, an unusual rock that will rise, assert itself as sign, leech into ancestor-old consciousness, punch a hole in the vein of eternity that leads us underground. The spirits are corn, and their demand is harvest. But while we finger dust brought near to uselessness by chemicals and the erosion of memory, mice have crept into the grain, corncobs mold in silos, rats climb ladders into the hay lofts of barns. It's not a question of exclusion: we can feed the rats and mice as well as ourselves. All creatures can be fed. The only question is, at what moment did we walk from light into forgetfulness? We turn aside as the sun nails our shadows into trees, earth, and the hitchhiking remains of running water. Edges like these are relentless. Calculating, then counting the whole thing out: complex numbers to measure our collection of fingers and toes, drop a plumb line from jaw to anklebone. We're too busy to step outside these transactions and bear witness, or chant a prayer for witness. In the city the church is empty and boarded up. A large black dog sits on the steps, a naked circle carved into its fur, naked skin targeted in red and white concentric circles.

When the Dalai Lama exchanged prophesies with Hopi elders, consulted on the preservation of culture and the future of sentient beings, he saw in the warm stone of sunset canyons and mesas a compassion as deep as the Buddha's. Huge blocks of stone, natural architecture. He heard them call out directions, not cardinal but intuitional, make adjustments to perceived cracks in air, chance openings that take us home. The Dalai Lama heard rumors in Hopi country of a previously undiscovered range of radio waves. It was so small, the entire history of energy and travel could be contained in a sigh, a drop of water. Can trees find safe haven? Can we count all the colors and still remember how necessary they are? Guitar and makeshift drum, skin over skull, columns of air held in the circled hand, struck into life by a descending palm. The Tibetan exile found the traveling blues, the ones that always hanker for a beginning (the hole we crawled from) and a resting place (the center where winds no longer tug us from side to side), a spot where we can sit in equilibrium. Only then do we see the cosmic butterflies that move pollen across the Milky Way, prepare us for its harvest of light.

Wandering alone in cities, suburbs, abandoned farm towns, we've forgotten to search for one another. We've forgotten the festivals of planting and harvest, how to celebrate them. The messages ancestors left pinned to trees have been eaten by squirrels. Those that appear on television screens are useless, eaten as fast as they appear, sucked into an electronic inversion of light, the Death Squad's holy of holies. Where is our community bulletin board? Where are the Ghost Dancers, their hands linked in the circle that will bring back the lonesome dead? Let's go south and find the conga line, thundering praise to Erzuli and Shangó. Or search for Damballah, his twin self emerging from a crystalline egg, playing music for a line dance that could bind us together like the vertebrae of an endless snake. The cave is full of colored eggs, and they will hatch into the Millennium. In the electronic chamber of horrors, where trash declares itself information, and narcissism is communication, we've forgotten skin. We need to touch its one hundred possible colors: the loops, wrinkles, and exquisite peculiarities that urge us to tell stories, design maps big enough to hold us all. When the dragon unbuttoned her blouse, pulled arms from sleeves, slipped it around her waist, the map on her shoulder told her lover all he needed to know. Its designed tenderness was large enough to hold the world. Her lips whispered, "All snakes love skin, even in the sloughing."

The winds come again, solar winds that transform farm and garden, drag us through the dust of millennia as comets pass, leave us in a universe of shooting stars. There's a line dance of planting, harvest, celebration. There's a dance of prayer and remembering. Since we've forgotten the songs, call in the kachina clowns. Striped in black and white, wearing tasseled horns, they mock selfishness, gluttony, stupidity, and presumption—and at the same time throw us packets of food. This is grace, the fertility of chance, lightning from the palms of hands, the moistened tongue, knees in their bending, holding all the erotic places on their secret list. There's so much power here, nerves begin to tremble within their sheaths, listen for new instructions, a way to repair their wounded circuitry. Out of the furrowed earth a marching multitude of grandmothers, a whole new human generation composed only of grandmothers. They're the legacy and the future; we must will all that we own to them. This ancient band marches us back to our proper places, to a circle of tents where we commit reckless and profligate acts of mutual adoption. Spider Grandmother laughs, sitting on the top of the butte, listening to the muddy Mother shift Her ankles below New Orleans, spread them to give birth. She laughs as she hears the mockingbird imitate a car alarm. No further payments, but total forgiveness— interest and principal. The white buffalo calf has been born in Wisconsin on a white man's farm. Our Mother thrusts knees upward, pulls back Her thighs. She's ready to deliver. We've sighted by stars, triangulated by landmarks, chanted back memory. We've come together for this: to hear the word and see it fulfilled.

Ethel Wright and Dierdra McDonald eating romaine-and-crouton salads in front of the TV, waiting for CNN to broadcast Jerry's news conference. Having disappeared from media scrutiny for over a week, he was back now. The pieces of his vision had finally come together, and the van painter was in Santa Ana, ready to address the world from La Estrella. Ethel pushed the bottle of Lite Italian dressing across the coffee table toward her colleague. They weren't taking notes, but Jerry's exploits at Crown Valley Parkway had changed their strike strategy for Midwestern State, and now they were eager for further inspiration. The cameras panned as he walked from the *taquería*'s kitchen door through a group of Laguna Niguel veterans, including Larry Smith, one of Midwestern State's own. Jerry, dressed in a white T-shirt and jeans, sat down at the table, a bouquet of microphones its only decoration. Camera flashes and the whir of mechanical advances set their own rhythm, but Jerry was grooving in another time.

"Mr. Martinez. Mr. Martinez. Where were you? Why did you go underground?"

Jerry had wanted to deliver a prepared statement before answering questions, but looked up from his notes. "Underground? I'd be glad to go underground if I could get a better view of the landscape. But the fact is, I just went traveling."

An interruption from the other side of the room. "There were rumors you had fled the country, or been kidnapped, or assassinated."

Jerry looked surprised, then laughed. "Assassinated? I thought you had to be a president or something to be assassinated." Now three or four voices spoke at once, demanding that he account for his time. Jerry raised both hands. "Look, I've got some stuff I want to say. When I'm finished, if you still have questions, I'll try to answer them."

The voices stopped, and the sounds of the cameras took over again. "I'm going to tell you a story I heard at First Mesa on the Hopi reservation. At the beginning of World War II, when everybody was getting drafted, there were six guys from the Hopi mesas who got their notices but wanted to file for conscientious objector status. There's a great warrior tradition among Indians of all different tribes, and they're proud of serving and coming back as decorated veterans. But these particular guys had a reason for not wanting to go overseas. They were the only ones who knew vital parts of the ceremonies that make up the Hopi religious calendar. Without them, the ceremonies the Hopis did to hold the world together—since it was always in danger of falling apart—couldn't be performed. So these six guys applied for religious deferments. The draft board didn't have much use for Indian religion, so they were all thrown in jail. There were a couple of court cases, but the conclusion was these guys were draft dodgers and traitors. In fact, the six of them stayed in prison through the whole war. Luckily, they were able to carry on a modified form of the ceremonies from inside the prison. Not good enough to stop the atomic bombs, or the other catastrophes of World War II, but good enough to keep the world from being destroyed. When the war ended, they went back to the villages and were heroes. The Hopis knew what they had done. Several of them are still alive. I talked to one of the six in Walpi.

"When I was traveling around Arizona and New Mexico—and that's where I was, for any of you who need to know—a lot of things started coming together for me. To be honest, when I organized the occupation of the Crown Valley Parkway, I was going mostly on anger and a general sense of injustice, not on any specific plan or vision. Now, with the help of the people I met out in the southwest—Hopi, Navajo, Zuni, and other Pueblo people—I have a specific vision, and a plan. I've always known we need to form a political coalition in this country that represents all the different kinds of people that we are. Working together—instead of fighting each other, which just gives the bosses more chances to pick our pockets. I hate it when I see Black people fighting Hispanics, for instance, or Asians, and everybody ignoring or beating up on Indians. If any group looks like it's going to get a leg up, the rest of us pull them down. Crabs in a barrel. It's always been that way. Sure has worked out well for the people who own everything and use us for cheap labor. But now I have a vision of the bosses' worst nightmare—a multicultural coalition that really works. It will be made up of Blacks, Hispanics, Asians, Indians, and progressive white people, but the Indians need to be at the center of the coalition. They need to be the mediators between the other groups that are always fighting each other. For all the hundreds of years Native Americans have held us together, culturally and socially, they've never gotten credit for it. Like the six Hopis that kept the world from exploding to pieces in the middle of the twentieth century."

Jerry paused, scanned the room of reporters and camera operators. They were all white, except for one Black behind a minicam. Almost all men. "Looking around the room, I just realized I'm probably making some of you nervous. Don't get me wrong; this is not about excluding anybody. The coalition I'm proposing is a true representation of who we Americans are as a people, and would be good for everybody, no matter what color. As far as I can see, it's the only way to put an end to racism, and that's the biggest problem we have in this country. Always has been. Not illegal immigration, not crime, not taxes, not the economy, but racism. That's really all I have to say. Any questions?"

The room rumbled, voices flew from all sides simultaneously. Jerry pointed at a woman in the front row. She stood and delivered her question. "How is what you propose different from Jesse Jackson's Rainbow Coalition?"

The man behind her said, "Because all the colors in his rainbow aren't black!" and the whole room burst into laughter.

Jerry stood up, leaned over the microphones. "Jesse Jackson's done a hell of a job swimming against the flood. When every other politician is sucking up to racists, he keeps trying to do the right thing. But the woman in the front row asked me a legitimate question. The main difference is we have the glue to hold the coalition together. Who has more experience bringing different kinds of people together than Indians? They're all different, but the tribes cooperated with each other when they had to. White people can't be the center of this coalition for obvious reasons. Not that they wouldn't want to. They've used people of color as fronts for years. That's what PC politics is about: tokenism to hide the real monopoly of power. Blacks can't be the center, because they've never been able to see the struggle from any other point of view. For them, history begins and ends with slavery, but not everybody else has been through that. Asians have their own peculiar truce with white people, who don't mind if some turn out to be doctors and engineers, and live in fancy neighborhoods with them. If Asians were at the center, that sweet deal would get in the way. And speaking for my own group, Hispanics have always had their own special point of view, that American history starts with the Mexican War and the violations of the Treaty of Guadalupe Hidalgo. And as for hating Blacks and Asians, some of my people outdo even the whites."

More questions flew, but two thousand miles away Ethel turned, broke the astonished Michigan silence. "Have you ever heard anything like this before?"

Dierdra held up her hand. "Wait, he's going to say something else." Jerry worked his way through the crowd of reporters and out the kitchen door, ignoring shouted questions. "Well, I guess not. Indians—where did he come up with that?"

Ethel pushed the remains of her salad across the table. "Did I ever tell you about my great grandfather? After the Civil War he went north into Dakota territory and married a Sioux woman. That's what my family says. When I went to the Pine Ridge reservation near Rapid City to find out more about it, I ran into a woman named Louise Wright. She visited us last Easter, but we never did figure out if we're related."

Dierdra stared at the CNN logo on the television screen. "No, he's talking about something more than mixed blood. In Trinidad we believe the spirits of dead Indians who were exterminated by the Spanish never left the island. I think this Martinez guy is onto something." She chewed on the end of her pen, then wrote two words on her note pad: "Arawak" and "coalition."

Walkingstick in the crystal cave: rising from the stream running through its heart, the outline of a man caught between substance and spirit. He's the bread that must be eaten. His flesh and bones are made of flour, water, and light; his blood is formed only by the spoken word. On wet skin engaging his congealed energies, the remains of eagle paint, but no feathers, fur, or cloth. Walkingstick stands naked, in a state of becoming, tattoos gleaming on hands, feet, and shoulders. Like the spirit release he has set in motion, his incarnation is irreversible. Caked over his skin is whitish gray grease the consistency of lard.

The chants he sends up echo the chamber into harmonic convergence, release spirits from the crystalline matrix, coax the splitting membranes of snake eggs into the blossom of chance. It is the moment of the Shift. This cave is stone and blood, the womb of time: a loop in the fabric of the universe, the cosmic snake swallowing its tail. Walkingstick's song mimics the star matrix, the web of connection between animals, plants, and rocks. Bears and raccoons listen outside, and a few human animals—the ones destined to seed memory caves within the four elements, the four faces of the wind. The Cherokee chanter sends ringing notes to bring back Nancy, basket weavers, stars, and corn. He instructs us that each kernel is a star, an egg, a pocket-sized crystal that will teach teeth to pray and the tongue to consider its music of silence.

Recalled souls swelled the numbers at Crown Valley Parkway, but this cave's release of bats, birds, the alchemy of stories and woven signs, is no longer dress rehearsal. When the souls fly up, rush down all channels of the Network grid, bears will lift their heads from streams, cease bathing and their search for fish. Lonesome sojourners in the fragmented world will feel their shoulders mounted by enabling fire. The strength of human memory will push down the walls that have been built around it. When water runs free, it becomes larger than any container that can be imagined. Chant praise for the underground river binding East and West in an ecstatic embrace that never ends. Praise the Mississippi as She raises Her thighs to give birth to the Shift that will deliver the nation. Memory is a gathering of water, sensitive as the deepest well. Its wet fingers feel textures of sand, woven marsh cane, tanned deerskin, and the edges of the crystals themselves. The temple of remembering is mobile and ready for action but remains invisible to Death Squad electronic devices. People raise inner eyes and see the shape this temple wraps around them. Our communal immune system is recharging: there's a new shield against viral invasions from the information highway.

A spinning motion, a whine as the new world prepares to leave the cave: bees set off to make honey for the Millennium. If a mountain hiker in North Carolina were to happen by the mouth of that cave when its ectoplasmic pulse hit air and sunlight, nerves would light up, brain flash into fire. She'd receive baptism in all the frequencies of the stars.

Jerry stood at Gate 25, Terminal 2 of Los Angeles International Airport in disguise as Latin America's guru of liberation theology, Gustavo Gutierrez. White clerical collar, long black traditional cassock. He received the usual polite smiles that priests despise, but no one recognized him for the nation's current celebrity troublemaker. When Ethel Wright and Dierdra McDonald emerged from the cluster of hugging families and lovers at the gate, he signaled them with a slight wave of the hand and roll of his eyes. Dierdra laughed, and was about to comment out loud, but Ethel yanked her arm and she went silent. As he walked them across the street to the parking structure, he apologized for the lack of space they'd have to endure in the drive to their motel. His van would have been perfect, but it had become such a TV icon, sometimes presented as an overlay on his face, universally recognized as a symbol of the movement, he could no longer drive it anywhere. Might as well be put right into a museum.

Ethel said she'd heard a story about a man who sent Picasso a check for ten thousand dollars and asked the artist to send him any scribbled thing in return. Picasso drew a naked devil on the back of the check, added "Money is the root of all evil," and returned it. The art collector was delighted; the drawing was immediately valued at fifty thousand dollars and hadn't cost him a cent. Dierdra said she'd heard that merchants don't cash the smaller checks of famous people, because their signatures are worth more than the value of the check. It makes bookkeeping impossible. Jerry laughed, said he was no Picasso, just a van painter from Santa Ana. He apologized again for the car, which he'd borrowed from Chaco, his boss. When they arrived at the parking space and Dierdra saw the classic white '61 T-bird convertible, cherried out to mint condition, she let out a squeal that turned into a long swooping laugh. "Shut up, Jerry, and put down the top!"

Ethel offered to take the cramped back seat because of Dierdra's long legs. She and the baggage were wedged in sideways as they drove down Century Boulevard and jumped into late-afternoon traffic on the 405. Jerry shouted a few questions. "Listen, how tired are you folks?"

Dierdra reached her arms up into the wind, then pulled them down and collapsed into laughter. "Doing just great! How about you, Ethel?"

Ethel was feeling the full force of wind and car speed in the back seat. She couldn't hear a word, so she cupped her ear. Dierdra shouted, "Are you tired?" Ethel smiled and raised her thumb.

Dierdra slapped Jerry on the arm. "Man, we're both in good shape. What do you have in mind?"

"There's a really good restaurant near the motel I booked for you. It's called Mariscos los Cabos, and the guy that runs the place is a friend of mine. I could take you back to your motel to wash up and settle in, then to Mariscos, and then to a jazz concert, if you want. I've got extra tickets."

"What is *mariscos*?"

"That's Spanish for seafood. And Ralph does amazing stuff with it. You can't get better food than he makes."

Watching a freeway full of Southern Californians, interpreting their cryptic vanity license plates, Ethel was enjoying sunshine in the back seat. She tilted her head back, absorbed the full force of the sky, enough free power to rise above the convertible and shadow it like a hawk. Catching the phrase "jazz concert" from the conversation in the front seat, the gumbo expert pushed forward and asked for details. "Who're we going to hear?"

Jerry turned and shouted. "I don't know if you're interested, but I've got extra tickets. She's a piano player with her own trio named Rachel Yorita. They say she sounds just like Thelonious Monk."

Dierdra grabbed the top of the windshield, pulled herself up and looked over it, caught the shock of the wind on her face, then dropped back into the seat. "Oh, oh, silly me—I forgot to buckle in. Yeah, I'm crazy about Thelonious Monk. Any good bebop or blues. Is this Yorita woman related to Toshiko Akioshi?"

Ethel thrust her head between the two of them. "Bebop is not my favorite, but I'm willing to give it a try."

Jerry shouted over his shoulder. "Believe me, I'm not a big bebop fan either. Salsa and Afro-Cuban are my thing. But this girl is a phenomenon: she's only twelve years old."

Dierdra and Ethel showered and changed as Jerry rested on one of the double beds. Later, at Mariscos los Cabos, munching tortilla chips and salsa, Ethel and Dierdra began to declare their enthusiasm for Jerry's proposed coalition. They offered to be midwestern representatives. Ethel suggested that with the current pressure on unions, those organizations would be natural allies. At least some of the more liberal unions, like the UAW.

Ralph walked up to their table, stared at Jerry and his costume, was about to comment but stopped when the holy van painter raised two fingers in the sign of benediction. The restaurateur caught on, offered the father and two ladies bottles of Dos Equis on the house.

An hour and a half later, in the concert hall at Chapman University, they watched a small girl with long straight black hair step up to the piano, bow, then do solo renditions of "Little Rootie Tootie," "Ruby My Dear," and "Nice Work If You Can Get It." After finishing, she stood up and bowed again, to enthusiastic applause. Then her sidemen came out; a lanky Black man with gray hair took his seat behind the trap set, and a young man with kinky blond hair and designer clothes picked up the bass that had been resting on its side. They jumped into a rendition of "Criss-Cross" and filled the hall with a sound so big, it left no room for the audience's amazement.

Dierdra leaned over to Jerry. "Damn! Nobody can play Monk without sounding like a fool, or sounding like somebody trying to play like Monk and missing. This girl is actually doing it. She's got the timing—coming in after the beat, the double rests. Wow. And she hasn't memorized the records. I've got them all, and she's doing her own versions."

Ethel tried to shout over the applause. "Who is this girl? Where is she from?"

Jerry leaned across Dierdra. "She's local, from a place called Villa Park. But she's got a following all over the West Coast now."

Before the audience calmed down, the trio tore into "Hackensack." Rachel gave the bassist and drummer chances to stretch out with long solos, got up and stood at the end of the piano bench, jigging, holding her arms up like a boxer, directing her sidemen with signals from shoulders, eyes, hands, and by pointing lips. When the musicians momentarily stumbled into her groove, she drew back her mouth into the pouty smile of a twelve year old. Then she sat down, ran her solo into breathless loops and digressions, landed square on the melody, and brought it home. The crowd leaped up and cheered.

Rachel got up from her seat, pulled up the piano microphone and spoke. "Thank you. Please give a hand to Marty Richards on bass and Gary Higginson on drums." She paused. "The next two numbers are my personal compositions: 'Dream Tobacco' and 'Virtual Tree.'"

As she sat and played the first song, Dierdra leaned over to Jerry. "I've never heard this one before, but it's got to be Monk."

Jerry watched Dierdra scrutinize the prodigy as she performed. He saw her skeptical expression change to fear or amazement, he wasn't sure which. He grabbed her elbow. "What is it?"

"Can you see it, Ethel?"

Ethel nodded. Jerry looked, but all he saw was a trio playing something called "Dream Tobacco." Ethel pulled Jerry over Dierdra's lap, put her chin on his shoulder. "Do you see that shadow arching over her? It wasn't there before, and it's not from the lights. Just look, right there."

Jerry began to make out the amorphous dark form. It pulsated, rose up, then settled back. As he stared, he could see extensions reach out like arms and touch Rachel as she performed, then drop to the keyboard. The shadow resolved into the shape of a man, became so clearly defined Jerry could see a fur hat, a beard, and from his lips a hanging cigarette. It hugged the prodigy as her improvisation took a particularly risky side path. Then a flash of light and the shadow reincorporated into the body of the girl.

They'd come together in the back room of La Estrella: the heart of the coalition. Discussing possibilities as Alva served coffee and *churros* to Jerry Martinez, Carla Abruzzese—who'd been sick since returning from Mongolia, but insisted on coming—Larry Smith, Wilbur Lum, Ethel Wright, Dierdra McDonald, and Maxine Hong Kingston and Gerald Vizenor, who'd flown down from Berkeley. Smith had introduced the two writers, asked Ethel and Dierdra how strike preparations were going at Midwestern State. Chewing on *churros*, chatting, everyone waited for Jerry's pronouncement. Now that the coalition had been officially declared, what would be the next move?

The van painter got up from the table and left the room. Returning, he sat down, rubbed his hands over his face, and sighed. Everyone around the long table went silent and stared at him. "You don't need to advertise this to anybody, but I haven't got the slightest idea where to go from here. Visions only take you so far, no matter how good they are. There are always demonstrations, but we already did that at Laguna Niguel. There's got to be some other direction."

Maxine leaned forward on her elbows, long silver hair falling over her arms, eyes widening as she spoke. "What you're talking about is bringing people together, right? Building community. That's what I was doing with my veterans' group: peace veterans and war veterans together. If that works, and it did, then anything can happen. We need to gather the tribes together, or invent a new tribe."

Jerry leaned back in his seat, looked at the ceiling, envisioned a crowd of people in white cotton clothes and beads. "Like a festival, or a be-in or something. To tell you the truth, I like that sort of thing. I liked it in the sixties, and it sounds good now. But don't we run the risk of people saying we're on a nostalgia trip, living in the past?"

Maxine grabbed the hair on the top of her head. "No, Jerry, I'm not talking hippy dippy. You're not hearing me."

Carla snickered. "I'm going to remember what he just said about nostalgia the next time he tells one of his Brown Beret stories." She glanced around the table. "You may not know it, but Jerry is a sucker for stories with a moral to them."

Vizenor shifted in his seat, cleared his throat. "Oh, I don't know. Most of my stories don't have any particular moral, other than the uselessness of terminal creeds."

Carla looked at the Berkeley writer, startled. "I'm sorry, I forgot there were two Jerrys here. I was referring to the guy at the head of the table—Martinez."

There was uncomfortable laughter, then a long silence as the assembled activists eyed one another and sipped coffee.

Jerry Vizenor leaned forward on his elbows and massaged his temples. "This is a playful group. I'm really happy I flew down here with Maxine. Reminds me of a bunch of plant impersonators I knew back in Minnesota. They worked out of the Leech Lake area. Screw bean, sumac, wild rice, ginseng. The woman who did ginseng was outstanding. The whole group did such a marvelous job, nobody noticed them. Of course, strategically that was an enormous advantage." Jerry V. closed his eyes, smiled beneficently, put his hands behind his head. All the people around the table looked at him expectantly, except Larry Smith, who shook his head in amused disbelief.

Carla asked what happened to the impersonators, wanted him to finish the story. The writer paused, as if listening to a far-off sound. "Oh, that's all there is to it. They were just very good, and a really playful, enjoyable bunch of people to be with."

The other Jerry groaned and Ethel clucked her tongue. Dierdra released a stage sigh, looked down as she spoke. "I don't know if this is the proper time to talk about this, but there are a lot of angry white folks who think they're being excluded from their own history. They're not going to be happy about any sort of multicultural coalition."

Wilbur twisted himself sideways on his chair. "What history? Whose version? I'm getting really sick and tired of hearing about angry white people. Same old stuff at UCLA over ethnic studies, but there it's white liberals instead of rednecks. What do they have to be mad about? Besides, Jerry—I mean, Jerry Martinez—has already said progressive whites need to be a part of the coalition. And that's fine with me, as long as they don't try to run everything."

Larry signed his impatience with the discussion. "We're getting back to the same old arguments again. Rainbow Coalition stuff. What happened to Jerry M.'s Indian mediators? Where are they? That's the next step, I'd say. Working on that aspect of the coalition."

When eyes shifted to Jerry Vizenor for further clarification, he threw up his hands. "Don't look at me. I didn't come down here to be a crossblood mediator. I just came to see what you people were up to."

Ethel straightened her spine and folded her arms across her chest. "Let's not get into one of these white people things. There isn't anybody at this table who doesn't have some white blood, more than likely."

Wilbur turned and faced Ethel. "Wait a second, I don't have any white blood. At least, not that I know of."

Maxine joined in. "I have a sister-in-law who says she's Chinese by injection."

Wilbur raised his eyebrows, then began to laugh. "OK, we should allow them in as long as they don't use Scotch tape on their eyes and try to be Asian. Like that Broadway production of *Flower Drum Song* where they didn't cast one Asian actor."

Maxine put a finger moustache on her upper lip. "Or Charlie Chan. White people are always thinking they can be better Chinese than Chinese."

Jerry Martinez pulled one knee up to his chin. "What about Marlon Brando as Zapata?"

Gathering energy, Maxine began to lift off her chair. The discussion had turned into one of her favorite games—movie trivia. "Or doing that sleazy house boy in *Tea House of the August Moon.*"

Ethel jumped in. "Don't forget *Amos and Andy.*"

Larry dropped his palms on the table. "I get it, I get it. White people are like Bottom in *A Midsummer Night's Dream.* They don't want much; they just want to play all the roles."

Everyone at the table laughed, but Ethel went into hysterics. She got a handkerchief out of her purse and began to dab her eyes, then laughed uncontrollably again. Finally, she held her face in a rigid expression. "Oh, Larry, you're so funny. You always forget that you're white!"

He blushed and rolled his eyes, shrugged his shoulders, dropped his forehead to the table in mock humiliation, signed his approval that the morning's tensions had been dispersed by laughing at him. When Smith pulled upright, he could see her standing in the doorway. The laughter died and everyone turned to look. She was at least six feet tall, sunglasses, a brown leather bomber jacket with frayed knit cuffs, dusty jeans and cowboy boots. Her long dark hair pulled back in a ponytail. She had a duffel bag over her shoulder, which she swung down, dropped to the floor.

"Name is Walker Thompkins. Just got off the Greyhound—coming straight to you from Oglala, Lakota Nation."

Jerry M., being the closest to her, had to crane his neck to stare at her face. He was trying to interpret the scar on her right cheek. It was puckered and nasty, made him think of mean bars and knife fights. Did it mean this woman was dangerous? He decided to address her. "How did you find out about this meeting?"

The woman put her hands on her hips and laughed. "Don't get worked over it, man. You were easy to find. And lucky for you, because I'm the one you're looking for. Now we can pack up this coalition thing and take it on the road."

Maxine got up and introduced herself and the others at the table. Then she glanced around, counted heads with her finger. "How many people are in this room anyway? I'd swear there's an even dozen, but I only count nine heads."

Carla leaned back and crossed her arms. "Nothing to worry about, happens in La Estrella all the time. There's always a crowd, even if the place is empty. You know, around here nobody is ever dead and gone. We could ask Alva about it, but I'm not sure even she can tell us why."

Dierdra studied Carla for a moment, then turned to Jerry. "You got to listen to me, folks, because I know what I'm talking about. We can't pretend things are business as usual. There's a lot of weird stuff going on out here in California."

They all turned to watch in silence as Dierdra's forehead wrinkled fiercely. Everyone at the table had forgotten how to breathe. When the jukebox in the front of the empty restaurant suddenly ripped into a salsa song, Dierdra listened seriously for a few moments, then lost control and burst into high whooping laughter. The grace of mirth and pregnant chance moved quickly through the coalition brain trust. Walker pulled out a chair and sat down.

The Shift

| CHAPTER XV | # THE BIRTH OF A NATION |

Bjarni, drunk on berries and dew, in his perpetual orgasm of half light and hidden creatures, never left the Vinland shores. He chose to stay behind, let other presences enact his drowning in the Atlantic west of Greenland; he chose to remain in the loop of narration that wrote itself across his eyes and called itself an earthly paradise. Bjarni's laughter tugged at margins drawn through trees and stones; it privileged chance, kept all the doors of felicitous entrance and escape wide open. Freydis shared Bjarni's passion for the land, arrived in Vinland before her boat did: spirit traveling night beast. Even after she returned to Greenland with an extra boat and homicidal booty, marked as an outlaw for all time, she lingered around the Viking stockades in the land that became Rhode Island. She played at havoc, cataclysm, the spectacular and explosive end of things. As Bjarni's laughter opened doors and windows, Freydis stood by his side, reached between the spread legs of time, and midwifed rotten blood. Leaning hard on swollen flesh, she breaks the sac. First sacred waters, then the birth rushes out—more blood, such a grievous loss the mother's body is delivered into darkness. Blood, but no child. In Freydis's hand there is a detached umbilical, good for nothing but strangling dreams. For one thousand years Freydis has choreographed the dance of Europe and America, midwifed collisions and comings together. She's served the Death Squad beyond its greatest expectations. The masters have regretted only the few live births that have slipped through—rising into the air, soaring over lakes and forests, then falling back as seed. But those of us without spiritual wings, our feet planted in asphalt and concrete, can see only blood. Freydis has washed the sky in blood, drowned the light, and we've admired her artistry as sunset. The blood of her deliveries is in our eyes. As it dries on our hands and cheeks, we become convinced of our complicity, begin to love despair. In such depths our own darkness embraces the fire-haired demon, leading to even more births of blood.

In Detroit a sacred crossing of water and earth is buried beneath a poisoned city. The midwife there is Tyree Guyton. A car, a street, a house married to one another by virtue of the same huge polka dots. Maimed dolls, in pieces, collectivized on the sides of a house. The riots of '67, the ancestral riots of '42, lives from daily skirmishes lying broken in the street. But Tyree paints the street, the curb, the sidewalk. He teaches us that all colors are not blood and death. The harmonic Traveler brings back the colors, conjures music, fills the air with sounds of Bird, the bebop that was invented there. Trees sprouting shoes instead of leaves, pendulous fruit of tires, bicycles, and chairs. This artist has *connaissance*. The houses talk to him, the orishas show him the way. Erzuli jitterbugs in her red dress while Tyree paints the street and watches the wind. In a metropolis the Death Squad made, through the mechanical hands and eyes of Henry Ford and Thomas Edison, Guyton releases the sacred, frees colors, washes the blood from our living eyes. Redeemed junk cascades like water over the sides of abandoned houses: a new life, a baptism of spiritual fire. Not torching houses for profit or despair, but a baptism. Tyree has painted the streets.

He is as angry as Coltrane and Monk, whose music soars out windows on the top story of the Fun House; like them he transforms the burnt-out, ruined, and maimed into rapture. He never leaves Heidelberg Street, but he is a Traveler. He's taking names, calling on Papa Legba, the opener of gates, to liberate us from broken words: LAPD, NBC, CNN, DNA, USA. He's conjuring both thunderstorm and rainbow. He calls on Damballah and Naanabodho, feels the approach of the underwater panther, the hidden power of the Anishinaabe, descending from the northern lakes into the Detroit River.

Another press conference at La Estrella. Tables stacked, pushed to one side, reporters jammed in, transmitters and equipment trucks parked along Fourth Street. Jerry made an entrance from the kitchen, said he was only there to introduce the next stage of the movement that had begun with the occupation of the Crown Valley Parkway. He explained that a woman had arrived during a meeting of an ad hoc committee on the new coalition. She'd presented herself for a leadership position, and after some discussion the committee endorsed her unanimously. Jerry said he now planned to step back and assist, and that he should no longer be considered the leader of the movement. He signaled the kitchen, and Walker Thompkins strode in, dressed in a sports jacket and tie, the same jeans and cowboy boots she'd arrived in. The tempo of flashes and whirring camera advances increased.

"Jerry forgot to tell you my name is Walker Thompkins. I don't have a prepared statement, so let's move right to the questions."

A reporter shouted from the back of the room. "How are we supposed to interpret your name, and the way you dress?"

Walker leaned against the podium with its cluster of microphones. When it began to tip forward, she caught it and set it right. "Guess I don't know my own strength." There was some laughter. "Getting back to the question, are you asking me about my sexual preference?"

"Yes."

"Well, I'd say mostly human beings, but I'm willing to make an exception if the situation is interesting enough." There was a pause, the flashes and shutter noise stopped. A woman in the front row laughed, and the flashes resumed.

Another man shouted. "Have you ever been married?"

Walker straightened her tie. "Is this what I get for dressing up in my best tie and jacket? Actually, it's my only tie and jacket. OK, I guess we'll talk about the coalition later. This is obviously more important. Yes, I was married to a man once. Didn't work out. I've had lovers of both sexes before and since. You're probably going to ask me about drugs next, so let me just say I've got drunk, messed around a lot, smoked marijuana, chewed peyote. All of these experiences have made me a better person, more qualified to be a leader in the new coalition."

Several people asked for clarification at the same time.

"Well, all those experiences have kept me from being a self-righteous bigot. And, believe me, there's a bunch of Indians who fit into that category. What's more, all those things have kept me from taking myself too seriously."

Another male voice from the back of the room. "If you don't take yourself seriously, then what makes you think people will listen to you?"

Walker squeezed her nose, looked down for a moment. "I've never asked anyone to listen to me in my life. I figure that's up to them, whether they want to listen or not."

The woman in the front row raised her pencil. "Ms. Thompkins. Ms. Thompkins. From some of the things you've said, I assume you're Native American. Could you tell us something about that? For instance, is Thompkins your real name?"

"Yeah. It's the one I got when I was born on Pine Ridge in 1955. My grandmother had this dream of a man in a black suit. When she asked him his name, he said, 'Thompkins.'" There was laughter from the kitchen, particularly notable was Dierdra's squealing crescendo. "I don't want to disappoint you folks, but we don't all have descriptive names, like White Dove and Running Bear and so on. Do you remember Jay Silverheels, the guy that played Tonto? His real name was Jay Smith. Most of us are just plain old Smith or Jones or Peltier."

The woman reporter jumped back in. "Do you mean Leonard Peltier, the imprisoned activist? Does that mean you're a member of AIM, the American Indian Movement?"

Walker turned and rested her hand against the wall. "I wish I had charts and stuff, or at least a blackboard. The target population for this new coalition is one hundred and fifty million people, folks of all kinds. That's more than voted in the last presidential election. Do any of you think that might be interesting?"

A smirking man in the front row shouted, "Miss Thompkins?" then recrossed his legs. "Back to the question of credibility. With all of your involvement in drugs and radical politics, how do you expect the government to cooperate with you on implementing the goals of this new coalition?"

The Lakota woman threw up her hands in mock horror. "I hope the government doesn't cooperate with us. If they do, we don't have a chance in hell of succeeding."

The front row woman was back. "How can you create social change without the help of the government?"

Walker turned and began to draw on the wall with her finger, great loops and flourishes. "Oh, it'll work out. Government is always trying to catch up with what's already happened. We're way out ahead of them on this one."

The smirking man in the front row spoke up again. "Since you've obviously been involved in gay issues yourself, could you tell us why gays and lesbians haven't been included in this new coalition?"

Walker gripped both sides of the podium, stared over it at the questioner. "You folks seem to have run out of serious questions, but I'll give you one more chance. This is the last press conference I'm going to give."

Another male voice from the back. "Then how do you plan to communicate with the American people?"

She undid her tie, looped it over her thumb, folded it twice, then unbuttoned her collar. "If people want to know something, they'll sure as hell stumble on a way to find out. Press conferences are not about communication. A good interview, with someone who's done her homework, is something else. Communication is about respectful dialogue. The next time you hear from me it'll be on an interview. And the only person I'm interested in talking to is Connie Chung."

Walker tucked the tie into her jacket pocket, walked into the kitchen, and the door swung closed behind her.

Tyree Guyton pours a libation from his can of beer. He has built the house, and he's a child of this same house. He serves the orishas and their fellow Travelers, calling on Robert Johnson, Prince of the Crossroads, calling on Papa Legba to open the gate for all of Detroit, cause the sacred crossroads buried beneath the city to be unearthed. He creates layers of sacred trash because it shows us the Damballah power of transforming imagination, takes us to the bottom layer, where all truth lies. Heidelberg Street, the Guyton project, is a nexus on the Network grid. This man has the gift of eyes. Like a Hopi sacred clown, he carries dolls of himself and all the rest of us. Tyree sets up the snaky pole, the center, he paints the earth, he holds our hands against the packed grains of the mother so we can see and hear again. Open the gate! He nails us, along with the dolls, to the abandoned walls of our own making, the wounds of our forgetfulness. Together we will remember the ancestors, free ourselves into this discipline. In his bones there is a beating time, inevitable as a Monk composition, a song that plants him in our remaining earth like a dagger into a sheath. Doll House, Fun House, O. J. House, Street House, Sky House. The master of eyes and wind is building power. His rituals have set in motion a force that cannot be reversed.

In 1991 Detroit Mayor Coleman Young bulldozed three of Tyree's urban masterpieces: his treatments for the sick, the healings promised and prophesied by Tecumseh. One of the flattened houses held all his paintings and freestanding sculpture. The Death Squad has beaten Tyree around the head and eyes, but they can't stop him from seeing. As he paints, neighborhood children join in. The streets are speaking, and the children hear it too. Tyree's colors, the colors of generations, sing the music of transforming fire. It's promise, it's *connaissance*. He's called on the ancestors, and they have delivered their cosmic polka dots. The master will perform a marriage of sky, street, and fresh water; Tyree Guyton is midwifing the new American soul.

Jerry walked into the kitchen and yelled for Carla. On the counter: cut vegetables in a steel bowl, a glass one with flour and two sticks of butter, an open cookbook next to the ingredients. There'd been no response to his call, so he walked into the hallway, shouted again. No answer. He stuck his head into the bathroom, but there was no one. When he walked through the bedroom door, he heard cardboard boxes slamming against one another inside the walk-in closet.

"Carla?"

The voice, but not the woman, came out. "Yeah?"

"Didn't you hear me when I called?"

"I heard you and I answered. Listen, I'm in the midst of sorting out these shoes and getting rid of some of them. There's no more space."

Jerry leaned in the closet doorway, watched Carla on her knees, shifting stacks of boxes—opening some, then closing lids and restacking them, or throwing them out the door. An orange box hit Jerry in the shin. When he remarked on the unfinished project in the kitchen, Carla looked up for the first time, gave him a get-lost look, and returned to her boxes. He waited for further speech, and even angry words would have been OK, because he needed someone to listen to his troubles. When she refused to stop her energetic shuffling, he did a Joey wiggle with nose and eyebrows in silent protest behind her back, asked if she were playing Imelda Marcos. Without turning her head, she replied, "Tell me about it, Mr. Noriega." Watching her work in silence for several minutes, he gave up and explicitly asked for attention, and she replied that she was listening. The van painter and retired coalition leader began to list complaints against Walker Thompkins: her arrogance and presumption of absolute authority, her refusal to consult with others before making decisions, her constant self-contradiction. He said she was driving him crazy. Carla's response was unsympathetic, suggesting that he get rid of her if he didn't like what she was doing.

Hands in his pockets, looking down on the floor, Jerry began to narrate the incident that had put him in his present state. "We were sitting there, talking about the Crown Valley Parkway. I was laughing, saying I never dreamed how much attention I was going to get from it all. Then she told me that was pretty much over, since I'm John the Baptist to her coming."

Carla looked up at Jerry's childish wounded expression and laughed. "Walker is really good. I like it, a female Jesus."

"Yeah, when I looked at her—you know, after she said that— she piled it on even more. 'You think that's blasphemous because I'm a woman, right?' How can I go on working with her now?"

Carla turned to face Jerry, folded her legs under her. The short skirt she wore shifted up to the tops of her thighs. "You need to quit complaining about Walker. It's over a week now you've been doing this. Of course, she's unpredictable and arbitrary. You know you'd be the same way if you could get away with it."

Jerry dropped his seat down to the carpet on the closet floor. "Who says I can't?"

Carla reached out and caressed his cheek. "I thought you wanted to be a follower, not a leader. Looks like you want it both ways. What happened to being sick of the media attention? Now that Walker's getting all of it, be happy. Let her handle it. Besides, I've got much more important news than your little tiffs with Walker."

He lifted his eyes from the carpet's weave. "Like what?"

She drew in a long breath, dropping her diaphragm and pushing out her stomach. "Like why I'm always throwing up. My parasite tests came back from the lab, and they're all negative. Dr. Chu told me to get a drugstore pregnancy kit and try that. So I did, and I'm pregnant."

Jerry stared at the bottoms of her panties, as if he might be able to see some external sign. "How can you be pregnant? Did you forget to take your pills in Mongolia?"

"How can I forget to take birth control pills? There's one marked out for every day, and I finished the package. I didn't forget anything."

He pulled his knees up, rested his head on them, sensing the walls of the closet, listening to the sound of his own breath, and Carla's.

Carla slipped off her flats, hitched up her skirt, and pulled her legs into a lotus position. "There's something I didn't tell you about the trip. You remember, I said I met some strange people in the mountains, but they weren't Neanderthals. Now I think they were. They never took off their masks, but that's what they were. Well, one of them took off his mask. You won't believe this, but he looked just like Joey Patchouli. At first I thought the high altitude was making me hallucinate. But I'm sure of it now; they were Neanderthals. They did a ceremony with me and I blacked out. I mean, I had no choice. They didn't ask my permission. When they were through, they left me at a village at the base of the mountain." She unfolded her legs and stretched them out, touched Jerry's thighs with her chocolate-colored toenails.

"Are you trying to tell me they fucked you?"

"No, I don't think so. It didn't feel like it, and there were no signs of it."

Jerry laughed, reached out, and grabbed one foot in each hand. "I hope you kept your boots on, Sweetie. If they saw these feet, they couldn't resist." He leaned down and held her second toe—significantly longer than the big toe—gently between his teeth. If her feet were his biggest turn-on, the long second toe was the most dangerous hook in that foot fetish. He chanted with the toe still between his teeth. "This big piggy's going to market."

Carla pulled back her feet, slipped her panties down over her legs. "Now that I'm pregnant, does that mean you're not going to fuck me anymore?"

He put his hands over his face, peeked through his fingers. "Are you going to make me wear a mask?"

"That would be a very nice idea."

Jerry lowered his head to the floor, began to lick the inside of her legs, working from the anklebone upward, stopping occasionally to make a comment. "Why don't you just imagine the mask? Which do you want this time, a big monkey or a Neanderthal?" He reared back and snorted, until his eyes came to rest on the tattoo on her hip. It was a duplicate of the glowing turquoise symbol on Joey's right hand. Its loops and arrow looked like it was part of the legend on a map, suggesting a hidden direction. He went quiet, then dropped down and continued his slow wet crawl up her leg. When he reached the area just above the knee on the inside of her left leg, he lingered, kissing, licking, and sucking. Carla's muscles contracted by reflex, and she shouted, "Oh!" When he lifted her knees slightly, clusters of jolts and shivers passed through her body.

She pulled her skirt into a band around her waist, unbuttoned her blouse, and opened the front clasp on her bra. Looking down, she watched him close in on her dark forest. "Don't be in such a rush down there, Mr. Silver Tongue. You've got a couple of old friends up here that would like to talk to you."

After he came north on command, she grabbed him by the ears and pulled his face into her right breast, held him while he sucked, circled the nipple with his lips. Later, back in the forest, flickering his tongue at high frequency over her magic pearl, her legs wrapped around his head in a hammerlock. But Carla suddenly released her grip and cried out, said she could feel something flutter in her abdomen.

Jerry lifted his face, looked up at her. "How could that be possible in just a few weeks?" If he'd have listened more carefully, he would have heard it himself. Gills slashed into neck, a being climbed out of the sacred waters and began to make its way up the mountainside. Even though he couldn't entirely sense the connection, Jerry became thoughtful, pulled himself up on his knees, then sat back on his heels.

Carla put her hands behind her head, flexed pectorals and made her breasts jump one at a time. "Is this a rest stop, or are you out of the mood?"

He looked down at her. "I don't know whether I'm in the mood or not."

"How about a nice outfit to put you back into the mood?"

"What do you have in mind, a corset and fishnet stockings?"

"No, no, a costume for you, Generalissimo Noriega. Slip your clothes off. I've got just the thing." Carla got up, pulled a hanger off the rack, draped the outfit over his arm as he leaned over to untie his shoes. It was a long cotton cloak, like a caftan, but open all the way down the front. Its vertical stripes mimicked the colors and sequence of a rainbow.

He stood up and put it on. "Wow! A cloak of many colors. Where did you get this, in Berkeley or something?"

"I made it for you." Carla was down on the floor again, legs spread, hands behind her head. "Stand over me, and open it slowly."

He stood for a moment without moving. As she stared at his rainbow, she could see energy vibrating on the north-south axis. There was a calling, and she knew what she'd find when he opened the curtain. Wrapped around and around his waist, the dragon, the feathered serpent, the big-headed snake. She pulled herself up and took the snake head in her mouth, sucked it, held it tenderly between her teeth. And through her teeth the voices came. At first it was one, singing a chant of lamentation, then there was a chorus. It was the mudheads, the Neanderthals. They were beckoning, calling for her to come back home. She groaned, threw her shoulders against the carpet, thrust her feet wide apart, one touching each wall. When Jerry caught up with her, she inserted him roughly.

Carla was whining, emitting a strange childish sound she'd never made before. Jerry looked into her eyes. The lids were wide open, giving her an exaggerated bug-eyed look, as if she'd been frightened. But she wasn't looking at him, or at anything else in the closet. When his eyes dropped down to her forest, Jerry could see the muscles in her legs and around her vagina flex and tense. She held him so tightly, he began to feel himself go numb inside her. When he came, she convulsed violently but didn't make a sound. He lay his sweating chest again her breasts, and she put her arms around him, held him like a baby. She ran her fingers over the hair on his arms. She loved hair, and she could feel the power of it in the ancient creature growing within her belly.

CHAPTER XVI | **C-SECTION**

Chicago in swirling October looked east over a lonely lake—a city full of people who'd forgotten how to imagine the other shore. Walker Thompkins zagged through the heartland with her charter bus convoy, doing scheduled speaking gigs, surprise appearances at cafés and local talk shows. Her insights and proposals, the wake she kicked up by passing through, replayed each night on the national news. The more government officials denied their feasibility, the more people were convinced her schemes would work, and deliver them from their burdens. News editors bet on how long it would take for the country to get sick of her. But right now Walker Thompkins is all the people want; she even fascinates the ones she terrifies most. Outside the Chicago amphitheater, vendors at tables selling posters, T-shirts, an unauthorized biography, and a selection of bumper stickers. The most popular is WALKER THOMPKINS FOR PRESIDENT. At the beginning of every speech, when the crowd takes up the chant, her response is the same: "I already get more attention than anybody in Washington, so why should I take the demotion?" Warm-up rock bands, usually bad ones, brass bands, country and western or rhythm and blues ensembles, depending on the location. Walker Thompkins floats in and out of these scenes, leaving an ambiguous trail of images and speech fragments. Witnesses who spend days trying to reconstruct her appearance and message debate among themselves but learn not to trust television recaps. The growing band of followers searches for a collective memory, a practical knowledge of human interaction they can share with one another. They seize on each fragmentary clue in the treasure hunt.

Walker told audiences to stop worrying about enemies: there was no individual or group that could do them harm. She said the only enemies were greed and fear: the carrot and stick that bosses use to make us act against ourselves. For the disease of greed she suggested giveaways, a cure tribal people had figured out years ago. If anybody got too much, they'd just turn some over to others and even things out. Potlatches, those incredible giveaways thrown by families in the Northwestern tribes, were considered so dangerous and subversive the government banned them entirely. When Walker told this story, she'd always stop, pull back from the podium, stare at the floor and tug at her upper lip. "Yep. Give a lot of stuff away, and make sure you let the FBI know about it."

The Lakota Traveler talked about fear, asking what exactly people were so afraid of, then she answered for them. "You think you'll lose your security, right? Hell, why worry about something that doesn't even exist? Some folks in this building will die in the next month—or next week, or even tomorrow. Not a thing we can do about it. Retirement or medical insurance? They've got you convinced that if you just shut up and work, you'll be taken care of. You don't get the joke until you try to collect. Listen, if you took all the money you pay for insurance and shit like that, pooled it among yourselves, you could take care of each other. And when you're too sick to get better, we'll throw you a party, then let you go home and die with dignity. Believe me, people have been doing that for thousands of years without spending a lot of money.

Crossing over to the other world's not nearly as scary as the bosses want you to believe. But they know the moment you figure that out, their whole game will collapse on itself. Stop letting these guys sell you your death. When you finally catch on, that'll be the revolution, and not a bullet needs to be fired.

"For starters, you got to get to know each other. Introduce yourself to everybody in your apartment or condo, then everybody on your block. Get yourselves together and throw a block party." Walker talked about retribalizing the cities, not by blood lines but by recognition of community, reforming a network of responsibility and mutual respect, a ritual circle.

Two weeks before the Chicago speech she'd walked uninvited into a meeting of conservative Republicans at a Newport Beach hotel. The cameras and microphones clustered around the spot where she stood by the door. She said she knew Republicans were troubled by the issues of poverty and welfare, but she had an easy solution. Why not index the top income tax bracket to the percentage of people who are unemployed or below the poverty level? The fewer people in those categories, the lower the taxes for that upper bracket; the more people, the higher. The tall Lakota woman said if that idea were made law, she'd personally guarantee enough hiring into real, private sector jobs to resurrect the American work force. She added that no corporate executive would ever again be tempted to send jobs out of the country.

Sometimes when she'd taken a crowd to a particularly intense moment, she'd talk about the old belief that everyone in the world has a medicine bag waiting somewhere. Not only Indians. She said make sure to keep your eyes open, so when you get there you'll find it; if people aren't careful, they'll walk right by their destiny like a dirty penny on the street. Walker described the United States as if it were an enormous person—female, dark-skinned, but confused about who her children were. The United States had a medicine bag waiting for her too. Then she asked the audience to imagine what would happen if Mother found that bag and put it around Her neck.

On the evening in the Chicago amphitheater, after she'd worked the crowd into a few minutes of heady call and response, they were ready to march out over Lake Michigan to find Atlantis. The coalition chief told them reservation and street corner stories that made them angry, others that burned at the edges of their own secret dreams. But when she was through, she'd convinced them they had the power to change everything—more power by far than corporations or the government. Just when that Chicago crowd's energy was ready to spill into action, potentially violent and certainly unpredictable, she pulled a letter from her black leather vest, unfolded it slowly, and raised it above her head.

"I got a letter today asking me if I'm the reincarnation of Crazy Horse. Crazy Horse! Must be they noticed the scar on my cheek. Sure can't be my horsemanship, because I don't think any of you ever saw me ride. But it takes more than a scar to be Crazy Horse. Maybe the person who wrote this letter understands how a spirit can jump on your back, become a part of you. Let me just say this: could be one of you out there in the audience—black, white, or tan—is Crazy Horse. He could be riding one of you right now, hard, like he rode his war pony. Or maybe one of you out there is Wovoka, coming back to fulfill the prophesy of the Ghost Dance. You don't have to be Indian for the spirits to enter inside you and give you a good ride.

"Another thing I've got to say. You Chicago folks keep asking where coalition stuff is happening around the Midwest. I know most of you've heard about the return of the White Buffalo Calf Woman on that white man's farm in Wisconsin. Don't need to tell you all what that's about. But do you know Tyree Guyton in Detroit? The man is reimagining that ruined city, and he's most definitely what's happening in the Midwest. Things are changing all over the country, and Tyree is a whole lot of the power, beauty, and energy making that change. Drive over there and see what he's doing. His Great Work has put such a surge on the Network lines, changes are happening faster than anybody ever figured, including me. Go talk to Tyree, talk to yourselves. You all know more than you think you do. OK, that's it for tonight." Walker grabbed her ponytail, tugged on it, pushed away from the podium, walked offstage, stooping to pick up the leather jacket she'd dropped by the stairs. She was out the door, into a car, and gone before the crowd could react.

Five minutes later, Jerry sat on the edge of the stage watching Carla whisper to Joey in the front row, empty seats all around them. She put her arm around the boy man's neck, pulled his head down, and kissed him on the cheek. The Patchouli healer was looking elsewhere, maybe in the direction of the hands that rested on his knees like tired birds, but birds he could never seem to locate. Jerry caught himself as he began to mimic Joey's characteristic facial grimace. He forced himself to raise his eyes above their heads, look at the remains of the crowd, chattering in clusters all around the amphitheater. He watched the people who lingered to exchange enthusiasms forcibly driven out by the building staff. Jerry felt shitty, wondered if there was anyone left in the world he could talk to. He didn't dare say what was on his mind to anyone but Carla, and she had no patience with his grumpiness or complaints about Walker's ego and irresponsibility. Two months before, Jerry couldn't have walked into a supermarket anywhere in the country without causing a media event. Now his activist life was devoted to being an invisible advance person for the "Walkman." And her highhanded attitude wasn't making the transition any easier.

Handsome Bear shouted suggestions to the seaman pulling the reins attached to the first two horses, struggling to get them on board the junk. These weren't the stubby Mongolian ponies he'd ridden into the mountains with Marco Polo, but the fine, long-legged horses from Khan's capital city. Not sky dogs, but eagles with hooves as light as wings. They'd take you to another world and bring you back before the sun could go down twice. These horses burned their pure energy so recklessly, the memory hero believed he could smell blood in their sweat. That was why he called the emperor's select breed "blood horses," and that amused Khan, preased him enough to give the Bear Caller three breeding pairs for the voyage home. Beyond that, axes, tripods, porcelain plates and vases, carved statuary, seeds of the fruits and vegetables he had come to enjoy in the jade kingdom. Khan had sent enough gifts to fill half the ship's hold, ballast it snug into the water. The rest of the space was devoted to the rice, salted fish, pickled vegetables, and water that would sustain them across the blue desert.

The first pair of breeders didn't want to board the junk. They yanked at their reins, whinnied and reared, kicked the loading ramp into a frenzied clatter. Handsome Bear felt a twinge as he watched the sensual flexing of the horses' chests; their beauty made him even more aware of what he'd lose by leaving Khan's kingdom. Ping Shang-lien had been sent away over a month before. Now he and his expedition were in the huge seaport to the southeast of the capital, waiting for final preparations and favorable winds. The seamen tried a new strategy, tying cloth hoods over the horses' eyes, and successfully led the first pair on board. The Bear Caller wondered what omen the animals' initial resistance, followed by blind compliance, held for his journey back to Beautiful Village.

Besides the Chinese crew there were two salmon people who'd lingered in the jade kingdom after their countrymen had built, with the help of Khan's shipwrights, three new hybrid sea craft, then returned home. The rest of the original sun people expedition—except for Eagle Claw and Red Stone, who died in the desert on the way to the abalone people, and Crow, who was lost at sea—were ready to return. Rabbit and Cold Moon Fire had distinguished themselves in the jade kingdom. Both had been given fine embroidered silk clothes, fur hats, jewelry made of various semiprecious stones. Their company and conversation, as much as their broken Chinese would allow, was sought among the elite of the capital. Magpie Girl had also made a name for herself, slipping away with a rich merchant on a trading expedition to India, but she'd been returned to the capital when Khan had made his displeasure known to the merchant. Two Bucks, Descending Cloud, Dancer, Little Ram, and Broken Hand had enjoyed their new lives for most of the first year. However, since they'd been maintained modestly as members of Handsome Bear's retinue, rather than as celebrities—like Cold Moon Fire and Rabbit—they'd been ready to return home for a long while.

After the junk sailed out to sea, Handsome Bear watched every morning for the one-eyed dragon dawn that led them, teased their quilted sails into tautness. Clear weather and strong winds kept the captain busy maximizing their good fortune, and the ship ran the current faster than expected. Of course, the one hundred years they'd previously gained were lost when they traveled back over the north-south hotwire on the Network grid, the erratic dragon path now called the International Dateline. After crossing it, Handsome Bear felt shudders and wrenching shifts beneath the water. He suspected his old friend with the spinning eyes, and also partly guessed that the area around the line was prone to short circuits, the sudden opening of gates into possibility. But the circuitry wasn't the cause of the undersea rumblings. The memory hero gazed at burning water to the west one evening, saw fire slide down the troughs of waves. He leaned over the stern to catch a glimpse of the dragon, but noticed instead the appearance of his own bare arm. The movements of the waves were mimicked by motion within his flesh—skin-covered oceans containing feathered serpents, the underwater sliders responsible for storms and impossible breakers. He held out his hands, palm up, toward the sunset, watched bone and flesh disintegrate and reform, each time in new combinations of hair, feathers, and scales. The Big Baby felt changes within him, and they were pulling him away from any life he'd known until that moment. He was becoming a creature so different from the painter, chanter, mover of memory stones, it would take an entirely new dimension to hold him. Like his journeying ancestors, he was about to cross over, but the circuitry of the next world, the system that would give that place shape and light, was still in the process of formation. Getting there would require inventing a new way to travel. A shimmering hole opened in the air before him, and he knew this opening was the gift of pregnant chance. Handsome Bear grasped the stern railing and laughed. "Haw . . . haw! haw! Haw . . . haw! haw!" But the gift also felt like a loss, because he knew if he crossed over he'd never be able to join Sun Girl in the otherworld below this one. There wasn't enough of his spirit to inhabit both places. The hole closed before his eyes, and a powerful loneliness drove him to the edge of song. At first he tried pushing multiple notes through his throat, like the horsemen he'd heard on his Mongolian expedition with Marco Polo. He could hold the low note, but couldn't produce the dance of the upper harmonics. Then he began to chant to the Grandmother in the old way. This feeble attempt to recall the Song of Creation set his eyes drifting back to the horizon. They were lost there a long while until the light congealed into two figures: Sun Girl and Red Swallow kneeling, washing each other's hair with flame. As he watched them caress one another, demonstrate a shocking intimacy, he felt a brittle cold seep into his bones. Then the first roll of thunder.

It swirled in on them, the attack from all directions at once, wind-carried upheavals of water that should have been impossible.

In the middle of the night, the junk was so spun by the storm, catapulted from the crest of one wave to another, the animals in the hold began to scream. Handsome Bear tied himself to the stern railing to keep from being washed overboard, and was often held underwater to the limits of his breath. He'd lost the sacred directions, all connection with the Network; there was nothing in the world to feel or see but chaos. All the Snake clan chief could hear was the mad jumble of stories the storm was telling, and a sorrowful chorus provided by the cries of the blood horses. How long the storm lasted was impossible to tell, because there was no light. When the skies finally cleared, winds ceased, and the ocean returned to a rolling blue, the expedition leader was astonished that none of the seamen or sun people had been lost. But when they opened the hatches and looked below decks, they saw that the wind walkers had stolen all beauty from Khan's magnificent creatures, along with their breath, leaving only sculptures of terror. The crew used a block and tackle to hoist each of the six stiff clumps of bone, muscle, and skin onto the deck, then pushed them over the railing into the sea. Handsome Bear knew the dragon that followed beneath their wake would accept each tortured offering as a dumpling to pop into his mouth. Or her mouth, since the dragon was all genders at once: snake, bird, and star simultaneously. Sometimes when you watch a dragon, it's hard to tell if it's devouring prey or giving birth.

In the silent world that followed the storm, air became so heavy it was almost impossible to draw it in or expel it from the body. The crew and expedition members watched one another struggle with their ribs, squeezing, pushing, or pulling in an attempt to stay alive. Above their heads the slack sails sickened with a glistening rose-colored dew. It was clear the wind walkers were hungry for more death. The two salmon people who'd originally helped carry them to the jade kingdom passed quickly into the otherworld. Their bodies were pitched over the side, following the horses as sacrifice to a dragon determined to chase them all into oblivion. Most of the sun people became dragon food within days, each one turning weak, pale skin blossoming into bruises. The end always came with a sudden sitting up, a startled look, the storm of convulsion pushing a mush of guts through the mouth. Avoiding the diseased as if they were cursed, the Chinese seamen insisted that sun people dispose of their own dead, until there was no one strong enough to do so. The only sun person who didn't fall prey to this sickness was Handsome Bear. He grieved as he watched each body drop over the side, sensing a betrayal of his responsibility to the families back in Beautiful Village. But no matter what chants and prayers he offered, to the Grandmother or to other spirit powers, he couldn't keep the runners from dying. Tending Cold Moon Fire, the last survivor, he fanned the hot, unbreathable air over her face. Her red embroidered bib undergarment, tied around neck and waist, was soaked with sweat that smelled like urine. She no longer looked like a champion runner; her flesh was shriveled and grotesquely splotched, the death demon practicing with brush and ink inside her skin. But Handsome Bear refused to read that calligraphy, continued to wipe down her slack arms, pull up the loose silk pants and wash her legs with cold seawater. He sang songs he'd never heard before.

At dawn, four days after the storm passed, Cold Moon Fire opened her eyes and stared at the Bear Caller. He was so stunned at the hatred her eyes poured on him, he touched his hand to her shoulder and asked for forgiveness. She licked her dry lips and rasped, but he couldn't hear what she was trying to say. He put his ear close to her mouth. "I want you to burn with me in the fire where I live." Handsome Bear pulled back quickly, dodging the strike of a rattlesnake. He wanted to ask her what she meant, but her eyes weakened and closed. Cold Moon Fire had grown from a child into a powerful and beautiful woman, but the healer believed a bad spirit had found its way into her. He wondered if the woman's anger was also the work of the wind walkers, if they'd left her a double heart, made her into a witch. Cold Moon Fire was beginning to remind him of Red Swallow as a young woman. He leaned down, put his ear to her chest to listen for a double beat, but heard only the careening flutter of one exhausted heart.

Three more days of Handsome Bear's nursing and the woman opened her eyes again, sat up, rubbed her face into ruddiness. The healer saw that the splotches on her face and body were entirely gone but knew he had nothing to do with the cure. After another day, she was walking and behaving as if she'd never been sick, chatting with Handsome Bear and the crew. She refused to talk about the loss of the rest of the expedition—even her brother,

Rabbit. When they sighted the western land mass, began to coast southward, Handsome Bear wondered if the two of them would be enough to make the trip back to Beautiful Village. If they could avoid fights along the way, it was possible. Maybe they could travel by night, navigate by the stars. The two of them certainly could not bring back the Chinese treasure. But he hadn't forgotten his mission, even after all the years that had passed; the only things that mattered were the two bronze axes wrapped in coarse blue cloth, the color of twilight. The porcelain ware, perfumes, spices, and statues he'd give to Acorn Teeth and the other abalone people in return for supplies to take them home.

Lying on the deck, smelling the land, he watched the afternoon clouds and sea birds. On the edge of a cloud he could discern a woman's face. Not Sun Girl, because she seemed hopelessly far away from him now, even as he got nearer to home. It was Acorn Teeth's daughter, the girl with the sensitive knees. He called up images of the tattoos around her eyes and sensual mouth, the double ring of dots and stars around each nipple. As he imagined standing with her on the weed-strewn beach, laughing at the children who played in the sunset waves, Handsome Bear's cock pushed against the silk of his trousers.

Dr. Babs, aka Queen Babs, slammed the knocker harder against the red door. She'd slipped the deskman at the Meridien a hundred-dollar bill to direct her to a mambo, a real voodoo priestess. He gave her a name and directions but suggested she wait until the next day. Babs looked around her; it was ten o'clock in the morning, and she still felt nervous. The ramshackle wood frame houses, the clusters of Black people staring at her from porches, or as they leaned against cars in the street: it was clear to this white girl that she was a long way from home, and she was afraid everyone else had figured out the same thing. One of her women's studies courses at Midwestern State University was entitled "African Spirituality in the New World: The Voodoo Priestess and the Role of Haitian Women as Primary Breadwinners." Dr. Babs had written a number of articles on the subject and was working on a book. She'd even performed secret rituals with her woman's group, using a gutted chicken from the supermarket instead of a live rooster, but she'd never found a woman to whom she could apprentice herself, one who had true *connaissance*. There was always her colleague Dierdra McDonald, the English Department professor from Trinidad, known to some as the "Voodoo Queen of Midwestern State," but Babs had never understood why Dierdra wouldn't discuss voodoo with her, no matter what the situation or context. Even after a campus slide lecture she'd given on voodoom banners, Dierdra chatted with students, answering their questions, but wouldn't respond to her colleague's comment about the connection between goddess power and Erzuli. Dr. Babs wondered if it were female envy, the queen bee syndrome. Maybe the Trinidadian didn't think there was room enough for two mambos on one campus. But the cold shoulder puzzled the aspiring scholar, because Dierdra McDonald was considered a generous person and a respectable feminist. She even taught a course in the women's studies program.

The door opened, and half a face the color of a good praline peeked out. "Yeah?"

"My name is Babs—I mean, Professor Barbara Carter. Bobby Pontchartrain at the Hotel Meridien sent me. He said you'd help."

The woman opened the door farther, stood flat-footed in a black lace slip. "Bobby who? Bobby? Oh, shit, you mean Snake Boy, don't you now. OK, sweetie, come in and sit over at the table. I got to get ready."

Barbara walked into a small area that had once served as a dining room. Beneath a round oak table with an elephantine base, the dusky hardwood floor bowed with the weight. Newspapers, magazines, and old telephone books stacked around the periphery of the room and in the window seat had turned the sizable room into an alcove. On one end of the table was a jumble of liquor bottles and squat unlit candles. As Babs's eyes adjusted to the darkness, she saw that the walls were covered with posters from Preservation Hall and pictures of the Virgin Mary and various saints, geometric designs beaten into their metal frames with a sharp point. As she sat down, Babs felt electricity in the back of her neck. She knew from her library studies that these pictures were the tip-off, voodoo gods in Catholic disguise.

When the woman returned, wrapped in a black robe, with her hair turbaned into a red bandanna, she announced herself officially.

"I am Queen Matilda. If you're looking for power or revenge, you come to the right place."

Babs straightened her back, opened her purse, and pulled out a small notebook and a pen. "Queen Matilda . . . Or should I call you Queen Matilda Mather?" The mambo crossed her arms and gave the Yankee visitor an angry look. "Queen Matilda, I've been looking for you my whole life. You must believe me: all I want is true information. Know what I mean? Knowledge is power. Let me be your apprentice and I'll pay you anything you want."

Mama Matilda sat down, looked Babs in the eye, then pulled her visitor's hands to the center of the table. She spit over her right shoulder, leaned down and scrutinized the knuckles, pulled off Babs's turquoise Navajo shaman's ring and a gold pinkie with incised Wiccan designs, tossed them over her shoulder. The initiate gasped, reached for her purse. Matilda raised her right hand and made a gesture with two fingers. Babs relaxed, let the purse slip from lap to floor.

Matilda got up, retrieved a bottle from the end of the table, poured some of its contents on the floor, took a swig, then passed the bottle to Babs. "Take a drink, child. Don't you worry, I won't rob you. You got to free yourself of metal to pass the gate. We're going to make a great journey, you and me. Yes, we are. You're the messenger they been talking about sending me. I can see it and smell it. You're the chosen one."

The young man with the blond brush cut banged on the nursery windows. "That's not my baby! That's not the one, you idiots!" He pointed at the card he'd pressed to the glass, JENKINS printed in large block letters. The masked nurse turned the metal cart holding the plastic tray filled with a squalling baby. She pointed at the attached sign—JENKINS.

"You idiots, how can that be my baby? It's black. Can't you see?" Red-faced, pounding the windows. The viewing room had cleared minutes before. Now two security officers came through the door, seized the raving man by either arm. He was taken to the administration offices of Albuquerque General Hospital until matters could be looked into. But when they'd verified that the footprint taken at birth matched the child in question, the man was still unsatisfied. He exploded again, threatened revenge for the hospital's mistake, the kidnapping.

Bob and Jill Jenkins sued Albuquerque General Hospital for five million dollars: gross negligence, pain and suffering. They offered a ten-thousand-dollar reward to anyone who could find their real baby. The day after the story hit the Albuquerque newspaper, the tabloid people were there—both print and televised. Jill, who swore she'd never had sexual relations with anyone other than her husband, took the reporters on a tour through the family photo album, verifying pure white bread for at least two generations back. The whole fiasco was a media natural. Headlines began to leap from the minds of reporters even before Jill had finished telling her tale—the hostility of the Mexican and Filipina nurses in the hospital, and her suspicion they'd taken her baby to torment her. "Switcherooni." "A Mother's Heartbreak: They Took My Beautiful Baby and Gave Me a Welfare Child." Although the hospital denied the possibility of a switch, and offered physical evidence to substantiate their claim, the story was too good to let die. When the networks picked it up, they were careful to add the "allegeds," but also gave it enough play to significantly boost their ratings for a week. On National Public Radio a commentator theorized on the popularity of the controversy. She said white America had seized on the story because it turned their worst paranoid fantasy, that people of color would edge them out, into a simple parable.

Then the other stories began to come in. At first it looked like me-toos, but by the end of the second week there were more than ten thousand couples who presented babies who did not appear to be genetically compatible. There were white couples with babies who appeared to be Native American, Hispanic, or Asian, as well as a wealth of dark-skinned children. The Asian babies displayed certificates of authenticity on the upper parts of their buttocks: the blue-black bruise called the Mongolian spot. White babies born to people of color had caused just as much trouble. There'd been so many lawsuits filed against hospitals that an emergency summit meeting of the five biggest insurance companies had taken place in New York.

When he'd first heard the Jenkins story, Jerry had been amused. He thought the bigoted rednecks were getting just what they deserved. But the more he thought about it, the more concerned he became for the children of all these couples. What would happen to them? Either they'd be abandoned to foster homes or they'd be brought up in an atmosphere of hatred and abuse, maybe worse. The cruel things the Jenkins guy had said about his child, during every interview, made Jerry want to travel to Albuquerque and thrash the jerk personally. Visions of troubled mixed families ran a bridge over the wall between his conscious and unconscious. It had become so complex, he didn't really know how to feel about the phenomenon. But as Carla, Joey, and Jerry sat in an Atlanta hotel room watching a television news magazine devoted to the subject, a whole new dimension to the controversy came to light. After a number of experts solemnly offered sociological explanations, all variations on a hypothesis of mass hysteria, a Johns Hopkins researcher told about his work with DNA samples from a hundred babies of the "switch phenomenon." Dr. Tien hypothesized that genes had "come unhinged." He didn't understand the physiological mechanism but suggested that the American gene pool had somehow gone over the levees, allowing genes to cross from one individual to another spontaneously, without the usual mechanism of sexual intercourse and offspring.

Jerry laughed and shook his head. "Do you think this guy is making it up?"

Carla stared at the screen. "Does he strike you as the type that jokes around?" She turned and contemplated Joey's profile, a marvel of genetic chance, put her hand on his arm. Joey's eyes couldn't focus on the TV screen, seemed to be following something outside the window. When she looked to see if there were birds, she could see nothing but buildings and sky.

Recognizing the intimacy between Joey and Carla, Jerry felt the old queasiness again—anger and then guilt over being angry. He tried to make out the contours under Carla's loose sleeveless dress. What kind of child was she carrying? If Tien was right, the whole thing was up for grabs. He wondered how much you could find out with an ultrasound examination, but didn't dare mention his idea to Carla. She wouldn't even talk about marriage yet. Was this the modern way, have the baby first and then decide whether or not to make it official?

After the program was over, Carla got up and turned off the television, took Joey by the hand, told Jerry she was going to take a walk, get some fresh air, and look for a park. The coalition organizer watched them leave, then lay back on the rumpled bed. Walking sounded like a good idea, but he didn't have the energy for it. He'd been spending most of his time in hotel rooms, setting things up for Walker's speeches in arenas, amphitheaters, or football stadiums. A lot of work without much exercise, and no pleasant diversions. Until the switch phenomenon had surfaced, Walker had entirely dominated the various media. Now there was another story, but he was sure that it was a related story. Jerry stared at the hotel room's textured ceiling, tried to think of a way for them to make it their issue. He was fading from thought into sleep when the charismatic Lakota walked through the door from her adjoining room. Jerry turned his head lazily, watched her carry in a box, throw it on the coffee table. Her T-shirt accented the impressive flex of her arm muscles.

"Hey, Walker, you ever pump iron?"

She gave him a disgusted look, pointed at the box. "Go through that stuff. There's a bunch of unauthorized pamphlets and posters. Could be a lot of nothing, but on the other hand that'd be the best way for enemies to discredit us—put out junk with our name on it."

Jerry sat up, rubbed his tousled hair. "I thought we didn't have any enemies."

She walked to the door, not bothering to turn around. "Fuck off, Jerry. Just get this done by tonight."

He jumped off the bed. "Wait a second, Walker!" She paused in the doorway. "What about this switch phenomenon thing? The unhinged genes. Have any ideas? I was thinking we could do something with it."

"It's part of what's happening: White Buffalo Calf Woman on every street corner. I've got it under control. Just take care of the stuff in that box." Walker slammed the door behind her.

Jerry walked to the window and moved his eyes over the Atlanta skyline. He could feel them moisten, and the helplessness of that reaction disgusted him. He hated whatever it was that had happened to him. When he made the commitment a couple of months before, how could he have guessed the trouble he'd have with Walker Thompkins? Like everyone else, he'd been caught up in her charismatic wake. She was the perfect guru: iconoclastic but full of positive vision. The day-to-day with her, however, had become intolerable. Jerry noticed how generous she was with people she'd never met before, people on the street, but she treated the coalition organizers like relatives who'd overstayed their welcome. It was time for him to go. Even if Carla didn't want to listen, he decided to talk about it with her when she got back from the walk. Running over the schedule in his mind, he figured most of the advance work for the Tuesday Houston Astrodome appearance was done, and that would take Walker through the next week. Wilbur could take over, or Ethel, or Dierdra. They could all work together and get the job done at least as well as he could. He had no illusions about being indispensable, not anymore.

Back on the bed, staring at the ceiling, trying to clear static from his mind. Searching the corners for some portable light, a reflection of open sky, untethered flight, a way to detox from the anger and meanspiritedness that was strangling him, go back to the optimist he always thought he was. He ignored the soft knocking at the door for several minutes but finally got up and sighted through the peephole. The man outside was holding his face up to the same hole, so Jerry could only catch successive glimpses of eyes, Asian he thought, and swatches of gray, close-cropped hair. He opened the door, and the man walked in, took a seat without invitation.

Jerry sat on the edge of the bed. "Do I know you?"

Wong Fu Gee leaned back and folded his arms. "How can I tell you that? You know Handsome Bear, certainly. But there's a whole list of Travelers you know nothing about; they're making alchemical adjustments, moving spirits back and forth in the pulse you still interpret as time."

Jerry heard a low whirring noise. It began to hurt his ears, but when he covered them with his hands the sound increased. Holding his head, searching for a steady point, he watched the visitor vibrate at a frequency so high his edges blurred. "Do you have anything to do with that noise?"

The gray-haired image came to rest. "Sorry. Sometimes a few adjustments and calibrations are necessary. But all the gates are open now, the circuits at full voltage. It's hard to keep things fine-tuned."

"Does that mean you're a spirit?"

Wong Fu Gee showed his teeth, the closest his face came to a smile. "No, I'm flesh. I'll be with you in this state, on and off, until the Shift is completed."

Jerry looked at the bed to make sure his body wasn't still lying there taking a nap, then turned back to his visitor. The noise was gone, but it had badly wrenched his neural system, and he felt irritable. "Maybe you're talking to the wrong guy. Walker Thompkins is the one in charge now; she's the whole show. If you've got important information, I'd say you should go straight to her. Let me arrange a meeting."

Wong Fu Gee raised his hand. "No reason to talk to Walker. She already knows what's going on."

The van painter noticed the stranger's face was becoming increasingly unstable. There were flashes of feminine beauty beneath the weather-lined skin: a young woman's eyes, cheeks, lips, ears. Jerry felt an urge to reach inside the man's flesh and pull out the woman he saw lurking there. "OK, then. Whoever you are, tell me what I need to know."

"You don't need to know anything. We wanted you to open the gate in Laguna Niguel, and you did a good job. Now you've got to step back. Have you read the book of Revelations? That's the script. Not so much the violent effects, but the new kingdom. Walkingstick wanted to give them what they've been talking about all these years. Those hypocritical Christians fronting for the Death Squad—with a few exceptions, like Saint Francis of Assisi and the liberation theology priests."

Jerry watched the visitor, his red-and-yellow flannel shirt buttoned at the cuffs, leaning elbows on the arms of the chair, shaping hands into a triangle to hold before his eyes. Eyes that looked like they'd been laughing forever. The disheartened coalition organizer tried to find breath for his question, finally pushed it into words. "What am I supposed to do now?"

"Find a new project. Why not something to do with birds and sea creatures, or dream pillows, the relationship between air and human seed? You're a man of imagination, it's up to you."

Jerry noticed that the air in the hotel room was full of suspended glitter, like an exploding firework, or the more subtle shimmer he'd once seen in the upper reaches of Alaska, where the air itself can freeze. The glitter pulsed at the same rate as the visitor; particles of the two merged together. Jerry was afraid the man would fade out before answering his questions. "Don't go yet! Just tell me, are you the one behind the gene switch?"

The constellation Wong Fu Gee had become rose from the chair and moved toward the door. "I know John Walkingstick's plan to release spirits and join them to the living. That's already out there, and you've seen it. I know Tyree Guyton's conjurations. There are others as well. The Shift has passed the pivot point; it can't be reversed. I have no idea who's doing the unhinged genes. I wish I'd thought of it myself. Good luck in your new alchemical studies, young man."

Wong Fu Gee let himself out, pulled the door closed so quietly Jerry couldn't hear the click. The organizer got up from the bed, went to check the door, pulled it open, and looked into the hall.

"Ah, ha! There he is!" Elbows high, Carla was truckin' solo down the fake Persian runner, a comic book smile on her face. Her companion of choice paused to change gears, then leaped dramatically into the hall, hanging his arms and scratching one armpit. Animal noises.

Carla rushed up, circled her arms around his waist and pulled him to her. "Is this the same monkey I left moping in the hotel room? I don't think so. This one has a lot more jazz in his pants." She slipped one hand down the front of his jeans, swatted him on the rear with the other. "A road test is the only way I can find out for sure if this one is mine. What do you think?"

Jerry grunted enthusiastically, directed Carla's hand to his stick shift, backed inside the hotel room with an Italian hillbilly in tow. As they hit the bed, Carla watched high-energy fallout glitter through the air, black and white feathers tumble, then scatter themselves over the carpet.

CHAPTER XVII | # AT THE ASTRODOME

A dome of stars arches over the town named for Sam Houston, an adventurer raised by Cherokees, taught to live in this world with both ally and enemy, pass over the plant he wanted twice before taking the third, ask permission of the small forest people before touching anything. Of course, power lingers there in Houston, even after all these years, but not where the Johnson Space Center assembles teams to calculate moon shots, or take aim at planets and stars. Oil rigs that surround this city built on stars rip through the crusty mantle, suck out enough liquid to fuel the greed machine another few months. Back at the Space Center, scientists and politicians consult on how to fire tin cans filled with human confusion into earth orbit or beyond, veering toward the crystalline Network of stars. The dome in this city is named for astral projection, but in the fall the athletic team that plays there is called the Oilers, not the Astros. Stars are often talked about but hard to see in Houston.

The city of Houston tour guide makes no mention of John Walkingstick's master plan, nor the location of his activities here. At his unofficial space center he researches destined links among the real players: humans, animals, plants, and stars. His Great Work is near completion. He's on line with Tyree Guyton and Wong Fu Gee: alchemical transformations, the conjurations of light. No official updates from this Houston control, just a lot of hard dream-work, day and night. There's sweat behind the eyes of various creatures he employs: the Night Bird, the dragon, and a legion of their assistants. Teeth are on edge, skins burst with the ripeness of knowledge, *connaissance*. Louisiana drops the west end of its bayous on Houston's back porch. If you stand at that boundary, you can hear gates opening: new harmonics, the multiple vibratos of plant songs that heal the damage plotted by animals in their just anger over human rapacity. Bears will be the last to forgive, but the time for reconciliation has come. Not far from the Astrodome, Walkingstick reimagines a time of common language, before humans were thrown out of the family of creatures and revenge began. Stomp dances, staged for the retrieval of old stories, illuminate veins inside the memory dome, lines traced by shooting stars. There are links between all sentient beings, whether rooted in the ground or mobile on air, earth, or water. They are the children of the Network, transcending the apparent difference between animal and vegetable, climbing up the mountain into a universal frequency, the Mind of God.

Drawings anthropologists call petroglyphs decorate the inside of this dome—not the steel structure built to keep rain off football games, but the larger one that mimics it, covers all of Sam Houston's city. This structure is the rotated arch of our collective imagination, blueprints for entry into the next world, the fifth one that will arrive with the Great Millennial Shift. The gates are open, and this time we'll all be ridden. Secrets will be revealed and eaten like the bread of fulfilled prophesy. Bridges, tunnels, and passages will join every corner of the sky—wires, struts, and beams transparent as night. The eagle and hawk instructing, foxglove and slippery elm reciting to stones and bears. Clouds on the horizon at sunset, clouds of stars at night: they release clusters of lonesome spirits eager to reinhabit flesh, full speech, and breath. Stored for over a century in Walkingstick's cave, they've finally come home.

Dr. Babs drove into the Houston outskirts thinking about her mission. It was right in her daily planner: "Wednesday, November 14—put a number on Walker Thompkins at the Astrodome, stop the coalition dead in its tracks." Babs had spent two weeks studying under Queen Matilda in New Orleans. The professor from Midwestern State was impressed; she'd seen and heard things you could never find in books. It was glorious to learn about the gods of blood and mammon. Matilda would sit in her darkened dining room, lay palms flat on the oak table, make it shift and jump, chant an overwhelming mass of information from between the pages of those stacked papers, magazines, and phone books. The power of the experience was so seductive, the professor felt her panties moisten, touched her skirt to make sure it wasn't soaking through. Names and numbers marched across the floor and up onto the candlelit table. Dr. Babs was convinced she was watching a voodoo Disney animation. Queen Matilda crooned on, explaining how people were numbers and numbers were money when merged and assessed by the right personnel using the right program. Put numbers on numbers, turn blood into gold. Matilda raised her hands, threw her head back and screamed, opened her throat and channeled an opaque guttural language. The mambo pulled her dress up around her hips, took a straight razor from the table, cut the insides of both thighs. Lifting head and eyes, a drunken smile invited Babs to join her, "bleed and do the darkness" too. The novice was so excited when she cut herself, juice from her crotch ran down the inside of her thighs to mix with blood. Who was this Freydis, the Blood Queen, speaking through Matilda's mouth? In all her lectures, Dierdra McDonald had never mentioned such an orisha. Maybe her existence was too deep a secret for public consumption. Or maybe the Blood Queen was a power even Dierdra didn't know about. The idea that she, a fresh initiate, a small new leaf on the voodoo tree, might know things Dierdra did not, pleased Dr. Babs immensely.

The box holding the curse sat next to her on the car seat. She'd seen its contents when Queen Matilda sealed it the night before: two red feathers, a newborn's mummified right hand and nose, graveyard dirt, a piece of red-and-gold cloth with elaborately interwoven symbols, most of which Dr. Babs had never seen before. And poured over it all, a heavy oil that stunk of putrefaction. Now that the box had been sealed, there was no trace of that horrific smell, the leakage of waterlogged caskets. The midwestern professor had wondered if she could put up with it on the trip but was so eager to please her new mentor that she refused to worry about details. The box was also much heavier than it had been before, but she assumed that was the burgeoning weight of the curse, the power of blood and mammon to overtake enemies and destroy them. Babs had been somewhat troubled by the choice of target for this curse. She'd admired Walker Thompkins from the beginning, when she'd surfaced earlier that summer and become the coalition's leader. The South Dakota charismatic was a feminist's dream. She told the truth about everything, especially how women felt, in spite of repercussions—made no compromises with the dominant male hierarchy. After admiring Walker's weatherworn pair, Dr. Babs had even bought herself a pair of cowboy boots. But Queen Matilda had revealed the conspiracy behind the coalition, added weight and logic to the Houston mission, the opportunity to prove herself worthy of further instruction in the Mysteries. The New Orleans mambo said Walker Thompkins was the mouthpiece for a foreign power that wished to destroy the economic and social stability of the United States. The very fact that Walker was so appealing necessitated quick action, before the damage became irreversible.

Dr. Babs hit the brakes as traffic in the fast lane suddenly slowed. Her hand reached to catch the box on the passenger side, but even in the sudden deceleration it did not shift. As she tried to lift her hand from the box, Babs felt the pulse of a force so enormous, so fierce, it could be caged only in a closed canyon, an abandoned salt dome filled with crude oil, a silo of nuclear missiles directed at every living thing in the world. The hand she lifted from the box felt unwhole, partially decayed. She looked at it, expecting flesh to fall away, as it did from the bones of victims at Hiroshima and Nagasaki. She lifted the hand to her nose and smelled death, then raised her eyes, saw the squat monster of the Astrodome.

Transmissions cranking through power lines in the Travelers' Network, ionizing the air around Houston. If you looked into the sky, you might discern a smoke ring or halo, a tease at the edges of second sight. But Death Squad minions are stationed at points of interception. They're setting up line taps, planting ingenious bugs in the system, using even the best of the coalition as mules to smuggle darkness into the realm of light. Neanderthal code talkers work counterespionage along the sacred frequencies, redirect transmissions into the five hues of sound and light. But slips are inevitable. There have been intelligence leaks at the convergence of threads that weave to determine the dream. The cactus vision prepared the way. Before hauling those Fusang agave treasures back to China a millennium and a half ago, Hui Shen, the lotus preacher, moved across the desert, heard the same thunder walkers that now stroll along this Texas horizon, dancing with twisters, a wind that steals both breath and memory through your eyes. Look away, pray to the merciful rose for safe passage, squeeze through the slots that hide within unmarked coordinates between the six directions, their edgeways snaking, inference and permutation, complex variables offering sudden windows through darkness or in light. There's some serious trucking on the big Network power lines: spirit freight and convergence, the lost frequencies that loop tunnels and passages through earth, air, and water. They mend and reweave by interpenetration, make their flights invisible to everything but harmonic fire.

Travelers sing the sacred directions, clusters of quarter tones pulling the future into place. They compose psalms on the Shift and its integration of all elements: star fire, flesh, bones, and sinews; constellations of rock, water, and air in their various illuminations; the crawlers, leapers, striders, and swimmers that arch bridges through clouds and air, guide us along perpetual rainbow vectors. Work songs and sleep songs, dreamtime construction and recovery. Fill the universe with song, dissolve static information and chunks of dead energy the Death Squad uses to strangle memory channels like cholesterol, block vessels and tribal interconnections until the mind implodes. Silence the psychic jammers who work for Radio Free Death.

J. P. Morgan has sent a high-level delegation to Space City, and they're preparing for a showdown with Walker Thompkins and the coalition gang. There's Chester Long, Orange County District Attorney, who has completed his metamorphosis into J. Edgar Hoover, the Master's bastard son. He stands before a full-length mirror in his Hilton suite, trying to decide between his naughty red dress and a more tasteful black knit. At the insistence of Thomas Edison, the master of black boxes, Morgan has called in a key Disney executive. He's already made his connection in Memphis, and is the first to step off Northwest #795 at Houston Hobby. Derwood Wall and his insecurity force have arrived by Lear jet, on loan from a consortium of Southern California developers. Imperfecto Ruiz squats in the Astrodome parking lot beside his '75 Ford Granada, the authorized biography of Pope Pius XII open on his knees. Media people, working blood and doing their own darkness, fly in from everywhere, accumulate frequent-flyer miles and premium points on their gold cards. There are others here beyond human recognition. No one has the whole list.

Carla and her favorite Neanderthal companion sat in the front row of the VIP section, rows of metal chairs facing the elevated speaker's platform. Carla smoothed the big collar on Joey's shirt—actually more of a smock—ran a hand down its large vertical red and green stripes. Since she'd made it for him, he didn't want to wear anything else, except of course his trademark baggy denim overalls and custom-fit leather sandals. The Patchouli healer scraped his sandals against the floor, was amazed all over again at the number and variety of his toenails, then looked up in surprise at the massive crowd filling the arena seats. Carla continued to smooth his clothes, speak soothingly in his ear. She'd never seen him this edgy before. Usually he'd find something to groove on and get lost in it, quietly entertain himself until she came to escort him away. For the last hour his hands had shaken and fluttered uncontrollably, had risen up and bumped at the limits of his arm span, birds trying to fly out of a locked cage. Carla kissed him on the cheek, held his neck in the crook of one arm, and cradled her swollen belly with the other.

Checking the speaker's platform, the specialist on Mongolia saw Dierdra and Ethel, waved to catch their eyes, but gave up when she saw that their heads were turned in the opposite direction, waiting for Walker to appear at the west end of the arena. No one saw Dr. Babs coming, carrying a wooden box painted like a gift package from Nieman Marcus. The pleats of her red-and-white checked dress swung back and forth as she sashayed down the aisle. If anyone noticed this new blood lady, there was no show of interest, not even from the security guards with their heavy looks and red armbands. Suddenly the crowd shouted, jumped up, and swayed toward the entry tunnel, where a troop of New Orleans Mardi Gras Indians made their grand entry, dancing around and around Walker as they escorted her toward the podium. A band and thundering second line rhythm section struck up "Iko Iko." They were talking about hey now, hey now, whooping on the holiday, about a host of testifying grandmas and how they were going to set flags on fire. After a couple of choruses, most of the crowd joined in. The Mardi Gras Indians whirled, high-stepped, leaped into splits, backed by a second line of eighty thousand: singing, cheering, sending up a thunderous stomp with their feet.

It was time to get drunk on Walkman words and ideas again. She could quote the New Testament, Wovoka, or renditions of tribal stories, sometimes all in the same sentence. "If your daughter asked for a fish, would you give her a snake, or keep the snake for truth, make its eggs hatch into millennium?" She'd demand a list of good things corporations have done for people—facts, not what they've promised or suggested in television and magazine ads. "Burn the tree that won't bear good fruit, can't tell the truth. Burn the tree that can't sing the Song of Creation." In the air over the eager crowds she'd build invisible cities, retribalize them, start communal organic farms in collapsed and burnt-out pockets of old cities, return parks to native wilderness, replace the widening rings of urban blight with waves of regeneration. "Let the forests begin where the centers of our cities died." She described the journey from butterfly to snake, the way the two could make love in their double flight, and the holy penetration of sky and earth, how it kept things going. She laughed at the phenomenon of unhinged genes, predicted a majority of American families would soon be identified as mixed-race, said it was too bad it had taken us so long to figure out what Wovoka was saying. No one has to be driven off the continent; it's just that everyone who stays will be different. She sang praise to the invisible, immanent, and everlasting utopia of the present. She sang strange harmonies of astral frequencies, saying, "Who needs the Internet, we have the Network." Walker put talk shows, televangelists, late nights, and soaps almost out of business. Who could compete with her? The thunder of dance, song, and anticipation rocked the Astrodome.

Ethel grabbed Dierdra by the elbow, yelling against the noise, pointed out George Johnson, chief of the Wild Magnolias, leading his gang in a celebration of brother and sisterhood. He was the charming man they'd met at the White Rose Inn during Mardi Gras. In the whirl of fine white breath feathers that covered the dancers' bodies, Dierdra could not make him out, but as she pulled back in an attempt to resight along Ethel's pointing arm, Dr. Babs and her box tugged at the corner of her eye. The neophyte mambo was turning down the aisle that separated the seats from the speaker's platform. As Babs cruised toward the podium, a spectator from the VIP section jumped up and danced with her, spun her around, box and all. Dierdra pulled at Ethel's shoulder, redirected her attention from the tumultuous grand entry to the unexpected appearance of their colleague. Carla saw Dierdra gesturing, waved back, raised Joey's hand as if he were a victorious prizefighter. She and her Neanderthal friend did not see Queen Matilda's delivery girl and the package as it crossed their field of vision. When Dierdra glimpsed a skeleton, a momentary flash beneath Dr. Babs's flesh, she jumped down the steps of the platform, walked with tremendous strides toward the intruder. Queen Matilda's protégé was hoisting the box to slide it onstage when she spotted Dierdra closing on her. Two security guards ran down the center aisle. The messenger girl clutched the box to her chest, arms paralyzed with its heavy energy, turned, and began to run back the way she came. A flash and concussion took the dome's breath away, dropped it from joy to oblivion. Dierdra was lifted off her feet, sailed lazily back toward the speaker's platform, moving so slowly she could count the flying chairs and bodies in midair, two or three times over. There was smoke and silence for a long second or a short minute, or maybe this impenetrable thickness of air was completely out of time. Then a sudden rupture, sound and motion returned—screaming and a mad scramble along the floor and up through the arena. The seats and spectators on the left side of the VIP section had been blown back fifty feet, and were mounded in a small hill of tangled metal and body parts. All that was left of Dr. Babs were bits of red checked fabric.

Jerry, who'd been sitting with the sound panel operators behind the stage, was slammed to the floor, his legs taken out by a chair that shot under the speaker's platform. Torn wires sparking around him, he got to his hands and knees in the shattered glass, tried to expand his damaged ribs and draw in breath. Finally he stood, stumbled around the buckled platform toward the center of the Astrodome's wound. Walker fought through the scattering crowd, sprinted toward ground zero. She and Jerry arrived at the same time.

He fell to his knees before the heap, cried out for Carla, began to tug at a woman's leg, naked and bent the wrong way. Jerry collapsed on the disarticulated leg and moaned.

Walker gave him a boot kick in the hip. "Get the fuck up, Martinez. People are alive in there. Can't you hear them?"

Security guards and state police were moving into the tangle, trying to separate chairs from people, a game of grotesque pickup sticks. Jerry lay still, face into the floor, an empty high-heel shoe inches from his neck. He continued to moan, felt cold move from the center of his chest and creep into every limb. His spirit looked down from above, saw a painting of his body, heart cut out of his chest, held high in the air by a bloody hand. The hand belonged to a gray-haired man wearing a striped morning coat, vest, and scarlet cravat. His walrus moustache released a groan of joy, the song of J. P. Morgan's last triumph.

Walker refused to talk to reporters for two days after the bombing but finally agreed to a brief press conference in the lobby of Ben Taub General Hospital. After she'd finished with the reporters, Jerry caught up with her walking down a hospital corridor, pushed her into the wall. She was unprepared for the attack, but regaining balance, she whirled, whipped a leg against the backs of his knees, and brought him to the floor.

"What are you trying to do, you crazy bastard?"

He lay there, clenched teeth, hands over face. Catching his breath, he screamed, "You're the bastard! How can you tell those reporters this is a victory? The end of the Death Squad! Carla's the one who's dead. Did you miss that somehow?"

Walker leaned over, grabbed Jerry by the collar of his jacket, and pulled the sobbing man to his feet. "Shut up. I'm not going to fight with you out here in the hall. Just shut up for a second. Let's find a place where we can talk."

They walked to the lounge, but it was filled with family and friends of the victims, still stunned and waiting for a new story that would give them hope. The death count was five, including Joey and Carla, with many more critically injured, barely hanging on. Down the hall Walker found an empty linen closet, pushed Jerry in, closed the door, and turned on the light.

"Want to fight me now? Punch away. This'll be the best chance you ever get."

Jerry leaned back against a stack of towels, his arms at his sides. "I can't believe how cruel you are. Nothing means anything to you. Where's the baby? Those doctors said there was no baby inside Carla."

Walker took off her leather jacket and threw it against the door. "What do you want me to do, scratch my face bloody and pull out my hair?" She dug her fingernails into her cheeks and left claw marks as she pulled them downward. "There, how's that? Do I care as much as you now? Damn it, Martinez, Joey's dead, too. I loved Joey, and I loved Carla. I'm sorry about the baby. You said yourself we wouldn't get through this without casualties. It could've just as easily been you that got blown to pieces; and you know they meant the bomb for me."

"I was talking with them about five minutes before, then went over to the sound panel. It should have been me in that pile." Jerry let his back slide down the stack of towels until he was sitting on the closet floor. "It didn't have to be Carla. Why did they have to take her?"

Walker squatted, pushed Jerry's head back. "Listen, I know it's going to take a long time before you pull back from this. Just accept that. No matter what you do, it's not going to get better until you're finally ready to move on." Jerry fixed her with a furious look, began to twist his mouth into speech, but Walker covered it with her hand. "Now, just shut up. Listen to me. I don't want to hear any more about how cruel I am. This was the last battle, and we've almost won. Even if you wanted to sabotage everything right now, you couldn't. You think Carla would like you fucking up all the stuff we've been trying to do?"

Jerry pushed her hand away from his mouth. "You heartless son of a bitch."

The coalition leader pushed her hand back over the assistant's mouth. "Shut up and listen. I'm going to Dallas next week. No cancellations. Are you hearing this? Everybody's going to be watching now to see what happens. You don't need to worry about the Dallas date, I'll take care of that. But I want you to fly back to L.A. with the bodies. Do you understand what I'm saying to you?"

Jerry looked into her eyes, confused. His raised one hand to his forehead, then dropped it.

"You understand you've got to take care of the arrangements for both Joey and Carla. They're not going to be forgotten. I don't believe in heroes, but that's exactly what's going to happen. Understand? What I want you to do is arrange for a big outdoor meeting in Watts, the place where they bulldozed all the houses for that big project. I don't think anybody's going to give you trouble on it. Set everything up for the week after next, Thanksgiving week. Set it up on Thanksgiving."

Jerry watched as Walker stood up, moved to the door. He stuttered. "You mean you're going to give the memorial service yourself?"

"Yeah, why not? Who better? Listen, you've been carrying some bad shit against me for a while now, but you've got to let it go. The stuff on Joey, too. He saved both you and Carla, even though you didn't know it."

Getting up on one knee, Jerry made a gesture of dismissal. "What kind of bullshit are you talking about?"

Walker squatted down again. "You're always talking about Hopis. Now I'm going to give you a Hopi story. There was a young guy who was crazy about this widow. But she loved her dead husband so much, she decided never to get married again. Being a persistent type, the young guy finally talked her into it. Unfortunately, a witch, one of the guys she had turned down, hated how happy they were and made her deathly sick. The new husband did everything he could to save his wife, but she died at the end of the second day of her sickness. But he didn't want to let go, so he chased her spirit through the brush as it traveled to the otherworld, shredding his skin in the process. He ran at full speed for two whole days, all the way to the land of the dead, and only at the very end did he lose sight of his wife. When he finally got there, he saw her with the first husband. They were hugging each other, happy to be together again. That sight gave the young guy such terrible pain, he went back to the land of the living and began a new life."

Jerry looked at Walker, tried to speak, but couldn't.

Walker leaned her hands against both of his shoulders. "Listen, we don't have time for self-indulgence and jealousy. Leave Joey alone, and let Carla go. Things are working for us, the gates are all open, but it's not finished yet. Set up the L.A. date. That's where it's going to happen."

Walker stood, shut off the light, and left Jerry in his darkness. He reached up, felt around, grabbed the binding strap on a stack of towels and tried to pull himself up. But the strap broke and the towels collapsed, knocking him flat on his back. He pushed them away from his face, spit out lint that tasted like chlorine bleach, then relaxed and took a deep breath of hospital sterility. The weight of the towels on his body and the darkness of the closet began to feel good. This strange embrace released him from so much of his pain, he was drawn into sleep. In a dream he saw Carla and Joey climbing the sheer rocky face of a mountain. Below them white clouds formed a rich carpet. Jerry called out to his woman and her companion in his dream, but either they didn't hear or they simply ignored him and continued their ascent. The next morning, he told Walker about his vision. After a long silence, she gave him the story he needed. "We're moving toward the invisible city, but Joey and Carla are already there."

After sighting the butte that rose from the middle of the canyon of their birth, Handsome Bear and Cold Moon Fire ran at top speed. Their gear bounced furiously as they sprinted, eyes enraptured, drawing light from the monument at the center of the sun people's world, where ancestors still kept vigil, marking solstices and other measures of time. When she surged ahead of him on the southwest road, he made no attempt to keep up with her, deciding to let her arrive first, tell the people anything she wanted to say— that she was Bear Caller, that Handsome Bear was an imposter, a witch who brought death with him wherever he went. He watched her run, pulling away, drawing on the power of her youth, even though she'd now passed a long way beyond girlhood. Cold Moon Fire tripped on a clump of sage brush growing through the road, caught herself with one hand and the opposite foot as she hit the earth, bounced, then regained her stride and accelerated. They were under Beautiful Village's sky now, different from any other in the world. It was the deep polished blue of turquoise, the blue of their sky's infinite longing.

As Handsome Bear ran behind Cold Moon Fire, he watched her, wondered if her spirit, the one that had been lost on the jade kingdom sailing ship, would return to her when she saw home again. She was still convinced she was the leader of his expedition, calling herself Handsome Bear, Bear Caller, telling anyone who listened she was a shaman and memory hero, the only survivor of impossible travels. She'd tried to kill him three times since they'd left the abalone people's village. The concentration necessary to sleep and still remain aware of her movements each night was exhausting, hampering his power to run during the day. She wanted to murder him, even though the healer had saved her life after she attacked Acorn Teeth's daughter, now the mother of four children. The attack had been sexual in nature, and had outraged the chief and his people. Handsome Bear pleaded her insanity and left the village immediately, before they had time to plot against them. To avoid being pursued, he took an alternative route eastward, one that lay to the south of the usual trading paths.

Handsome Bear lagged behind Cold Moon Fire, but his legs were still powerful, his eyes too. Snakes scrambled off the road out of Cold Moon Fire's way—a good omen: welcoming ancestors sunning themselves in the road. Snakes who were not functioning as messengers from the spirits always stayed in the rocks and brush. As he rounded the last turn in the west wall of the canyon, Beautiful Village came into view. The excitement and the strain of running pounded blood against his famous fontanel. Looking for dogs, the Bear Caller tried to pick up their barking as the wind whistled by his ears. Their chorus of yelps at his arrival would bring everyone running to the walls. Cold Moon Fire had already reached the south wall, but there was no sound at all. She threw stones—not at dogs, but coyotes. Handsome Bear ran by his companion without comment, came to a stop when he reached the village's straight front wall. Fragments of a ladder lay scattered in the brush. But no ladder was necessary; one of the arches, which had been filled with dressed stone to keep out marauders, had collapsed. Handsome Bear moved toward the opening, checked hidden angles for possible ambush; then, as he walked through, his fear-knotted stomach relaxed into the nausea of total loss. His eyes witnessed what his inner sight had imaged for most of the trip through the desert: Beautiful Village was no longer a place for the living. It could never be empty of spirits—that scramble of voices just at the edge of hearing—but the clans, his relatives, all the people he knew were gone.

A ladder with two broken rungs reached up to the second level of apartments; it was the only workable one in the village. Handsome Bear had to pull it up after him and use it to reach the next level. As he pulled it up behind him once again, he saw Cold Moon Fire sitting outside the walls, looking toward the butte. He climbed to the third level, made his way over two sections of collapsed wall to his own apartment. It was filled with stones and rubble, mixed with trash—broken pots, disintegrated mats, bones, scraps of cloth, and broken feathers. The plaster he'd used to dress the walls had broken away and scattered across the rubbish. In the few sections where it was still clinging, he could see image fragments from his sacred paintings. On the ceiling one wing of the Night Bird remained, offering inadequate protection over the ruins that lay below. Handsome Bear felt spirits surround him, looked over his shoulder for a glimpse of Sun Girl, or Red Swallow's plump figure disappearing into a doorway. He felt pressed on all sides by overwhelming numbers, a mob of spirits, but when he held his head still and looked, there was nothing. In the jade kingdom he'd finally admitted that his daughter was lost to him. Now he wondered if Bird Grass was alive and with the villagers somewhere else. Maybe out by High Ground River, or south, in the canyons where some of the other clans had settled before he left on his search for the carved axes.

The memory hero climbed down, removing and lowering the ladder from level to level, until he reached the courtyard. He picked up the axes, untied their bindings, removed the cloth that had protected them on the journey. Handsome Bear held them above his head, one in each hand. "I brought these axes back to save you!" He shook the axes in the air, waiting for a miraculous sign. "These are the power axes I swore I'd bring you!" There were no clouds, no thunder, no wind, no signs of reply of any sort; the sky was as empty as the village. He fell to his knees, dropped the axes to the ground, leaned against their hafts. The man felt a desperate need for song, a chant to some benevolent power, if there were any left in this world. But no words or vocables rose through his throat to pass the gate of his teeth. The stillness inside his chest matched the stillness of the strangling dust and filth that surrounded him. Out of the corner of his eye he saw Cold Moon Fire lower herself into a kiva. He started to warn her about the violation but stopped. It was impossible to act as an interpreter of the sacred under these circumstances, and he felt his authority was now gone.

Handsome Bear stared at one of the axe heads, its elegant intertwined patterns. They could be snakes, or plants with the power to heal. He felt the edge with his thumb, found it just as sharp as when he'd wrapped them in the jade kingdom. Sharp enough to cut down a tree or take off a man's head. He looked at his own sorry flesh, caked with dust and dried sweat. It was not hard to imagine how quickly that blade would slice into the flesh, pare it away from the bone, reduce him to a minimal state where there would be no more pain, no more intolerable emptiness. He picked up the axe, prepared to draw the blade over a forearm, but stopped when he saw the green band of light move along the ground and dive into one of the kivas. Jumping up, he took a step in that direction, then whirled to see the face of the apartments on the second level pulsing with purple light. Streaks, walls, rivers of light—rolling balls and fluted columns, humming, crackling with power and life. Handsome Bear was surrounded by a chorus of light. Streaks of it swirled around his arms and legs, made them feel solid and alive again. He wanted to sing, praise the Grandmother, but when he opened his mouth, it was the voice of Eagle Claw that did the singing. "The colors are still here, Handsome Bear. They're here when you see them, and when you can't. In all this desolation, nothing has stopped living."

The sound that had leaped from Handsome Bear's throat stopped, and in the silence he tried to find his own voice and question his uncle. But this was not going to be dialogue: Eagle Claw's voice started up again. "Sleep in the Snake clan kiva tonight, but first put it in order. Say prayers and do things as they should be done."

Handsome Bear was on his knees, his skin and internal organs still tingling. He looked up and saw a few puddles of color left in the abandoned village, but these were the leavings of an earthly sunset. He tried to stand but couldn't move his legs. Rolling on one hip, he pushed them out, pounded blood into his thighs, flexed stiff muscles until they could do what he wanted. He called out for Cold Moon Fire, searched for her inside the walls and without. Finally he convinced himself that she'd gone, probably toward High Ground River to find village people, living creatures who would know her. It was a relief. Handsome Bear used the one ladder in the village to enter the Snake clan kiva. He called out, "Light on your hands and face," before entering, but there was no reply. Once inside, he cleared debris from the floor and the circular bench that ringed the kiva, smoothed the sand with a long flat piece of wood. He did his best to reconstruct the altar, planting the handles of both axes on either side of it, their blades facing each other, made a large *paho* with feathers and string he'd found blown into niches around the courtyard. When it was too dark to see, he lay on the stone bench and fell asleep.

Handsome Bear woke up, saw the window of dawn that entered the kiva roof. He stared at it. It seemed like a moon, or a sun sickened by the kind of mist wind walkers bring with them. He thought he was in the dragon's sea for a moment, but dropped his hand to the sandy floor and was reassured. A flush of happiness at realizing he was home passed over him, until he remembered the circumstances. Beautiful Village had become the boneyard he'd foreseen in the axe dream years ago. He wondered how many years it had been—after counting, he knew the singers of the sun people had saved the world from darkness eight times since he'd left. It didn't seem like enough time for such an enormous change. When he climbed the ladder out of the kiva, he looked across the courtyard; it was still rubble and trash, just as it had been the day before. The memory hero hung on the longer pole of the ladder, not wanting to step back into the cruel dream.

Her strange voice clattered in his ears, then echoed in sun people language. "Don't be despondent. What you see here doesn't matter the way you think it does."

Handsome Bear turned his head, saw the Chinese woman sitting on a wooden stool a few paces from the kiva entrance, arms wrapped around knees, a light like blue water shimmering over her body. At first he thought it was Ping Shang-lien, tried to greet her in Chinese, but the woman replied that he wasn't speaking her dialect. He looked again, realized the face was different—younger, and at the same time possessed by a hovering gray shadow under the skin. Her clothes were different, like the strange tight-fitting clothes the painter wore, the one he'd spoken to in another time, crossing over walls of light in his dream. On the lobes of her ears this woman wore dancing jade monkeys. Shang-lien was magical, but she never wore living jewelry. Suddenly he was afraid Cold Moon Fire really possessed the shapeshifting powers she'd bragged about in her madness, among the abalone people and on the trip home across mountains and desert. "Who are you? What happened to Cold Moon Fire?"

She laughed a garbled laugh. "Gone to find the living. You know that. I'm here because of the act you're about to commit."

Handsome Bear stepped off the ladder onto the ground, walked a few steps toward the woman, then squatted, chanting quietly to himself. He considered the possibility of witchcraft and remained cautious. "All I want to do is to find my people."

As the sun rose higher and shone more strongly on the woman, her hair grew shorter and grayer, the face more sinewy and bony. Out of the blur of change emerged Wong Fu Gee, looking just a little to one side of Handsome Bear as he spoke. "You think your expedition was a failure because no one is here."

Handsome Bear sat on his heels. Rather than being shocked by the age and gender transformation he'd just witnessed, he now seemed more at ease. "I know you're not an ancestor, so you must be from the coming time."

"No, I've always been here. That's why you recognize me, in both my male and female forms. The point where we stand, this calibration people read as time, is a bridge. Cross it now, voluntarily, and you'll put such a load on the Network circuits, a surge so large, that the Shift that has always been happening, always on the verge of happening, will wrap the seed of human grief with new flesh and skin. A redemptive incarnation. This time the colors of that skin will have a more miraculous configuration than your sacred corn."

Handsome Bear scrutinized the wiry alchemist, wondered how their powers would match up if it came to a fight. He hadn't forgotten the comment about the act someone wanted him to commit. "I know about redemption. That's why I went to the jade kingdom for the snake-carved axes."

Wong Fu Gee shook his head. "You went in the wrong direction. You dreamed about Vikings, not Chinese. But in this world there are no mistakes; the way you led your expedition was exactly right. Now you need to finish your travel by opening yourself, making a perpetual beginning that will move stale blood out of the limbs that have become sickened and weak, push new blood into the heart."

Handsome Bear stood up. "Are you asking me to sacrifice my heart and blood? With all the people I've lost, do you think I'd be afraid of that?"

Wong Fu Gee stood too, and his image split and tipped to one side, then rejoined and righted itself. "I'm not asking you to die. Just a diaspora of those packets of energy you've been reading as flesh, a scattering of seed. A redistribution." The alchemist reached out his hand, and blue light pulsed beyond it. As Handsome Bear took a step back, Wong Fu Gee cautioned him. "This won't work if you think it is a defeat, the end of everything."

The memory hero scanned the ruins and in the shadowed doorways saw familiar faces: Sun Girl and Bird Grass; all the relatives, friends, and enemies of his life; the guiding ancestors who lived lives before him. Together their voices were the speaking wind: mournful, but full of excited energy. Sun Girl stepped out the door of their ruined apartment, held palms up in a gesture of encouragement, asking her husband to cross the bridge. The Bear Caller knew it would be a sudden walk on a lightning path. Standing with his back turned a few paces from Wong Fu Gee, the thought of witchcraft came back, but he dismissed it. He knew these spirits were true ones, had come to tell him Beautiful Village was gone, that there was no place for him to travel in this world. Handsome Bear faced Wong Fu Gee, stepped forward, and touched the light. His eyes washed a pure scalding white, then the white congealed into a sphere, rolled once around the top of the kiva, and soared over the broken village wall. Wind swirled around him; as he filled with that wind, he grew larger and more diffuse, a pulsing cluster of fireflies. It was joyous, ecstatic disintegration. In every particle of his body refined knowledge and perception: each increment possessed an eye different from every other. There was no way to sort and process these infinite points of view, but he understood the simultaneous possibilities, and that he existed in all of them. Knowledge exploded in the sacred six directions, passed through all divisions of the material world. It was a diaspora of time. Curving to conform to the Network lines, his presence was about to arrive and was already there. If people could see as the magpie speaks, they'd know the promised Shift had already come, and was named Handsome Bear.

CHAPTER XVIII

THE LOTUS, THE CACTUS, AND THE CRIMSON ROSE

Robert Johnson had been traveling for kalpas through immeasurable worlds. He dismounted a freight train near L.A. Chinatown, tracked the long boulevards down to Watts. Guitar strapped to back, cattle grits on the lapels, cuffs, and knees of his pinstriped suit, snakeskin shoes scarred from leaps into roadbed cinders, the greatest bluesman of this world or any other was in L.A. looking for Eagle Peak. He'd heard about the coalition powwow on Thanksgiving Day, the gathering of the tribes, had come all the way from Commerce, Mississippi, to see it for himself. This trip could have been in 1938, or through the fires and broken glass of 1965, but here he was at the finish of the millennium, the butt end of the boss man's dream. Useless, though, to talk about dates, lay them in a line like that, as if the great wheel of the universe did not

constantly turn back on itself. R. L. had known about the impossi-
bility of time since his ostensible death. Stated causes of that
illusion: poisoned whiskey, a knife slipped between the ribs, a
nasty number laid on by an evil-hearted woman, or the collapse
of an exhausted soul. When poor Bob moved his guitar from one
shoulder to the other, the earth trembled. Took three more steps,
hand on his black cat bone. A finishing jolt and the temblor was
over. In the aftermath, a dance of dust in air, a subtle scent of
sandalwood. He could feel the spirits gathering.

The mangled dog who'd shadowed him since Chinatown
trotted by his side, looked out the corner of its eye for a sign of
approval. But it scampered away as the troubadour pushed down
one foot, spun on that leg, landed with hands on knees. It was halt
and parade rest in the big-city ghetto. Bob's toes found Eagle Peak,
curled over the cliff at the edge of beginning. Good Lord have
mercy.

Old R. L. knew the realm toward which his births and deaths
were tending. He'd learned that words betray the sacred emptiness, the hole in the middle of all singing that is the pure reservoir
of truth. Not the hole power lines burn in the middle of your
favorite song: that's Death Squad–style bitter absence, not lotus
plentitude. Moving along the street toward the liquor store on the
corner, felt in his pockets for the key to that delight. They were full
of seashells, alms from the god of the sea. If he'd never been here
before, why did his feet recognize the street they traveled on? Like
the small roads that run between rows of ripe cotton in Mississippi,
or the one that leads to the abattoir, snaky guide to the blood
bucket at the heart of every city in the world. Broken bottles in the
gutter, he stooped, pushed back his hat, squinted and twisted his
head, tried to read the labels, see what Californians drank. Looked
up to palm trees, their untrimmed, sun-bleached fronds clinging
to trunks in a thousand deaths. The trees leaned at random,
loitered here and there in casual disgust. Then there were the
stunted, beat-up jacarandas, dusty oleanders, scruffy clumps of
jasmine spilling over the earth under iron-barred windows. All
these savior plants, with their mission to deliver humans from
suffering, living in disguise as neglect and degradation. Nonetheless, they directed their scents and seed toward heaven and the
king of trees.

Leaning his back against the black grate that stretched across the liquor store's window, man in a tight-fitting suit and lambskin cossack hat: Thelonious Monk on the job, scouting the area for Travelers. He offered Robert a swig from his pint of Chivas, all snugged up in a paper bag. "Sweet and smooth," remarked the newly arrived troubadour, wiping his chin with a cotton hanky. The bluesman traveled neat and proper, saw where he was going, knew how to choose his company. When their mutual *connaissance* first broke into words, they assessed the trembling weather, warm-up embraces between earth and sky. Was it the big one or just a sign? They talked hotlines, hidden frequencies, the coming together and adjustments that had to be made. They were voice hearers, meditating on the twelve-linked chain of causation, on the law of tranquil extinction. Old R. L. pulled his guitar from its canvas case, played "Stop Breakin' Down Blues," and beat its hollow body like the dharma drum.

Monk took the last swallow from his bottle, looked down the street where coalition enthusiasts were gathering in an area cleared for new projects. They waited for Walker Thompkins to arrive and preach the Lotus of the Wonderful Law. Turned back to Robert, dropped the empty to the sidewalk with a muffled shattering. "Maitreya, understand this. In all those lives turning on the Great Wheel, Bodhisattva Wonderfully Bright was nobody else but me myself. And Bodhisattva Seeker of Fame was you."

Jerry dodged shoulders and arms, sidled through the crowd, past tables and stands set up to sell Joey and Carla T-shirts in different designs and colors. There were also posters, the most interesting of which was a psychedelic elaboration of Carla hugging Joey, her inaccurately long hair transformed into blossoming tendrils as it looped around his right arm and shoulder. Hand-stitched banners with likenesses of the two martyrs, appropriate for hanging over the front door or from the second story of a house, were offered at an elaborate kiosk decorated with Coca-Cola signs. Jerry looked at the piles of banners that were, as advertised, handmade. He wondered what L.A. sweatshops had forced people to work around the clock to make so many on such short notice. Angry and sick to his stomach, he considered making a scourge, lashing these charlatan spirit merchants, overturning their tables, driving them out of the temple. But there were too many of them, and he had no time. The event was entirely under his supervision; he hadn't heard directly from Walker for over a week.

The crowd swarmed around the sales booths, wound around the encampments of the faithful, some having arrived the day before to get a spot close to the speakers' platform. The crowd looked happy and manic rather than mournful, even though the event had been advertised as a memorial for those who died in the Houston bombing; and it seemed even bigger than the strange coming together that transformed the Crown Valley Parkway in Laguna Niguel. The mood surprised Jerry, made him wonder if Walker was right and the Death Squad had really been defeated. There were also lines of portable toilets and hundreds of police in riot gear. People in lawn chairs, on blankets and newspapers spread across the expanse of cleared ground. If you'd been riding in television helicopters, or in the Goodyear blimp dispatched from its base by a Carson oil refinery, you could have seen the formation of human lotus petals around the central platform. The thrust of the flower was radiant expectation.

Reporters had been chasing Jerry all week, asking him if it was true Walker Thompkins was going to make a momentous announcement at the Thanksgiving Day gathering. He'd heard the rumors too, in the papers and within the organization, but had no idea if they were accurate or not. Walker, communicating with him through go-betweens, had mentioned nothing.

As he moved through the crowd, coalition supporters stopped him, pulled him into hugs, expressed their condolences over the loss of Carla. One woman pressed her teary face into his neck. Moments later, after he'd shaken her off, a man walked up, mumbled a few words, and shook his hand. He was dressed in denim shirt and pants, wore a baseball cap with the name of an extermination company printed above the bill. He sure looked to Jerry like an angry white male, but since the Houston bombing, even the people who'd previously raged against affirmative action and illegal immigration had begun to show up at the rallies. As the cameras played over the crowd at the Dallas rally the week before, Jerry could see that the impossible had happened. They were the last piece of the puzzle, the final words necessary to decode the new map's legend.

Within fifty yards of the speakers' platform, pushing toward his final checkdown in preparation for Walker's arrival, he kept eyes on the ground, hoping people would resist the temptation to commiserate with him. A firm hand on his shoulder halted his progress. As he turned and began to apologize for being too busy to talk, he realized it was Larry Smith.

"There sure are a lot of cops. How did that happen?"

Jerry slapped his forehead. "Are you kidding? These guys show up whether you want them or not. They were telling me there's going to be gang trouble. Which is bullshit, of course."

Larry leaned toward Jerry and spoke in a low voice. "Do you know where Walker is? Something came up I think she should know about."

"I've got no idea where she is. Haven't talked to her for a week. You know she'll probably make some grand entry at the last minute. I don't know how she's going to top the five thousand Catholic nuns and Buddhist monks in Dallas, but I'm not betting she won't try."

Ethel Wright walked up, lifted Jerry's left hand, and pressed a note into it. She smiled, shook her head, turned, then walked away. Jerry opened the piece of paper, stared at it, then excused himself, pushed to the edge of the platform, climbed it, signaled for the mike to be turned on.

"OK, people. Is this thing on? Can you hear me?" Whistles and laughter. "I have an important announcement, a message from Walker." Chants for the leader began to move through the crowd. "Just listen to me. I'll read what she's written here."

> I hear you're waiting for me to tell you something, but you should talk to each other instead. Look at yourselves. You're the miracle, the Shift, the thing itself. The battle's over—even the one who carried the bomb in Houston helped the transformation. Look at all the faces here and watch the changes. You don't need my parade anymore. Good-bye. It's over, and it's just beginning to happen. We're breaking in on the next world.

The crowd moaned when they realized Walker wasn't coming. By the time Jerry finished reading the note, there were waves of agitated human sound bouncing back and forth across the gathering. He held his hands over his head. "Listen to her. She's right. You're the important ones, not her or me or any other single person."

He'd barely gotten the words out when it hit. Everywhere the Buddha world quaked and trembled in six different ways. The sky blew the conch of the Great Law as electrical transformers flashed and exploded throughout the greater Los Angeles metropolitan area. Everyone felt the presence, much larger than when Walker had led them through the intoxication of possibilities, the ascending steps. The crowd was cleansed of doubt and open to the power of echoing intention. In looking at each other, they saw not an ordinary congregation—not even an ordinary if unusual coalition rally—but a gathering of heavenly beings, dragons, spirits, human and nonhuman beings. They existed out of time and place, in the full manifestation of the five transcendental powers. The wisdom that embraces all species, and calls down the blessings of the stars, was suddenly available to everyone. Wheels spoked by kalpas, stretching for eons, were beginning to turn. There was lotus truth, the beauty of compassion and transcendence. There was cactus vision, a world manifest in the timeless geometry of recycling light. There was the anthem of the mystic rose, hidden in the navel of the universe, blossoming to the eyes of the blessed, showing how the mercy of thorn-drawn blood nourishes the Sacred Heart.

The speakers' platform had been severely shaken but hadn't collapsed. Jerry stood on it, holding up his arms, pushing out the sky with a prayer to the powers of serpent, feather, and holy blood. When he fell to his knees there was a flash above his head, a bright blue light that resolved into two figures, a man and woman. Jerry began to watch the male apparition, who wore huge bracelets covering his forearms, gross-gartered boots of skin that came almost to his knees. As he grabbed playfully for the huge woman in red braids, she hitched her long tunic above her knees, laughed, circled him like a cautious tiger. They both laughed as she pulled the sleeves of her tunic from her shoulders and down around her waist. Her pendulous breasts shook and swung as the two figures made playful feints at one another. In the midst of their intimacies, they appeared as large as X-rated actors on a drive-in movie screen. The ground they cavorted on was midair, fifty feet above the platform where Jerry lay watching.

When Freydis went down on her hands and knees, squealing her invitations to Bjarni, he circled around back, kneeled, lifted her skirts and prepared to push his erection into place. At the precise moment Freydis shrieked with the penetration, a contingent of the riot squad clambered up the platform and demanded that Jerry turn off the pornographic projection. He replied that he had no control over it, had no idea where it came from. How could he turn anything on or off, when all the electricity had gone out in the first moments of the earthquake? The cops lifted their riot visors and stared at the playful couple above them. Now Bjarni was lying on his back, Freydis giving his face a rough ride, his telephone pole standing straight up, waiting to get back into action. Instead of mirrors on the ceiling, there were mirrors in the sky. You could see everything from all angles. After Freydis got back on her hands and knees, the two squealed, groaned, and collided in ecstasy, colors of all shades playing across their bodies—a light show more spectacular than any Fourth of July. Freydis was nearing her climax, laughing joyfully, breathlessly, until she let out one final whoop and they both disappeared.

At the close of the magnificent copulation, the cops turned their attention back to Jerry, who was sitting on the platform, arms around his knees, looking at the sky. One of the riot squad grabbed him by the back of his shirt, pulled him to his feet. In the middle of this action, the dazzling love light that had been playing over Bjarni and Freydis dove into the tough cop's helmet, began to invade his face. The punisher released Jerry's shirt, pulled off his helmet, and screamed, trying to wipe the pulsing light from his face. The other officers had also received the light, and were discarding their helmets, scampering over the platform, grasping their faces, struggling to control the storms thrashing under skin. Like the recent unexpected permutations in the American gene pool, the facial features of the police had also become unhinged. Parts of the Black cop appeared on the faces of the white officers, and a short blonde woman distributed some of her best features to at least two of the men. Then they all became women, rippling skin tones moving from pale pink to beige to brown to black, and in an instant replay found new gradations in between. They all had to be tuned to the same frequency, because the hundreds of cops who were spread around the crowd, stationed by paddy wagons and squad cars, began the same remarkable process. Everyone watched as the police went through a metamorphosis that was completely beyond their control. Then the panic. All those cops shed helmets and flack jackets, pulled off shirts, struggled directly with their own bodies, trying to keep them under control. Some wrestled themselves to the ground. Finally, a majority of them ran—all of their vehicles having been completely disabled since the appearance of Bjarni and Freydis—disappeared down every street in the neighborhood. Those few that stayed touched each other's faces and bodies in wonder, and began to laugh.

The colors rose up to the sky once more, danced briefly with the Night Bird, then descended on the upturned faces at Eagle Peak. The people had come for the word, the truth, and they had seen the visual music performed by Bjarni and Freydis, enacted by the mutating cops. Now, feeling the transformations in themselves, the barriers of race and gender disappeared, as skin, eyes, hair leaped from one face to another. They smelled the alchemical light, with its hint of sandalwood, and it calmed them. People in the crowd touched their own faces and the faces of others around them—wives and husbands, friends and strangers—realizing this was the marvel Walker was talking about. The promise of revelation. Then flowers raining from above, released not from planes but from the immutable law of nondualism, the inviolable unity of emptiness. Birds of paradise, gardenias, plumeria, hibiscus, fragrant hybrids never seen in this world before, tumbled through the electrified air. Above the transforming mortals, their faces shifting quickly, unpredictably, the sky itself shifted. Its dome of light was penetrated by a greater light, stars poised like a manna of fire ready to descend and feed the righteous converts. In this new light all illusions of separation and difference—between stars, plants, humans, and animals—fell away.

Jerry drew his eyes from the show in the sky, watched remarkable changes sweep back and forth among thousands of people. There was laughter in the light as it played across their faces. Everyone was in motion, except the man sitting on the steps to the platform, a figure Jerry had not previously noticed. He wore a brass helmet on his head, held a metal rod in each hand. When Jerry walked toward the stranger, the honking began. Inching along, the old school bus persisted in its racket, waiting for the crowd to part and let it through. Painted red violet, covered with stylized depictions of animals and rock formations, abstract symbols and showers of light, Jerry recognized many of his own motifs. But he knew he had nothing to do with the painting of the magic bus; this one came straight from the ancestors. It honked and revved its engine, slowly working its way toward the platform. The crowd, at first irritated by the intrusion that had broken its spell, now started to cheer the new arrivals. Jerry walked to the edge of the platform, strained to see who was inside the bus, but could not. When it finally came to rest by the stairs, the doors opened, and the first rider descended: a mudhead kachina. Following, one kachina after another: clowns, abstract maidens holding melons and stalks of corn, the feathered memory heroes, and guardians of the Great Snake. They danced and drummed. Some were somber, some playful. A young girl descended from the bus, her braided auburn hair interwoven with feathers and honeysuckle. She wore cotton clothing with bright vertical stripes, carried an elaborate double-weave basket in each hand. She strutted, danced, and kicked, showed off her strength and flexibility. John Walkingstick, who sat on a support strut under the south edge of the platform, recognized her; it was his daughter, Nancy. So did Antonio and his tattooed child assistant from the Cantina Rosarita, but they thought the dancing girl was the Virgin of Guadalupe. Wong Fu Gee, who remained on the steps, lifted his helmet from his head and set it down at his side. He bowed his head, rubbed his gray brush cut. White Buffalo Calf Woman appeared in the crowd, walked toward the bus, along with Snake Boy and Erzuli, the guardians of the Shift. Emily Roebling, Gertrude Stein, and William Carlos Williams observed the bridge as it formed itself but had nothing more to say. Chief Seattle, surrounded by eagle men, danced and chanted prophesy into physical substance. Thelonious Monk, Robert Johnson, Charlie Mingus, and Duke Ellington worked their way through the crowd toward the platform—as always, keeping perfect time. Hui Shen danced in the area by the food concessions, beating the dharma drum. Sun Girl, Red Swallow, Bird Grass, and Cold Moon Fire closed in on the platform from the north side, walking arm in arm. They laughed like sacred crows, singing, "Haw . . . haw! haw! Haw . . . haw! haw!" Ezekiel Smith and Siu Lan Eng cuddled by the *churros* stand. Imperfecto Ruiz joined Francisco Torres, who healed ailments of environmental poisoning and immunal collapse as he walked through the color-pulsing crowd, among hands reaching out to touch his garment. Queen Matilda followed in the wake of these healing frequencies, leading three old women: J. P. Morgan, Thomas Edison, and J. Edgar Hoover masquerading as the Three Fates. Even they could not hold back the laughter of their joy and release. There were those who had fallen into hell alive, and those who had made the evolutionary climb from trenches beneath the sea up to the mountaintops, becoming paragons of compassion and enlightenment. There were more presences in Watts on this Thanksgiving Day than a voice-hearing namer could enumerate in a long kalpa. And the discrete, unnameable particles of Handsome Bear's power, the sum of his transformational surge, permeated all flesh and spirit in the convocation. His spiritual diaspora electrified a city that no longer possessed a single watt of conventional power.

The horn began honking wildly again, and the attention of the crowd turned from the revelations at every hand back to the noisy bus. One last kachina—a *koshare*, a Hano clown—descended the steps with a white cloth bundle in his hands. The package burst into blossom, pushed out petals that became limbs—an infant dressed in lightning, its head crowned with a shock of straight black hair. Preceded by the other kachinas, the *koshare* clown marched up the stairs of the platform, holding the child above his head. Jerry looked at the offering, heard the sound of Tuvan throat singing, different songs simultaneously from one voice. Unlike the sounds he heard when he touched Carla's swollen belly, this was not a private experience of the Song of Creation. The whole crowd heard it as well as Jerry, because the singer's throat was L.A. and the sky its motive breath. This was the child that had disappeared after Carla's death. Jerry stopped breathing when he looked into its face. It was not like any human he'd ever seen. He stood in awe for a time, a ghost of a moment, then took the child from the clown, held it above his own head. The crowd cheered. A voice came through Jerry's body and exited his mouth, made the child's name echo through the air, the utterance a combination of vowels and consonants that had never been heard before. The gathering of shifting people, redelineating the map with every moment of their metamorphosis, knew the child had good plans for them, and for all the sentient beings that linked them to the Network. It was a world of Travelers, compassionate bodhisattvas. They knew the child had good plans for them, and she did.